PANORAMA

PANORAMA

A NOVEL

STEVE KISTULENTZ

Little, Brown and Company

New York   Boston   London

Copyright © 2018 by Steve Kistulentz

Hachette Book Group supports the right to free expression and the value of copyright. The purpose of copyright is to encourage writers and artists to produce the creative works that enrich our culture.

The scanning, uploading, and distribution of this book without permission is a theft of the author's intellectual property. If you would like permission to use material from the book (other than for review purposes), please contact permissions@hbgusa.com. Thank you for your support of the author's rights.

Little, Brown and Company
Hachette Book Group
1290 Sixth Avenue, New York NY 10104
littlebrown.com

First Edition: March 2018

Little, Brown and Company is a division of Hachette Book Group, Inc. The Little, Brown name and logo are trademarks of Hachette Book Group, Inc.

The publisher is not responsible for websites (or their content) that are not owned by the publisher.

The Hachette Speakers Bureau provides a wide range of authors for speaking events. To find out more, go to hachettespeakersbureau.com or call (866) 376-6591.

Portions of this book appeared, in different form, as stories in *Crab Orchard Review* and *Quarter After Eight*. The author thanks those editors.

ISBN 978-0-316-55176-2
LCCN 2017945031

10 9 8 7 6 5 4 3 2 1

LSC-C

Printed in the United States of America

For Tracy, first reader, favorite reader

The trouble with us Americans is we always want a tragedy with a happy ending.
                    —Hal Hartley, *Surviving Desire*

PART I

1

THIS HAPPENED on the last day of the last year when we still felt safe, with the American skyline brilliantine, the entire panorama still rendered in its familiar postcard wholeness.

The two years bisected by this particular New Year's Eve would come and go without fanfare, no shock in the timeline, no Dealey Plaza or Ambassador Hotel, no Miracle Mets or miracles on ice, no archdukes or mad monks, no anarchists or secessionists, no Treaty of Versailles, no surrender, no peace, no Sputnik or man on the moon, no heiresses turned into gun-toting molls, no *Giants Win the Pennant!* or *Nixon Resigns!*

The names of the infamous airports of the past became, at a distance, a roll call of crises: Tel Aviv, Kennedy, Sioux City, Hanoi, Tripoli, Athens, Entebbe, all those historical locales that conjured up grainy, United Press International photos of smuggled handguns, heroic pilots negotiating out the cockpit window while hijackers demanded unencumbered passage to Beirut, Havana. In San Juan, the narco dogs barked at every piece of luggage; in Geneva, armored personnel carriers stood sentry between the runways, a response to the vaguely threatening nature of our time.

We could have been anywhere. But for the purposes of this particular holiday and its hurried arrangements and contingencies, we need to choose a benign location. Salt Lake City, the middle of the Great Basin, in the valley sandwiched between the natural fortress of the Wasatch and Oquirrh Mountains. A sprawling city on the bottom of what was once a tremendous prehistoric lake.

Even on a holiday, the town rolled up its sidewalks just after dark. Whatever celebrating was to be done was likely a solitary pursuit. Disgruntled airport workers smoked their last cigarettes of the year alarmingly close to thirty-thousand-gallon tanks of jet-A fuel. The terminal was empty except for employees so close to the margins that these few hours of overtime meant the difference for the next month.

And what are New Year's resolutions but our simplest prayers? *Help me give this shit up,* uttered by forty-eight-year-old airline mechanic Arnold Bright as he wandered the tarmac of the Salt Lake City International Airport these silent hours of late evening. A pledge to quit made for the fourth year in a row while digging behind his lip to remove an hour-stale pack of chewing tobacco, *just a pinch between his cheek and gum.* His wife would refuse to kiss him when he got home, and it was, after all, New Year's Eve. He swirled tepid coffee in his mouth, trying to extract the grit of tobacco and coarse coffee grounds from his teeth, then spattered the mess onto the concrete.

This burden he carried: at home, everything he did or said was a disappointment. He was worn out, too, from family squabbles, a wife he could not seem to please either emotionally or sexually, a teenaged daughter who now refused to go to church, whose newest set of complaints included not getting a car for Christmas, not having her own cell phone. New Year's

Eve meant another night as last man on the tarmac, a duty his wife would see not as a practical effort to pay the bills but as just another way he had conspired to stay out of the house.

He hoped she could be assuaged with a nine-dollar bottle of champagne, a neck rub, and a pre-midnight arrival home. He was just four hours from union-mandated double time, and besides, every conversation at home reminded him how much they needed the money. But his week already included sixteen hours of overtime, so his decision to cut corners seemed without consequence. It wasn't that he'd forgotten to do something; instead, he'd actively decided not to roll out the ladder, not to take a closer look at the entire tail rudder assembly. This human gesture—Arnold Bright's inclination toward home and family on the last night of the year—set in motion a series of events with their own unstoppable momentums.

Arnold busied himself initialing the ground crew's preflight checklist, making cursory marks with a twenty-nine-cent BIC pen. One of tomorrow afternoon's early departures, one of the airline's decades-old workhorses, a 727, was already attached to the Jetway at gate B14. He picked up the basic tool of his job: a clipboard, its metal jaw straining to hold the nearly inch-thick pile of recent airworthiness directives and safety bulletins. There was newfound concern about the older 727s, the potential malfunction of a servo control valve that might cause the *sudden deflection of the rudder.* A known defect that could result in *uncontrolled flight into terrain.* The airline took these government-issued documents and translated them into new preflight inspection procedures. But today's memos, written in the Esperanto of bureaucracy, appeared in commonplace batches of ten or twelve, which made Arnold Bright think none of them was cause for alarm.

He ought to have been more attentive. An understandable

oversight, one that would no doubt have been corrected if he could only have seen the next afternoon's breaking news.

A plane down on approach to Dallas–Fort Worth.

What Arnold Bright would see on television: ranchland scattered with the detritus of wreckage, briefcases, a lone running shoe, the live network feed from a camera stationed at a discreet-enough distance to insinuate a burning fuselage, its cyclone of smoke visible over the reporter's right shoulder. In that field, the camera would find its narrative in garbage, air sickness bags and in-flight magazines, luggage thrown clear of the debris field, a teddy bear and some sort of melted personal electronic device, a leather portfolio stamped with the name of a property and casualty insurance company, its corporate logotype intact despite the presence of soot and ash and oozing plastic and blood spatter, the implied presence of human remains.

Those broadcast images would never leave him; the insurance logo would always evoke for him not the image of a blanket or a fireman's hat or a *piece of the rock*, but an airplane short of the runway, the end of his career as a burning field.

Months after the accident, once reports had been written about the failure to notice the stain of bright-purple hydraulic fluid visible against the predominantly white and orange paint of the Panorama Airlines' color scheme, and blame officially assigned, the livelihood of a forty-eight-year-old airline mechanic, a union and family man, would become the final casualty of Flight 503.

2

RICHARD MACMURRAY—moderately well-known television pundit, part-time gadfly, prized Washington cocktail-party guest, owner of more than a hundred neckties in a palette of screaming oranges and purples, forty-two years old and once divorced, a Capricorn, former criminal defense attorney turned professional advocate—sat in a director's chair trying to regulate his breathing, hoping his forehead sweat wouldn't pop through his makeup.

He was a guest, live and in studio, on a cable news show debating the issue of mandatory sentencing. Eight weeks ago, at the beginning of the November sweeps, he'd appeared on the same program supporting the inalienable right of a bakery owner in Madison, Wisconsin, to sell pastries shaped like human genitalia. A cupcake frosted to look like a breast was guaranteed airtime, guaranteed ratings, maybe a two-point spike in the overnight share. Tonight's topic, legal and esoteric, meant that no one would watch. During the commercial break between segments, he found himself wondering what the lowest possible rating on the Nielsen scale could be. He wasn't breaking news or making memorable television here, just cashing a check. He hadn't even told his sister about it, and she recorded nearly all of his appearances.

A foundation for criminal justice reform had hired Richard as their television mouthpiece, given him contractually defined talking points simple enough to memorize: mandatory sentences handcuffed the judiciary, put a disproportionate burden on youth and minority offenders, gave too much discretionary power to the police, to prosecutors. But he'd hit all the high notes in the first segment, closing with, "If absolute power corrupts absolutely, then absolute discretion divvied up between police and prosecutors is a power that will be absolutely abused. We all want safer schools, safer streets. But those good intentions haven't led, in this case, to good public policy."

On the adjacent set, Max Peterson, tonight's anchorman, fiddled with papers; Richard knew from experience the papers were blank, a prop. A former Marine and a Rhodes scholar, Peterson could be counted on to digress eloquently on anything from the Stanley Cup finals to the risks inherent in American naval presence in the Persian Gulf. His appearance as a substitute anchor tended to evoke a similar reaction in most viewers: *I thought he'd retired.* Among the inside-the-Beltway talent, Peterson was famous for trying to get his guests to crack, interrupting arguments about the serious issues of the day with a discrete flash of a hand-drawn pornographic cartoon, something like Uncle Sam sporting a monstrous erection. No shenanigans tonight, however, which made the attorney in Richard suspect that maybe Peterson had been spoken to by human resources.

Richard stood and smoothed his suit, eavesdropping as the anchor mumbled monosyllabic responses to his in-ear instructions. *Forty-five seconds back.* The director would probably offer him some comments as well; the previous segment featured

Richard talking over the flustered objections of the other guest, Vance Hiddell, a United States attorney from Alabama.

"One last segment, boys," the director said. Richard realized he didn't know a face to put with the voice in his ear. "Let's try to share our little sandbox. We'll treat it like congressional debate, two minutes and forty-five seconds, divided equally. Then we'll go back to Max for wrap-up and his final thought."

Hiddell stood close by, tapped on the wooden armrest of Richard's chair. He smelled like a barbershop. "Congratulations. We're the featured guests on the lowest-rated network-television program of the year."

"At least we'll be done in time to join in the festivities. Any plans?"

"Reservations at the Old Ebbitt. My wife insisted. Even though the crab cake that's twenty dollars every other day of the year is now part of a two-hundred-fifty-dollar fixed-price romantic adventure," Hiddell said.

Richard nodded in a way that he hoped suggested agreement. New Year's was always difficult, had been for years. The imaginary pressure to invent happy occasions with his now ex-wife had given way to an equally imagined fear that people would judge him if he admitted to his usual habit of spending the holidays alone.

Alone. He repeated the word to himself as he reached for his bottled water.

He heard the shuffle on the studio floor that meant they were going live, the count in his ear, *five, four, three.* The red light on the anchor's camera went hot, and Max Peterson set up the final segment. On the reference monitor, the split screen suggested that Richard and his opponent had been brought together by the miracle of satellite, when in fact they sat on the same riser, in identical chairs five feet apart.

"Welcome back. We're talking about possible revisions to federal sentencing guidelines, what the lawyers might call mandatory minimums. Our guests are Washington-based defense attorney Richard MacMurray and longtime federal prosecutor Vance Hiddell, Alabama Republican and candidate for the United States Senate. Mr. Hiddell, how do you respond to the charge some legal scholars have leveled that mandatory minimums undermine the very premise of equal justice for all?"

"Mandatory minimums are the absolute guarantee of equal justice. They serve as a deterrent to crime and add a system of checks and balances against activist federal judges, one that keeps them from handing out unduly lenient sentences."

"Or," Richard interrupted, "mandatory sentencing laws undermine the very purpose of the judiciary, which is to allow our learned men and women the chance to display wisdom, compassion, and judgment. We're building prisons faster than Stalin, and filling them with college kids who made the fatal error of smoking a joint, or housewives who stole a seven-dollar lipstick."

Hiddell took an unsubtle detour into his stump speech. "It's almost as if my friend has forgotten where these laws came from. They keep violent offenders off the streets. They keep our wives and mothers safe from recidivists. And the prisons we send career criminals to are nicer than the hotel I stayed in last night. It costs taxpayers nearly twenty-five thousand dollars a year per prisoner in the federal system, and those felons get three square meals and cable TV. What we need to bring back is discipline. The sense that prison is not a vacation but a punishment. Because right now, we're not reforming or rehabilitating, we're simply coddling *these people*. Sending a three-time loser to a work farm for ten years is nothing more than justice."

Richard took the reference to *these people* as a typical us-versus-them gambit, designed to rile up the pickup-truck-and-shotgun crowd. Hiddell probably had polling data in his briefcase that showed how those voters were exactly the kind of people who might put him over the top on election day.

Richard did not know he would pull the stunt until he was out of his chair and crossing the stage. The director shouted through his earpiece, an airburst of profanity followed by the begging of all three cameras to stay with the shot. Richard walked the two steps across the riser, stopped next to the candidate. "Thirty-eight years ago, a teenager pled guilty to a pair of nonviolent felonies for some youthful mischief involving fireworks and bad decisions. Since then, he's graduated from high school and college, earned a master's degree, and become a licensed pharmacist. And this week," Richard said, "a district court in California sentenced this fifty-seven-year-old pharmacist to life in prison. His crime? Stealing a Snickers bar."

Hiddell prattled on, "We don't need to send career criminals off to camp. We need them to pay their debt to society."

Richard dug into the pocket of his suit pants and extracted some change. When he extended his hand, Hiddell reflexively stuck out his own. Richard dropped the coins in, one by one. "Twenty-five, fifty, seventy-five, seventy-six, seventy-seven, and seventy-eight."

"What's this shit?" the candidate demanded. The anchor blanched, but all three heard the director answer, "Easy," into their earpiece.

"One criminal's debt to society, paid in full."

They'd end the segment, Richard knew, no matter how much time was left. A slogan popped into his head: *More Americans get their news from our network than any other news organization.* He knew too that the clip would be picked up on free media and repeated in a seemingly perpetual loop, the candidate sitting there in his chair, dumbfounded and visibly furious, trying to decide whether or not to stand, still holding on to the spare change.

In a year when everything else would go his party's way, Vance Hiddell would lose his September primary by twelve percentage points.

Richard walked past camera two, unclipped his IFB, then headed through the narrow corridor behind the control room, where he was surrounded by stagehands offering back slaps, laughs, murmurs of congratulations.

In the reference monitor, Richard saw Max Peterson stack the papers of his fake script one last time and smile at the camera. "We'll return in a moment."

3

AT THE deserted concourse gates of the Salt Lake City International Airport, the waiting areas flickered with the light of soundless televisions blinking out the last of the year's news. A science correspondent talked about the prevailing winds, the patterns of frigid Pacific currents, the historical increase in temperatures, all to an audience of empty plastic chairs. At each gate, video terminals predicted the on-time departure of tomorrow morning's earliest flights. Maintenance personnel tended to the business of cleaning; their slapping mops and whirling floor polishers, their muffled whistles of boredom and melancholy, all reverberated off the terminal's exposed girder-and-crossbeam ceiling. Forty-gallon garbage bags stuffed with stale cinnamon rolls sat abandoned near an unattended customer-service kiosk.

Because the most delicious cigarette is a surreptitious one, the workers inside smoked too; cigarettes dangled from their pursed lips as they completed the last items on a checklist of second-shift chores. Behind the closed pull-down gate of an airport shop, a twentysomething employee they called Heavy Metal Bob stacked and tied together bundles of the previous morning's newspapers, December 31 headed for the recycling bin. Tomorrow's travelers would congregate over a stack of them, four different varieties with the same set of headlines: *Sri Lankan Ferry Disaster Claims Hundreds; Heat Wave Dominates for Third Straight Day; For California Businesses, Everything Turns Up Roses.*

They called him Heavy Metal Bob thanks to his long, straight hair and endless supply of concert T-shirts. Behind his back, co-workers scoffed at his ratty jeans and the navy suede sneakers that on rainy days left his white tube socks stained at the toes and heels. The people he worked with assumed he was high, but he'd gotten and stayed clean, if only to spite the naysayers. He blocked out their sniping comments and the day-to-day sounds of the airport with an old Walkman he'd found near gate A18, and worked with the perpetual slowness of someone barely awake.

Bob spent the end of his New Year's Eve shift dusting around shelves of souvenirs, stuffed animals, shot glasses and snow globes, bric-a-brac labeled with the city's name, purple T-shirts emblazoned with the incongruous words *Utah Jazz.* He'd volunteered to work, to give the family men on the custodial staff the evening off, and in the near solitude of late evening, he did what so many others across the nation were doing at that exact moment, using the year's waning hours for self-assessment—this personal inventory his only distraction as he counted his way through a rack of paperback bestsellers. His resolutions were meager—put away a few dollars for the future, stop wasting so many on 900 numbers and late fees at the video store, get a few more fresh vegetables into the diet.

Bob dreamed of an airline job, counter agent or baggage thrower, one that might mean someone to talk to at work. All he'd ever wanted was to help people, to be dependable; in the parlance of the cop show he'd watched last night at 2:00 a.m., you could say anything you wanted about Bob Denovo, but he was a *stand-up guy,* the kind of guy who'd bail you out of the city lockup, no questions asked, the kind of guy who, if there was one sandwich left in all the world, would offer you half. How easy it had become to ignore the guy with the garbage bags and the headphones; most evenings, as he passed the women who worked at the hamburger joint on the A concourse, he received only a nod in return to his greetings. Someday, he hoped, one of them would wave him over and say thank you for carrying out the bags of stale buns and rancid meat. They might talk for a few minutes, but it wouldn't be anything like working on the ramp.

Maybe he could be the guy with the flashlights, steering the pilots toward the Jetway. He had no idea what the guys with ear protection and fluorescent vests actually did, just a peculiar confidence: whatever it was, he could do it too. Besides, no way you could sit out on the ramp all day, loading and unloading planes, and never find anything to talk about.

His plans were for an evening of television and a modest splurge, delivered pizza and a Sprite (he wasn't Mormon but had adopted some of the Latter-Day disciplines, such as skipping caffeine, mostly to avoid strangers who might ask the question of his faith). As he watched the illuminated ball descend over the Times Square throng, he would feel the total absence of human contact in his life, a longing for someone, anyone, to kiss at midnight. What else could he do besides watch television? A cable network offered a marathon of reruns, this science fiction series he was trying to catch up on, where government agents were complicit in the cover-up of an impending alien invasion. This plot made perfect sense to Bob; on the edge of the high desert, he'd seen inexplicable displays of celestial lights, phenomena known by obtuse-sounding titles that combined numbers and initials. The only other thing on TV was going to be the news, and whenever he could help it, Bob paid no attention to the events of the world outside.

At the top of the ten o'clock news, a fat weatherman—the standard-issue avuncular type—offered a scientific explanation for the week's weather pattern. We were just two days away from perihelion, the time when the earth moved closest to the sun; B-roll video showed coastal North Carolina, buffeted by a week's worth of unusually strong surf, the result of a convergence of the latest nor'easter and the tidal pull of a full moon. Under the constancy of fifty-knot winds, a handful of million-dollar homes had already toppled into the sea near Wrightsville Beach, but those disembodied images were the nation's only bit of bad news this New Year's Eve.

The optimism of the New Year was reflected in the forecast: the jet stream crept farther north across Canada's prairie provinces, flooding the states below with an abundance of surprising warmth; the weatherman spoke of the prospects for record high temperatures, a dearth of snow. The first day of January would arrive from sea to shining sea under the brightest spotlight of clear winter, American sunlight, no chance of foul weather.

4

THE HOTEL, an elegant stone high-rise off Temple Square, stood just feet from the spot where the city of Salt Lake began. Tourists gathered in the shadows of the six steeples of the great temple and took photographs of the statue of the angel Moroni as he beckoned the faithful to arms with his blazing golden trumpet.

In the dead hours just before dinner, the lower floors of the hotel bustled with preparations for the evening's festivities. Uniformed employees vacuumed ballrooms while men in jeans and black T-shirts assembled modular stages; bar backs sliced limes, and $6.74-an-hour kitchen help wrapped frozen scallops in bacon slices. The musicians in cover bands—a schoolteacher, a car salesman, the produce manager of a local market, a hired-gun horn section that had once, in an emergency, played behind Chuck Berry—geared up for their various New Year's Eve parties, restringing guitars and reviewing their cheat sheets, the charts that would allow them to churn out perfunctory versions of the *top hits of yesterday and today.*

And on the seventh floor, Mary Beth Blumenthal primped for a night out. She opened her room's window to release the accumulated steam of her shower and admit the lush breeze of a warm December night, pausing in her preparations to admire the precise layout of the city. In front of a vanity mirror that made her look ten pounds heavier, she vowed to be remarried by this time next year, a preamble to her next New Year's resolution: provide a strong male role model for her son, Gabriel, who on his next birthday would be seven years old and had never known his biological father.

Mary Beth's strongest prospect was Mike Renfro, the Texas insurance man who also happened to be her boss. They'd been dating clandestinely for months, but this weekend was the first inkling she'd gotten that their future contained something more, maybe even something permanent. Mike was the only reason she would be in Salt Lake City. She could think of only one other reason people might come to Utah on holiday—skiing—and she hadn't been much for winter sports except for a few college-era trips down the bunny slopes. A romantic getaway meant the islands, St. Barts maybe, or dinner and a show on Broadway. Mary Beth had a tough time picturing romance in Utah. She had been meaning to ask about this strange destination ever since Mike snuck into her office the Wednesday before Christmas and left her an envelope stuffed with colorful brochures and airline tickets; there had been only two tickets, Mike's and Mary Beth's, and she'd been angry that he'd made no accommodations for Gabriel.

It had taken intense bilateral negotiations before Mary Beth agreed to leave her son with Sarah Hensley, one of Mike's cadre of just-out-of-college assistants. They would stay at Mike's house, where Gabriel could avail himself of the big-screen television and the heated pool, all under adequate supervision. Still, her worries had dominated the last three days, feelings of guilt about being apart from her son for the first time in his six years, a sense of remorse tempering the joy she felt at relaxing in the hotel-provided terry-cloth robe, the snacks of fourteen-dollar macadamias and honey-roasted cashews from the minibar.

In the evenings, Mike ministered to her feet, massaging them with peppermint-scented cream. They sipped mimosas and Bloody Marys with breakfast, quaffed Irish coffees after the last run down the slopes. She'd decided to be a gamer, what her late father would have called a good egg, and gone along with Mike's every suggestion, even ordering a Flintstone-size New York strip, slathered the way all mediocre hotel steaks are in a sauce whose main ingredient was a stick of butter, as her holiday dinner. The austerity program could always start tomorrow. What was the New Year for if not solemn pledges, draconian diets, another chance for reinvention?

She knew herself well enough to call this creeping feeling entitlement. The truth of her guilt: she felt she was entitled to exactly nothing, and she had felt that way ever since her ex-husband had moved out almost seven years ago. Six weeks after his departure, she discovered she was pregnant, her morning beginning with the sign of the cross, the symbol on the home pregnancy test that she stared at in disbelief, thinking of all the worrisome precautions she'd taken for some fifteen years to avoid an unplanned pregnancy. She'd sat through that particular set of holidays on her own, living off her savings, trying to minimize her interaction with the modern world. Ever since, New Year's Eve had always been a reminder to Mary Beth of the paucity of her romantic prospects, and now, on the last evening of her short holiday, she wanted to enjoy herself. She could not help but think that being away from her son at this time of the year served as evidential proof—she was a bad mother. But she'd made her choice, and Gabriel was safe in the custody of a good friend, so tonight Mary Beth intended to head downstairs to the hotel ballroom, to drink and sweat and grind suggestively up against her stodgy boyfriend and boss in a way she knew couples around her would think undignified.

For this holiday evening, she would not deny herself anything. She wanted to beat perfection—or at least the illusion of it—into her body. In the bath, she ground away the frayed edges of her heels with a pumice stone. She wielded a triple-blade razor to smooth over her legs, underarms, bikini area. She wanted nothing more than to misbehave—she still thought of sex as something to be embarrassed about, something to hide. Just as she rarely hit the dance floor anymore, it had been years since she had found herself lost in the animal compunctions that came over her younger self, the way the twenty-year-old Mary Beth occasionally lingered in the bath or her own bed, masturbating through the melancholy of an anxious Sunday evening. Sex was still an adventure but no longer a thrill ride, a train about to leave the tracks. Now it required preparations—shopping, shaving, personal lubricants—and happened with all the spontaneity of an Everest expedition.

At the end of her ritual, she tended to her hair, molding it in place with a combination of fixatives, including a space-age goo that contained micropolymers designed to add an illusory, silk-like finish; the combination of dry air and winter sun had fried her frosted locks, leaving them as thirsty as an abandoned houseplant. Her eyes received similar detailing: she filled the half-moons of her lids with two tones of color called Shimmering Smoke. The blush that amplified the domes and arches of her cheeks could not hide that her weight had been creeping upward. As she traced the outline of her lips with a deep burgundy pencil, she made her second resolution for the New Year: *Lose the baby weight.*

She fetched a tube of hand cream from her bag, then collapsed into a wingback chair striped in a pink-and-black fabric that reminded her of carnival tents and children's games. She sat there listening to the forecast for tomorrow's good weather, kneading her calves. She did not even like to ski—that was Mike's thing, this almost comically large man careening down a mountain—and her knees and quadriceps ached after a long weekend learning to flex with the lifts and falls of the slopes. Nor did she care much for the strange homogeneous nature of Utah; it was self-defeating, comparing herself to the flotilla of impossibly lithe blondes who swooshed across the icy slopes, a sorority of phosphorescent teeth and pastel ski jackets. They hightailed past her on both sides, showering her legs with a fusillade of wet snow and ice crystals.

Mary Beth tucked her hair behind her shoulder, then added a reserve of fragrance to her pulse points. She practiced the small talk of New Year's Eve parties, the explanations of who she was and what she did that would dominate the evening's conversations. She did not want to talk in the language of Mike's business, about retirement plans, employee benefit administration, policies for whole and term life insurance, or accidental death and dismemberment. She wondered if she could even talk about anything else, the volatile stock market, the recent presidential race, the prospects for a unified Europe. She'd once had the confidence that she was an intriguing and complex woman; that confidence had gone, she suspected, with her ex-husband. Before him, she went to museums, concerts, farmers' markets, lectures, charity events, and she'd done it all on her own. The soundtrack of her childhood had been Rostropovich conducting the National Symphony Orchestra. She could manage to sit by herself in a restaurant, shielded behind a paperback, and not feel the weight of self-consciousness. At the movies, the old Mary Beth could buy a drink and a large buttered popcorn and sit by herself through an afternoon of subtitled films, but now, at age forty-seven, she was a single mother on some sort of inadvertent vacation, and she could not remember the last decent film she had seen, or when she'd had time to finish a book.

Mary Beth was using her hair dryer to cure the top coat of her nails when she noticed the blinking message light on her hotel-room phone. Her son and his sitter were the only ones who knew she was in Salt Lake; no one else had the number or the name of the hotel.

So she dialed and listened to what she immediately knew would be a hurry-up reminder from Mike Renfro. His message was nearly lost in the noise of the bar, the clinking of glasses and the liturgical commotion of small talk, all of which made her think of Mike's familiar hands, likely as not cupping a tumbler of bourbon, then throwing down a handful of salted peanuts. She pictured him tapping his index finger against the crystal of his watch, a gesture he often made around the office. His recorded voice told her, *You're going to need to shake it. And bring my briefcase with you.*

That was the quintessential Mike Renfro. Always on the debit. That was what the insurance guys called it, trying to make the sale. An old-fashioned term, but then again, he was kind of an old-fashioned guy. He drove nondescript American cars, the leather seats the only nod to luxury. His latest Cadillac had nearly two hundred thousand highway miles on it from client trips all over north and east Texas. He had a routine and a cocktail of choice and a favorite restaurant where he always ordered the same meal, a New York strip, medium rare, and a baked potato crusted in sea salt and slathered in both butter and sour cream. She liked to tease him that vegetables were not poisonous. Yet he never took a sick day and rarely managed a vacation. He walked in the office each morning at 7:30, wore conservative dark suits and a white shirt, his ties always one of those French patterns with repetitive rows of small fish, birds, or turtles. He was the kind of guy who, although he did not know it, wanted to be a husband, a father. He wanted someone he loved to remind him where he'd left his briefcase and car keys, to brush off the shoulders of his suit jacket as he headed out the door each morning, and at the office, he needed someone to remind him about his lunch meetings and quarterly payroll-tax deadlines. He was in obvious need of two wives, one at the office and one at home, and here she was in the vague land of being a candidate for both.

She pressed the Delete button, then thought of checking on her son one last time. Ten times in three days, Mary Beth had called to remind Sarah that she was as close as the telephone. Gabriel wasn't much of a conversationalist, but his one-word answers and the pattern of his breathing as amplified by the telephone made the separation tolerable. She thought of a cartoon from her own childhood, Winnie the Pooh offering his nubbly paw to Christopher Robin, the two of them holding hands. New Year's Eve should have been a family night and was no time to be doing business. She certainly didn't need Mike asking for his briefcase, a reminder that, above all other things, Mike was still her boss.

There were sentences she could say to Mike, her boyfriend, that she could never speak to Mike Renfro of the Mike Renfro Agency. She knew the opposite to be true as well, and that only fueled her doubt; everything she knew about business and men both told her that dating her boss was a bad idea. She still remembered a story that her father, who had been dead for more than twenty years, had once told. Her father's college roommate, this guy they called the Maverick, worked as a vice president for a Fortune 500 behemoth that manufactured industrial lubricants. At a hotel along the San Antonio River Walk, the Maverick, emboldened by a quartet of strong Manhattans, made certain mistakes with his assistant. If it was a parable, it was about consequences: the necessary investigations, the divorce, the children testifying in open court as to which parent they preferred, the dissolution of community property, the recriminations. Amid all that destruction Mary Beth remembered only the blunt advice of her father, the career political hack: *Don't shit where you eat.*

Still, Mike had more than his status as her boss to recommend him: there was his attentiveness and his work ethic, his luxuriously abundant hair, the way he kept focus on the details both big and small. His briefcase was like an emergency kit on how to be a grown-up, filled with work papers and tiny bottles of hand sanitizer, wet wipes, a travel-size toothbrush. He was prepared for every eventuality. He himself was covered with $2 million in term life insurance, a line he'd mention in his sales calls, but on this New Year's Eve, Mary Beth realized that he'd never mentioned who the beneficiary might be. She suspected an ex-wife out there, somewhere nebulous, one day to be surprised by a sudden windfall. There were always these warning signs, but then, there were always enough positives to overlook the questionable things she already knew, a pair of acrimonious divorces (at sales conferences, he liked to joke that his next wife should be named Plaintiff, just to save the time), the house bereft of furniture save for giant televisions and leather sofas, a refrigerator filled only with beer, mixers, and condiments, the appearance and disappearance of twentysomething women who worked for six months, tops, as Mike Renfro's "personal assistant."

Calling him a boyfriend made what she was doing here feel

illicit and ill advised. Nor was he on some inevitable path to becoming her fiancé. Calling Mike her date was inadequate; he was one of the few constants in her life since the morning eight years ago when she answered a *Dallas Morning News* advertisement for an entry-level sales position and found herself being talked into taking the job as his office manager.

In the few awkward months when she referred to Mike as just a good friend, he'd courted her intermittently with small gifts, trinkets from his every business trip. Any weekend he spent at his condo near Galveston, Mike always returned with boxes of saltwater taffy. Mary Beth mentioned once that she preferred the peppermint-flavored pieces, white with red stripes, like some hybrid toothpaste. After his next trip, Mike put a box in the reception area and another at the front desk for the rest of the women, but not before liberating all the peppermint pieces, spiriting them into a sandwich bag that he left on Mary Beth's desk. She told him, "The taffy was great. But next time I want fudge, two boxes. One for here and one for home," and he had remembered that too, showing up a month later with a pound each of light- and dark-chocolate fudge and a bonus pound of peanut butter. They opened all three boxes and mixed the pieces together so that Mary Beth could take home a little of each. Between the two of them, they ate nearly a pound, leaving Mary Beth with a sugar- and salt-loaded tongue that could not be satisfied even after three glasses of water.

Then, somehow, they were dating. Now her presence in Salt Lake City made her feel as if she had not been courted but defeated, her resistance poked through by his persistence and ardor. She liked the physical pleasure of being around Mike too, both the lovemaking and, more recently, the reassuring way his solid frame dominated her bed. She liked the feel of a man next to her, especially now that Gabriel was no longer a toddler appearing in her doorframe in the night, seeking the solace of his mother and her queen-size bed. Just once Mary Beth wished Mike would stay for breakfast, for all the rituals of a family, but what Gabriel might make of that she did not know. Her son had no idea what to call him either. Mike insisted on being called Mike, whether he was talking to a six-year-old or to a client, but whenever Mike arrived to watch a movie or take Mary Beth and Gabriel out to dinner, the kid still referred to him as Mr. Mike.

She decided that New Year's Eve was exactly the time to put labels on things; they could stay up all night if they had to without worrying about waking up the kid in the next room. They had become a regular thing, but usually just on Thursday and Saturday evenings. Their interactions occurred almost exclusively on neutral turf; the only times she'd been to his house fell under the pretense of her professional duties, and that meant she had a hard time picturing her son roaming the bland suburban expanses of Mike's house. In Mike's list of personal and professional obligations, she had no idea where she fell. She knew too his upcoming calendar, and there wasn't much room in there for her, for Gabriel. She wasn't even sure how much she would see of him in January, given Mike's other plans: a trip to his mother's (the first in twenty-one months), a sales conference in Houston, a Hawaiian vacation (apparently, he hadn't thought of inviting her).

So if Mike wanted something more, starting at midnight he was going to have to ask for it. They had no excuse not to take some time and figure out where Mary Beth fit in, or whether she was going to fit in at all.

Mike lived in the city of his own future, a city designed with a distinctly Renfro-centric vision. Mary Beth saw herself demanding a bit more, wanted more of his presence, his attention. She clicked the television set off and reflected that it had been the better part of a decade since she spent this holiday in the arms of a man, her hair done and nails polished, since she had crossed the threshold of midnight somewhere other than on her sofa in front of *Dick Clark's New Year's Rockin' Eve*. Mike was free to tell the world about her. She was happy to have an evening where she allowed her wants to come first. It seemed so obvious that she shook her head at the thought. How little she'd allowed herself since her divorce. And that part could start now, she thought, so she said to herself, *Fuck the briefcase*. It was a holiday, for God's sake.

5

BY THE time Richard successfully hailed a cab outside the news bureau, he'd listened to seven messages, each shorter than ten seconds, all expressing reactions best summarized as *holy shit.* The first message came from his booking agent, a blunt rejoinder that Monday would almost certainly begin with a call from the chairman of the sentencing-reform coalition terminating his contract; the last was his agent calling back with the information that the group had already called with the announcement that they would seek a legal remedy to keep from paying Richard the $12,000 he was still owed.

From the television studio to his Adams Morgan home, a little more than three miles, a cab normally took fifteen minutes; tonight it took that long to travel just five blocks. He ditched the taxi and walked through the busy intersection of Connecticut and Florida, deciding against a pit stop into the corner market for a celebratory six-pack. He'd get a few hours' head start on his New Year's resolutions, the austerity program he'd been cultivating and refining for the past few months. Besides, he had precious little to celebrate.

He turned onto his hilly side street only to be confronted by a pair of women emerging from a pricey sedan. Georgetown students, Richard thought, based solely on the value of the car. The first girl, dressed in black cigarette pants and a spangly top that fell off one of her shoulders, pointed at Richard with her silver evening clutch, then stopped her friend with a violent yank at the elbow. They leaned together, whispering, and then the two of them gave him an enthusiastic wave and started to cross the street toward him.

He could not get used to being recognized on the street, even though it happened maybe once a day. Being familiar or even, he supposed, quasi-famous, meant that Richard could never be forgiven the sin of a bad mood, so he geared up to be the television version of himself, chatty, open. He was aware that it was television which had conveyed to him this authority; in bars, he was often called upon to settle arguments over things he knew nothing about, like who was the left fielder for the '79 Phillies, or who played bass in Mott the Hoople. And that authority, Richard knew from experience, attracted a certain type of girl, one of Washington's army of fit, ambitious, pencil-skirted young professionals. They all were organized, styled, and well coiffed, and walked as if they were late for a meeting that had started ten minutes before. Like the two now marching toward him.

He responded with a quasi-military salute, which he immediately regretted. The wave should have allowed him to make a quick exit, but leaving meant showing the two girls which building he lived in, and now he worried about the fact that his name was lettered on the directory panel next to the security buzzer. So he waited for the pair to catch up.

The first girl lurched toward him, demanding, "So where are you headed tonight?"

But Richard was not headed to some glamorous undisclosed

location, the kind that got written up in the Style section of the *Washington Post;* he wanted nothing more than to shed his suit, relax in a sweater and venerable chinos. Every sincere invitation he had received for New Year's meant an event where the hosts expected him to arrive as the televised version of himself. In other words, *work.* This holiday season, Richard had backed entirely out of the social swing, even skipping the three-week period of lavish and decadent Christmas parties thrown by the lawyers and the lobbyists he knew because, in his heart, he felt he was just too old for the false camaraderie of two a.m. What Richard liked most about Washington was that he finally understood the way it worked; sooner or later the city defeated everyone's idealized view of it and became an elaborate game of playacting. Friendships, even romantic relationships, lasted in predictable increments, two years or four, like election cycles. With Cadence, it had been two. And she had not returned his last four phone calls.

He didn't have the courage to say all that, so he settled for the modified truth. "I'm headed upstairs for a glass of wine and a steak lovingly prepared on my George Foreman grill. At midnight, I'm going to call my sister and wish her a happy New Year, watch the ball drop, make a wish for peace, and then at about 12:02, I'm going to bed."

"Peace? That's very political. But not very exciting," said the one in the spangly top, but both girls wore a look on their faces that said they did not believe his story. The head tilt and the hip that she thrust toward him implied a confidence that said she was older than he thought, late twenties. The friend, a streaky blonde in a navy-blue dress that skimmed the ground, thrust a business card at him. "My cell number's on there. We're going to some place around the corner called the Red Room." She showed him the open palm of her right hand and flexed her fingers wide. "Five of us. All extremely fuckable. Wherever it is that you're really going, if you want to join us for a drink later, you should call."

The girls left in a wake of chatter and the competition of two close-smelling fragrances (Richard thought of limes and burning firewood). He watched as they trotted around the corner to the Eighteenth Street bars that specialized in retro music and pink drinks. Richard thought he heard one of them say something about how he looked different than on television, and the other agreed, saying, *Taller.*

The girls were right. It wasn't a very exciting plan. A glass of wine and a steak, alone.

But Richard wasn't interested in flirtations, even those of attractive strangers. He imagined any number of excuses for bumping into them later that night; the New Year provided an opening for us to admit our longings, even if it was just the simple desire for the tradition of a midnight kiss.

His building seemed empty. No sounds of parties, no one in the hallways. Inside, the colonial moldings, plaster walls, and black-and-white deco tiles in the kitchen and bathroom always made Richard think that his bachelor quarters had been cobbled together from the rooms of a once-grand house. In the living room, a monstrous overstuffed sofa stood like an island. His queen-size bed, an antique Queen Anne dresser that had belonged to his grandfather, and a dilapidated pine armoire that hid a television and a DVD-CD-player combo, were his only other items of furniture, as if minimalist decor were the most logical side effect of divorce. Richard could not look at his apartment—inside or out—without thinking of it as the home of a man living in temporary internal exile. He was a dissident.

Inside, he turned on the television and had the momentarily

disconcerting feeling of seeing himself on screen, an edited highlight of his stunt being used to tease the news at the top of the hour.

He opened a bottle of wine and thought honestly about not even bothering with a glass. He would be the only one to know. There should be *two* glasses, that much was obvious; the holiday season felt like a weeks-long reminder of how adrift, how uncoupled, he was. There should be, he knew, more. It felt as if the only gifts that Christmas would ever deliver to him were reminders of how much was missing: a spouse, a family, a dog, a home. He hadn't bothered to put up a tree, and the wreath on his door was a gift from a producer at one of the Sunday-morning news shows. It was the end of another year in which he'd tried his best to ignore the season. On Christmas Day, he'd forgotten to call his sister, and the only holiday cards that showed up in his mailbox were from casual acquaintances looking to promote their law practice or their candidacy for Ward 2 city council. The photos on the cards became advertisements for a life he would not get to lead, no one in his bed, no fireplace, no elderly family dog wheezing contentedly at his feet, no child to watch in the anxious race to tear open every Christmas present with maximum destructive force. Alone at a time when the world told him again how he should be celebrating.

The wine he drank, a highly tannic California Cabernet, from the first sip tasted corky and left a fine silt at the lip of his glass, on the edge between simply not good and turned. It served him right. His ex-wife used to complain about his behavior, his constant introspection, as if he were some long-suffering character in a Russian novel. He thought the changes he'd made in the last year had conquered it, but the malaise (what else would he call it?) returned. His wine had turned. He thought about tossing it, but it was from a decent vintage and the bottle had cost something on the order of sixty dollars, and unless it had gone completely vinegar, he was going to tough it out. Petty crimes deserve petty punishments. So much around him had turned to acid in the past few years.

He powered through the wine because he'd given up everything else. In the past three years, he'd cut down on bourbon; at midnight, it would be exactly a year since his last borrowed smoke. He justified the wine on the basis of its alleged heart-healthy antioxidant properties. He knew too that he'd finish the bottle tonight. Already, on his tentative list of resolutions, this would be the year to cut out the wine, learn half a dozen different and flavorful ways to prepare steamed or broiled fish, walk to the office three days a week (these are the foxhole prayers of a man just beginning to fear his own death). He would learn not to be such a sentimental sap.

These desires for himself were not solely his; they had been his girlfriend's too. He went to the trouble to dig out a yellow legal pad from under the morass of bills and unread magazines on his desk and wrote down his first official resolution: he would not call his ex-girlfriend, Cadence Willeford, not tonight, not in the New Year. Maybe it was easiest to let Cadence and her demands, her thrills, settle into the fond memories of the recent past.

But that wasn't going to be his strategy. He had his legal pad and could add to his list of resolutions throughout the evening, but already he sensed a theme. He was trying to mold himself into the imaginary man she'd been demanding.

To wit, she said how the constancy of Richard's presence, their suffocating weekends, had left her feeling "close to overwhelmed."

"Not quite overwhelmed," Richard had repeated, and she laughed.

"Not quite. As of now, I think I'm not overwhelmed, just *whelmed*."

A few weeks after that, she'd called time out.

While he waited for the grill to heat, he emptied the refrigerator of its hoard of abandoned takeout containers. Awash in the flicker of the refrigerator's defective automatic light, he added a codicil to his resolutions: eat more fresh fruit, broccoli three times a week. He scrubbed the toilet, the tub, and wiped down the bathroom floor. He coated the insides of his oven with a foaming cleaner that made his kitchen smell like a swimming pool.

Then he filled two big bags with trash: year-old utility bills, unreadable taxi receipts, junk mail, a dozen delivery menus, the plastic wrap that the dry cleaner used to protect his laundered shirts, scores of ancient and unread magazines. His pack-rat tendencies meant that even his hall closet was filled with old clothes: a bespoke tuxedo purchased at a thrift shop during his sophomore year of college; a pair of red twenty-year-old Puma Clydes still grass-stained from mowing the lawn of a house he no longer owned. He took some well-frayed oxford shirts, a pair of too-small khaki pants, some stained undershirts, and a hideous blue parka that advanced fiber testing might have dated to the high school era, stuffed them into an old nylon bag, and headed out into the night.

The temperature was nearly sixty, record heat, a good omen for the New Year. Along his street, he walked past partygoers who lounged in summerlike fashion, enjoying cocktails on the front stoops. He passed living room windows flung open. Early revelers shouted down at him from adjacent rooftops. He crossed a vacant lot to a clothing-donation bin that looked like a lime-green dumpster, and tossed the whole pile, blue bag and all, through its swinging metal door.

The truth was that he wasn't meant for change. He longed for the familiar, specifically the presence of Cadence Willeford, who had excised herself from his life seven weeks ago, a decision that he still did not understand. To say that he'd been stunned was to underestimate the impact. He'd thought they were on an easy path to a future. She thought he needed to make changes.

The discussions still percolated in his memory, variations on a fugue of things he needed to improve, correct, revise. Which gave cleaning his apartment such significance. End of an era and all that. The first step felt obvious. He needed to remove everything from the apartment that reminded him of Cadence. Everything needed to be new. He'd been searching for a word to summarize her chief complaint, and as he opened his refrigerator door to remove a nearly month-old carton of 2 percent milk that had congealed into a curdled mess, it came to him. He'd been *stagnant*.

Richard knew she was right. Cadence managed to make all the places she inhabited into a home; even her office, in a nondescript black glass building on upper Connecticut Avenue, had been outfitted with oriental rugs, posters from National Gallery exhibitions, a few framed photographs of her father, a Depression-glass vase that her assistant filled with cut flowers each Monday. His office felt temporary, and he'd been living in that state for four years.

Maybe on Tuesday, he'd go look for a coffee table. He moved on to the bedroom, working methodically, and began folding the clean laundry that had sat unattended for nearly a week. He dumped his underwear drawer onto the bed, and from beneath a tumble of T-shirts yellowed with age and sweat fell a black vinyl envelope containing seventeen Polaroids of Cadence; the photos ranged from racy to what any court of appeals judge would be tempted to identify as hard-core pornography. But they were not like that to Richard. They were just another thing he had held on to, as if by this physical evidence that Cadence had once been a regular presence in his apartment and bed, she might somehow return, if only to claim the few items she had left behind: sweatpants, a bottle of eye-makeup remover, a nearly empty antiperspirant, a T-shirt advertising a five-kilometer fund-raiser walk, a collection of the metal clips and elastic ponytail holders she used to secure the flying tendrils of her hair, these photographs.

He sat on the edge of the mattress and scattered the Polaroids beside him. His favorite fell out on top, the great plane of Cadence's surprisingly tan torso from ribcage to hip bone, a spot that he loved to kiss. Even though he possessed other, more graphic pictures of her, some pantomimed from men's magazines, this snapshot held the strongest erotic charge for him; twice in the past week he had looked at these pictures, and it was this tame one that still stirred his orphaned cock. That he was the only person who could know it was Cadence's stomach made the resultant manual relief he'd given himself feel not just emptying but tremendously sad.

There was something pathetic, he knew, in his compulsion to conceal these pictures like some pimply teen stashing *Playboys* under his mattress. Richard did not want the Polaroids to be a reminder of loss. He suspected that his immediate future would contain a conversation in which Cadence demanded the return of the photographs, with all the ceremony and enjoyment of a prisoner-of-war exchange.

Now, on this New Year's Eve, Richard could not conjure any solid recollection of the past seven weeks; Thanksgiving had passed both unnoticed and uncelebrated, and he'd worked on an amicus brief throughout the better part of a Christmas Day on which he'd had no invitations and his phone did not ring. The days became unremarkable, a hodgepodge of half-finished work, bookended by that one painful evening when Cadence had declared her need to, as she put it, *reassess,* and now by this last holiday of the year.

His resolutions were simple: to address all of Cadence's complaints, the things she had said to him about his diet, his general inertia, his professional tendencies to fly off the handle on live television, defending things she suspected that he did not truly believe. Lately it was getting more difficult to work himself up into the froth that television demanded. Had she seen tonight's stunt, she probably would have turned off the set.

He left the photos on the bed and stepped into the galley kitchen to tend to his bachelor supper. After throwing together a green salad with just a tablespoon of an oil-and-vinegar dressing, he checked his steak; even though he liked things on the cool side of medium rare, it needed another couple of minutes. Enough of a window to call his sister. That was part of the plan too. Keep up with the remnants of his family, remember every important occasion, every birthday. There were only two to remember now, anyway: his sister, Mary Beth, and his nephew, Gabriel. They would be at home, certainly. But after four rings, he found himself talking to the answering machine: "Hey, it's your brother. You must be out and about. I just wanted to wish you guys a happy New Year and all that, swap resolutions. Oh yeah, I'll be on TV tomorrow. The usual shouting match, right around three o'clock Eastern Time, between the bowl games. I'm breaking out a new suit, custom made. I finally have proper attire for the budding pundit."

He hated the sound of his voice, the lonely echo it made against the ancient plaster walls of his apartment. It reminded him of how he sounded on television, syllables reverberating in his earpiece, the tautologies he was well paid to parrot, as if what he said might find some meaning if only he repeated it often enough. He carried his dinner into the living room, took up residence on the couch, and dug into what he swore would be his last piece of red meat.

For seven weeks Richard had tried to be hard-boiled about losing Cadence, as the breakup was reinforced by her refusal of dinner invitations that he'd meant to appear spontaneous, her abject unwillingness to reveal her simplest plans or whereabouts, the disappearance of his phone calls into her voicemail. She wanted, she said, a clean break. Time to think. Alone at the turn of the year, the point exactly where past, present, and future came together, he could no longer put up a stoic front. That was the real reason he wasn't out celebrating. He wanted to call Cadence, use all his skills in oral argument, tell her how much he was willing to change for her. But he did not. He suffered, as he feared he always might, from a thickness of heart and tongue.

6

THE LOBBY bar of Mike and Mary Beth's hotel—with its low-slung round tables topped with green felt, dark wood veneer paneling festooned with horseshoes, antlers, and framed posters of Ansel Adams photographs—was an anachronistic disaster. For a few years it had been a British pub, and when that idea went sour, only the dartboards stayed. Then the room had been known as the Capital Club and tried to pass itself off as the place where state legislators came to unwind. Now it was called the Canyon Room, but the decor hadn't changed. The furniture had been accessorized with Navajo blankets and the barstools covered in recycled denim, the menu heavy on exotic grilled meats and Irish coffees spiked with crème liqueurs. It was a casual room, and, despite the holiday, only a few men, Mike Renfro and two others, wore suits. And those three men were the oldest in the room.

When Mary Beth entered the bar, the first thing she saw was Mike, saying to a waitress, "The hardest part of my job is telling people the bad news."

Mary Beth stepped behind Mike and tapped him on the shoulder. He stood to greet her, taking her hands while announcing,

"You look exactly right—perfect," a compliment she accepted even though she suspected it was rote.

"*Perfect* is a little much, but thanks."

"How about *stunning?*"

"I'll settle for *passable.* No runs in my stockings, no chips in my nail polish, and no stray lipstick," Mary Beth said, whipping her tongue across her teeth. "And one of whatever you're drinking."

"A pair of bourbons, with a little splash of branch water," he said.

The bartender shuffled a new drink in front of him, handed one over to Mary Beth, then topped off the bowl of mixed nuts. "Just what is branch water anyway?"

Mary Beth said, "A Texas thing. Water from a freshwater stream. Or at least it's supposed to be."

The bartender grinned. "The other day, some elderly guy comes in, maybe seventy-five, and asks for a highball. Hadn't heard that one in a while. My old man used to call it that. A little bourbon, a little ginger ale." The bartender busied himself with a dingy towel, wiping it along the bar rail, then folding it into thirds.

Mike chomped through a couple of cashews. "I thought bartenders knew how to make everything."

"I'm not a bartender, I just play one on TV. I'm trying to make a few bucks while I study for the bar exam. And I like to keep it simple. When I was in college, I worked with a guy who refused to make any drink that wasn't named after its ingredients."

Mary Beth said, "My father always told me never to drink anything with more than three ingredients. Bourbon, water, ice. Ice counted as an ingredient. Keeps things predictable. The way I like it. What happens when somebody orders something that you don't know how to make?"

The bartender pulled out a Mr. Boston bartending guide from

beside the register. "I've got it covered. I believe in being pre-pared for any eventuality." Mike noticed the plain gold band on the bartender's hand. Married. Which meant he was a prospect.

"Me too," Mike said. "It's part of my job. Insurance." His hand went back into his jacket pocket, a nervous habit. He liked to turn the solid pile of business cards with his fingers, feel the embossed print, the way he used to fidget with his cigarettes back in his smoking days. Mike filched one card, a practiced movement, and laid it in front of his drink. "Mike Renfro," he said, and the bartender wiped his hand on his leg before return-ing the handshake.

"Warren Ashburton. My friends call me Ash."

"How long have you been married, Ash?"

"As of tomorrow, seven months."

"Well, I'm going to tell you what I'd tell anyone in your shoes, Ash. Any newlywed. If you've thought enough about the fu-ture to get married, you've already proven that you're capable of making concrete plans. The smart ones always do. You're off to a good start, education and everything, but you've got to make sure that you have that solid foundation, especially if"—and here Mike lowered his head, looked at Ash by raising his eyes—"the *unthinkable* happens."

Then Mike took a hit off his drink, held it in his mouth as if it were bracingly strong, another bit of practiced drama.

The bartender raised his hand before saying to Mike, "Hold that thought. I need to get Sherri over to hear this." Ash whis-tled gently and waved over the waitress, a blonde in a red bro-cade vest and short black skirt. She stopped gathering empty glasses from an abandoned table and, tucking her tray under her arm, headed over to the bar.

The introductions went like this: Sherri told Mike that Utah would be a great place to get settled, start a family, once Ash the bartender passed the bar. "He's going to work in the city, and I'm going to stay home with the family. Eventually." Ash looked at his wife, a questioning glance that Mike noticed, but she kept right on. "Well, I am. We're going to be pretty old-fashioned about things," she said. "I'm not letting my kids be raised by babysitters and television."

Ash couldn't resist chiming in. "That's because Sherri knows what kind of trouble we used to get into after school. We spent most of high school making out in her parents' basement. Me, I grew up on television. Smoked a lot of weed watching *Bugs Bunny*, specifically."

Sherri laughed. "We were so busy having fun that it took Ash years to muster up the courage to propose."

"It's true," Ash said. "Off and on through college, and then after I got out of school, I waited tables and skied for a few years. Sherri didn't want to get married until I got *serious*. Her word."

Mike smiled. "Tonight is the perfect time to think about this stuff. New year, new plans. You get real long-term benefits from starting a solid financial plan now, when the sacrifices aren't as noticeable. Being proactive about the future is a pretty sober way of thinking. It shows that you're serious people."

Ash tapped on the marble bar top and pointed at Mike's empty drink, and when Mike nodded for a refill, Ash said, "This one's on the house."

Mary Beth thought the conversation looked like a sales conference. The bartender pulled at the front of his red Spencer jacket, then leaned forward to watch Mike scribble on a napkin. Mary Beth knew Mike's spiel well enough to know that he was drawing a graph on a paper napkin, life expectancies, telling the two prospects some anecdotage. "Financially, it's women who suffer the most when the unthinkable happens, especially women who do not work," Mike said, "outside the home."

"And the sacrifices you have to make are always painful," Mary Beth added.

"Of course," Mike answered. He tapped at the place on the napkin where he'd drawn a set of small parallel lines that moved off toward the napkin's edge. "Your basic lifelines. One for you, Ash, one for Sherri. The only problem is that neither of you knows which line is which, and you can never know for certain which one is going to end first. Most people call what I sell *insurance*. But I call it *assurance*. Or, more accurately, reassurance."

Ash tugged at the cuff of his shirt. "I go first. It's been decided. After a brief illness. After, say, fifty-two years of marriage."

Mike took a belt of his drink. "Do you ever play cards, Ash?"

Mary Beth knew Mike was deep into his sales rap here; he could always be counted on to turn the discussion back to odds. He liked to tell his prospective clients—especially the young married couples who took him into their homes and stared expectantly across at him from a couch paid for on revolving credit—how life insurance was like gambling in a casino, except that you went to the table knowing the next turn of the card, the next roll of the dice. No insurance product yet had come to market that was capable of defeating inevitability.

Insurance, in Mike's eyes, was the only way to beat the house. Sometimes long-shot odds meant you were the only survivor; other times they meant you were almost certain to die. Mike Renfro talked to people about these things, showed them what side of the equation they wanted to be on. Part of his genius as a salesman was that he could talk to anyone about anything. His business depended on it. Early in his career he'd learned by listening how to talk to farmers about sorghum and the latest thresher attachments, knew instinctively who rooted for the Longhorns and who for the Aggies, talked with honest reverence to homemakers about the way his grandmother used to add a touch of real Vermont maple syrup to her oatmeal raisin cookies. But to Mary Beth now, there seemed something plastic and unforgivable about the charade.

Mike pointed again at the two lines on his napkin. Then he drew an X in the middle of the top line. "Who is that going to be, Ash? You? Can you really be sure about that? Four days ago, I gave a widow a check for five hundred thousand dollars because the husband had the good common sense to plan ahead. Forty-two years old, and he dropped dead at his desk. His secretary found him, face down in a chocolate doughnut."

Sherri the waitress mumbled, "Jesus. Any kids?"

"A boy. Eight," Mike said. "At least now the kid has a chance. I can't help but think where that family would be if it weren't for that check. His mom can pay off the house and still have a little bit of a nest egg. Without that, their situation would be, well, unthinkable."

Mike merely shook his head when he said the word *unthinkable,* with enough emphasis that all of them knew he was saying that the unthinkable happens on a regular basis. And none of them could say when it might happen again.

Sherri the waitress leaned back in. "This is a pretty morbid subject for New Year's Eve. This is supposed to be a night of festivities. Maybe we could plan to get together on Monday."

Mike rapped twice on the bar's wooden edge. "Would that it could always be like that. Take your time, get things squared away. After you've met all your goals, seen your children get married. That's the exact problem I'm talking about, Sherri. People always put things off. The hard things, the hard discussions. There isn't a person alive who doesn't think they'll be the exception."

That's when Mary Beth said, "But they never are. You never see it, anyway. Never."

She knew before Mike did that the prospect of a sale here was lost. Mary Beth imagined Sherri and Ash thinking about protracted illnesses, ninety-minute drives for chemotherapy, dialysis, losing a foot to diabetic gangrene, a sudden, shocking death by stroke. Mike was about to fold the tent too, she could tell. What little she knew about sales she had learned from him.

Mike balled up the napkin, used it to polish small circles on the marble bar top. "Sherri's right. No need to bring the party down. Not tonight."

"Oh, I don't know about that. It's as good a time as any to make plans. Tomorrow is the only day I have off between now and spring break," said Ash. "Otherwise, when are we going to think about this stuff?"

Mike reached for the check, threw down a pair of twenties. Then he pressed another business card onto Sherri's tray. He said to Ash, "Thinking about this shit comes with being married, or at least it ought to." Mike turned to Sherri and said, "When you guys are ready for action, you call me. I'll help you out."

On their way out of the bar, Mike and Mary Beth did not talk. Instead, she clutched his elbow and wondered if he had taken her interruptions as an attempt to sabotage the sale. She was a little bit angry, and the feeling suited her. She steamed over his attention to work, his morbid insistence on reminding people of their own upcoming death, as if he could never see beyond himself. He viewed every marriage, every partnership, in terms of its eventual collapse. Mike's philosophy of sales meant convincing people to buy life insurance by thinking about nothing except death.

To Mike, twenty-plus years of selling insurance meant that

the unthinkable always morphed into the inevitable. He would not even consider the alternatives. As they took the escalator down one level toward the raucous party sounds drifting out of the main ballroom, Mary Beth turned to Mike, and asked him, "Why don't you ever draw more lines on that graph?" and when Mike gave her a questioning look, she continued. "In the whole time I've worked for you, all the times I've watched you close, you've never drawn a line on that graph for children."

Mike stammered the beginnings of a defense, but Mary Beth raised her index finger, and he fell silent. "Someday you'll realize that scaring the shit out of people maybe isn't the best sales technique."

"Death and taxes," Mike said. "Why shouldn't I be realistic with these people? I'm sorry, but the unthinkable happens. More often than you could ever believe."

7

CADENCE WILLEFORD sold bomb-detection machines, behemoths the size of a delivery van, to large international airports in the U.S. They were designed to sniff the plastics, leathers, and ripstop nylons of checked baggage for the subatomic chemical taint left by certain types of Czech-manufactured high-tech explosives. Her job was to keep the nation's airline passengers safe in the skies.

The job meant travel, big city to big city, three weeks out of four. And travel meant she'd adopted certain behaviors. She drank bourbon on the rocks, because her career meant selling $30-million machines to committees of older white men who were easily impressed by a woman who could hold her liquor. The men who bought the machines liked to jokingly offer questions about mass spectrometry and gas chromatography, and because she had a master's degree from Johns Hopkins (she never mentioned that it was in English) and wore severe suits in navy or charcoal, their jackets winged with lapels that looked primed for takeoff like the vertical doors of an Italian sports car, they assumed she knew what she was talking about. She didn't.

The technology was beyond her. It had taken only a few weeks for her to realize that she would never have to talk about subatomic particles and molecular traces and chemical off-gases. All she had to do was talk about liability, the implied question of who would be responsible for another Lockerbie, and the fact that the ED60 system was the only one of its kind, and she'd somehow accomplished the hardest part, which was to sell the first machine to the first airport. The others she could sell on fear; *Cincinnati is protected, why not Denver?* The rest fell in line, and she got a commission check from her company and a royalty for every year that the annual service contract was renewed. It was a more-than-comfortable living but not exactly a vocation. No one ever dreamed as a teenager about a life spent selling machines designed to detect the residue of explosive compounds.

Her professional life—hotel to hotel, airport to airport—left her catching bits of breaking news wherever she could, taking up residence in a frequent-flyer lounge to watch live coverage of a high-speed police chase, the aftermath of a tornado, the attempted rescue of a child trapped in an abandoned well.

She reconstructed each vagabond month from her day planner and a stack of wrinkled credit card receipts. Her vacations were financed with frequent-flyer miles and hotel points. On weekdays, she had become accustomed to deciphering what city she was in based on the newspaper she found in front of her hotel-room door. But sometime in the last year or so, the chains had all begun to deliver *USA Today*, so she was never sure where she was except that on this New Year's Eve she was in Chicago, in a room on the twenty-seventh floor of the InterContinental Hotel. And because it was New Year's Eve and a Monday, she decided to take some time off, relax.

Since Cadence wasn't trying to make a sale, she'd been wasting time with this guy Chadley. A boy, really. A temporary measure. Cadence no longer trusted her own judgment—her judgment had led her to Richard MacMurray, and she was still questioning the wisdom of that decision. So for the past two months, Cadence had depended on a simple strategy to fill the hours that had once belonged to Richard; on Thursday nights, she met girlfriends to drink wine, eat prosciutto-wrapped asparagus and cornmeal-dipped calamari, and pretend to discuss the novel of the month. She stuffed her social calendar with happy hours and dinners out, reconnecting with the friends she had neglected as the infection that was her relationship with Richard grew. On one of those outings, Chadley made his move.

Chadley had presented himself on the first of December, a day to notice the oncoming winter's lengthening darkness. Cadence tagged along with a bunch of younger coworkers to after-work drinks, standing in the crush at a bar that offered a view of the Georgetown waterfront. The event showed up on the shared electronic calendar of her department. Cadence often suspected that her presence wasn't truly welcome, merely tolerated, and now the kids who worked for her didn't have the temerity to disinvite her.

But hanging out for a half hour bought her some street credibility at work. She'd throw down her credit card for a couple of rounds for her team and leave early. It was, like so much of what happened in her adopted city, an elaborate charade. She figured on escaping in a taxi, undoing the damage of cocktails with a salad and, later, forty-five minutes on the treadmill that dominated the corner of her bedroom nearest her overstuffed closet.

The crowd made her anxious; she knew she was being appraised, hip deep in a line of men and women a decade younger. The conversations around her were about where to find the best bargain happy hour, who needed a summer share in a beach house at Dewey, and, for the younger women, how to avoid further inflaming the married creeps from marketing who populated middle management. Socializing with her coworkers might be less stilted if Cadence had adopted one of the staff assistants to mentor; she could choose from a horde of entry-level college graduates who came and went in regular cycles each September and June. They referred to themselves as cogs.

She had been preparing excuses for her departure when this boy wandered over, tilting toward her to ask loudly, "So here's a typical Washington question. What is it you do? Who do you work for?" A wave of his drink came spilling over the edge of his glass, nearly hitting her, and she jumped about a foot backward. "Shit," he said. "Sorry. I'm somewhat drunk."

It felt like the first honest thing she'd been told in months. She decided then to answer him in kind. "I sell humongous, multi-million-dollar machines to the quasi-governmental entities that run our largest international airports," she said.

"What kind of machines?"

"The kind that detect the subatomic residues of certain non-metallic explosive compounds on passenger baggage."

The look on his face told her he either did not understand or did not believe her.

"You sell freedom," he said.

"Exactly. I sell the concept of safety. You can stop kids from shoving a .22 down their pants, and you can stop the guy from getting on board the plane with a parachute and a few sticks of dynamite, and you can reinforce the airframe so that a blast at altitude would require so much explosive that the mere bulk of it would make even the most narcoleptic security guard turn his head. You can train the pilot and the flight attendants in close combat techniques and put air marshals on every flight, and still no one is going to have faith."

"That's because faith requires a machine." He smiled the kind of self-satisfied grin that Cadence took as encouragement.

"People need the machine. A doctor can tell you about the

tumor, he can recognize its fibrous mass just by palpating it. He can say how it's the size of a walnut or a baseball or even a grapefruit because all tumors have to be compared to the totems of our everyday life, and everyday life is nothing but sports and fruit. He knows just from the look of it that it's malignant, but no one believes him until they take a biopsy or a cold-frozen segment or a needle extraction and run it through a machine. The machine gives me credibility. They believe me because I believe in the machine."

He regarded her. "I'm almost sorry I asked. Almost." He smiled, showing off bright-white teeth of an extraordinary symmetry. They looked so unnatural that Cadence thought they might be dentures.

"Why? It's a typical Washington question." Cadence cut him off. "But you're not a typical Washington guy, right? This is an ironic stance."

"How did you know? I'm Chadley, by the way."

"The purple tie. That's supposed to say how you're not really all about your day job—you have a band that plays out on weekends, or you're sitting on an idea, trying to get some VC together for the start-up, get parole from the nine-to-five world. But what you really want to do is write a book." Cadence knew she was being harsh, but Chadley looked willing to take the abuse. The alcoholic flush of his complexion said that he was a couple of drinks ahead of her. This was actionable intelligence.

"Actually, I've always thought I had a decent book in me."

"Everyone says that. They also say things like, *I'm not looking for anything serious right now,* or, *My job is in transition.*" Cadence folded sixty dollars together and slid it across to the bartender.

"You're done? Without even letting me buy you a drink?"

"Barring a drastic shift in the prevailing winds, I'm gone."

"Too bad. I'm thinking I should ask you to lunch. A limited-time trial offer. You know, low pressure."

"Low pressure is good," Cadence said.

"I'm all about low pressure. I'm an auditor. Even when I go in and find that the books are fucked, you know, the CFO has been writing some questionable checks, or the big boss has a five-thousand-dollar shower curtain in his executive washroom, all I ever get to do is hand the bad news over to someone else. My entire career consists of saying things like, *I think you ought to take a closer look at this, Dave.*"

She liked that Chadley wasn't serious. Richard was many things, and serious was right at the top of the fucking list. With Richard, she'd gotten used to conversations in which he and his friends commanded the bar, riffing about Senate confirmations, appeals-court decisions, the prospects for peace in Ireland, home rule, defense appropriations, a four-hundred-ship navy, the market prospects for securitized mortgage instruments, the two-state solution to the Palestinian question.

Somehow, she stayed for a drink. Almost immediately, Chadley told her he lived in the suburbs, not anywhere near her neighborhood. His condominium consumed almost the entirety of one of his twice-monthly paychecks. He described the expansive view from his balcony in the marzipan-and-spun-sugar suburb of Crystal City. The neighborhood turned itself off at 5:30 each night as parades of military officers and Defense Department bureaucrats trudged from office building to subway through a series of tunnels, rarely venturing to the hotel-lined streets above.

"The only problem might be the nightlife. Or lack thereof. The place is like a test site for the neutron bomb," Chadley told her. "The only time I see anyone is on the subway, on the way to the airport."

"Which airport?" Cadence asked, meaning it as a test. Maybe half the poster-size subway maps had been changed to add *Ronald Reagan* to the airport's name.

"National," he said. "I can't pronounce the name Reagan without bursting into flames."

"You just did, Skippy. Besides, I'm thinking," Cadence said, "you're probably a closet Republican."

"I don't make enough money to be a Republican."

Chadley offered a certain safety. He was obviously younger, uninterested in talk of children or commitments. Which made him ideal as a *temporary* distraction.

After two weeks, she knew that Chadley Billings was yet another of her strange enthusiasms. Dressing for their dates, she would sing a line from a song she had loved in college, a lyric she thought described the situation perfectly. *A simple prop, to occupy my time.* She thought of it as a disorder, these frequently appearing mini-obsessions. Because she feared the traditional holiday gain of five pounds, December's fixation had been her new diet, an implausible combination of high-protein vegetarianism that equaled gallons of yogurt and tofu in a million impossible ways. But for the New Year, sequestered with Chadley on the twenty-seventh floor of Chicago's InterContinental Hotel, in the heart of Michigan Avenue's Magnificent Mile, she had a craving.

"We're going for red meat," she announced from in front of the bathroom mirror. Chadley had busied himself flipping through the tourist guides he'd found on the desk in the room's corner, and Cadence knew by the time he'd decided on a restaurant it would be impossible to get a table. He hadn't made dinner reservations either, which, given the holiday, she found mildly irritating. Wasn't the New Year built around the idea of elaborate plans?

After a couple of days being cooped up together in a hotel room, she was beginning to notice the specific disadvantages of dating a younger man. Not *all* younger men, just this one. Chadley had a difficult time committing, an equally hard time letting go. He possessed surprising inhibitions. Even their fuck-ing had been far too choreographed. He couldn't go with the moment, couldn't even let it slide that somewhere in Cadence's recent past was an ex-boyfriend; he wasn't perceptive enough to notice that she had never asked about his recent past.

Chadley might learn in the next few years to appreciate the difference between fucking and making love, something all older men knew, something Richard understood intuitively, but God knows how long that would take. And as she went over the rims of her eyes with pencil, she mumbled his name, Chadley, and the thought struck her, *What sort of name is Chadley any-way?* She worried that she might have asked the question aloud.

In front of the bureau mirror, Chadley tended to his hair in an intricate ritual involving two different styling products and a series of contortions with the blow-dryer. As Cadence poked her head out the bathroom door, he clicked the machine off and asked, "What?"

She walked to the television, where a cable news channel was showing a clip of an on-air confrontation between two men in suits, the younger one standing in front of the older, looking for all the world as if he was about to take a swing. She couldn't get the context without turning up the volume, and she wasn't about to do that, because the younger man was Richard. The screen filled with chyron titles: IRATE DEBATE.

Cadence clicked off the TV, announcing, "I have a craving," then retrieved her skirt from the paisley armchair at the foot of the bed. She held the skirt in front of her, snapping it out like a matador, but before she could step into it, Chadley wan-dered over, kneeled to plant his face just beneath her navel, and started kissing his way down. To her, this was performance.

He looked up long enough to whisper, "I have a craving myself."

8

For Mary Beth Blumenthal and Mike Renfro, the New Year arrived like this: they and two hundred other couples packed themselves into a hotel ballroom ringed in green-and-white awning-striped wallpaper; Salt Lake City meant the New Year's Eve crowd was lily white, and there was no line at the bar, because the citizens of Utah prided themselves on restraint. That applied to their dancing too, tentative maneuverings that reminded Mary Beth of the cautious classmates she'd watched at her twenty-year high school reunion, moving stiffly with hands and elbows tucked to their sides.

Atop a temporary knee-high stage at the far end of the ballroom, a dance band robed in matching purple jackets meandered through a catalog of familiar songs from the last five decades; when they weren't playing, the four-piece horn section jerked together in stiff choreography, white boys imitating the Four Tops. During the twenty-year-old tunes, couples bounced and circled on the dance floor, percolating gently, singing along as the vocalist slurred out his urge to *celebrate good times, come on!*

That was exactly what Mary Beth wanted to do.

She attributed her giddiness to the altitude, or maybe the

remarkably pleasant weather, not to the bourbons or the champagne she'd had at the table. She felt relaxed, confident, her face radiant with a good, even suntan. Without the pressing demands of her child pulling at her hem, her worry lines had eased. She could not describe the relief of a four-day vacation, no obligations and no hurrying to the telephone. Tomorrow she would return to Texas, to her responsibilities and her routine, but tonight she wanted to give herself over to the occasion.

Mike and Mary Beth staked their claim to a table near the back of the ballroom. Mike retrieved a pair of cocktails, and they nibbled selections from the hors d'oeuvre trays of passing waiters. Mary Beth led Mike back to the dance floor as he chewed a scallop wrapped in bacon. But he didn't protest, just discreetly palmed the toothpick from his snack and fell in behind her, hands on her hips, as they conga-ed toward the band.

When the next song sped up, Mike dabbed at his hairline with his ubiquitous clean handkerchief. She liked that Mike did not have the big man's usual reticence to strut; he moved with a grace he inhabited easily despite his size. So many of the men looked flustered by the up-tempo music, but Mike moved with the confidence of a man armed with more than just lessons in the Arthur Murray method of dance; he was a surprisingly competent dancer, and that was the word that best summed up Mary Beth's feelings about Mike as a partner: *competent,* a possessor of minor but nonetheless impressive skills. He could choose a patterned tie that matched a striped shirt, make a decent dinner that did not include red meat, fillet any number of small, bony fish; he never forgot the birthdays of any of the girls who worked at the Mike Renfro Agency; he wasn't fazed by the cartons of Mary Beth's Swedish furniture that arrived labeled SOME ASSEMBLY REQUIRED; tonight, he demonstrated the secrets to dance steps that lived on in the films of the forties, the fox trot, the Lindy.

Since there wasn't some great passion, Mary Beth knew she was feeling a sort of Cinderella effect. She'd been treated well for the past three days and hoped both the feeling and the treatment wouldn't vanish once they returned to Dallas. Maybe it was the alcohol, the way they gulped the last of their drinks before heading out to dance, but Mary Beth could not help but feel she was on the precipice of some important change, a way she had not felt since her high school days, when she gave too easily of her heart and body. How refreshing it was to learn that under the weighted yoke of decades of minor disappointments might lurk an optimist.

Mary Beth swayed along with Mike, surveying the crowd, writing histories for each blank face she saw. The party was filled with couples, long- and short-term, alliances of permanence or convenience, anniversaries ranging from paper to gold. The song morphed into something newish; the younger couples nodded their heads in agreement, mouthed the words. She was one of the very few who did not know the song. Mary Beth limited her movements to half arcs in front of Mike, who danced behind the beat, then lurched to a stop.

He checked his watch and stopped in place and shouted at her over the squawk of the horn section. "Jesus Christ. They're missing it."

"Missing what?" Mary Beth too stopped dancing and leaned in to hear Mike over the thrum of the party.

Mike tapped the dial of his watch then pointed as a man in a well-worn tuxedo bounded onto the stage, waving his arms over his head in a panic to stop the band, flashing two inches of white shirt cuff from beneath his too-short jacket sleeve. "The goddamn New Year. It's already midnight."

Knowing that her New Year's kiss would arrive late felt like the evening was offering her a peculiar brand of betrayal. How often real life fell short of even her slightest expectations. She had a moment of guilt, the passing thought that perhaps she should have been watching the ball drop on television, on her own couch, with her son, nested in a huge swaddle of blankets and pillows. She'd kiss him on the forehead and carry him to her room, let him sleep the rest of the night in the big bed. Soon he'd be too old for that particular comfort, and that would be another disappointment to add to her list.

Onstage, the emcee's voice counted down the last seconds of another year—"Three, two, one"—filling the air around them, but the timing was off, too late. Even though it was just seconds, it was a ridiculous mistake, an Apollo rocket already off the launch pad while the voices at mission control kept on counting.

Half a minute into January, the band managed "Auld Lang Syne," the music rising over the noisemakers and the report of champagne corks. Mary Beth tilted her head to accept Mike's incoming kiss. He slipped his arms around her waist, slid a step closer, reached a hand into the stripes of her hair near her temple. She craved an epic kiss, if only because the other kisses that surrounded her—the dancing couples with their homogeneous, perfunctory pecks—were so disappointing, the loveless duties she remembered of her parents. She opened her lips and waited for Mike's tentative introduction of his tongue. His hand crossed her back, his warm fingers circling to touch the skin left exposed by her cocktail dress. The song's melody, funereal, dirgelike, now swelled as an overture, a call to arms, a battle cry to bury the disappointments of the past year and embrace the promise of the new. The nearby couples sang along, and Mary Beth opened her eyes to find that she and Mike were the only ones still in the clutches of their kiss. She had kissed Mike hundreds of times, kisses as a necessary thing, kisses as a prelude to roaming hands or more advanced activities. She snuck a moment's peek at Mike's face because she wanted to capture the kiss in her memory.

Mary Beth wished everyone could witness the beauty of their kiss. Tomorrow, replaying the moment from an outsider's view, she would see them in the center of the ballroom, sharing a noteworthy embrace, a life-shaping event. Already she was comparing it to a scene in that French movie, *Un Homme et Une Femme,* a man and woman kissing on the beach as the camera swirled around them in vertiginous loops. She kept both those images together, allowing them to blend into one, something to recall, replay, savor. Their long kiss ended with a second, shorter kiss—Mary Beth pulling Mike back to her with a two-handed grip on his lapels—touching his moist lips quickly, then pulling away with an audible smack. She could not help but feel that she was getting carried away to the soundtrack of a good-bye song.

After the kiss, as the band segued into a song from her childhood, one Mary Beth remembered from the AM radio of her father's Oldsmobile Delta 88. Mike settled for an awkward version of slow dancing. His hands fell on Mary Beth in the expected position of a dance instructor, holding her at a length far enough removed to remind Mary Beth of the childhood lessons she received from her father, living room waltzes with her feet across his instep, to the strains of the string-heavy arrangements of the easy-listening hits of the day. Mike puffed a bit with each step, and Mary Beth pulled him in close, conserving his movements, as the song ended in a flourish of cymbals, the elephant-like bleat of horns. He drew back, then glanced again at his watch and said, "You'd think, for two hundred and fifty dollars a couple, someone could have wheeled in a fucking TV."

9

ON RICHARD'S television, revelers pressed against a temporary barricade, cops and drunks side by side and staring skyward as fireworks exploded in a towering penumbra, casting the amusements of the Navy Pier in a cascade of red-and-white firelight. Richard could not fathom why he was seeing Chicago on his screen, the John Hancock Center and the Carbide and Carbon Tower bathed in celebratory flashes that boomed out over the great lake. He'd slept through the New Year and now was watching as the television networks chased midnight into the Central Time Zone.

The last thing he remembered, a pair of stories at the end of *Eyewitness News at 11,* had told of a Nebraska man who had built a lovely modern residence in an old Nike missile silo. A New York City policeman had been accused of taking $500 from the pocket of a man who'd died in the backseat of a Lexington Avenue taxi on Christmas Eve. He'd also slipped the cabdriver $100, telling him, in front of witnesses, "No need to ruin everyone's day."

Richard stood, then watched as the remote control fell from his chest, toppling his half-full wineglass, a few ounces of

Cabernet spreading across his rug. As he hurried to retrieve some paper towels, he put his right foot down onto a piece of glass, and his brain registered the pain before he even saw the shard protruding from the ball of his foot. The interjection, a basic *shit, shit, shit.* He hopped to the kitchen on his uninjured foot. He leaned against the counter and cradled his right heel in his hand, then watched as a few drops of blood appeared, soaking through his gym sock. He thought of such things not as accidents but as part of a grand conspiracy, the same trickster forces that made toothpaste fall from his mouth onto his tie, or left small puddles of water on his bathroom floor, unnoticed land mines for his stockinged feet.

He unfurled the bloody sock and gritted his teeth to extract a toothpick-long sliver of glass sunk half an inch into his foot. Immediately he thought of the story of the lion with the thorny paw. Richard could not count on anyone, had somehow managed never to have made a dependable friend in the city. The people he'd once relied on were gone: McDermott, cocaine. Schiek, Valence, Randall, all suicides. Hemphill, colon cancer. Cavanaugh, car accident. The Michaels twins had given up drinking and fled to Colorado. Kassner lived in Jakarta, Hanzel married and went to Virginia's horse country. McKalip kept threatening to leave the army but never had, was stationed somewhere in Germany, a living remnant of Cold War strategic planning. Up until a few months ago, Richard still talked to his college roommate, but more often than not the calls ended with Wentworth berating him for staying in the city, saying, "Man, you say hello to someone in the elevator, and they act like you're trying to steal their purse." Wentworth himself was married to a girl from high school; they'd moved to a Sears bungalow in one of those small North Carolina cities that always showed up on some magazine's list of Best Places to Live. The last time they'd talked, Wentworth called Richard a liar, said, "I can't even talk to you, man," and Richard had lost a friend without ever knowing what the argument had actually been about.

As he tended to the wine spill, blotting it with paper towels and covering it with a thick spread of table salt, the network news was showing the late-night preparations for a party in Seattle. It was nearly 1:15 a.m. Eastern Time when he finished with the mess, rinsed and stacked his dinner plate, and he still hadn't heard from his sister.

After the commercial break, he started flipping channels, managing to hit a block where all of the two-hundred-something networks of his cable TV seemed to have gone to commercial. A weight loss pill; *Are you paying too much for car insurance?; Accident or DWI? We can help.* He paused at a come-on for a 900 number, $4.99 for the first minute and $1.50 for each additional minute; his cock greeted the ad with a welcoming and familiar twitch, but he could think of nothing sadder than ringing in the New Year with a self-induced orgasm. Richard wondered how the supervisors over at 1-900-WET-BABE got anyone to stay home and service customers. His only interest, real conversation, wasn't going to happen. A girl of the sort he might like to talk to was already out on the town. Christ, he'd had two of them practically hand delivered, and now they were out, sucking down apple martinis at eleven bucks a pop, ridiculing the Washington men who went out for New Year's Eve wearing their best pinstriped suit. In this mood, he doubted he could even get hard.

And if he could concentrate long enough to picture the distinctly hard-core things that these women pretended to want, he had a problem. Cadence. He had tried this type of manual relief before, and somehow Cadence always intruded on the fantasy scenario: Cadence as a plaid-skirted schoolgirl, Cadence as a flight attendant. Soon, Richard figured, the women on the other end of these lines would be from India, perplexed by all the elaborate fantasy scenarios demanded by American men. It was the logical consequence of outsourcing. The accent might work for him, though. At least it wouldn't sound like Cadence. However much he imagined himself as a noble barbarian, even masturbating wouldn't help tonight. A couple of Tylenol PMs, washed down with another ounce or two of wine, might.

10

MARY BETH and Mike continued kissing in the corridor, kissed some more while staggering through the lobby, past a handful of disapproving guests. In the reflection of the elevator's polished brass doors, Mary Beth watched as her hands roamed across Mike's wide shoulders. His hands acquired a beachhead at the lower half of her ass, began a playful attempt to raise her skirt. At the ding of the bell indicating their arrival at the seventh floor, they separated, as if by instinct; at home in Texas, they'd become well practiced in the art of keeping their relationship away from prying eyes.

They kissed again, once outside the room and once inside, before Mary Beth shivered at the shock of the room's temperature. Her complaints about the cold were lost in the hum of hotel machinery. She flipped on the lamp at the edge of the dresser and turned to Mike, repeating herself. "Jesus. Did you turn down the heat?"

"I'm planning on being a human bedwarmer," Mike said as he tugged at his necktie.

Mary Beth slipped out of her evening clothes and shimmied between the sheets, improvising a bolster out of the king-size bed's four pillows. She pulled the comforter to her shoulders, then discharged her underclothes with a flourish, tossing them on the corner chair. Tomorrow she planned to return to Dallas and the demands of her son, but her flight wasn't until 8:00 p.m., and she was thrilled at the prospect of eggs Benedict from room service, watching the Tournament of Roses parade, not getting out of bed until sometime around noon, maybe even more champagne, a last day of decadence.

The sounds of Mike urinating with sudden urgency echoed out of the bathroom, so she turned on the television and ratcheted through the channels, stopping when she heard the last ten seconds of an anchorman wrapping it up before the commercial break. Then Mike stood naked at the foot of the bed. He was thick across the beam, the skin of his chest a bright, milky white, especially in contrast to the windburn that bloomed on his cheeks.

She threw back the covers, and Mike clambered in, pressing against her. His skin felt warm, vaguely moist. She admired how he'd always been at ease with his body, willing to walk from kitchen to bedroom, even out to the pool, without a stitch. Back in Texas, Mary Beth kept a robe on the back of the bathroom door, swam in Mike's pool encased in a navy-blue one-piece suit, the kind advertised as providing full coverage for the curvier woman.

On the television, the update at the top of the 1:00 a.m. hour showed footage of a protest gone wrong, two masked students hurling a galvanized garbage can through the plate glass of a chain coffee house, a phalanx of police in full riot gear milling languidly a block away. Taking the shattering glass as their cue, the police consolidated into an orderly mob, marching with linked elbows toward the disorderly. Mike pointed at the TV. "Why do they always do that? Go after the Starbucks first. Set the McDonald's on fire."

"Symbolism," Mary Beth said. "My brother and I saw a riot once. The start of one, anyway. In DC. We're at this little Mexican place when a rumor started to go through the neighborhood that a cop had shot an unarmed man. A Salvadoran. The guy was drinking in public, and the cop, a black woman, told him about five times to put it away. He didn't speak English, and she didn't speak any Spanish. How he got shot, they never really figured out. But by the time the cameras got there, about three hundred people were in the street, banging on garbage cans, shouting slogans. The cops broke out the gas, but then the wind shifted and blew it right back at them, and when they ran away, it was a free-for-all. A busload of kids ushered the driver off a Metrobus, then turned it over in the street."

Mike said, "They burned it, of course. Every riot starts with a burning bus."

"Then they turned and went after the lamp store on the corner. A hot dog cart, a Seven-Eleven. Then the Salvadoran bank, and finally the Western Union office where they all go to wire money to relatives back home. Only then did they go after the Kentucky Fried Chicken."

Mike laughed. "Looking for the Colonel's secret recipe?"

"Who knows?" Mary Beth pointed the remote at the TV, kicked the volume up. "The KFC was four blocks from that bus. They sought it out. It was a political act."

"For no good reason?"

"That KFC had to represent something. Oppression, colonialism, slavery, the whole plantation culture. They went after it. It was worth picking up a brick and throwing it through a window."

Mike reached for the remote, but Mary Beth showed him a palm that meant *stop*. "What did they expect?"

She answered. "Maybe not to get gunned down for drinking a two-dollar bottle of malt liquor."

"You sound like your brother. You should be making this argument on *Meet the Press*."

"Our dad had a strong libertarian streak. That's the cornerstone of history. The inalienable right to be left alone. There are times when that's all anyone wants in the world."

"I take it you've been there." Mike rolled onto his elbow.

"Wanting to be left alone? Sure. Like tonight, I just wanted it to be us. I didn't want a party. I barely wanted to talk to anyone else. I can't trust someone who pretends to be overly interested in talking to the office manager of an insurance agent."

"*Agency*," Mike said. "You work for an insurance agency. We represent safety, security. We're a symbol."

Mary Beth shook her head. "I don't want to be a symbol. I don't want things that stand in for something else, or clever little phrases that are supposed to represent some larger whole. I want pithy little sentences that break your heart, that warn me about the roadblocks ahead. I want something short and sweet that's going to make me cry."

"I have a hard enough time telling anybody what it is that I want as it is."

"No one else is going to do it for you. I learned that a long time ago. Like in sales. You have to ask for the commitment; that's part of being a closer. I learned that from you, Mike."

"Are you asking for a commitment?" Mike gave her a raised eyebrow.

"I'm asking you what exactly you think we have here."

"What we have here is something fantastic. This," Mike said, pointing at the floor, "this is where it's happening. Utah is the future. New jobs, new roads. All the modern amenities. What we have together is maybe a chance for a future. I just don't know if I want any future to be in Texas."

Mary Beth sat farther up, straight and stiff against the headboard. She wanted him to be a champion and a stalwart, but now she knew he was, at his core, simply afraid. "Are you breaking up with me? Is this one of your resolutions—bring a woman to Utah to do the thing you couldn't do in the comfort of your own home?"

Mike smiled, a look Mary Beth took as nerves. "I wanted you to come with me because it's time for answers. Someone needs to figure out exactly what's happening here. Are we a weekend thing, or are we a more permanent thing? Or are you never going to be happy unless that thing has a name? We never talk about this stuff. I try to bring it up, and you tell me not to, at least not in front of the kid. So to answer your question, I'm not trying to do anything."

She let out a heavy breath and stared at the ceiling, its painted-over water stains. "We don't talk about these things because most people, most adult couples, have conversations like this at the dinner table. Or in bed, next to each other, after the kid goes to sleep and the TV gets turned off. This isn't something that we're going to talk about at work. The only thing that we've established for certain is that we've turned into a living cliché."

"What does that mean?"

"You've said everything short of 'It's not you, it's me.' The next thing I know, you'll be telling me how you need some space."

"I do"—Mike laughed—"but I'm not talking about the kind of space that you're thinking about. I need space in the no-freeways, no forty-five-minutes-to-go-five-miles sort of way. No gang shootings. No midafternoon trips to the bank that end in sudden violence. No one jostling me from behind at the ATM, looking over my shoulder to steal my PIN code. The Utah kind of space."

On the television, the police dispersed a milky cloud of gas that settled over the protesters in a yellowing mist. Mary Beth couldn't look away from the violence; it wasn't until she saw the faces of the police, cartoonish and distorted beneath the space-age polymers of their riot shields and helmet visors, that she figured out the scene was from South Korea, a student protest. A young man in khakis and red sneakers, his face hidden behind a red bandanna, ducked under the swing of a police baton and picked up a gas canister, tossed it back toward the police lines. The news went to commercial before she started in on Mike again. "Why Utah? What kind of wide-open spaces are there in Utah that you can't find in Texas?"

"It's not the space itself. It's what the space suggests. You can hardly find any Texas in Texas anymore; it's all filled with people from Connecticut and New York. Guys who grew up wearing Topsiders now wear boots with their suits."

"Christ. You sound just like my father. We're sitting having breakfast, the summer before he died. He looks out the window toward the other houses on our block and says, 'Who put those other fucking houses there?' And they'd been there all along. Before we were. For about a hundred and forty years."

"Exactly. No matter how much I sell, how much money I make, I'm never going to be a part of the old Texas, all that Stetson-hat and Sons of the Alamo crap. I didn't go to school up in Austin. Daddy wasn't a federal judge, there isn't a library or post office named after my great-great-great-uncle somewhere. The real Texas is closed to people like me."

"That's a little dramatic, don't you think? You have every advantage I can think of. Every one."

"Maybe thirty years ago that was true. Nowadays you can't even buy the idea of Texas. Costs too much, for one. And it's stupid to think things will be any different in Utah, any better. But I want to try. I want clean air and jolting winds and peace. Peace most of all. That's the whole point. Look at these people here, these Mormons, with their eternal marriage and their principles of modesty. The army drove them out of Iowa and Missouri, and do you know what they did? They came all the way to Utah just to be left alone." He gave her a sheepish laugh, unfolded himself out of the bed, went to fetch a glass of water. He drank and let his other hand rest on his hip. Mary Beth saw how the width of Mike's shoulders almost matched his waist. He was rectangular, larger than Texas himself. He was Alaska.

"But you could go anywhere. Seattle. Upstate New York. Why not Montana? Or Colorado?" Mary Beth sighed and slid down flat on her back, still staring at the ceiling.

Mike climbed back on the bed, pulled at his trunklike legs until they folded into a yoga-like pretzel. "Seattle is over. And the assholes have already gotten to Colorado. Filled to the brim with Californians."

Mary Beth relaxed, showing some of her well-appointed teeth. "That's because there's no space left in California."

"I don't really know how this happened. Texas went all sour on me. Like a song that I'd heard all summer on the radio. You're never sure when it happens, but by the time Labor Day rolls around, the thing is ruined forever."

"So there's only going to be space enough in Utah?"

"There has to be a chance."

For Mary Beth, the discussion existed like the moment between burning a finger and actually registering the sensation. She was still debating how much of a reaction she would allow herself to show. "How far have you looked into this? I'm just hoping that you haven't found anything yet. That you haven't made commitments."

Mike said, "I haven't done much of anything. But I'm sticking around. That's the one resolution I made. I came here to stake a claim, find a Utah homestead."

Mary Beth pulled a pillow to her lap, petted it like a cat. "I think that's excellent. I really do. Sounds like a more ambitious resolution, as opposed to the usual 'I've got to lose twenty pounds' crap. When does this little surveying project begin?" She kept expecting a more specific invitation. But she wasn't going to spell it out for him. There were any number of ways he could say the right thing. *Help me find a house. Help us find our house.* His vagueness was exasperating. She had spent years imagining her future, and Gabriel's, and even the most fanciful versions of what she imagined had never included Utah. She wasn't even certain that she'd imagined Mike as part of it. And maybe he was being obtuse, but he wasn't exactly spelling out where she and her son fit in to all of this. He hadn't said anything explicitly, and to her, her future and that of her son were far too important to assume she belonged in someone else's future too.

"Tomorrow morning. After I drop you off, I'm meeting a guy. The guru of Great Basin real estate. We're taking out the Jeep and scouting for a homestead."

Her passing thought: their coming to an end was logical, even inevitable. She should have said no, no to the idea of the trip, no to the idea of taking up with Mike in the first place; her late father called that way of thinking "paralysis by analysis," yet here she was, in bed, next to a man who was her boss and her lover and who apparently did not think of himself as her future husband. She'd come to Utah filled with questions, and now the answers she was most afraid of were here, taking up space beside her in a hotel bed.

There wasn't much else to say. Soon Mike rolled away, perhaps feigning sleep but certainly showing that the discussion had been tabled for now. She wondered what New Year's Eve at Mike's house would have looked like, Mary Beth in a simple black dress serving a dinner that she'd labored over for hours. She wanted all the comforts of home, to dice the shallots and herbs for the sauce, to cook a five-course feast on the $4,000 range that Mike used only as a storage cabinet for his pots and pans. She wanted Gabriel helping in the kitchen, tasting sauces and batters out of stainless steel bowls, decorating sugar cookies with rainbow-colored sugar sprinkles. She didn't want to head home alone and have an almost three-hour flight to think about where she'd gone wrong.

Utah would be solely his decision, and even in the middle of the night, Mary Beth couldn't fault his reasoning. He wasn't a Texan any more than she was, so maybe leaving wasn't a bad idea, not for Mike and maybe not for her. She just wished she'd been a party to the decisions he'd already made. In his new home, wherever it might be, she would not be a partner or a helpmate. She would be nothing more than another of his accessories.

She felt restless, consumed by her inability to sleep. Mike wasn't having that problem. He breathed with a rhythm like a shallow purring, a melody that, in her own bed, Mary Beth had always found soothing. Not tonight, though, so she threw back the blanket, slipped from the bed, and headed to the bathroom.

She hadn't been able to sleep without difficulty for years. She needed the cool side of the pillow, clean sheets, the occasional ten milligrams of diazepam, the calm of a controlled environment. In her own apartment, Mary Beth let the air conditioner, a window unit that spat a fine black dust onto the floor, console her with its autonomic noises. Even in optimum conditions, sleep never came in torrents, as she suspected it did for Mike and most normal people. The world was too intrusive, her heart too insistent, to allow more than an hour or two of sleep at a time. When she was lucky, she could string together three or four of these breaks in a night and be a reasonable facsimile of herself in the morning, after, say, three cups of coffee. She had tried everything, prescriptions that left her muzzy-headed, exercise, valerian root, a black satin sleep mask and yellow foam earplugs to block out the world. The world came anyway.

She knew only one reliable remedy. She eased herself into the empty bath, the plastic of the molded tub cold against her skin. She piled together a temporary bed of ample, plush towels, then made a pillow out of the white terry hotel robe and sprawled out, tensing and relaxing her legs. The small knot of muscle in her midcalf burned with a pleasant feeling that bordered on overexertion, a consequence of the evening's dancing in high heels.

She bit into a towel, the texture raw on her tongue. She liked the idea of him walking in, knew how much he would enjoy watching the rest of the performance. That's what she was picturing as her hand began to work a little faster, as her legs moved wider to accommodate her movements. She wanted to make him feel hungry, carnivorous.

She slithered lower in the tub and jumped at feeling the plastic—the simulated porcelain—against her thigh. She wanted something real, a clawfoot tub, real tile walls. She wanted a *home*. The summit of her own climax moved perceptibly closer; she did not need a finger inside her any more than she needed to add details to the fantasy in her mind: Mike standing over her, watching. A husband. As she worked at that most sensitive part of her anatomy, the noise came from her in one long, shallow exhalation, and her orgasm was there, tepid, as furious as a damp sparkler, something left over from the year before.

11

ROOM-SERVICE dinners fell into two categories, romantic and necessary, and now, in the middle of the night, Cadence could see nothing romantic in the sediment-choked dregs of her empty wineglass, the grease-smeared plates. A glance at the clock radio told her the New Year was nearly two hours old in the Central Time Zone, that its occasion had come and gone without her noticing. She'd slept through it.

At least it was quiet, Michigan Avenue some twenty-seven floors below no longer ringing with the evening's sonata of car horns and the occasional drunken shout.

She was angry because she'd gone to bed with him again and hadn't said anything. If they were going to keep fooling around, then Cadence wanted to do it in her own particular manner. She was willing to permit access to her body, but she was going to demand certain attentions, a minimum of his ham-handed groping. Thinking of how to explain this to Chadley, how to correct his errant techniques, Cadence's mind drifted to Richard.

Richard's habits—browsing the Sunday *Times* naked save for his tortoiseshell reading glasses, bringing a glass of wine to the

bedside table and never drinking it, even his more earthy pro-
clivity toward cleaning his toenails with the tines of a dinner
fork—seemed endearing quirks now that she could view him
from seven weeks' distance. She felt a comfortable abandon
when they were together. He could make her laugh too, even
during the awkward moments of their lovemaking when his
feet tangled into a maze of sheets and blankets and threatened
to throw them both onto his apartment's hardwood floor.

It was never going to be like that with Chadley, even with the
lubrication of three stiff cocktails. She looked at Chadley's face
and saw only the imperfections, the small places where he was
not careful enough with his shaving, the one stray hair always
poking out of his left nostril. And then there was the fucking.

At least there had been some recent improvement, less of the
thrust and counterattack approach that reminded Cadence of
the worst of her drunken college couplings. Too much of how
Chadley performed was just prelude to something else, the next
thing implied by the placement of his fingers or the pushing of
his hands. Cadence showed her frustration by simply picking
up Chadley's hand and putting it where she desired. Richard
had never needed such remedial instruction.

She missed Richard's way of expressing his needs, when she
would beg him to tell her what he thought about, what secret
film loop rolled in his head, while he masturbated. She asked
him to tell her everything as long as she appeared in the fantasy
somewhere; whatever he asked of her, she would gladly try.

With Chadley, each new encounter felt more like she was
in survival mode, their lovemaking an awkward mix of reck-
lessness and sensible precautions. She could not imagine how
the provisional approaches they were taking might dissolve into
a sea of spontaneity. They used condoms, and Chadley never
broached the subject of feeling skin on skin.

Cadence could give herself over to a man in any manner she chose—she would tell them they could have her any way they pleased, and for most of them, that was enough. By the time most of the men she had known were able to give voice to their desires, it was too late, too late for Cadence anyway. Only Richard could let the darkness out of himself and know that in the morning he would still be able to close the lid on that box. He announced his desires—*I am going to fuck you hard*—and then acted; the hottest thing she could think about was Richard whispering in her ear about how desperate he was to taste her, to fuck her. The appearance on his face, the concentration and release, became something she always thought about when she was with Richard, and now those thoughts of Richard intruded on her moments with Chadley. Eventually, she supposed, it would be this way when she was alone and her hands started their fundamental ministrations to the needs of her body. It would become a need, and the need would become imperative. And she would think of Richard. And thinking of Richard, she knew, was the part that turned her on.

Chadley rose up on his elbows. "What are you doing?"

"Couldn't sleep," Cadence admitted. The thought of waking to a plate of day-old French fries congealed in grease made her want to retch, as did the pile of tissues next to the bed, all lacquered with the fluids of half-inspired lovemaking. She took the greasy plate, the tissues, all of it, and dumped the pile onto the room-service cart, pushed it into the cavernous hallway.

"What time is it?"

Cadence returned, shimmied under the covers. "Almost two. We missed it. I didn't come all the way to Chicago just to miss the New Year."

Chadley turned and gave her a garlic-and-booze-riddled kiss before saying, "You didn't miss it. You were otherwise occupied."

"Okay, fine, I didn't miss it, exactly. But isn't the point of New Year's Eve that you're there, right at the moment? The moment is what makes it special." Cadence could tell Chadley was more focused on what they had been doing at the stroke of midnight.

"I thought it was a pretty good moment. But let me be the first. Happy New Year." He leaned in for a kiss again, and Cadence withdrew, watching the telltale point of his persistent tongue rising from between his lips, then departing quickly, a rodent emerging from its burrow.

Chadley hopped out of bed and carried his condom to the bathroom garbage can. He yelled back at her, "There's champagne in the fridge. You can't have an occasion without champagne."

Cadence grabbed the bottle by its neck and inspected the label. It was one of the usual brand names that most guys Chadley's age had memorized from films; that meant he'd been too shy to ask for help. Richard would have consulted the hotel's sommelier, had something delivered. "Impressive," she said, picking at the bottle's foil cap.

When Chadley came out of the bathroom naked, a white hotel towel draped over his shoulders, she noticed how the girdle of his hips looked boyish, slim, almost hairless. All she could think of was the other men she had been with, men she had loved, Richard especially, their musculature, their entirely manly appearance.

"I didn't think you were going to stay," he said. "I just kept thinking that something would come up. I keep expecting for us to be interrupted."

So he was smart enough to feel her ambivalence. When she'd spent the night in Richard's bed, she could often feel the gentle waves of nervousness roll off Richard, as if he was always anticipating the worst possible news from her. She could calm him with a touch, a hand on the flat of his chest. But what she felt from Chadley was different, a timidity that reminded her he was a stand-in.

She wanted to be alone, *now,* to open the windows to Chicago's blasting cold, extract the spare blankets from the closet, and cocoon herself against the harshest winter she could imagine; she wanted to watch the city buses sloshing diagonally up the street in a sudden squall, businessmen in trilbys and fedoras turning up the collars of their Chesterfield coats and struggling up the avenue against the wind. She would watch until the city ground to a halt and then wake to room-service coffee and a bath as hot as she could stand. Or, better yet, she could leave. A forty-dollar cab ride to O'Hare and the first flight home would fix everything. Among all her impulsive enthusiasms, this might have been the dumbest, thinking that she could spend the weekend with a near-stranger and distract herself with the mildest of hedonisms, a few cocktails, a good steak.

She turned the television to a news channel and put the volume on low, just loud enough for her to distinguish between the newscasters and the commercials, and hoped the blink of the screen might hypnotize her into something resembling rest. She did not think she could sleep with this quiet. She wanted all those familiar noises to fill her up.

Still, she'd never really shared any of these domestic visions with Chadley, and she couldn't see that changing. "What were you going to do if you were stuck here alone?"

"Probably order more food, watch a movie."

"What kind of movie would that be?" she said, adjusting the sheet to cover her breasts.

Chadley grabbed the remote control and pulled up the menu for the 'adult films. "The businessman's special, of course." But Cadence winced at the titles: *Where the Boys Weren't, A Taste of Chocolate, Naughty Newcummers 17, Rocco Goes to Romania.* They all held a curiosity for her, but this was a longing she would rather keep to herself. She and Richard had even watched one of those *Faces of Death* videos, which left her understanding two things simultaneously: first, how distasteful it was that someone was making money off those videos, and, second, how her own voyeuristic gaze had proven that the human psyche had a remarkable capacity for getting, and staying, numb.

But this curiosity was not for sharing with Chadley. She knew how he liked to think of himself as a charming rogue, convincing enough to talk a random woman—the kind he flirted with in the laundry room or the grocery store—into performing for the camera. Cadence doubted he had any particular gift for persuasion; nothing he said could convince a woman to try the secret things these movies suggested to him—women with comical dimensions and artificially lightened hair who claimed to want to take on Chadley and all his friends, who enjoyed taking it *anywhere he wanted to put it.*

Cadence could not help but think that porn had ruined an entire crop of otherwise fuckable men; she didn't need the Chadleys of the world, their baldly imitative techniques: a quick slap of her ass, or going down on her with a flapping, clownlike tongue. She wasn't about to perform for him either. Cadence did not want to play any role other than herself. Already she imagined her return flight in a wistful way. Chadley wouldn't know enough to say his good-byes at curbside, to offer only a modest kiss. She pictured him ruining the moment, doing something crass that only he could assume might be sexy, like bringing his fingers to his face, telling her that he could smell the traces of her that remained. She shivered because she had him figured as the kind of boy-man who thought whispering could make the word *cunt* sound sexy.

Cadence took the remote from Chadley's hand, skipped past a few titles with *Hustler* in them, and found the next page of possibilities. "Amateurs? I mean, Jesus, there are some people you just shouldn't see naked."

Chadley snorted a bit. "Like who?"

"I don't know. Anyone who looks like a high school P.E. teacher. Some guy with a mustache who takes his wife to a swingers' party for her birthday. You know, the ones right at the cutting edge of fashion."

Chadley nodded as if he knew what she was driving at. "If it was 1978."

"Exactly." She clicked to another choice. "And just who is this Rocco guy anyway? Is that the one who calls every girl he meets a whore? Charming. There's nothing hot about a guy who stuffs it into you and says, 'Take it, bitch.'"

Nothing could be more of a buzz kill than a woman who wanted to discuss the politics of erotic art on New Year's Eve, but here she was, thinking in terms of exploitation, coercion, the hegemonic and male-driven industry of pornography promoting an image of women's bodies—tan, enhanced, hairless—that could be achieved only through the diligent patronage of plastic surgeons and aesthetic technicians. She wanted to impress upon Chadley the absurdity of the situation, ask him to read books she hadn't thought about since college, *Sexual Politics*, *Backlash*, *The Feminine Mystique*. She wasn't opposed to pornography. She was simply opposed to situations, the situations of most of those movies and the situations she found herself in now, their contrived nature, this boy next to her with the insistent cock and utter lack of romance.

She could forgive the cock. The body was always the body,

and wanted what it wanted; the people who spoke of what the heart wanted were often proven fools. Lately she had been dividing humanity into two categories: those who were fools and those who weren't. At this moment, she was realizing in which category her recent behavior had placed her.

So, like countless other women in the course of history, she knew the rest of her trip had become something to endure. She pressed the Purchase button for what felt like the most innocuous choice, and the screen filled with two couples fucking side by side at a swimming pool somewhere in the plastic diorama of the San Fernando Valley.

Chadley turned the volume down a bit. "We should make our own movie. Get a camera and a tripod. You can see what it really looks like."

"I have a pretty good idea what it looks like."

"Only in your head. It would be more interesting if we were in it."

"Maybe," Cadence said, knowing that even though Chadley was still as enthralled with her as he would be with any new lover, he'd likely take her reluctance as a disappointment. "Maybe it would help you to learn what it looks like when it's real."

Just then the camera went back to a shot featuring a pre-eminent view of a guy's muscular and completely hairless ass. "Okay, that's real, but that's disturbing. The guy has a tan line. From a thong," Chadley said, punctuating his thoughts with an *eeeeeewww*. The camera focused on the first couple, the man sitting on the edge of the pool deck, dangling his feet in the water, while the woman lowered herself on top of him.

Cadence laughed, knowing he'd missed the point of her comment. "And what's up with the way she's shaved?" The woman's pubic hair had been whittled down to a single, pencil-thin line that ran a half inch straight up and down.

Chadley said, "We live in an era of intricate grooming. What do they call that anyway?"

"Whatever you call it, it's awful." Cadence nestled into the crook of Chadley's left arm. "That girl is just straight-off-the-bus-from-Topeka skanky. Those press-on nails could put an eye out. But Christ, this is boring. They're not even really showing anything."

She knew in her heart that she didn't mean that the movie was boring; it was the company. She'd thought she had the temperament for a meaningless fling, someone who would be attentive and grateful, and here Chadley seemed bent on being neither. Cadence knew too she would become a story told to his friends, guys he played pickup basketball with, whatever he did to fill up his Saturdays; she'd be the older woman who'd curled his toes for a while, a tale to be told, the same way her father, when he finally put down the drinking for good, substituted stories of his drinking for an actual drink.

And that's when it hit her—Chadley already was a story, one she hadn't quite finished. But she knew how it would end. Just then, one of the men reared up and announced that he was going to come, and Chadley and Cadence stopped talking as the camera moved in for a close-up of his eyes as they wrinkled tightly shut.

"That's worse than stupid guitar-player face," Cadence said.

She was willing to let Chadley fuck her one last time and managed not to worry about her makeup, or that she was down to a last pair of clean underwear. She touched herself discreetly to make sure she was ready, then climbed on top of Chadley, who immediately began with his usual furious grindings. As she took his fingers from around her neck, she finally found a way to say it to him. "Can we just fuck like normal people for once? Make an effort at normal anyway?" And when Chadley raised himself up to argue with her, she pressed a finger to his mouth, which he licked a few times, stopping only when she told him, "Spare me the histrionics."

He extracted himself from under her, and she fell back on the bed. He kissed his way down across her stomach, and that's when she touched him under the chin, pulled him back up until his head came to rest on her shoulder, and told him that was enough.

12

THE VOICE on the phone kept referring to Ash as Warren. He bit his tongue. He hated to be called Warren.

A doctor was explaining, and Ash kept telling him to go back to the beginning, which he obligingly did. That was how Ash knew it was bad. The hospital, the doctor said, has Warren Eugene Ashburton, thirty-four, lately of Salt Lake City, Utah, on record as the possessor of both durable and medical powers of attorney over his mother, Geneva. He was the sole contact in case of emergency.

Warren listened as the resident physician explained the events of the morning. Apparently, his mother had been suffering some nonspecific confusion (Warren wrote a note to look up what exactly Lewy body dementia was). The resident had diagnosed Geneva with three possible fractures—each wrist (X-rays would later confirm cracks in the hamate and sesamoid bones of the right wrist, which had absorbed the brunt of the impact) and the left hip. There was more news to come, and the news would get worse before it got better.

The hip would be problematic, an orthopod would need to see the film, but, he was explaining on the phone to Warren—

Can I call you Warren?—Geneva was likely to spend New Year's Day having emergency surgery to insert a series of screws into the compromised socket of her hip.

The guilt of children too, with regard to the treatment of their elderly parents, is commonplace, as was Ash's first thought upon hearing of his mother's injury; her broken hip was retribution, karmic payback for his decision not to travel home to Texas for Christmas. He was studying for the bar, after all, an excuse that two weeks ago had seemed legitimate. Guilt on this scale is what makes the Wednesday before Thanksgiving and the Saturday before Christmas the busiest travel days of the year.

But Ash and Sherri hadn't flown to Texas this year. Instead they'd spent thirty-seven dollars to send a large box overnight, and the box had arrived on Christmas Eve, its tardiness making Geneva wonder if her only child had even bothered with a token remembrance of her for the holiday. She'd said as much on the phone, *I thought you'd forgotten about me,* in a depressed yet even tone that reminded Ash of Eeyore and his end-of-the-world pronouncements.

The fact that she'd said all of this while narrating her unwrapping of a cashmere cardigan sweater in her favorite color (lilac) made Ash wish that he'd done nothing at all, not even made the phone call. If he'd shown up with a catered dinner, a marching band, and the president of the United States in tow, Geneva would have complained about the fuss. Whatever he managed was never enough.

What made it worse was that she knew how tough it was on Ash and Sherri. Sometimes Geneva resorted to a particularly passive-aggressive kind of blackmail, sending money for one plane ticket, not two; Ash suspected that his mother knew that he had neither the cash nor the available credit to buy a second ticket for his wife.

Ash asked the doctor, who spoke with the lilt of colonial India in his voice, to run through the probabilities again.

"It is almost certainly surgery," the doctor said. He had a four-syllable last name that Ash hadn't caught. "She will need to start physical therapy as soon as possible after surgery if she wants to continue to walk unassisted."

Nine forty-seven a.m. Mountain Central Time, and Ash was on the phone making plans for an emergency trip to Dallas. Sherri moved past him to the bathroom and started the shower; only when he heard her turn the water off did he realize that he'd been on hold with the airline for more than ten minutes. The airlines made contingency plans for grieving relatives, half-off fares and customer service representatives who seemed to actually give a damn, but a broken hip was to them an everyday occurrence and didn't have anything to do with whether Warren Ashburton possessed the $874 available credit for the ticket home.

While the customer service agent looked again for a cheaper fare, Ash thought about his mother. He hadn't realized how nebulous a concept *home* could become. Home wasn't where his mother lived; in the years since his father's death, she'd shed nearly everything that had once belonged to the both of them. Once she'd moved into the care facility, she seemed to spend her afternoons handing off her personal items to whoever happened by for a visit; Ash himself had collected pot holders and odd photographs and stainless-steel flatware and a patriotically colored afghan that his great-aunt had knit out of acrylic yarn in celebration of the Bicentennial. The reservation agent apologized for having nothing cheaper, advised him to check at the gate; there was still time for him to make the noon flight if he was willing to hold the seat now with a major credit card.

Sherri exited the bathroom and walked naked to the bedside.

Ash wrote flight numbers and a total on a blow-in card that had fallen out of her most recent issue of *Vogue*. She took the towel from around her head and wrung the excess water from her hair into it, and Ash pulled her close by snaking his left arm around her waist. He kept talking to the reservation agent, and even as he was confirming the expiration date of a MasterCard that was nearly at its limit, he was kissing his wife on the stomach, just above the hip bone, and then down toward the feathered tail of her appendectomy scar. He covered the receiver, whispered, "It's Mom."

13

FEAR. IT was part of the dialectic now, the foundation of the language. Fear of terrorist strikes, fear of the devaluation of currencies in the developing world, fear of the twenty-four-hour news cycle, fear of carcinogens lurking in our food supply, fear of Alar and malathion and sodium laureth sulfate, fear of nitrates and nitrites, fear of genetically modified foodstuffs, fear of high-fructose corn syrup, of partially hydrogenated oils, artificial sweeteners, fear of crumbling infrastructure, fear of human immunodeficiency virus and dwindling T-cell counts, *fear of fear,* fear of a vague and unidentifiable spot on a chest X-ray, fear of teenagers in hip-hop regalia crossing an unlit street, fear of sleeping alone, fear of the inevitable prostate problems and urinary difficulties, *fear of a black planet,* fear of a dwindling Nielsen or an irrelevant Q rating, fear of thinning hair and drooping jowls, fear of being discovered, fear of being ignored, fear of the hard truths, fear of death and dying and especially of dying alone. Fear was the exact way we were being taken apart, this fear that cleaved the country in two, the runny albumen from the solid core of the yolk, fear of *us versus them.*

And Richard's entire professional life was *us versus them.* He wanted for once to find a way to win an argument without re-sorting to cheap stunts, theatrics, or rhetorical flourishes, or just by being lucky enough to get the last word before the commercial break. He dreamed of the day his opponent would simply scratch his head and say, "You know, you're right," a phrase he figured he had never actually heard uttered in all his years in Washington.

In other words, Richard MacMurray had qualms about the product he was selling.

He settled in for coffee and a survey of the morning news. One network thought the most important story of the week was the death of a comic actor—cause undetermined but suspected to be blunt head trauma, the result of a drunken fall in his own bathroom—as narrated by film clips and interviews with the *coroner to the stars,* who had managed to present himself and this theory on three different networks in just under ninety minutes.

Another network ran a story recapping a year's worth of disappearances of young blond girls. The missing that year had always been girls, never any older than fourteen, affluent in their youth and beauty. From the moment they disappeared, it was even-money odds: for every family made whole, another would be left heartbroken, and somehow it all came back to the image. The anecdote of one rescue: The wife of a policeman in Fort Durango worked part-time at a local Wendy's. From her perch at the register in the drive-through window, she saw a girl from northern Arizona cowering in the backseat. She couldn't have been more than twelve.

The face was familiar only from the news broadcasts, but that had to be the missing girl, shaking gently against the restraint of her own arms, her hair already cut and dyed. Because this wife of a policeman knew the image—the slightly buck teeth, the coltish legs—the girl had been saved. The news had been broadcasting home video of the girl at a church picnic, shying away from her father's camera; her picture had been superimposed behind the left shoulder of dozens of anchors. The image moved, evolved; in the case of this particular girl, the jump cut went to video of a tearful reunion with her parents, the father's emotional thanks to a local sheriff, the refusal to speculate on what had happened to her in captivity, the usual wild gratitude.

More often, the girl, the body, was never found.

A family waited for answers that never came. A grieving mother gave a year-end interview, sitting on her plastic-wrapped couch; her daughter's room remained a shrine, pristine, untouched. The only thing left was the image, the seventh-grade school portrait of a girl everyone knew was dead. The gap between her front teeth meant she wasn't quite through her course of orthodontia, forever thirteen monthly payments away from the removal of her braces. The image was photocopied, faxed, emailed, broadcast; state troopers with creased hats stopped traffic at shopping malls and interstate on-ramps, hopefully comparing faces. Dogs used their noses to rout the undercarpet of desiccated leaves and moss in the nearest forest, their handlers hoping for the type of definitive answers that could only be provided by a body encased in the coroner's black polymer bag.

The morning anchor did a live read promoting Richard's next gig, an afternoon slot defending two Texas high school seniors who'd published an underground newspaper that even Richard thought fell on the wrong side of tasteless. For the past week, Richard had been giving it the hard sell, making the rounds of the cable news shows, pounding the same talking point over and over: *Freedom of speech doesn't stop at the front door of our public schools.* It didn't matter much that case law had proven him wrong on countless occasions, or that the two students in question were arrogant shits gifted with spectacularly bad judgment. It wasn't the newspaper, just the kids and their preeminent sense of entitlement. Their little underground paper ended up in the legitimate news once the principal confiscated all its copies and suspended the pair indefinitely; the students got themselves called on the carpet by the local school board, which was rumored to be considering expulsion. And what was the crime, exactly? With its crude cartoons and sarcastic headlines, the stunt was hardly enough to foment revolution—the most controversial things it advocated were free condoms in the school clinic and the reinstatement of an assistant principal who had resigned after pictures of him were found on websites "promoting leather, motorcycles, and homosexuality."

But because the week between Christmas and New Year's was the dead time for the news—the top-of-the-hour broadcasts filled with B-roll video of dogs singing "Jingle Bells," Good Samaritan stories about families who lost everything in a fire only to have their Christmas presents replaced by a millionaire benefactor—Richard had been on the air eight times on three different networks. The students were a spicy story that seemed to have a little of everything: race, class, the light and heat of a 1960s protest.

Richard secretly longed for marches in the streets and students seizing the university president's office, putting their feet up on the desk, drinking his brandy, and smoking his cigars. He wanted flowers in rifle barrels and rioters overturning buses.

If these kids wanted to exercise their First Amendment rights, if they were willing to live up to the obligation to be truthful, then he would live up to his obligation to defend them. The principal had gone on *Nightline* and made the mistake of calling the paper libelous. Richard, in the following segment, told Ted Koppel, "There can be no such thing as libel when what you write is the truth." Even though he didn't much care for the attitude of his clients, he couldn't help but egg them on; his advice was to do everything short of protesting at the school board meeting carrying sandwich boards that read *I Am a Man*.

Which meant that ever since Richard and his team of activists had taken up the cause, things had gotten worse for the two kids; their expulsion was upheld, and one of them had his acceptance to the University of Texas rescinded. The story's place in the news cycle would soon be assumed by an outrage of newer vintage, but Richard's strategy here was still slash-and-burn; he expected in every interview to throw out the word *Nazi* a time or two, mostly for the shock value, but also because it was one of the few ways to make a school board nervous.

So he advised the students not to back down. He had a law school classmate, a federal judge, whom he could turn to for a temporary injunction, at least to get the one kid back into college.

In an ideal world, the whole thing might turn into a show trial, wall-to-wall coverage that would provide Richard with the chance to parade and shout, a full contingent of press outside waiting for a news conference on the courthouse steps.

He knew that his histrionics could make good television. He'd started this phase of his career by writing amicus briefs to the Supreme Court in support of constitutional protection for even those types of free expression that he personally found to be in bad taste. He fancied himself an advocate, a watchdog of the state. This put his name out at the very edges of public consciousness; now, because he gave good television, the same arguments he once made on paper he now spouted on cable news programs, debating Tipper Gore–styled housewife activists or local prosecutors-cum-political aspirants who wanted to thin a library's collection, put warning stickers on nearly everything, shut down the local porno shop. From these appearances Richard was on the record in support of medical marijuana, decriminalizing drugs and paroling drug offenders from over-crowded prisons, repealing three-strikes laws, protecting in-terstate commerce in adult videos and novelties, and the inalienable right to wear a diaper gathered from the stars and stripes of the American flag. Low crimes, all.

In the past few years, Richard had made almost nothing from the practice of actual law; most of his money came from these appearances on television, or short trips to conventions of ac-tivists and attorneys where he defended what his sister called the indefensible. She didn't much care for what he was selling, and most of their attempts at conversation ended in arguments. Now they talked only on birthdays and holidays, and it was the fault of his burgeoning career. That and the fact that now she was fucking her boss.

With his head done up in a bonnet of foamy shampoo, Richard thought of who might play him in the motion picture, alter-nately dismissing Bruce Willis (too old) and Kevin Bacon (too skinny) before pausing to consider Kiefer Sutherland. A definite possibility. He was lathering up for his morning shave when the telephone rang.

"I've managed to wake up one of those back-bencher con-gressmen you're so fond of yelling at to be your sparring part-ner," Toni White said, her Australian accent far stronger than Richard remembered. On the other end of the line, he heard a crunch that registered as *celery stick*.

"You're in early for a holiday," Richard said. "I thought most Australians couldn't resist the opportunity to hoist a few."

"Up late, actually. I took a twenty-four-hour shift. Lots of people on vacation, and since I wasn't going home, I volunteered. I don't have to be here today, so I'm hoping you'll do me the professional courtesy of keeping the theatrics on ice and give me some serious debate this afternoon." She produced almost all of the higher-profile dayparts that originated from the Washington bureau. Richard wasn't really surprised that she would be working on a holiday.

"I'm all about serious," Richard answered, then missed about half of Toni's reply as he wiped stray peaks of shaving foam from the mouthpiece.

"No one who saw you yesterday thinks that. You've got to stay on message. Keep to facts, keep it tight, nothing longer than twenty seconds."

"So you're just calling to make sure I'm up, on my way down, that sort of thing. You do realize it's only ten o'clock? My call time is two p.m."

"Actually, I'm making sure you're at the top of your game. A friend of mine is going to be here this morning. Scouting for new talent."

"America's news channel gearing up for another line of layoffs?"

"Richard," Toni White said in a tone that reminded him of an exasperated high school teacher. "He's coming to look at you. An anchor job, news at six and eleven. A small-town gig."

"I'm not a news guy or a small-town guy. I'm all opinion. If he's coming to look at me, they must be pretty desperate."

"Don't big-time me. I sent him a tape. Some tapes. A bunch of people, and you were on there, and you're the guy they like. They're looking to replace the news-and-comment guy with a brilliant curmudgeon. 'Brilliant and young.' His words, not mine."

"I have plenty of opinions," Richard said, "but I didn't know anyone did commentaries anymore."

Toni laughed. "They don't. No one outside of Paul Harvey, anyway. Like I said, this is a distinctly small-town operation. Small-town, small-time. You get the commentary, one minute, once a week, at the end of the Thursday-night news. But there is a catch."

"There would have to be. *The opinions in this commentary do not necessarily represent those of the management of W-so-and-so TV,*" Richard said in his best faux-announcer's voice. "What happened to the last guy?"

"The last guy has been there for eighteen years. He's on his way out," Toni said.

"Retirement?"

"Lung cancer. Last of the hard-drinking, hard-smoking news guys. Won an Emmy for his reports from Cambodia. Spent time in Lebanon. He was there when the barracks blew up. He's seen some shit." Richard heard the hint of admiration in her voice, wondered if he could ever live up to those standards. Before he could ask another question, Toni spoke up. "Look. He's on his way out, but he's still working. He can hand-hold you through the breaking-in period. You'd get to co-anchor with him for three months, work together on a series about his treatment, advances in medical science. Death, the final frontier."

"So what do I need to do?" Richard pictured animated graphics with Toni's last words floating in, DEATH spelled out in yellow on the chyron.

Toni said, "Today, you need to show up early, do a little gripping and grinning with the headhunter, and look like a guy who's not out of his depth with hard news."

"That's it? I don't need to solve the crisis in the Middle East?"

"Nope. Just wear a serious suit, and when the congressman yells at you, don't stoop to his level. Come down early, and I'll introduce you, pump you up a bit."

"Why the break to me? I'm not at all qualified for this."

Toni *tsk-tsk*ed. "Maybe, just maybe, in the twenty-two years I've worked in news, I've learned how to spot someone who has a feel for this shit. Someone who has a feel for the people." Richard did the math. He'd figured Toni to be in her late thirties, but twenty-two years in the business probably put her closer to forty-five.

"I really don't have a feel for people. In fact, I generally don't like them. Well, most of them, anyway."

"Which is why you'd be a great small-town newsman. You'd have to learn to treat them with respect. Give them dignity in a way that some kid who wants to make it to New York would never bother with."

"That's a lot of faith," Richard said before asking, "Just where is this dream job?"

"Wilkes-Barre, Pennsylvania."

The foothills of the Poconos, dead coal towns. Small cities with great granite buildings downtown, their facades chiseled with the names of banks that no longer existed, furniture and department stores that had long been bankrupted by the national chains. Missouri, Kansas, Iowa, they were all that way. That was all Richard knew. Pennsylvania was probably the worst. Wilkes-Barre, where they lopped the tops off mountains and blasted them hollow and carted away the rock and, when they were finished, left the trucks and the rail cars and the front-end loaders to rust at the bottom of an empty pit. That had been thirty years ago, but, to a man, everyone there was convinced that the mines would reopen, that someone could find the money, the ways around the blasting laws and the storm-water regulations. They could get those towns moving again. They could not fathom that the land might be like the people, ruined and empty.

Still, being a local celebrity there didn't seem like such a bad life—free beers from the bartender at the VFW or the American Legion, throwing out the first pitch at a minor-league baseball game, riding in a vintage Cadillac in parades at St. Patrick's Day, stuffing himself with sausages and pierogies at the annual Saint Mary's Slavic-American picnic. Cadence's father had grown up in that area, Luzerne County, and the only time Cadence had taken Richard home to visit, Curtis Willeford spent the afternoon sitting in an old Barcalounger he had moved onto the front porch, throwing crabapples out onto the reddish macadam of the highway and rewarding himself with a stiff pull off a pony bottle of Rolling Rock each time a car ran over one of them. Curtis Willeford thought the mines were coming back too.

Richard made careful work of choosing a tie for today's television appearance; under the overhead lighting sometimes even the most luxuriant red silk looked flat, something out of J. C. Penney's. Anything garish became a costume, an affectation. It took him five minutes of scrolling through his tie rack before he settled on an egg-yolk yellow tie with woven burgundy pin dots, a bit of color to pop against the background of his navy chalk-stripe suit. The tie had been a gift from his nephew, and Richard extracted a notepad from his suit jacket and wrote a reminder, another temporary resolution: *Call G and wish him happy New Year.*

At least he was making progress. For the first time in seven or eight years, Richard would not spend New Year's Day recounting the half-baked resolutions of the night before. His days as a smoker were years past, yet his morning wasn't ninety minutes old before he broke a New Year's resolution—to get more exercise—and decided to plunge into a cab for the crosstown trip to the television studios. He knew the medical and anecdotal reasons that he needed to spend some time patrolling his neighborhood on foot, lingering in the natural foods aisle as much as he did at happy hours, trying one of those brunches with Gospel music on Sunday mornings or lurking among the Impressionists at the National Gallery on Sunday afternoons; all in all, he ought to try to get out more, avoid what faced him, avoid the hard truths he was starting to see in the mirror, stay away from his empty apartment, his empty bed.

He had seen every random event a big city had to offer—a trio of street fights, a bank robbery, a hit-and-run car wreck— and had learned to be attuned to the city's mild ejaculations of violence, the fender benders between cabdrivers screaming heavily accented profanities that morphed into comical shoving matches (the Hindustani man he'd seen pounding on a stoned Rastaman, shouting, *I am looking pissed!*), bicycle messengers who serpentined the wrong way through traffic, the occasional liquor-store robbery or purse snatcher who tore down Eighteenth Street in the midafternoon rush of the luncheon crowd. He'd even witnessed the beginning of a riot, a lifetime ago, watched it start in the streets and then watched the rest of it on *Eyewitness News at 6* and again on *Eyewitness News at 11*.

But he was not prepared for what greeted him on New Year's morning, the streets of his sometimes overly festive neighborhood littered with broken beer bottles and empty plastic cups, all smothering in a stench he could not place until he stepped over a huge pile of curbside vomit baking in the lukewarm January sun, and the correlation came to him: New Orleans, the French Quarter in the false dawn light of a Sunday, just as foul and deserted. He headed down his small street, then right on Eighteenth and south a block to the corner of Florida Avenue. He was waiting to hail a taxi when he wandered into another of these random scenes, a drunk staggering out of the corner bodega, followed by the white-aproned owner, wielding a straw broom.

That's when the drunk excused himself from the scene, setting down an unopened pint of Velikov, the cheapest available vodka, and raised his hands, wiping them on his pants, Pilate erasing his troubles, and backed away in surrender. This drunk still had enough firepower for his addled mind to know that somehow four-dollar vodka just wasn't worth all this trouble, getting beaten for it here and probably again at the mission dinner on Fourteenth Street and again later as he shuffled through the line of the shelter at Third and D Streets.

The drunk said only, "Fuck you, Chico," before the owner headed back into the store, then reemerged carrying an abruptly shortened Louisville Slugger. He removed his apron, taking the time to fold it in quarters before picking up the bat and waving it around, shouting, "It's on, it's on!"

The drunk disappeared into the alley behind a long-abandoned auto-parts store, and the bodega owner pulled his apron overhead, tied it neatly back into place, and swiped his hands together as if brushing off dried mud. He picked up the broom again and waved as Richard climbed into the only cab around.

14

AFTER JUST five hours of a spasmodic, champagne-addled sleep, Mary Beth's optimism for the New Year was a remnant of the night before, replaced by the usual morning-after remorse. The empty feeling had to be a result of the drinks, the drinks her excuse for getting carried away in the imperfect moment of that midnight kiss. Her first waking thought of the New Year: *Go home.*

She stretched in the tub, then tried to work the kinks out of her neck. She moved back to the bedroom and reached for the light nearest her bedside table, and as Mike shielded his forehead with a spare pillow, Mary Beth found herself making a quick phone call to check on Gabriel.

The answer came after five rings, a muffled and bleary, "Hello?"

"Sarah? It's me. Just calling to say happy New Year."

"MB?" Sarah's voice sounded scratchy, heavy with sleep. "Yeah, you too. Happy New Year. Fuck. What time is it?"

"About ten o'clock your time. How's Gabriel? Did he behave last night?" Mary Beth pictured Sarah padding down the long hallway nearest Mike's bedroom, headed for the guest room to check on Gabriel.

"The kid was most excellent. Seriously, he's been great. We threw a junior version of a New Year's Eve party, complete with pizza and sparkling cider. Then we watched some movie about a boy who builds a robot dog. In bed by ten o'clock. At least, he was. Wish I could say the same."

"That movie has been in heavy rotation for a while. Sorry about that."

Sarah yawned. "It's fine. I had a few people over. We dug it. It makes sense on so many levels, like there's something there for the kids and for the parents too. Though it probably would be better if you were high."

Mary Beth found Sarah's laughter alarming. This sense of responsibility revealed itself in surprising ways; since Gabriel's birth, Mary Beth had come to realize that it had been there all along. Her feelings were inconsistent, since she'd sat through *Fantasia* and *Fantastic Voyage* and even *101 Dalmatians* under the influence, but that was years ago, when she was a high school student worried about getting caught. She hadn't even seen weed in fifteen years, knew that Sarah and her friends probably didn't even call it weed anymore. She wasn't clued in on the vocabulary, and she took pride in that. She was as aware of the changes in her attitudes as she was of the changes in her body, even though she noticed them slowly, as if she were translating secrets from some ancient text.

"MB? Do you want to talk to Gabe?" Sarah asked.

"Sorry. I kind of drifted there for a minute. It's always Gabriel. Never Gabe. But don't bother him. Just say that I love him and that I'll be home tonight."

"Are you going to need someone to meet you at the airport?"

Mary Beth gripped a ballpoint pen, tapping it on the notepad next to the phone. "I'll grab a cab. You've already done enough."

With the phone safely back in its cradle, Mary Beth thought

it might have been a mistake not to tell Sarah of her early arrival. She'd already made the decision to march in there straight from the airport. She couldn't help but fear that her child had been neglected, hadn't been properly supervised, all weekend; from the moment she awoke in the hotel bathtub, she'd found herself morose and sluggish, the stink of cigarettes still in her hair and the accumulation of last night's alcohol muddying her thoughts, but the pictures of Gabriel she conjured were crystal clear: her child playing with matches in Mike's kitchen, her child being coaxed into a waiting van, her child—unwashed, no shirt—sitting amid a pile of broken glass.

Irrational, she knew. But she was changing her plans for her son, and she did not expect Mike Renfro or Sarah or anyone who did not have a child of their own to understand her need to hurry home. Gabriel would be happy, or happier, and that was all that was important. She pictured him on the floor of Mike's den, enthralled with his Christmas toys; he had the typical six-year-old's fascination with all forms of motorized transportation—passenger cars, over-the-road trucks, construction equipment, jumbo-jet aircraft. Gabriel collected these vehicles in miniature, carrying them from Mary Beth's apartment to Mike Renfro's house and all destinations in between in a blue plastic case he referred to, aping Mike, as his attaché.

Mary Beth hoped she might have time to fetch Gabriel a souvenir on the way home, another model plane or even a miniature Utah license plate that spelled out his first name. He owned seventeen of the fifty states now.

Mike raised himself to his elbows and asked, "How are things at the old homestead?"

"She was still in bed, dammit. Who knows what that kid is

getting into. He hasn't slept past seven a.m. in his life. Could have burned the house down by now."

Mike reached for Mary Beth's nearest shoulder before he said, "He's probably sitting in the game room watching *Bugs Bunny.*"

"I don't know. I clearly woke her up."

"Last night *was* New Year's Eve."

"I remember," Mary Beth said, pinching the phone between her neck and shoulder and punching out the toll-free number for her airline. "But I'm still going to see if I can't get on an earlier flight."

The change of arrangements cost Mary Beth seventy-five dollars, and after she hung up, she told Mike, "My flight's at noon."

"Good. Then you have time to come back to bed."

15

As SHE moved through the center hallway of Mike Renfro's home, running her hand along its textured, coffee-colored walls, Sarah Hensley listened for the stirrings of the child. Since he'd been in her care, Gabriel had established a routine, helping himself to a bowl of Cap'n Crunch and stationing himself in front of the den's battleship-size television. But this morning the television was off. Sarah retraced her steps back to the guest bedrooms, where she found Gabriel sitting up in bed, running a toy ambulance across his covers, over the tops of his legs. He slept on a pull-out leather couch in a room crowded with all the accoutrements of a businessman who occasionally works from home.

Sarah had learned that the best way to deal with him was to ask simple questions, try to have no agenda, so she said, "What are you playing?"

"I'm playing disaster. The ambulance comes to pick up the injured, but there aren't any, so they get to drive fast back to the fire station."

"There aren't any injured?"

"Everybody is dead. Nobody needs an ambulance. That's what makes it a disaster."

"What else have you been playing this morning?"

He pointed at Mike's desk, a mahogany behemoth riddled with cubbyholes for documents, even two brass inserts for inkwells. Across the top of the desk were strewn several feet of paper, old adding-machine tape. Sarah picked one up and looked at the numbers, random seven- and eight-figure sums that did not compute. "I've been playing insurance," Gabriel answered.

No question her charge was a weird kid. An eater of paste, a loner, the kind of kid who carried to school a lunch pail (as opposed to his peers and their neon lunch boxes that pledged allegiance to dolls, superheroes, boy bands, and NFL franchises and came with a matching backpack); he could be counted on to switch to a briefcase in high school. To Sarah, the kid was a *type,* an only child now and forever permeated with a simultaneous sense of entitlement and a last-to-be-picked-for-dodgeball kind of awkwardness. He talked in complete sentences, forswore slang, did not watch cartoons, and sounded in all ways like he was already consumed with his ratio of good cholesterol to bad, with the demands of paying for whole life insurance, saddled with a thirty-year mortgage, and saving to put his own children through college. Each time Sarah had asked Gabriel what he wanted to do, put in a movie (Mike had provided an impressive stack of Disney fare on DVD) or take a nap or walk to the park, he'd answered her with a weighty sigh, telling her, "That's kid stuff."

At his next birthday, in just a few weeks, Gabriel Blumenthal would be seven years old. He had the hair typical of his mother's side of the family, an ample mop that gently faded from blond to medium brown close to the scalp. Only Mary Beth could see any semblance of Gabriel's father in the boy. Quiet. Gabriel was lithe, thin. He didn't have much to say.

Sarah had no idea what to do with him. The entire weekend, Gabriel had shown his usual disdain for the constructs of organized play. He was not interested in Candy Land, Chutes and Ladders, video games, anything that required the participants to take turns. He indulged only in the common, solitary escapisms—building elaborate planned communities of Lego and Lincoln Logs, clogging their imaginary commuter arteries with Matchbox cars. Sarah had been warned about this: his mother hoped he might move on to a more constructive hobby in a year or two, say, building model aircraft and miniature versions of the muscle cars of the past, each hand painted with Testors enamels using a fine-point brush.

Then there was the matter of his name, Gabriel. Sarah thought he carried it around as his own private burden, treating it as if it were an adversary. He would not permit his classmates or teachers to call him by a nickname or the more familiar Gabe, and he kept reminding them—and Sarah—that the name belonged to one of the four archangels. She could imagine how well this went over with the other children. Sarah spent the weekend trying to coax him into behaving more like her definition of normal. They talked football. He sampled liberally from a plate of foods he had never tried before, exotic fare like spring rolls and caramel chicken, along with staples of the American childhood, cheese puffs and Oreos and pretzel rods. How in the name of God could a little boy be six and never once have savored a pretzel rod liberally slathered in creamy peanut butter? She'd had to bribe him to do it. She tried to plant a seed, an idea, that he needed to become more like a boy before he could become a man; he needed a dog as his constant companion, a sidekick (like all great heroes), and he needed to be responsible for the dog, teach it to fetch and shake and only to bark at strangers.

Sarah sat on the bed next to him and noticed that the front of his pajama top was crusted with a bib of boogers and snot. And she laughed, because she was thinking how children never call things by their proper names. *Booger* was itself a word from her childhood, from all childhoods, really, and then eventually Booger was her favorite nickname for her younger brother; she did not know if there was some medical term for what was on the front of Gabriel's shirt, but she helped him undress. He did not unbutton the top but rather raised both arms to the sky, and Sarah pulled it over his head. "Come on. We need to wash this, and then I'll make breakfast. Huevos rancheros."

"What are huevos?" It came out *way-views*.

"Seriously? You can't be a Texan without knowing what huevos rancheros are. Eggs, Mexican-style. It's breakfast."

"Who says I want to be a Texan?"

Sarah pointed at a Dallas Cowboys T-shirt that hung over the back of the desk chair, and Gabriel obligingly put it on. "You are a Texan. That's what they call people who were born here."

The last thing he asked Sarah as they headed to the kitchen for breakfast was, "Was that my mom?"

16

THE WEATHER forecast promised Mary Beth an uneventful flight home. The Utah sun was bright, the air warm and dry, with the occasional gust biting down into the valley. Still, she preferred to travel on overcast days, chilled in the cool whirl of a car air conditioner, a sensual memory of a childhood spent criss-crossing the eastern United States in a wood-paneled Chrysler wagon, fighting her brother for elbow room in the backseat. Now, at the end of her getaway with Mike, she was thinking about this trip in terms of a mistake, an ill-advised decision. She had come to Utah seeking definition, and she'd gotten it, even if it wasn't the result she'd hoped for. She prayed the fifteen-minute ride to the airport would pass in silence.

Surely all over America, other couples were headed home from romantic excursions, last-minute jaunts famous for room service and the abandon of hotel-room sex, the ability to be someone other than yourself for a few days. But Mary Beth felt as if she was one of the few anxious to get home. She did not resent the urge; stunned as she had been by Gabriel's sudden ar-rival, after two years of trying for a child and then two years of trying to extricate herself from a dying marriage, she now better understood the instinctive drives of motherhood: the urge to protect her son, to know where he was at all times, to make sure he ate a balanced diet and watched a minimum of television, and, finally, this New Year's morning, her sudden unwillingness to consign him to even one more hour under Sarah's care.

In the silence of the car ride, Mary Beth pledged to herself that her child would never be a latchkey kid, shrugged off to the auxiliary world of gum-chewing teenaged sitters in their baby tees and low-riding sweatpants. Putting Gabriel first among all things was going to be this year's main resolution. It was already part of the arrangement at the office, the reason Mary Beth arrived at 9:30 and departed at 3:00 and took liberal amounts of time off for parent-teacher conferences, doctor's appointments, Cub Scout meetings; she left early to deposit him at soccer practice in the fall, T-ball in the spring. She had no desire to be a superwoman.

Nothing could ever become more serious with Mike, at least not while they worked together. She was tired of the power differential—he knew too much about her, her past, her family situation, even her checking-account balance. But to her, he remained impenetrable. She had little idea about his finances, his previous loves, where he'd gone to school, whether he'd been raised in a church. Which meant the New Year was as good a time as any to reconsider everything, a time to pursue every option. She was going to remain his employee for the foreseeable future, for practical reasons: health insurance, flexible hours, the stable routine that she so desired for her son. But in the passenger seat of a rented Jeep Cherokee, she made another resolution for the New Year. She'd put her résumé together.

Once their car fell into the flow of the minimal traffic of a holiday lunchtime, Mike let out a sigh and said, "Christ, I'm getting fat. These pants are killing me." He hooked a thumb into the waistband of his weathered chinos, the ancient garment soon to be retired to raking leaves on a Saturday, touching up the paint in the garage.

"Too much red meat," Mary Beth said.

"Too much everything. We're starting a new regimen as of today. Fruits, whole grains, something. An austerity program."

"How is this surprising? You give your life over to doughnuts and pastries at a breakfast meeting, a large coffee with cream and three sugars on the way back to the office, something from the drive-through for lunch. Someone leaves the firm or has a birthday or makes the big sale, and there are brownies in the kitchen at midafternoon, but you don't finish the second brownie because you've got to hurry up and get out to a happy-hour meeting with some guys from Blue Cross or Travelers or something." Mary Beth cracked her window, taking refuge in the cool air ruffling through her bangs. She knew just by saying it out loud that she was really talking about herself.

"Exactly. I bought this muffin last week. Banana oat bran. It sounded healthy, at least. Except that after I finished it, I decided to look at the nutrition label. And it says calories per serving are something like six hundred. Serving size, one-third of a muffin. Who eats one-third of a muffin? It's not like I'm going to split it with a couple of people at the office. Of course, all this information came too late for me to do anything about it. Plus, it was roughly the size of my head." Mike laughed at his own joke, the sound escaping from his prominent nostrils. When she didn't answer, he droned on. "The hazards of sales, I guess. But now is time to make changes. I don't want to be one of those fifty-two-year-old guys who suddenly has a doctor telling him to give up meat, booze, cigars, and fucking or else he'll be dead by next Thursday. What do you do then?"

"Find a new doctor," she said, laughing.

Mike ignored her vaudeville line. "Anyway, the program starts today. All things in moderation."

Mary Beth offered a quiet buzz through her lips, an agreeable *hmmm.*

"I've made progress already. Back when we met, I used to eat dinner standing up. I didn't have any furniture except for a television and this ancient recliner, and so I'd order takeout and eat standing up at the kitchen island while I watched *Monday Night Football.* Not going to do things like that ever again." Mike turned the radio on, then lowered the volume and asked, "Any resolutions you want to share?"

Mary Beth wondered if he meant something about her weight. Mike had never given her a reason to think this, at least nothing he'd said. But she lived with her own self-consciousness every day, making an effort to distract attention from her midsection with her somewhat overdone makeup and outlandish accessories. Today that meant a sweater in Popsicle orange and an oversize silver nylon purse stuffed with magazines, trail mix, throat lozenges, and travel-size tissues for the trip home. "Nope. Nothing. Anything I'm going to change is something I'm going to just do. I'll leave it up to you to decide if it's an improvement."

"Like what?"

"Maybe I'll get a couple of pink stripes dyed in my hair. I don't know."

"I'd like that," Mike said, with a touch of a leer.

"Or not. I never tell people my resolutions. That way they don't judge me if I don't follow through. All my life I've felt like I was moving toward something inevitable. In high school, college was inevitable. After college, it was a job, and then, when I was married, I thought I was moving toward being a mom. Then in about two months, I got pregnant and divorced, and abandoned in Texas, not really knowing a soul."

"But that's just the point. You don't get to know what's next."

"But I've always known what's next. My life has been moving from one obvious thing to the next. When I came to work for you, for a while, doing well at the job, having a career, that became inevitable. But now, it's like I don't know what I'm supposed to be going for. And I'm not sure I want to make any specific plans right now. I'm going home, and I'm going to enjoy the rest of my week off. The only thing I've got planned is doing whatever Gabriel wants to do."

"So you're worried about things being inevitable," Mike said, repeating the word a few times. "*Inevitable.* Sounds like the name of a ghost town."

She didn't want her malaise to be what he would think about as he drove away. She tried taking a lighter tack. "Or a place to build your dream house. You can get your mail general delivery. Mike Renfro, Rural Route One, Inevitable, Utah."

Mike veered toward the off-ramp that fed them the final mile to the airport. "I can't believe that's all you've got planned."

What Mike really wanted to know, she assumed, was how Mary Beth might fill the days without him. She did not want to provide the disappointing specifics—she'd fall back into the same routine she had every week, whether or not Mike was involved. Laundry, an inventory of her son's clothes, some light shopping, organizing her receipts for tax purposes.

Mary Beth visualized the framed picture she kept on her desk, one taken right after she gave birth. Gabriel nestled on her chest, the cotton cap that the nurses stuck on diagonally trailing across his forehead. He had been fussy, jaundiced but loud, a wailer, really, until the nurses put him back with his mother. That first moment of quiet—that was what that picture was about. But the lack of photographs from the rest of his life felt directly contrary to MacMurray family tradition. Each year of her childhood, her parents had added another formal portrait, an eight-by-ten from the latest special at the Sears photographic studios. Her father and her brother in matching navy pinstripe suits from J. Press. They made an evening of it, got their picture taken, rewarded themselves with dessert from Baskin-Robbins.

Mary Beth's father kept pictures of his two children under the glass top of his desk, rotating in selections from a new batch maybe once a month—school photos: Richard in his basketball warm-ups, Richard in the basement, tinkering with one of his arsenal of guitars, Mary Beth with her glockenspiel in the marching band, her forehead and eyes obscured by the rise of her white wool hat, a giant cotton swab on top of the Green Giant–colored uniforms.

"We're going to get our picture taken," she said, a meek offering that started as a fib but now seemed organic, believable.

"What for? I mean, you get a school picture each year, don't you?"

"That was September." Mary Beth had forgotten about picture day. She'd shipped Gabriel off to school in a worn but serviceable Spider-Man T-shirt. Among his scrubbed, starched, and ironed classmates, Gabriel stood out, the cowlick at the crown of his hair giving the illusion of another inch of height. Her forgetfulness was a mark against her, a sign of inattentiveness, a warning that she'd been distracted from the important things. The picture took up residence in her office and on her refrigerator at home as if it were proof of her parental inadequacies. "Kids change so fast at this age."

17

MOST OF the neighborhood around Capitol Hill stood quiet, the only sound the grinding of the taxi's ancient brakes, metal against metal, as it slowed through the circles along Massachusetts Avenue. At the turn onto North Capitol Street, Richard spotted the familiar corner window of the Russell Senate Office Building and smiled; on television, the window had belonged to Oscar Goldman, the bureaucrat who kept the Six Million Dollar Man in line. These bits of knowledge made Richard feel proprietary about his city.

The news bureau was squirreled away in a bland office building, a common late-1960s box with a marble facade. Outside, a custodian sat against a concrete planter full of boxwoods and ornamental cabbage, waving a garden hose in front of him, the insistent stream of water pushing cigarette butts, stray leaves, and the foil wrappers from chewing gum off to the curb. He was the only person Richard passed on his way inside.

At the empty receptionist's desk, Richard ventured a few half-shouted hellos before Toni White came out to greet him. He felt the taut muscles across her upper back as they embraced in an A-framed hug.

"How do I look?" Richard smoothed his lapels, tugged down on his jacket hem.

Toni fingered the lapel of Richard's jacket, a discriminating shopper examining high-end merchandise. "Top-notch. Like a trusted newsman. Come on, there's someone I want you to meet," she said, glancing at her watch.

Toni led him past the newsroom, where desks were pushed together in clumps of four, as in a fourth-grade classroom; sometimes during the workday, correspondents did live fills sitting at their desk. Behind each cluster you could see the dominant curvature of the Capitol's marble dome through the two windows at the back of the room. Richard thought it was funny that his interview would be conducted in front of a green screen that would be filled with a graphic to make him appear as if he too were just outside the Capitol, when the real one sat across a grove of trees and two streets, less than six hundred yards away.

In the rear corner of the studio, a folding table covered with a blue tablecloth had been set up, and a decent party spread of crudités sat at one end, opposite a dozen bottles of top-shelf liquor.

"Leftovers?" Richard asked as two stagehands busied themselves making drinks. One poured a Bloody Mary from a pitcher into a clear plastic cup, tracing his finger up the side of the cup to catch a stray drop.

"Don't ask, don't tell. A little bonus compensation for having to work today. Most of these guys came in at four o'clock this morning. They get twelve hours at double-time to pay for all the Christmas presents they've bought. Or they're pulling a double shift, like me. I've worked every day for nineteen straight days. So what's the big toy this year, anyway?"

"How would I know? The last time I got wound up about

that sort of thing was 1977. Mattel electronic football. I didn't get one, but my next-door neighbor Dale Whiteis did."

"Do you want something to eat?" Toni steered Richard to the buffet table.

He picked through the dozen or so fifths, grabbed a bottle of Pimm's, and read aloud the printed instructions from the side panel, how to make a Pimm's Cup. "What is this stuff, anyway? You're supposed to know these things. Australians are part of the empire, right?"

"Castoffs of the empire. At university, I did a summer program at Cambridge, and we drank gallons of that stuff at brunch. You put a splash of seltzer and a cucumber stick in it. I'd ask the guy who owned this pub near Christ College what Pimm's was, and he'd say, 'Brilliant. It's brilliant.' And then I'd ask what was in it, and he'd say, 'Genius.'"

Richard let the bottle settle in his hand, then replaced it on the table and took a bottled water from a tray of ice. "I don't know about brilliant. But this open bar could make some good reality TV. Bring on some members of Congress, give them a few drinks, let them fight it out. Last man standing wins."

Toni gave Richard a look that he took to mean something along the lines of *get serious*. "What's the latest with your Texas kiddies?"

Richard poured himself a cup of coffee. "Oh, the subversives. A city councilman keeps saying they were planning to go Columbine on everyone. And the principal found out that they used the computers and printers in the journalism room to make the newsletter. Then they broke into the faculty lounge to photocopy it. He wants them to reimburse the school district at forty cents a copy."

"How's this all going to work out? Litigation? Do I need to send a camera crew somewhere?"

"Doubtful. The kids are going to go to college and become even more disillusioned with me, the principal, the whole system. If we're lucky, they'll continue on to law school." Richard snorted out a laugh, hoped this wasn't how Toni saw him, just another well-paid cynic. "Don't worry about these kids," Richard told her between sips. "They're pretty resilient. In the end, the smart one runs for Congress and gives his life over to children's issues and winds up with a post office or a courthouse named after him."

"Are you sure? Why can't this be the beginning of the long downward spiral? They barely make it out of community college, end up selling Chryslers at the auto mall, get picked up for drunk driving every four or five years." Toni pinched her banana peel in half, tossed it in the small steel can.

"That's not how this is going to end," Richard said. "The dean of some journalism school is going to sweep in and give these kids a scholarship, liberate them from Texas. This is their ticket out, the admission to a life of comfortable northeastern liberalism. They'll buy corduroy suits at the Salvation Army thrift shop, join Students for a Democratic Society, intern for some network. They'll report from war-torn Beirut, work for the *Christian Science Monitor* or NPR."

"You sound pretty confident," Toni said.

Richard laughed. "I'm a firm believer in the happy ending."

18

MIKE WAS aware that he rarely thought about the practical issues of child-rearing, just as he was aware Mary Beth might see it as a deficiency in his character. Perhaps that would explain her minor outbursts, the fact that all morning, her expression had consisted of wetter-than-usual eyes and the slight downturn of her lips that usually led to a full-on quiver. He had no idea how to interject himself into that part of Mary Beth's life. He'd been an only child, had no children of his own. In his heart, the begrudging confession to himself: children were inconvenient, alien. But a more recent portrait of the boy seemed both motherly and practical. The boy. How often did he even say his name? Even in his deepest thoughts and especially in his conversations with Mary Beth, Gabriel was always *the boy*. And what was the point of another formal picture? School pictures were artifacts that came in the mail a few times each month, postcards in search of abducted children, bearing the heartbroken plea *Have you seen me?*

Why didn't Mary Beth take more pictures of her son? God knows every young couple these days managed to document their child's most mundane achievements on video: first steps and first day of school, sure, but also first day of chicken pox, first solo shit. Sometimes on sales calls he had to watch and pretend to be enthralled by the ordinary things, just because they'd been committed to video. He much preferred the snapshot era he'd grown up in, four-by-four Kodachrome prints, the month and year stamped at the bottom edge. Permanent memories.

Mike had taken the last photo of his own father, Artie Renfro, sitting in a plastic lawn chair, the collar of his camp shirt loose enough that the fabric fell away to reveal his tracheotomy scar. Was it an exaggeration for Mike to think that he'd photographed death itself, Artie gaunt in the way that only the chronically ill can be, savaged by esophageal cancer and its poisonous treatments?

On his dad's knee sat a half-drained bottle of Lone Star, the last basic pleasure he could tolerate. Mike was fourteen, maybe fifteen—he could not remember without doing the math—and the camera was his father's old Brownie, the kind with a flash-arm attachment; the picture had to be taken outside because the night before, a bored Mike had gathered all the flashbulbs and thrown them up in the air, shot them with a pellet pistol, watching the phosphorescent burst rain down on him like fallout. Mike did not know how to load the roll of 126 film; his father had to do it, beer sheltered between his legs. Artie wanted a picture of his scarred throat. His "war wound," he called it. But his shaking hands spilled his beer, and his cursing, his retreat inside for a dry pair of slacks—that last picture almost didn't get taken at all. Instead, his father returned a few minutes later wearing dark-brown pants, the same pair he wore in all of Mike's memories. Artie eased himself down into the chair with a sigh, a slight grimace that the adult Mike knew he should have understood as a sign of metastasis; the tumors had spread to his pelvis, his lower spine. He took a sip from a new beer and flinched, as if the beer had turned on him, and he turned to Mike and said, "I can't even enjoy this."

It would have been nice to have a snapshot of him and Mary Beth on New Year's Eve, but he didn't own a camera, and his father was the reason.

Now, as Mike Renfro drove along the access road at the entrance to Salt Lake City International Airport, the silence became a third passenger in the car. He wanted the comfort of small talk, an assertion that everything was okay. He pointed to the mountains that rose on Mary Beth's side of the highway. "They look like a rib cage, don't they?"

"Oh, yeah. We're right in the belly of the beast," Mary Beth said, then pulled down the visor and squinted at her reflection in the makeup mirror. "Sorry. I just don't feel much like being profound right now."

The flatlands around the airport glimmered in the direct wash of the noonday sun, the light dancing in reflection across the fuselages of the various jets. Mike pulled to the curb lane in front of the terminal and shifted into park, let the engine idle. He hurried out of the car, fetching Mary Beth's bag and leaving it in front of the curbside kiosk. In the background, the public-address system alternated between issuing the usual red-zone parking warnings and paging random travelers: *Mr. Agajanian, Tamar Shelton, Captain Cliff Ellis.*

Mary Beth stood in front of Mike. "I should call my brother and wish him a happy New Year. I didn't even talk to him on Christmas."

"How is Richard these days?"

"Still trying to save the world, I guess. Or remake it in his own image. I haven't talked to him in a couple months. You're back in the office Friday?"

Mike nodded. "You've got my cell phone in the meantime. But I can't imagine there'll be a reason to call. At least not work related. The billing is done, and no one's working the rest of the week. Take Monday off and let the voicemail pick up everything."

"I just might do that. Take Gabriel to school and have a day of leisure."

"An excellent plan." Mike turned to the rear passenger door, opened it, and handed over a black plastic bag. "It's not much. Just a little something for the boy."

Mary Beth reached into the bag and, with the flourish of a stage magician, extracted a stuffed brown bear with ears that stuck out in half-moons from the nine- and three-o'clock positions on its oversize, nubbly head. The bear had a pink T-shirt that said UTAH in letters of raised felt. "He's kind of, I don't know, pathetic. The bear equivalent of Charlie Brown's Christmas tree," Mary Beth said, showing her warmest smile. She felt a bit like a salesperson, certain Mike would see through her facade.

Mike thought of the bear as slightly off, defective yet charming; it seemed cruelly blunt to admit that the bear, with its large head and protruding features, could remind him of a six-year-old, a comparison that was, at the least, honest, but one he knew he could never explain to the child's mother. That Charlie Brown comment was exactly how Mike pictured Gabriel; he was the kid flailing at a yanked-away football, knocked ass over teakettle off the pitcher's mound by a screaming line drive. But Mike knew that Mary Beth could understand how the bear's defects, even his ears, might seem endearing.

"I don't know if I ever told you about Whit Carrboro," he said. "My first boss, with this agency in Houston. I go to this conference one time and I see this promotional bear, and I take

121

one because he looks a little like a bear I had when I was three. Back in the office, I prop the bear up against the electric pencil sharpener in the corner of my cubicle, behind the phone. One day at a staff meeting, we come in and the boss hands out this memo outlining the proper decor of cubicles. And specifically outlawed are *stuffed animals or other quaint items.*"

"Well, this one is very cute," Mary Beth said, giving the bear a hug. "When my brother was a kid, he used to take all his bears into his crib and pick the fuzz off their heads until they were bald. He'd stop and hold up the bear and say that now that all the fur was gone, the bear looked like Dad."

"Hopefully this guy will get to keep all his fur. It's just a little something. A quaint item. So, will I see you on Friday?"

"I promise. You'll have the weekly schedule on your desk. The accountants come in around ten-thirty."

"I don't want to drive away thinking that the last thing we talked about was work."

"What else are we going to say? That's the beauty of it, don't you think? I finally met someone smart enough to know that there's no point in talking something to death when it's already dead." She shook her head at the end of the sentence; her memory felt edgy, vibrant, her anger justified. It wouldn't be until she was in her seat on Flight 503 that she would realize this: she'd talked to Mike the same way her ex-husband used to talk to her.

There wasn't a lot of bustle for the middle of the day, no three lanes of traffic, no diffident-looking flight attendants sharing a smoke with ticket agents and airport cops, just two drivers in red tunics sitting near the terminal's automatic doors, keeping a watchful eye on their hotel-shuttle vans. They weren't listening. Neither was the skycap, standing a discreet distance behind Mary Beth's shoulder. Mike knew he must have seen worse, heard more embarrassing discussions. Nonetheless Mike whispered, "Do you really want to have this conversation here?"

An imported hatchback rolled by, the driver invisible behind tinted windows. The car rattled with the locked-down groove of bass and kick drum, some aggressively loud song burping out as it made the left turn to circle back toward the terminal. Mary Beth shook her head. "I don't. I don't want to have this conversation here, and I'm not sure I want to have it back in Dallas. I leave, I take the quaint item home to my son. You stay here and look for space."

Mary Beth handed her ticket to the skycap and, pointing at her only bag, said, "Dallas." Mike tried to hand over a tip, a trio of crumpled ones, but Mary Beth intercepted him by the wrist. "Relax. We'll be fine. I'm going to take care of things for myself for once. Maybe this is the beginning of a new era. One where I come first. A pro-MB phase."

Her thoughts: There had never really been a pro-MB phase. Everything she'd ever done, she felt, had been at the behest of the men in her life, the clothes she wore, the way she did her hair. She'd chosen a university and majored in international relations at the insistence of her father, and then he was dead. She'd moved to Atlanta, then Memphis, and finally Dallas following the vagaries of her ex-husband's career, or his political whims, or his firm belief that real estate or gold or crude-oil futures were going to skyrocket. Clark, her ex, had mandated even her choice of undergarments. There should have been a way to make that sexy, but instead it felt creepy.

Perhaps she would even have time to sit in the airport lounge, writing a postcard for Gabriel and having a quiet drink. She wasn't much of a drinker, never had been, first out of fear and later because of her husband's insistence; his attempts to control her behavior spiraled outward to include not just what she wore on her body but what she chose to eat and drink. A jingle popped into her head: *Schaefer is the one beer to have when you're having more than one.* Schaefer, the beer she had refused to buy for her brother when she was in college, because there were lines of propriety that Mary Beth wouldn't cross. Her reticence went away after a while; one weekend when Richard was in college, they'd actually smoked weed together. A week later—in an era when long-distance was expensive and people actually wrote lengthy and considered letters—she'd written to confess to her brother how her husband sometimes slapped her for "making a spectacle," and a few years later, the husband had stolen all of their money and disappeared six weeks before she'd discovered that she was pregnant.

But she'd never made that spectacle. Clark had made her feel silenced and small, so she behaved accordingly. She supposed that Mike had given her a voice. Mike, who discovered she was as good at navigating the little Byzantiums of insurance companies as she was at projecting a feeling of warmth to his clients. *Her* clients, she thought. Maybe she'd study for her licensure, write a few different lines of life insurance, workers' comp policies. She didn't want to be an office manager. Everything about her job felt limiting—its title, its responsibilities. Her inner dialogue about work relied heavily on the word *only,* as in, *I'm only the office manager.* He'd given her a voice, so why was she so reluctant to use it? She needed something she could call her own. Surely Mike could help her stand on her own feet in that one way. And if he couldn't, maybe a pro-MB phase was a no-Mike-Renfro phase too.

She tipped the skycap, then returned to her conversation with Mike. She wanted her face to be blank, not just to Mike but to the flight attendants, the other passengers, the world. She felt like a weary traveler between more exotic destinations, waiting for her luggage to catch up, hoping she could be rerouted through Helsinki. Her brother did that, lied to people on planes about his destination, his career; he thought of it as entertainment; he was a roughneck, a bond trader wanted in Hong Kong, the author of a forthcoming series of children's books about a purple Airedale terrier who taught at Harvard Law School and spent his evenings fighting crime. She wanted to be someone else, a retired figure skater, a courier carrying a diplomatic pouch. Anything except what she actually was, a middle-aged woman with limited prospects. She wanted just to be able to watch Mike Renfro drive away without hoping that he might turn back.

Standing on the curb with Mike at street level, she could see the expanse of scalp that threatened to emerge through his once-impressive head of lacquered black hair. And that's where she chose to place her kiss, on the top of his head, intimate but without the upheaval of romance. She did not want to stir herself that way, not before her flight. As she stepped in for the kiss, he moved toward her, forcing her to reacquire the target; he was too close now, and her lips came in inches off, a motherly landing point that left the outline of her lips stained across Mike's forehead. She didn't tell him about the lipstick above his Soviet-looking eyebrows and resisted the urge to forage through her handbag for a tissue. Mike pursed his lips, an expression Mary Beth assumed meant just what it did at the office: he was giving up. He wasn't going to fight.

When he retreated to the driver's side of the Jeep, he still had three dollars crumpled in his right hand. He stuffed the bills into his shirt pocket, then watched as Mary Beth disappeared behind the sweep of the automatic terminal doors.

19

IN THE green room, Richard passed time by flipping through Tuesday's issue of *Barron's*, last week's *U.S. News and World Report*, the most recent *Foreign Affairs*, all publications that in a normal, busy week he would have already read. The holidays made everything a bit more casual, and he was regretting his lack of preparation. It reinforced the idea that his career frequently felt like an elaborate charade. He wasn't being a pundit so much as pretending to be one. The guys who did the same thing for a living, the ones he saw on television every day, had staff, young lawyers, interns, assistants, all tasked with boiling down the issues of the day into talking points on a three-by-five card. Maybe, Richard thought, he should hire an intern.

Toni White appeared in the open doorway, arms crossed to hold a pile of videotapes. An overly tanned man in a black suit and gray shirt with an open collar leaned in behind her, and Toni dropped the pile on the makeup table, rested her hips against its edge, and began the introductions.

"Richard MacMurray, meet Don Keene, news director of the lowest-rated newscast in all of Pennsylvania."

Don laughed, showing teeth dingy yet perfectly straight. "Not all of Pennsylvania. Just the northeast."

Richard got up out of his chair for a handshake. "Lowest rated? I thought you had the dean of Pennsylvania anchormen up there."

"We do," Don said, holding Richard's hand a beat too long, a mannerism Richard associated with both politicians and television personalities. "It's not that we don't have a solid product, I just think people are tired of watching. They like to take some time and look around, watch a few weeks' worth of *Family Feud* and *Bowling for Dollars*. I'm down here casting around for what's going to bring them back."

"Come home to Channel Eleven's *Eyewitness News*," Richard said, a heavy emphasis on the *Eye-* in *Eyewitness*.

"Which brings us to you and your tape." Toni gestured to a pile of videos.

Richard said to Don, "Until this morning, I didn't know I had a tape."

"You don't, in the usual sense," Toni said. "I sent him a compilation of your greatest hits."

"I hope," Richard said, turning back to Don Keene and his black suit, "she didn't send you the thing with the candy bar. Not exactly my proudest moment."

"It might not have been on your reel"—Don laughed—"but goddamn, it was great television. I thought the anchorman might lose it. Anyway, nothing wrong with shaking things up a bit. Let's just hope you never get charged with a federal crime in Alabama, or else that prosecutor will fuck you but good."

Don's immediate pretense of familiarity suggested a man who had spent a lot of time in locker rooms. His suit, plus the tan face and the shirt with its open collar, contained all the trace elements of his past: all-state safety in high school, college in

California, a brief career as an on-air personality, even hosting an unsold game-show pilot, followed inexorably by divorce, cocaine, rehabilitation both personal and professional, which led to a fine executive job running the news division of a small-market station buried deep in anthracite coal country. Internal exile.

Richard got the game now; what Don wanted to hear was a profane version of the banter that passed between the anchor-man and the sports guy.

"Never arrested, never convicted," Richard said to Don's hearty and laughing approval. He turned to Toni. "I say that all the time, but I'm not really sure what it means."

Toni tapped her foot twice. "I hate to break this up, but we're going to be about a half hour. The game's running long, because that's what always happens. But we're all set to go. And, Richard, all you need to do is give me a little *Sturm* this afternoon. I've got work to do, but we'll fetch you about five minutes before." She fluttered in for an air-kiss.

"What about the *Drang*? There's always got to be some *Drang*," Don said, shaking Richard's hand again.

"People these days demand *fair and balanced*. We provide the *Drang*," Toni said. "In this case, a congressman from Orange County with the attention span of a tick. Last summer on *Crossfire* they're doing this special on mental illness, and Carville asked if he was advocating voluntary sterilization of the mentally disabled, and the guy said, 'There shouldn't be anything *voluntary* about it.' Despite three million dollars' worth of outside spending, he got re-elected by his largest margin yet."

Richard laughed. He explained to Don, "The only contact sport Toni knows is politics. She'd be completely happy to fill prime time with Burmese deputy ministers beating each other senseless with bamboo canes."

Toni turned to Richard. "Today's opponent may be a nutjob, but he shakes things up. It's good television. And, face it, unless we're saying something interesting, they're just going to flip right past us. Give them the conventional wisdom, and they'll tune out in favor of the Tostitos Fiesta Bowl."

Richard said, "You should be grateful there isn't a Smith and Wesson Bowl."

"That would be one hell of a halftime show," Don said with a grin, before he and Toni headed up the short hallway to the control booth.

Toni looked over her shoulder. "Someone will come get you to tape a cutaway. Max is anchoring. He'll give an overview, introduce both of you, then we'll do a sixty-second break and jump right in." Next came her traditional exit line, the only pep talk she ever managed: "Don't fuck it up."

Left alone in the green room, Richard fiddled with the morning's *Washington Post,* reading the annual New Year's list of what was in and out, all with a slight hope that it might say something along the lines of *James Carville out, Richard MacMurray in.* He thumbed through the spurious claims of a women's magazine, wondering who actually followed the advice—"Secret Sexual Tricks," "The One Thing He Can't Resist," "Twelve Ways to Spice Things Up" in a presumably mundane love life. *Cadence.* He picked up a pair of newsmagazines that would be in his mailbox the next day, nearly identical covers about diet and exercise studies. *Cadence.* Cadence, who ran four miles four times a week, who bought and ate all things organic, who subscribed to eleven different health and wellness newsletters, whose most prominent compulsion was opening a new toothbrush every other Monday.

Sometimes what Richard did not know about her bothered him as much as what he did. Like the etymology of her last name, Willeford, and its almost anti-ethnic sound—English, he supposed—but the subject had never come up. She was constantly working; the city did that to people, turned them into worker bees who went back to the office after happy hour. And he had no idea just how her family got by, a younger brother who'd managed the difficult trick of washing out of a junior college, a father who hadn't worked in seventeen years; he cashed a black-lung check plus Social Security and a pension from the mine workers, but that didn't seem like enough to keep the furnace bin filled with coal in winter, keep him in Jack Daniels and pony bottles of Rolling Rock, all that the old man asked for in the name of recreation.

And suddenly Richard understood the motivations of Cadence's career, that she was an old-fashioned girl who sent money home to her father each month without ever bothering to ask for the credit. How had he missed such obvious things? So many of his friends did these minor things for their aging parents, then acted as if they deserved a victory lap for bringing Mom flowers and candy on her birthday. Cadence didn't want or need the credit. She did what was required. Now, even seven weeks from the last time he had touched her, Richard kept thinking of new reasons to love her. Cadence, of the twenty-nine workout videos and almost as many pairs of athletic shoes. Cadence, who once pummeled a Somali cabdriver after he called her a bitch. It was Richard who had posted her bail, and Richard's mildly pushy phone calls to a deputy prosecutor that made the charges against her evaporate, another bit of the insider bartering he now performed most every day of his adult life.

A healthy-looking brunette swaddled in a tight, fuzzy black cashmere sweater appeared with a cup of coffee and without comment produced a stiff whisk broom to remove flakes of Krispy Kreme icing from Richard's navy suit. "I see they've given you the crucial job of the day," he said, eliciting a smile but no reply. It took a moment to register that she'd probably take that as an insult, and all he'd intended was to tell a gentle joke, to express that he was fully capable of doing it himself. But he could think of no other thing to say to extricate himself, so he sat quietly and waited. Part of her job description, he surmised, included never talking to the talent. He wondered how long it would take before he stopped assessing a woman's attractiveness by scrutinizing the ways in which her body differed from Cadence's.

A second production assistant lugged in a tackle box full of makeup and motioned Richard to a barber-style chair just off the set. While she patted concealer over the bluish half-moons beneath his eyes and dusted his face with powder, Richard took his IFB device out of its case, and another technician clipped a battery pack to Richard's belt. The IFB was a luxury, its plastic innards custom molded to fit the contours of Richard's left ear. Cadence had arranged the fitting for his last birthday. He couldn't stand to watch guests on these shows shuffle, trying to catch earpieces that popped out at awkward moments. This was a badge of office for his profession.

Toni materialized out of the control room, her arm draped proprietarily over a fat man in a plaid flannel shirt. "Wally here is going to tape a teaser—sit in the chair and look like an authority. And the game is running long. Which means the whole segment will be short—if you've got ammo, use it up front. We'll get about a four-minute warning, a College Football Scoreboard, and then we're live."

The production assistant pointed Richard to a second, slightly higher director's chair that sat in front of a blue chroma key screen. Wally toyed with his intricate Rollie Fingers mustache while moving in close with the camera dolly. "This won't hurt a bit."

Richard pulled his jacket taut and sat on its tail, then adjusted his bright-yellow tie. He checked himself in the monitor on the floor stage left.

"Try to look like a serious fucking guy with some serious shit to say. Look just over the lens to the left. There. Give me five seconds of that. You don't want to look like Congressman Mouthbreather over there." Wally nodded at a guy in a cheap gray suit perusing the buffet.

"Ready?" Wally said, and before Richard could reply, the red light came on. Richard cocked his head just slightly, a mannerism he had learned from videotape of his previous appearances; his media coach—the same person who had trained the would-be senator from Alabama on how to appear folksy yet serious—said it made Richard look studious, as if he were considering the evolution of his position at every moment.

When the red operating light on the camera disappeared, the light from its secondary spotlight dissolved into a blue-black glow, and Richard blinked his eyes clear. Cameraman Wally departed the darkened set, sipping a tall, ice-filled glass of orange juice that Richard figured was spiked with a good dose of vodka.

"What do we do now?" Richard asked of Wally's departing back.

Wally stopped. "The only thing we ever do. We wait."

20

SHERRI ASHBURTON began calculating just how much her mother-in-law's latest misadventure—Geneva's fall, her hospitalization, a last-minute plane ticket for Ash, his cab in from the Dallas airport—would cost. Ash hadn't even left yet, and already they were out $900 for a plane ticket and a few nights' worth of $60 motel rooms and restaurant food. She'd keep a running total in her head for the entirety of his trip, and she resented it. Being an adult, Sherri had once believed, would free her from having to worry about things like whether or not her bank card would go through. She felt guilty too.

Whether Ash flew in tonight or tomorrow or next Tuesday, Geneva's hip was still going to be broken, and she'd still need surgery, rehab. The hospital wasn't going to make her wait until Ash showed up to sign whatever paper they needed him to sign; the only reason Sherri had relented, the only reason she had chosen not to put her foot down about the money—despite the fact that she would have to cover his shift at the Canyon Room this afternoon and despite the fact that he was scheduled to sit for the bar exam in just three weeks—was that the doctor described Ash using one of the saddest phrases she'd ever heard: *only known living relative.*

She settled for helping him pack. She stopped him at the edge of the bed and made him remove his T-shirt, stuffed it under the pillow so that she could sleep with his scent. All Sherri Ashburton would do in his absence was watch television and eat cans of organic vegetable soup and wear his shirt while relishing the extra room in their full-size bed.

Ash hadn't spoken to her about his mother, not since the discussion about the plane ticket, about whether or not his presence would make any difference. "It's therapeutic," he argued, and Sherri suspected that he meant his absence would be therapeutic for both of them too.

Because Sherri was thinking about money as they drove in silence to the airport—whether or not she could survive for three or four days on the forty-seven dollars in tips that she'd squirreled away—she knew that she would not park the car (three dollars for the first thirty minutes) and walk Ash into the terminal. He'd be frugal once he got to Dallas; he'd even sleep in his mother's empty house if he could; the dust and the stale smell and the general creepiness never seemed to faze him. Geneva had been in the nursing facility for a while; how long, Sherri couldn't precisely remember. Seven months? This trip could work in their favor, even. She could encourage Ash to be assertive for once, to take control of his mother's finances on a day-to-day basis instead of letting things crop up the way her property tax bill had snuck up on them last spring.

Sherri made an almost involuntary noise she knew he would take as *harrumph*. "You need to talk to your mother. Between the taxes and utilities, she's paying maybe seven hundred dollars a month for nothing. For an empty house. Just pissing that money away."

"Please, not this. Not now. I grew up in that house."

"That house is empty now," she said, and immediately

wished she hadn't. His face registered a pained look that told her to back off. "Think of what a difference seven hundred dollars would make in our lives every month. Can we at least make a point of actually talking about it sometime, before it costs us more?"

Sherri popped the hatchback, and Ash extracted his duffel bag, a separate backpack with books on constitutional law and a mangled copy of *Black's Law Dictionary.* "When I get back. Right now, I figure I'll have three hours on the plane each way. Three hours, uninterrupted, just to study," he said, thumping at his books through the heavy canvas of his bag; he dropped the duffel at the curb and leaned in the driver's-side window for a final kiss. She pictured him rummaging in his mother's house for a pen to make notes, huddled over his books, sitting under the baked-enamel light on what had once been his father's desk. He would always be the smart boy from trigonometry class that she'd fallen in love with, the one who used to camp beneath her window, a subdivision Romeo throwing rocks and pennies. She nearly swooned as he ran his thumb along her jawline with the lightest pressure he could manage, his touch moving along with her memory. She loved that boy. Always had. He kissed her again, and said, "Thursday. I'll see you Thursday."

21

AT THE newsstand, Mary Beth stopped for a bottle of water and a new tin of peppermints. Farther down the C concourse, a woman sold coffee to a man in a turtleneck sweater and watermelon-colored nylon running shorts. Mary Beth made a quick stop at the restroom, and when she returned, saw the same man leaning against the wall, taking a call on the white courtesy phone. There wasn't even an agent at her gate, just a dozen other travelers, all wearing the mask of boredom they hoped might keep friendly conversation to a minimum.

Mary Beth took a seat and watched the television news, a reporter in a tweed cap and trench coat making his way through midtown Manhattan. He stopped in front of the retail display windows that lined Fifty-Seventh Street to confront passersby about their resolutions.

The top-of-the-hour broadcast recapped the lead stories from the past year—an assassination in the Middle East, a mining collapse in western Pennsylvania, the bombing of an Orthodox cathedral in Moscow by Chechen separatists, August's transoceanic flight of a billionaire in a shiny silver balloon, the summertime disappearances of a handful of young blond girls.

Next, set to the background music of Sinatra's "It Was a Very Good Year," came the usual year-end homage to dead celebrities, a slideshow of the last luminaries of a departed age, the tributes rendered in black and white—the stop-motion of an athlete dying young, the overdosed guitarist haloed and backlit in performance, a soundless clip of a pratfalling sitcom star, people both familiar and anonymous, even in death. A hockey player from a team Mary Beth had never heard of, the Green Hornets or Yellow Jackets or something, lay in a profound coma after being struck in the temple by an errant slapshot. In Washington, the president's daughter was recovering from mononucleosis, and the president himself waddled on crutches after tearing his Achilles tendon during some undescribed Camp David recreation. Goodland, Kansas, dug out after seventeen consecutive days of snow; the local McDonald's claimed to be sold out of everything but Filet-o-Fish sandwiches and orange soda.

Ten hours into the New Year, the airport began to fill with a smattering of travelers all plagued by the rescission of their pledges from the night before, already defaulting on the renouncement of tobacco, the promise of temperance. The bar even offered a midday special, *a double for a dollar more.* Most travelers would soon abandon the grandiose ambitions of midnight in favor of a more cautious optimism. New Year's Day meant negotiations, internal debates. One drink wouldn't hurt.

Shifting in her molded plastic seat, Mary Beth realized she was the loneliest kind of traveler. The worst part of being in an airport was being there alone, with no one to watch your luggage while you darted into an overcrowded and malodorous restroom, no one to laughingly point out the tabloid headlines about your favorite celebrities, no one to share the once-every-two-years pleasure of a box of Good & Plenty. She was flipping through a well-thumbed copy of the *USA Today* Life section when her eyes caught the image of her brother on the TV, seated in front of a computer-generated backdrop of the Capitol—a short promotional announcement for a scheduled television appearance.

A check of her watch told her she'd be on the way to Dallas by the time he made the air. She wondered when they'd taped the teaser (he'd taught her the whole vocabulary of his strange career) and whether he was going to wear that garish yellow tie before she remembered it was one Gabriel had picked out among the downtrodden orphans that littered the clearance table at Dillard's; she'd forwarded it along last Christmas, a tentative step toward reconciliation.

Richard made efforts too. A phone call on every occasion he could remember. They had stopped sending Christmas presents to each other years ago, though he managed small, DC-specific presents for his nephew, a Washington Capitals jersey, a T-shirt that said FBI. Sometime in the next few days, Richard would send her a tape of the broadcast, and she would watch him talking about the injustice of the week, sounding the alarm against some unseen evil.

His theatrics made good television. In a thank-you note for the yellow tie, he'd told her that he'd never forgotten a line from a media-studies class in college (she hadn't known they taught such things in Williamsburg in the early eighties), that television meant appealing to the lowest common denominator; any idiot, Richard said, could understand the theater of the absurd. She wondered if he meant that she was an idiot. She was used to the feeling, just as she was used to being underestimated by the men in her life.

That was certainly his reaction to her pregnancy. "What are you going to do without a husband?" he'd asked, as if thousands of women didn't raise children without help. Since her husband had gone missing, Richard delved into the literature. He called her with worrisome statistics on preeclampsia and gestational diabetes, mailed photocopied journal articles to her and her obstetrician, flew in for the delivery to feed Mary Beth ice chips, and help her pad slowly up and down the hall. Richard was capable of great gestures. He often forgot her birthday but never Gabriel's, sending along remembrances with various postmarks, springing sometimes for overnight delivery to ensure they arrived on time: football cards, an extensive set of Legos large enough to build an entire model community, miniature license plates from each state Richard visited. She didn't have the heart to tell him that the license plates meant more to her than to her son. She looked forward to the videotapes, to his infrequent mail, which came every three months or so; she recognized the arrival of a new plate by the heft of its envelope. She kept them all in her kitchen, used double-sided tape to affix them to the front of her yellowing refrigerator. Seventeen so far.

But this morning Richard MacMurray was not a priority, and she literally shook the thought of her brother out of her head. Now, she needed to figure out where she stood with Mike Renfro.

Why, after all these months of dating, did she still think of him by his first and last names? Even in their most intimate moments, she looked at him and thought *Mike Renfro*. He had no nickname, no diminutive. Mike had never called her anything more affectionate than MB. And she'd gotten a strong sense all morning, as she watched the city recede behind her into the periphery of the mountainous basin, and again at the curb of the passenger drop-off area in front of terminal 2, and as she waited to board her flight in the order demanded by the gate attendants, how she fell in among competing priorities: she was not at the top of Mike's, or anyone else's, list.

In 26C, on the aisle, Mary Beth deposited her carry-on and adjusted herself into the seat, happy that the plane was half-empty—she counted about eighty other intrepid souls. This counting of hers was a hobby, making guestimates of how many people filled the ballroom last night (four hundred) or were waiting in line for a chair on the ski lift Friday morning (eighteen).

With so many empty seats, Mary Beth felt entitled to spread out her magazines and claim the whole row for her comfort. She took out a leather portfolio containing the random fragments of work she had needlessly carried with her on vacation. The portfolio was stamped in gold with the logo of a large company that provided diversified financial services, a broad spectrum of solutions that meant term- and whole-life insurance, retirement plans for individuals and small businesses, long- and short-term disability. Each time Mary Beth looked at the logo or at the bar graphs and pie charts within, the tables of tobacco- and non-tobacco-based premiums, the actuarial predictions of longevity and quality of life, the accidental death and dismemberment plans and their graduated payment schemes—*$100,000 for one arm and one leg, or both arms or both legs, $50,000 for one hand and one eye*—she was reminded that she made her living as part of the machinery that tampered with the mathematics of death.

Being in this seat, for example, was a bona fide ten-thousand-to-one shot, completely unthinkable. Her son was six years old, and she'd never had a vacation without him until this ridiculous holiday weekend, where a man took her a thousand miles away apparently for the joint purposes of *not* asking her to marry him, *not* asking her to help pick out their new house. Whatever his intentions had been, the vacation was now over, and she'd been unable to contrive a way to make him actually say what he wanted. She'd chastise herself later for being so gullible, for letting such mundane fantasies creep into her thinking unrecognized, for craving the regular stability that she wanted for herself and her son, for thinking that anyone other than her would feel responsible enough to want to provide it. She was disappointed at herself for wanting such predictable things, and even more so by the fact that it had taken her so long to realize it. The entire chain of events that had brought her here—all the way back to that Monday morning seven years ago when she learned she was going to be a single mother—was unthinkable. She'd never told Gabriel about how hard she'd tried, in the first years of her marriage, to have a child. Maybe when he was older, she could have a conversation in which she explained the intrusive tests, the blood chemistries that seemed to happen biweekly, the ways she'd tracked her monthly cycle, even the unsympathetic doctor who'd told her that she had an inhospitable womb, a comment he'd apparently forgotten once she'd actually conceived. She'd overcome a recalcitrant husband, fibroids, an obstructed ovary, countless minor issues consigned to the marginalia of her medical records. Which meant that she still labeled her pregnancy a happy accident, the kind of long odds better suited to lottery jackpots and sweepstakes winnings.

The captain's voice on the public address system interrupted Mary Beth's reverie, telling Mary Beth and the other passengers that a small problem with the onboard computer was "a-okay" and their flight was number one for takeoff. The scheduled time for departure was ten minutes past. Mary Beth bided her time reading the directory of entertainment choices in the back of the magazine, thinking how Burt Lancaster films were never shown on airplanes. She wanted to sit in a cabin full of men in ties, women with hats; she wanted to rack up enough miles to earn platinum status, get upgraded to the front of the cabin, where she'd sit next to a cavalcade of stars, B-grade celebrities. Her brother liked to regale her with stories from his own travels, of run-ins with quasi-famous seatmates: the former Nixon aide who found Jesus in prison, the actor who played the bumbling spy Agent 86, a baseball player most famous for swapping wives with a teammate. Now air travel had all the glamour of a bus ride.

As the plane lumbered to reach V1, the speed required for flight, Mary Beth silently chanted the introduction to a pair of vague prayers, stumbling in the middle passages of both the Lord's Prayer and a Hail Mary. The words themselves were so familiar that she could not pinpoint her mistake, could not remember when the modern church melded *trespasses* into *debts,* only that she relied on prayer at each takeoff and landing to assuage her nerves. There was only the gentle rattle of normal turbulence once the landing gear retracted and the plane began to climb above the Great Basin, out toward the flat expanse of the Great Salt Lake.

22

TWO PEOPLE thinking simultaneously of the same unsatisfying kiss.

Near the point where the outskirting suburbs of Salt Lake City began to dissolve into high desert, west of the airport, Mike drove fast, fifteen miles per hour over the limit, headed for a rendezvous with a real estate agent who, it turned out, was a cousin of Sherri Ashburton, Mike's cocktail waitress from the night before. He remembered the name because he'd written it into his log of possible sales leads, made a note to follow up next week. The state seemed filled with these sorts of tangential relations, people who all knew each other, who shared a sense that the land itself was a special place. These small, happy coincidences Mike would take as additional proof that forces he did not understand were pushing him toward Utah as his obvious next stop.

He allowed himself any number of delusions that day: that he had enjoyed a perfect holiday weekend of revelry, that the adventure with Mary Beth that had for so long been on the periphery of his mind as a possibility had just begun. He could persuade her to come to Utah. The kiss had been nothing more

than a hurried contingency, a duty she needed to perform before she returned to her son. And he was willing to permit
that feeling, for now, the idea that he did not have to be first
among all her obligations. It would be only a few hours before
he would realize exactly how wrong he was. Nothing in his life
could prepare him. He had built an entire miniature empire on
anticipating every contingency for each prospect, and soon he'd
be confronted with proof that it was a skill he could not use for
his own benefit. That's what would burn in him, the knowledge
that she'd been saying good-bye the entire time. Mike could not
anticipate how, in just a few more hours, he would end up daz-
zled and beaten, remembering how Mary Beth had given him
a kiss at curbside, that solitary benediction placed on the forehead, as if she were purposefully avoiding the contradictions
and intimacies that came with open mouths, choosing instead
to give him this promise in the form of a kiss Mike Renfro
would always consider to be filled with meaning because of its
felicity, its grace, its finality.

And now, as her flight barreled above the Utah flats, headed
to its cruising altitude of thirty-seven thousand feet, Mary Beth
fixated on the kiss because it had been so perfunctory and
meaningless. How often in her life she had wanted more: more
passion, more commitment, more of a sense of destiny. Her college girlfriends used to debate what was worse, a life without
passion or a life without security; what she had learned in the
intervening two decades was that you could have an abundance
of either one, but if the other was lacking, you were still basi-
cally bankrupt. She'd allowed herself the luxury of pretending
her getaway had been a romantic vacation, which came with
the luxury of looking forward. Mike was the eternal optimist;
it came with his profession. He was always on the debit. She

could hear him saying, *No prospect was ever truly lost,* which meant he would never see her departure in the same concrete terms as she was beginning to, the start of one era, the end of another. That's what her kiss with Mike had been, a dividing line. She'd felt in her body and in the purse of her lips a kiss that felt defensive, one of custom and obligation, erected as a stop sign, chaste, motherly, and final.

23

PEOPLE MILLED together at the New Year's Day party with the randomness of charged particles. Sarah Hensley didn't even use the word *party*. Instead she welcomed guests by recounting how Mike Renfro, the owner of the house, had given her his blessing: *Why don't you just stay at the house? Have a few friends over, watch the Rose Bowl on the big screen.* Sarah and her friends planned on taking full advantage of both Mike's hospitality and his absence. Already, his sterile, modern kitchen was sullied with huddles of empty beers; ashtrays overflowed with Soviet-colored muck; three-quarter-empty cocktails were riddled with wounded slivers of citrus and dissolving cigarettes.

Sarah Hensley's only official duty on New Year's Day was to keep an eye on her coworker's kid. After spending two-thirds of the weekend trying to decipher the whims of a six-year-old, Sarah figured that today Gabriel Blumenthal could entertain *his own damn self.*

He sat in the midst of forty meandering guests, petulantly re-minding them to step over the cadre of stuffed bears he had nestled among the ancient, comfortable blankets piled on the floor of the great room. No one paid him much attention. On the concrete patio that abutted the great room, Sarah's friends sunned themselves, sleeping the dulcet sleep that came from too many margaritas in the early-afternoon sun of a freakishly warm January day. The poolside stereo churned out power-chord and hair-extension rock music ten years out of vogue, Sarah's guilty and ironic pleasure.

Another dozen people reclined inside on a passel of leather couches, staring up at the final minute of a lopsided bowl game. Between plays, the director cut away to a shot of the announcers in the booth eating Chick-fil-A sandwiches. Down on the field, two linemen hoisted a coach onto their shoulders before their other teammates could douse him with the Gatorade bucket. Which meant that what the linemen had intended as a Gatorade shower for the coach instead became an avalanche of sticky ice poured down his butt and over their teammates' heads. As the color commentator drew up the error on the Telestrator, he laughed and said, "What did you expect? They're big, dumb oxes, these linemen, every one of them. I should know. I played nose guard in college."

Like half the other women at the party, Sarah wore a swimsuit. Hers was a demure navy-blue bikini, and over that, she wrapped a flirty white terrycloth robe that fell open at midthigh. In between bouts of hot-tub frolicking, she elbowed her way through clusters of friends to retrieve a beer and found herself leaning over a small, mirrored tray striped with parallel lines of cocaine. Sarah considered her own reflection—a hint of wind and sun, her nostrils appended with a five-dollar bill—then looked around the house to ensure Gabriel was not watching before hoovering up two quick bumps of someone else's blow.

All morning, people had introduced themselves by their association—*I'm a friend of Jane's. We met in Mike's box out at the stadium. You must be Tim's girlfriend. Aren't you the guy who broke his wrist at Shelby's house? We've got room for one more here if you tell me who you work for. I play doubles with Terry on Tuesday nights.* A young man resplendent in a beer company T-shirt and baseball hat stepped next to her. She tried to place him, tried equally hard not to let her face betray that she did not recognize him.

"Great party. And great house. I like the decorations," he said, picking up a beer bottle that sat on its side. "Early American decadent. But the house ought to have a name, in black metal letters over the gate. Like a real ranch. Very casual and ironic. *Rancho Relaxo.*" He handed Sarah a bottle of Mexican beer and said, "Carter Lundy, at your service," turning on a high-watt smile.

After a quick handshake, Sarah realized how she knew Carter Lundy. Ever since she had moved to Texas, she had been part of a group of young professionals who rented a beach house in Galveston. The five-hour drive made less and less sense each summer, but Sarah did it anyway; there was nothing sadder than being the oldest single girl at the bar. Still, occasionally she led the procession in her ancient Volkswagen convertible, the top down and an Igloo cooler packed with cold beer nestled in the Beetle's backseat, all the while thinking she was too old for this kind of collegiate debauchery.

The romantic arrangements of those weekends tended to be temporary at best, and there was something temporary about Galveston too, its history, its architecture, its cast of characters. Every couple of decades, the town took it in the teeth from a hurricane, which meant, *voilà*—there was Dan Rather floating by in his yellow slicker, saying how nothing matched the destruction of the 1900 storm, when they'd had to weigh down the bodies and bury them at sea, only to have them float back up to the beach. Each time since, they rebuilt the island with bigger and better Kwikie Marts and Dairy Queens, T-shirt shops and all-you-can-eat fried-seafood emporiums. Sarah tried to remember if Carter had been part of the original beach house crowd—twenty-five-cent tacos and twenty-five-cent Bud Lights Friday night till midnight!—the Vegas-style justifications: *What happens at the beach stays at the beach.* Yet she could recall only fuzzy particulars: Carter worked for another insurance agency, but he had the gift, like Mike Renfro, of remembering names and birthdays and generally making people feel like they wanted to be around him.

She put it together as a question. "Galveston, right?"

Carter tapped his beer bottle against Sarah's and said in a mock British accent, "Cheers, then."

Sarah laughed. She worked her way around the kitchen collecting bottle caps and abandoned plastic cups.

Carter picked up a plastic trash bag and followed, holding it open for her. When she thanked him, he touched his forehead with his index finger, a gesture Sarah interpreted as Gary Cooper–esque, the taciturn cowboy tipping up his hat to better see the lady.

"Come on," she said, pulling the belt of her robe loose, "you can buy a girl a drink before kickoff."

Sarah motioned for Carter to sit at the end of the sofa, then draped herself over the sofa's arm, letting her legs fall across his. On the floor, Gabriel played with a model truck and a stuffed brown bear, alternately running over the bear or having it stand up and kick over the truck, an irradiated giant rampaging through a small town.

"So, what's the kid like?" Carter pointed. Sarah brushed his hand down from her upper thigh.

She had a theory—one that she might articulate once the

child was out of earshot—about his future: he would become a socially addled adolescent, unable to shake his awkwardness. She pictured him participating in elaborate role-playing games that used sixteen-sided dice. "I don't know. He pretty much does his own thing. His mom calls every four hours to remind me what to do next, what to make for dinner, when to put him to bed. But the kid and I negotiated an agreement."

"An agreement?" Carter fiddled with the dingy end of the belt from Sarah's robe.

"Not to tell his mom. I let him do his thing. He's on a kick, Vienna sausages wrapped in Pillsbury biscuits. He showed me how to make them, and as long as I watch the oven, that's what he wants for dinner. Three days in a row, it's been Vienna sausages and Cheez-Its for lunch and dinner." Sarah munched her way through some mixed nuts, then held up a Brazil nut, staring at it before throwing it back in the bowl.

"Do you think he has a peanut allergy? He looks like the type of kid who might have a peanut allergy."

"He's had a hard time. His dad is out of the picture," Sarah said.

Then Gabriel said, "Tell the general that Tokyo is a goner," before forcing the bear to kick over the truck again, this time adding the sound of mock-human screams.

When the big-screen television went to commercial, then returned to network-news headquarters, Carter said, "Shit. I thought the games went back to back. Walter-to-Walter coverage."

"What? What's that?"

"Something my granddad used to say."

Sarah shook her head. "Whatever. We've got time. There's this news thing. Maybe a half hour." Behind her, the giant screen split into two boxes, each filled with a nearly identical white male, around forty, one pristine in navy suit, white shirt, yellow tie, the other in a more traditional Washington uniform, gray suit, blue button-down oxford shirt, burgundy foulard-print tie.

Gabriel looked up from his toy bear's path of wanton destruction and pointed at the screen. "Uncle Richie."

Sarah stood. "Check it out," she said, catching herself before she uttered a more expletive-laden interjection in front of the kid. "It's actually the kid's uncle." The caption confirmed his identity: *Richard MacMurray, Free-Speech Advocate.* Sarah listened for the anchorman, who promised a spirited debate *right after these words, and an update from the college football scoreboard.* "How about a margarita, a beer, something?" she called over her shoulder.

Carter pulled Sarah through the hallway by her hand, leading her toward the open bathroom door. He pirouetted neatly behind her, shutting the door with a thrown-out hip. "I'll settle for something."

24

THE BLUE ROOF INN nearest the Dallas–Fort Worth airport was a squat, two-story motel that looked like it had been built from the same blueprint as every other 1970s-era motel, with its outside staircases, rusting aluminum railings, and doors alternately painted in forest green and pumpkin orange. The squat architecture and the safety railings and the L shape of the building gave off a bad vibe, as if it had been conjured from that picture taken just moments after Dr. King had been shot, men in crisp suits all pointing in the direction of the shooter.

Jeris McDougal and his girlfriend, Jenny Wilkins, walked along the second floor's outermost corridor, followed by Jenny's sister. Tara Wilkins worked at the motel as a part-time housekeeper, weekends and holidays. She'd gotten the job through a connection from the sober-living house she'd stayed in for a few months when she'd gotten out of the hospital.

"One hour. Don't pick up the phone. Don't take the matches from the ashtray and don't smoke and don't piss and, really, just don't leave a single sign that you were even here," Tara said, and she stepped forward to punctuate her comments with a finger to Jeris's chest. He caught her hand, turned her by the wrist until her palm opened, and because he laughed a deep and profound laugh, she did not take it as anything malevolent. Her whole life had been full of questionable choices, and this was one of the smaller ones, so she dropped the key into his other hand.

Jeris never once gave any indication that it might be strange that this woman was giving him the key to a motel room for the express purpose of fucking her sister. He was using Jenny, but he was also safe because he didn't drink and lived pretty straight-edge, spent most of his time reading about whey-protein isolates and carried around a plastic gallon jug of spring water as if his mantra were *Gotta stay hydrated.*

Inside the room, Jeris turned on the air conditioner. The unit rattled at the same tenor as the steady roar of incoming jets. He took a seat at the desk and started fussing with the display of his new digital video camera. The camera was a combination peace offering and Christmas gift from his mother because he had spent the past two weeks on restriction, after a day-long suspension from school for a shoving match about a girl—the same girl who sat next to him now on a double bed, flipping absentmindedly through twenty-eight channels of cable TV. Mama expected Jeris home by 3:00 in the afternoon; she kept warning him not to do anything that might fuck up his scholarship, his free ride to A&M that started next fall, but he kept getting in these little skirmishes at school. Last Friday his mother's workday had ended with a phone call from an assistant principal, warning her that Jeris was associating with *undesirables,* which by the principal's definition meant that Jeris had suddenly turned into an actual, verifiable teenager and was no longer behaving like a Cosby kid.

Jeris ordered Jenny to turn off the television and then tried to get her to pose for him on the orange-and-brown polyester bedspread. The motel was the only real place they could fuck, what with the way Jeris's mother watched over him and the sideways looks he had always gotten for dating white girls, from his mother and from everyone else.

Jenny's mother certainly did not like her daughter keeping up with a young black man, could not stomach that Jeris liked to tease her about his being black, *loud and proud.* Jenny's sister became their accomplice, but she could swing the young couple only an hour in one of those empty rooms, and Jeris was trying to both keep an eye on the time and not once look at his watch.

"You're not going to take pictures of me," Jenny said, her eyes following along with the movements of the lens as Jeris panned down past her breasts, toward the floor, pausing to slowly consider the length of her legs.

In the viewfinder, Jeris perfected a close-up of Jenny's lips and told her, "Let me see your tongue," and then moved in closer and said, "When are you going to show me something good? I'm going to need to see that shit."

He thought Jenny looked like a beer commercial come to life. Healthy. Jeris loved her name too; he'd never met a black girl named Jenny. She was a ticket to a life of pool tables and hot tubs and raunchy suburban sex in her parents' king-size bed while they spent the weekend at the casinos in Gulfport. A girl named Jenny could never live in a place like his mom's, with its orange countertops and striped wallpaper and plastic carpet protectors. In a few months, Jeris would figure out for himself that Jenny's family had neither money nor prospects, but on that New Year's Day he still remained enough in her thrall that the silver blouse she wore, a little glittery thing left over from the night before, looked to him like the very promise of better days.

She worked at the buttons, slowly and from the bottom hem, peering up at Jeris with each one as if pantomiming a training film she'd seen on how to seduce a boy. Jeris knew that she required this, that her effort to be sexy eventually passed into something that made her feel wanton and lusty; for now, she just mimicked what she had seen in the movies she and Jeris had watched, nothing too hard-core, a few late-night cable things with looped minutes of simulated bumping and grinding. They had already talked about watching themselves. In the early days of their dating, Jenny admitted that she wanted to see them fuck on tape, but he misread her curiosity for abject desire. She did not necessarily want to perform, she would explain to him whenever he raised the subject; she only wanted to see what she looked like, what it was that he saw when he looked at her in that animalistic way (he didn't know that with every movement she made, every button undone, every base that he went racing past, his tongue announced itself with an unconscious dart out over his lips, a reaction that Jenny registered as unthinking and reptilian).

By now they had wasted fifteen minutes of their hour together scouting out the angles, finding a place on the motel dresser where Jeris could set down the camera and still see most of the queen-size bed through the viewfinder. Jenny's slow maneuvering made Jeris anxious, impatient. When her blouse fell open to her waist, revealing a red-and-black bra with intricate embroidery, she stood at the foot of the bed and said, "Can you close the drapes? If I'm going to do this, I need some more darkness. I need it to be just us."

Jeris loved the way the motel drapes turned the room into a sensory deprivation tank, but he wanted to see all of Jenny, worried there would not be enough light for the camera. Too much of their sport fucking happened in the dark, in cars and basements, illuminated by televisions and dashboards. And at the most basic level, since she had asked, Jeris did not want to do it. Not without some negotiation. He pointed the camera at Jenny, who playfully ran her hands across her chest, then lowered first one bra strap, then the other, across her tanned and greatly freckled shoulders.

He stood at a ninety-degree angle to the window, looking at Jenny through the camera. "That looks so good. Are you going to put on a show for me? Are you going to suck me?" And then Jeris, in his peripheral vision, caught a glimpse of something moving across the brightness of a flat blue sky, as if the large window had turned into a television; the image blurred across the screen, moving downward diagonally from the upper right, a trail of black and orange. And before he realized that the contrail he saw was smoke, the surest sign of distress, he raised the camera, never even conscious that he was recording the incident. Jenny rushed to the window behind him and said, "What is that?" and then one or both of them were swearing repeatedly, almost autonomically, "Holy shit" and "Oh my fucking God," their words picked up by the open microphone. Across north-central Texas, at least a hundred people looked toward the sky, pointing, wondering. But Jeris was the first to understand what he saw and the only one to catch this moment on tape.

He was shirtless and shoeless and wearing only a pair of jeans, still rigid with their unwashed sizing, so it was hard for him to move with any speed, but he ran out the door, down the open staircase, and into the motel parking lot, and Tara, working the room next door, came out to see him running half-naked, his camera pointed almost at the sun. And the last thing Jeris said before the moving blur disappeared behind a horizon crowded with warehouses and office parks was, "That has to be a plane."

PART II

25

TEXAS, MIDAFTERNOON on New Year's Day, about to add another sad chapter to its history.

A commercial airliner on approach to Dallas–Fort Worth International, at that moment the world's fifth-busiest airport. Bathed in the strobing winter sun, the plane's fuselage glittered, a futuristic costume jewel left over from the night before. The passengers took in the perfect day, and the cabin crew, who put faith in technology above observation, scanned the associated readouts that provided scientific proof of what they saw outside their windows. Doppler radar confirmed the forecasts: no threat of microbursts, wind shear, thunderstorms, or sudden crosswinds. The temperature was nearly seventy, and visibility matched the prospects for the New Year—unlimited.

The plane took its numbered position in an orderly conga of incoming aircraft. Panorama Airlines Flight 503, as indicated on the strip placed directly underneath the oscillating screen of approach radar, the relevant details written on a piece of paper denoting the airline, flight number, type of equipment (a 727-200 with nearly four thousand hours of service), seventy-seven passengers and six crew, scheduled for arrival at 2:18 p.m. Central Standard Time, all in the heavily abbreviated jargon of flight control. Flight 503 was about to be shepherded from regional traffic control to the tower, and the controller offered the sort of unscripted good-bye that was against regulations: "This is TRACON passing you over to DFW tower control. Godspeed, 503, and happy New Year."

The pilot responded with a snippet of song—*"Should auld acquaintance be forgot"*—in a clear and steady tenor, surprising even himself; the tower controller and copilot joined in, everyone's headsets on that particular frequency filling with song.

Nearly one-fourth of the commercial-service airliners in the skies over Texas that afternoon were variations on the 727, but the one that wavered on approach to DFW seemed to the eyes of its captain a venerable lady, a dance-hall matron, filled with the kind of erotic flaws that could be appreciated only by old men wistful for lost chances. She might have been past her prime—the assembly line that built her was now devoted to making her unsightly and bulkier successors—but this old lady was a once-famous chanteuse known in nightclubs from Paris to Saigon, a celebrity slowly going to seed.

Dallas control signaled final approach, and Panorama 503 circled, two hundred miles out, beginning its final descent from flight level two-six-zero, twenty-six thousand feet.

Visual landing indicated.

The passenger in 3B was deadheading, a second-seat pilot returning to DFW to work an evening flight to Washington National. She slept soundly.

3E and 3F were colleagues of convenience, a developer and a moneyman intertwined in an elaborate plan to convert midrange apartments in the North Dallas exurbs into condominiums; they had spent the nearly two hours since boarding going over ad copy that promised a luxury lifestyle, the banner that hung from an overpass on the Thornton Freeway and swore, *If you lived here, you'd be home by now.*

4E, remembering his most minor assignation from the night before, a kiss with a stranger. He thought languorous thoughts—why had he never acted on his feelings for men before last night? The mere prospect of touching another man's skin left a taste like metal high in his throat.

5B, an accountant from a Big Six firm, admired the shapely legs of the woman across the aisle in 5E, who had removed her shoes and was stretching, pointing her stockinged toes in a variety of directions. Through the sheer hose, he could see that her toenails had been recently painted a brownish-red reminiscent of dried blood, a color 5B associated with the lips of a specific type of pale, raven-haired women. He was dreaming of what it might be like to sleep next to a woman with immaculately kept feet, all the calluses and corns soaked and shaved away with an array of potions and small tools. Then he waited for the shame, the self-admonishment that came whenever these mildly lewd thoughts entered his mind. This wasn't a middle-class longing. Even to his therapist, he could not admit the depths of his desire; he thought he might like to try being a submissive, and here in the aisle beside him was a pair of feet that practically demanded his worship. His wife, home in Plano, had tremendously ugly feet, like she'd spent twenty years as a cop walking a beat. Her toenails had gone yellow-gray with a persistent fungus.

In the window seat of the first row of coach, 6A felt the peculiar discomfort of travel, that pressing sensation in his bowels that meant, after three days of red wine and red meat, he desperately needed a good shit.

6C slept the dreamless sleep of a Xanax zombie.

7D turned to observe his children, a row behind (8A–C), and

wondered how they could have possibly gotten so fat. 8D was the beleaguered mother enduring the withering glances of 8F, the unspoken signifiers that clearly spelled out his desire for the children to *shut the hell up.*

9A and C looked silently over the same in-flight magazine, promising themselves a dinner at one of America's top-ten steakhouses.

9D waved for one last drink; 9E hissed at 9D, "Do you really need another?" before slumping across the empty seat to her right and staring out the window at the Texas flatlands.

The in-flight entertainments pumped out popular music. Six people on board (10A and B, 13C, 17A, 20D, and 28F) chose a meditative program of classical favorites, but it was 17A who began to daydream once he recognized a familiar theme from Debussy's *Doctor Gradus;* it wasn't so much a specific memory as an image of his sister, the way months of experience get condensed into one picture: she's at the piano bench, her long, straight hair parted in the middle (she would have been about eighteen, and this would have been the midseventies). She tried her best to teach him Debussy's wandering left-hand movements, the rollicking song for children, but he'd been impatient. An image of himself then, age seven, at the top of the stairs, listening to his sister practicing her scales on their modest upright piano. His own music room, in a five-bedroom house in the north Dallas suburb of Addison, had been designed around a seven-foot baby grand, but its keys had never felt more than the insistent banging of his unschooled children, the occasional riffing of "Chopsticks."

13F stared out the window and contemplated the mail he knew would be waiting for him, the latest settlement proposal in a series of divorce negotiations that had now lasted longer than the actual marriage; he scribbled figures on a yellow pad, added and subtracted various columns, and was resigning himself to giving his estranged wife everything she asked for, no matter her rationale. Arms-control agreements had taken less time. 13F was tired of arguing, tired of revisiting decisions he'd made two or four or even eight months ago, all for the purpose of deciding who owed what, who would be held responsible. He'd always been the one responsible for this relationship, responsible for its ill-considered beginning, responsible for the whimsical decision to get married, responsible for sitting his estranged wife down at the dinner table to tell her he wanted out. He was guilty of laughing a bit too hard at jokes about overbearing wives, nagging mothers-in-law. Now it was going to cost him, and he could use this legal pad to put together an actual dollar-cost estimate. The result of his analysis: he wanted out at any price.

14D dreamed of another trip, something that had nothing to do with the persistent movement required of him as a soldier of middle management, a week of repose poolside, dangling his feet into the edge of an ocean of warm, greenish water.

Row 16 was filled with four consultants in seats A, C, D, and F, each irritated that their frequent-flyer miles and platinum status had not gained them entrée to first class.

In 23A, a businessman pressed the buttons of his control panel indiscriminately, flipping through each channel until he settled on channel 14 to eavesdrop on the cockpit chatter, *Flight 503, cleared for final approach to DFW.*

Three people on the plane, moments apart, stared into the expanse of blue at flight level two-four-zero, each thinking that the color of the sky was the same azure tint that haloed Mrs. Kennedy as she descended the steps of Air Force One and waved to the assembled Love Field crowd on that sunny November day.

27C was a retired lieutenant who had joined the Dallas police force at the beginning of that November; thirty-six years and change since the morning he'd shaken the hand of an officer named Tippit, a no-nonsense crewcut type who for almost forty years now had been nothing more than history's trivia question.

25D debated whether to use the lavatory now or wait until he was off the plane and headed to the gold-status area of his preferred rental car company; he wondered which ubiquitous sedan waited under the yellow-green marquee that flashed out his last name, misspelled.

28D was knitting a six-foot scarf in blue-and-white wool.

30D, seated closest to the aft lavatory, wondered who he might complain to about the stench—stale wine, the ammonia of household cleaners and stray urine, even, he thought, the acrid smell of burning plastic.

The purser counted four-dollar miniature liquor bottles. The head flight attendant counted days until her retirement. The second flight attendant sipped bottled water and read a copy of *Shape* magazine.

Given a following wind and the anticipated movement of the jet stream to a southeasterly flow, the in-flight computer told Captain Grady Williston, fifty-five, of Westlake, Texas, that he could shave twenty-one minutes off the flight time. From the flight deck, he had already reported the prospects for an early arrival, but now, waiting for a vector for final approach, he began to regret it; Dallas was packed with end-of-season travelers, people heading home from Christmas with the family, which usually meant a crowded approach, having to take a sky lap or two before landing. Landing slots thirty-six seconds apart meant rush-hour traffic in the skies. Yet his own plane was only two-thirds full. The copilot had certified the count: seventy-seven passengers and six crew.

The navigator—Chuck Belk, forty-eight, of Chula Vista, California—confirmed a fuel reserve of nearly three hours, ten minutes, enough to circle Dallas four dozen times, enough, should events warrant, to allow for a diversion to Phoenix Sky Harbor, New Orleans, Sioux City. *In the event of an actual emergency.*

The rhythm of working with this familiar crew meant Captain Williston did not worry about the minor issues that bothered the flight attendants: passenger complaints about the seats, the assignations that led to entry in the mile-high club, an end-of-the-day shortage in the count of miniature liquor bottles. He feared the unpredictable: sudden turbulence, clouds exploding in microbursts, wind shear, bird and lightning strikes, runway incursions, and, as had happened last month on a long haul from Kennedy to Buenos Aires, a drunk and unruly passenger shitting on top of the beverage trolley; he worried about handheld missiles and passengers carting aboard Semtex-loaded backpacks, and, even though it had not happened in more than twenty years, he worried about an idealist brandishing a comically tiny handgun and demanding an audience with Brother Fidel, afternoon tea with Qaddafi. Captain Williston did not worry about the equipment itself.

Neither did the airline. After two more months of routine short hops, point to point between Salt Lake and the hub in Dallas, the plane was headed to a maintenance facility in Phoenix, where the logos and identifying marks and registry numbers would be sandblasted away, the skin of the airframe taken down to bare metal before repainting. The airline's business plan included pawning off the problems of this particular jet, known and unknown, to the Guinean national airline. Twice a week, the plane would fly its most glamorous route, triangulating between Conakry, Beirut, and Dubai. The retrofits and hush kits that quieted the voracious wail of the tri-engine jet had been stopgap measures at best.

The crew heard the broadcast on their headsets, air traffic control reporting to Flight 503, "Traffic in the area," an observation confirmed by First Officer Bill Zimmer with a lackluster "Check."

Navigator Belk chimed in from the third seat with his response, heard only on the flight deck and duly recorded on the cockpit voice recorder, "Duh." Belk, a former Marine, Annapolis graduate, took pains to get his work space squared away, stowing charts, filling out checklists. Only a small accident, dropping his pen, made him bend to the cockpit floor and, as he rose upward, notice the indicator light. An amber dome of plastic; replacement cost seventeen cents. A problem with the hydraulics. He pointed at it, and the captain gave it a quick series of taps with his index finger before the light flickered out.

How then to describe the sound of steel cable snapping, its pieces ricocheting against the aluminum skin of the airframe, tearing holes in the tail assembly, severing the hoses that fed the actuators of the hydraulic controls, those hollow pings and reports that meant total system failure? Perhaps it is best to describe noise by the absence that preceded it, the only sounds in the cabin the sharp, simultaneous inhalations of seventy-seven passengers and six crew, the short, automated trill of the *Fasten seatbelt* tone, the latches of galley compartments and lavatory doors boinging open, followed by the vacuum rush of rapid cabin decompression, the theatrical opening of the overhead panels that hid the plastic oxygen masks.

The flow of oxygen did not start, which meant that the level of pressure required to spring the masks from their housing was never achieved, but not a single passenger on

Flight 503 reached to remove the mask manually. Whatever it was, it would be over soon.

Captain Williston tried to coax the wheel, but the sound of engine response, he knew, was wrong. He had always thought of his planes as living beings, objects of desire, things he could cajole into their best behavior. The noise of the plane in flight, level and steady, should have been as natural as the quiet murmur of blood flowing past the eardrums.

They all wished they had paid closer attention to the flight attendant's instructions, closer attention to where the nearest exit was located, closer attention to the emergency instruction card located in the seat-back pocket in front of them: the six friends across row 19, the husband and wife in 20A and C, the young couple and their unticketed infant in seats 24D through F, and especially the young man in 26F, making an emergency pilgrimage to see his hospitalized mother. Warren Ashburton—*My friends call me Ash*—braced against the molded plastic wall nearest the window, now thinking not of his mother but of another time he almost died. He must have been seventeen. A winter's rain had blanketed the Dallas–Fort Worth Metroplex with a persistent coating of ice, the kind that brought the milk, bread, and toilet-paper panic to grocery stores all over the city. He'd spent the afternoon at a girlfriend's house, lost in the faux romanticism of black-and-white films on VHS cassette. He was expected home for dinner—family rules—but the roads were nearly impassable, and he'd pressed on as if nothing were different, no accommodation to the weather were required. His fingers now dug into the armrests of both 26E and F, but he was smiling at the memory, the cocksure arrogance of his teenaged immortality. Of course, he'd hit a spot of something he couldn't see; the car felt as if it had hopped sideways on the black ice, and then he was airborne. He remembered a doctor next, discussions of surgery for a fractured humerus and scapula, a compound break of the collarbone. His mother then, the hands he knew as comfort, holding his uninjured hand and making jokes—he'd do anything to get out of family dinner, wouldn't he?—the staleness of the hospital and the doubt he heard in her laughter scarier than anything else that had happened to him that day. The car had been a total loss. Doctors patted his legs after their cursory examinations and uttered the word *lucky* again and again. Indeed, he'd always been lucky. Admitted to law school on the wait list (he remembered the surprise of the admissions counselor, the way she'd told him that people as far down on the wait list as he was never made it in). He'd met Sherri in line at the campus bookstore the following month, their love the kind of bolt from the blue mythologized in fairy tales. He knew now there would be no happy ending.

The sounds of the plane's distress intruded. The nearly industrial soundtrack of man-made materials exceeding their mechanical limits, popping and cracking, the urgent scraping of metal against metal. He should be thinking of Sherri, but it was his mother that became his primary concern, and why wouldn't it be this way now that he was going to die? The ways in which his mother depended on him had always been a source of tension in his marriage, and now his sense of duty, of fealty, had brought him here to the very end of his time.

All these passengers with thoughts circling around one common idea—*What on earth? What is that noise?*—followed by a collective sense of relief as the plane leveled at flight level seven-zero, seven thousand feet, and the first officer announced that oxygen masks were no longer necessary. In the chaos, no one had told him that the masks had never deployed. Ash took a moment to chastise himself for being so dramatic.

*   *   *

A flurry of activity at the head of the cabin, the following of well-ordered procedures from a trio of memorized checklists. Navigator Chuck Belk shouted, *This is Panorama 503 declaring an emergency!* Tower control asked something about the stick, and Captain Williston did not hear the question; he focused only on his duty, announced they would try for runway 13L. Belk realized the captain hadn't transmitted the request to land, so he asked for clearance, told the tower to have the fire trucks ready to lay down a marshmallow of foam. *We're coming in hard and heavy,* Belk told flight control, and even he didn't know what he meant.

Bill Zimmer, first officer, fought with his stick, interpreted the warning lights and the cacophony of alarms to mean total hydraulic failure. He exhaled audibly, the noise picking up over the microphones of the flight-deck headset. Runway 13L was the short one. Captain Williston made some quick calculations about the glide path and, realizing that Flight 503 was still too hot and powered up, pulled the stick back hard. The plane gave faint response, enough to suggest hope. "We're going to be fine, ladies," he said. Zimmer exhaled again, the sound amplified through his headset, and Williston knew that he was trying only to control his physical response to pressure. All three of the cockpit crew had learned certain coping techniques in the military and would do anything to keep their blood pressure down; in the quick drop, they'd all probably taken three Gs, enough to force all the wind out of your lungs and even make you empty your bladder if you were caught unawares. Williston tried to match Zimmer's metronomic breathing, a short inhalation, a deep, cleansing exhalation. On his second inhalation, the stick began to respond, and Williston exhaled hugely, with a cough, in premature relief. The unmistakable sound of popping rivets, little staccato explosions, followed immediately, then sudden sideslip, the plane taking a hard and unplanned bank to the left.

For Mary Beth Blumenthal, in 26C, there would be no sudden realizations in this moment, just a gradual awareness, as if Death had taken a seat in 26B, produced from its attaché a package of cheese crackers with peanut butter and begun with the kind of small talk so familiar on airplanes, the who-are-yous and where-are-you-froms and where-you-headeds. Now only the sounds of a plane reaching its mechanical limits and, in the cabin, a woeful silence. Time took on its well-reported elastic qualities.

Mary Beth began to pray. She had not managed Mass or the confession of her sins in a decade. She interrupted her own prayer to try to calculate the last time she had set foot among the good offices of the Catholic Church. She was thinking she might say whatever she could remember of the rosary. The words themselves, their unsettling familiarity, surprised her. She found in them comfort, as they had been the mantra that ushered her to sleep for the first twenty years of her life. How logical, then, that the prayer she repeated was the Hail Mary, because mothers, whether through history or experience, are inexorably tied to their children.

Through her sweater her fingers sought out the ampleness of her gut. She pushed her hands under the thin fabric to touch the small stretch marks that surrounded her navel in an almost symmetrical radius, like the darker green stripes in a summer watermelon. Now she dragged her hand across her stomach, just above her waist, the same places where Gabriel's feet had kicked her from the inside, the striations where her abdomen had grown impossibly elastic and inflated. Richard had come to the hospital and fed her ice chips and wet a washcloth for her head and had generally performed the duties of her absent husband, and she wished now that she had taken his hand and placed it there, on her belly, encouraged him to follow the highways that appeared on her lower abdomen, asked him to rub lotions into the marks to tame their angry redness. Where her brother was concerned, there were a lot of things she wished she'd done. Then and now.

She'd been just old enough to regard him as a nuisance, a thing to be tolerated. As a boy, he seemed to have so little to protect him from the world other than his brains, and she told herself then that it was not her concern if he were to head out into the world unarmored. Then Lew was dead, and everything turned, as if the entire family could be identified only by their relationship to the deceased. And now the same thing would happen to her son. Now, she thought only of who might tell Gabriel about it, and here for the first time she thought the words: *the crash.* Someday he would stand in a field and gaze upon the site of his mother's death. Richard would bring Gabriel here and hold his hand; they would come to the site like accident reconstructors, like the assassination buffs who climbed to the sixth-floor window of the Texas School Book Depository and squeezed off shots from an imaginary Mannlicher carbine. Richard would have to put his boots on the ground. She knew her brother that well.

Now she was thinking of her son, his six years, those early days with his persistent fussing, the vocalizations that she had to learn to decipher. Her brother had been in the birthing room, not her husband. He'd rested a hand on her stomach through the paper-thin dressing gown. He'd been the first to hold her son. She could picture them both, Richard's unruly hair flopped across his forehead, the same undulating cowlick that would poke forward in Gabriel's thick mop.

*   *   *

The pilot's stashed briefcase escaped from under the jump seat. The navigator tried to heel it back into place.

Captain Williston knew the jet's slide to be uncorrectable now—they would die—but still he worried only about work. Figuring out the cause was a job for later. He didn't have adequate training for this, and there was certainly going to be a lawsuit, though it would have no bearing on him. Part of the mantle of responsibility meant that every time he was in the first seat, he knew there was a chance that he might make a mistake, that his epitaph, as written by the various investigating authorities, might be reduced to two words: *pilot error.*

He couldn't think of any possible explanation for what was happening, the loss of power, the rudder swinging like a barn door, left, then right, then left again. As the airframe reached its maximum tolerance for stress, it suddenly became imperative to Williston that he develop a working theory of his own death. Cause and effect. Meanwhile, Captain Grady Williston, fifty-five, of Westlake, Texas, was about to become the only person onboard Panorama Airlines Flight 503 mentioned by name in every news article, every initial bulletin of the crash.

The noise then of metal being stressed, then the final severing of steel control cables. The fan disk of engine three, mounted on the tail assembly, broke from its moorings, and its shrapnel penetrated the cowling, the fuselage, shearing the last pinions that kept the rudder secured.

The head steward worried about his dog, ensconced in a kennel out in Plano—certainly none of his friends were ready to adopt an Airedale with a curmudgeonly disposition and fur like a well-handled Steiff bear. 3A rattled a set of turquoise worry beads.

4A had a mortgage nearing foreclosure, 5E admired the color of the polish on her toenails (Decadent Rose), 8C scratched under his arm, 9D and E kissed feverishly, 11C worried about his recent loss of bladder control, 14A looked out his exit-row window and imagined himself on the tarmac, guiding passengers down the deployed emergency chutes.

16D was scheduled to have a pacemaker implanted on Thursday morning, 17E wished he had not been stuck in the middle seat between two corpulent seniors who smelled of moldy bread; 24A and B, two men traveling separately, held hands and whispered prayers without self-consciousness or embarrassment.

One of the flight attendants sitting in the rear galley secured the bathroom doors, while the other ducked around a cabinet, avoiding the sharp edge of the open door, and braced herself in the space behind a beverage service cart. On VFR approach, in the warmth of the early afternoon sunshine, conditions ideal, visibility unlimited.

The deadheading pilot in 3B imagined the stick in her own hands, heard a voice (the navigator's) shouting, *Up, up, go around. Full power.* The captain's hands fought against the stick shaker, its vibration part of the built-in safety measures against stall. A quintet of overhead compartment doors on the right side of the aircraft sprang open, scattering a few bags, foam pillows, blankets. The plane began a sudden leftward roll. A collision alarm and a stall alarm sounding in unison. The aircraft, left wing low, headed for slapdown. The cockpit voice recorder, from an area microphone, captured the inelegant last words of the first officer: "Oh, shit."

Seventy-seven passengers and six crew.

Now and at the hour of our death.

26

EVERY TRAGEDY manufactures for itself a hero. Herewith the story of how Howdy Ard, chief of police at the Dallas–Fort Worth International Airport, became the best-known celebrity from the crash of Flight 503.

Daley "Howdy" Ard Jr. got his nickname as a child, following an afternoon trip with his mother to the airport. Daley Sr. got off the plane, and in the sparse Love Field crowd, Daley Jr. picked him out easily; he wore a bolo tie and a Resistol hat, and everyone in the airport, the gate attendant and the shoeshine man and the redcap at the baggage claim and the valet who brought around his mother's Plymouth, all greeted Daley Sr. with a cheerful "Howdy." In the logic that only six-year-old boys can have, Junior decided that his father's first name must really be Howdy. Which meant it was his name too.

Now, after twenty-seven years on the job with the Fort Worth Police Department, and two here at the airport, the only things in the world that identified him as Daley Ard were his laminated airport ID and his Social Security card; even his Texas driver's license referred to him as Howdy Ard Jr.

At work, Chief Howdy Ard was the only cop who wore a

white shirt, a thick elasticized double-knit polyester. Badge of office. Running the airport police was a cushy job, the easiest way to double-dip on his pension. Twenty-five years' experience had earned him the right not to spend his retirement sitting at the front desk of an office building asking people to sign their names in a three-ring binder. Because his wife was out of town, Howdy had volunteered to work the holiday, double-shifting on New Year's Day, covering for the family guys. It was easy duty, average passenger traffic and parking enforcement and swinging through the terminal every hour, his walk punctuated by the soundtrack of people calling out to him, *Hey, Howdy,* patrolmen tipping their hats to the boss.

When the plane hit, Howdy was at the food court in terminal C, which meant that he felt the impact before he heard it, a seismic event. His instinctive, spasmodic turn toward the sound knocked over his extra-large cup of coffee, light, with two sugars, sent it pouring across his white shirtsleeve. With the rush of adrenaline, he never felt its heat. Reflexively, he looked at his watch.

Seven minutes then at a near sprint from terminal C to the police garage on the air side, seven more by the time he'd hopped into his cruiser and driven the length of the two-lane limited-access road inside the fence that delineated the edge of FAA-protected property.

Of course, the aircraft rescue and firefighting personnel had already arrived; that was the whole point of being a first responder. Fire trucks sat motionless, emergency lights still blinking, sirens silenced. Howdy sped across the open tarmac, hoping to get as close as he could to the crash site. A firefighter held up two hands, and the chief parked his car, stepped out. The field had a slight crown to it, and the ruined tail section, Panorama Airlines' red-and-white logo still visible, loomed above him at the horizon.

Howdy did not have to see the rest of the airframe to know

how bad things were—the fire chief's helmet was tilted back on the crown of his head; its protective visor hadn't even been clipped on, and the chief was the kind of guy who liked to get his hands dirty. Howdy watched as more trucks arrived, moving with the urgency he expected. A half mile out in the flatlands, men from the pumper trucks sprayed the burning wreckage, then turned their attention to where the crash had ignited the field's dry grasses. In the minute or so it took Howdy to walk over to the fire chief, Tommie Perl, Howdy realized the men were simply looking for something to keep themselves occupied. There was nothing to be rescued, just a fire to be contained and an investigation to begin. The coroner had already sent out the vans.

Tommie gave him a nod, and Howdy said, "Bad?"

Tommie offered Howdy a bottle of water from the seat of his truck. "Yep," he said. They were natives, laconic in that Texas way, and Tommie motioned with his head in a manner that said to Howdy, *Hey, look around.*

It dawned on Howdy that he was looking for an airplane that wasn't there. There was evidence of a plane, melted pieces that suggested one. Not much else. He didn't have to be an engineer to know they'd hit hard and fast. "Shit," Howdy said.

"That's the word for it, all right," Tommie Perl said. He turned to his lieutenant, giving orders; the lieutenant repeated them into a walkie-talkie; the echo Howdy heard was the squawk of his own radio, slightly delayed voices coming back at him through the tinny speaker.

He reached to his belt clip and turned the squelch knob and said "Shit" again.

The fuselage had come to rest in three large parts; the wings had yet to be found; the nacelle of the tail engine looked as if it had been shot through by artillery fire, and because the event was going to go out on live television, a cameraman was wandering too close to the smoldering site for the chief's comfort. Howdy went to retrieve him. He put his hand on the cameraman's shoulder and steered him back a respectful distance. The cameraman had something in his left hand, a stuffed animal, and he handed it over. Howdy examined it for a minute, then tossed it aside. The bear left a residue on his hand, something jelly-like, and the horror of it struck Howdy. Blood, or worse, but the mess was a strawberry color, maybe a child's melted Fruit Roll-Up; it certainly smelled like fruit, and Howdy wiped his hand across his white shirt without thinking, leaving streaks of artificial color and soot.

Hours later, when the cameraman would return and ask for comment, when the pool reporters were assembled in a terminal 2 conference room, they would show a cover shot, Howdy Ard standing in the burned field, that same shirt stained with whatever had been smeared all over his hands and the rush of the coffee he'd spilled at the moment of the crash. As chief, he'd be the first to take questions, and the image was this: Howdy Ard backlit by temporary stage lights and in his stained shirt, tired from the events of the afternoon and unable to process the enormity of loss, and those millions watching *continuous live coverage of the crash of Panorama Airlines Flight 503* would remember this as the moment that the grizzled police chief began to cry. He looked tough, too tough to cry like that, like some old Texas Ranger with that bushy mustache he'd cultivated in retirement, the sun-lightened hair and the reddened face and a distinctly nonregulation Resistol hat in the same style and color that his father had once worn. And because Howdy did not answer any questions, he never disabused the viewers of their erroneous presumptions. He'd already begun to walk away when he paused and, looking into the camera, said "What else is there to say?"

27

ON THE short riser that was the newsroom set, Richard sat in a director's chair and strained to see the last few minutes of the football game on the live-feed monitor at the foot of camera one. He could hear the game audio, along with an occasional comment from Toni in his earpiece; he liked the way her voice insinuated itself in his ear, its quiet assertions of her authority. She'd remind him to sit on the edge of his suit jacket and lean forward slightly, to show 10 percent more of his left-side profile, to look not at the camera but the camera operator, which kept viewers from regarding him like a portrait that hung over the fireplace in an old Vincent Price movie. He imagined her saying these things to all her guests, the occasional ex-president, celebrities major and minor, the neighbors with human-interest stories to tell, the owners of the dog who traveled two hundred miles to return home, the teachers of the year, lottery winners, hero cops, hangers-on with memoirs to sell.

He looked up after an incomplete pass, and Richard could see Toni, behind the soundproof glass of the control booth, talking into a telephone, her hands darting to extract her cell phone from the pocket of her slacks and then typing into the keyboard on the broadcast command console. Around him, people began with the electronic setups for the upcoming news broadcast.

Another voice, from network control, in his ear, saying, "We'll be live after the next break," followed by the return of the audio feed of the football game, the familiar baritone of the sportscaster announcing the game's final time-out and promising *a doozy of a finish right after these commercial messages.*

Richard's opponent for the day, a backbench Republican congressman from Orange County, strode in and greeted him. "I can't believe you take this shit so seriously." The fact that the guy wasn't home in California over the holidays meant he'd decided against running again, was busy lining up clients for his turn through Washington's revolving door as a highly paid adviser to Fortune 500 companies.

Richard knew little about the congressman other than that he was a John Bircher. The shake was perfunctory, Richard worrying about whether his palm felt clammy; in the closeness of the greeting he thought he could smell booze on the congressman's breath, the aftermath of New Year's Eve. He hadn't known the congressman as a drinker, but then again, the guy was a bachelor and rarely traveled, so it would've been unlikely for Richard to run into him in steakhouses or on congressional fact-finding trips to tropical locations or other places he might drink. Rumor had it that he slept on a foldout sofa in his office in the Rayburn Building. Other rumors said that the congressman, when he was a member of the California state assembly, had been known by the nickname Steam Room Sammy. The most noteworthy accomplishment of his four undistinguished terms in the House was that he had never missed a vote, a fact the congressman would inevitably work into the argument.

A production assistant got the congressman settled into his chair, wired a lavaliere microphone to its battery pack. The monitor showing the live network feed broadcast a commercial for light beer, then went to black. Next came the preview of Richard's appearance that he'd taped just a few minutes before, and Richard had the disconcerting experience of watching his own face appear onscreen. He heard the network announcer begin the pre-recorded setup: *After the game, what happens when an underground newspaper hits too close to home? Taking sides, with Richard MacMurray from the left, and from the right, Congressman Sammy Bickley.*

"That's a total *Star Trek* moment there," the congressman offered, and when Richard raised an eyebrow at him, the congressman scooted forward and pointed back at the monitor. "Sorry. It's the kind of thing you see in the movies, the Sammy Bickley of the past meets the Sammy Bickley of the future."

This concept was an idea that would return to Richard again and again whenever he thought about the events of this New Year's Day. Perhaps he'd always been inclined to think this way. Richard had always wanted to be able to change his bad decisions into more benign events, to force things into a shapely resolution of his own making. That would be a worthy superpower. He could talk his father out of going on the trip that killed him. He could convince Cadence to stay. He'd always believed in his abilities as a persuader. That's why he'd chosen litigation over corporate law, then television over litigation. As a child, Richard sat in the cramped stall of his elementary school bathroom and believed that with concentration, he could transport himself across the space-time continuum away from the place where six-year-old boys learned how to be sadistic and back home to the talismanic comfort of a teddy bear. He'd always been uncomfortably aware that the Richard MacMurray of his childhood might look upon his career as something inexplicable—*You get paid to what?*—something with no allure in the outsized dreams of a fairly average boy. He'd wanted, even then, to be part of a team, to contribute, to belong. When he got recognized on the street, he knew his feelings to be exactly what they were, discomfort, unease, an awareness that he'd become an accidental pundit and inconsequential celebrity. He never dreamed of being the Hall of Fame outfielder, turning his back to home plate and making a running grab that made Vic Wertz into the answer to a trivia question; he wanted to be a slick-fielding utility infielder, a master of the dying art of the pinch hit; he wanted to be known for his drive, his enthusiasm, his hustle to leg out the extra base, the ability to move from first to third on the meekest of base hits. He wanted to be known for playing the game the right way.

He wanted to be a man people relied on.

He'd once (actually, more than once) asked Cadence to enumerate his appealing qualities, and she'd offered his earnestness, his sincerity, his *competence*. He didn't have her perspective. The discussion reminded him of a tepid letter of recommendation he'd found in his father's papers, wherein Lew MacMurray—veteran of Korea, paratrooper, holder of the Combat Infantry Badge and winner of the Bronze Star—had been described by his commanding officer as *trustworthy and loyal,* appellations, Richard thought, better reserved for the family dog.

You did something a hundred or a thousand times, and it became almost automatic, and you never observed any of the artificiality of the moment. And there it was, Richard watching his own image appear and disappear before the screen dissolved into a commercial for fabric softener. He saw himself for what he was, a commercial. What did it say about him that often he could think only in terms of the image of his irretrievable past and its impossibilities? Surely there was some magic that could return him to the most crucial moments of his past, the ghost of bad decisions that could steer the university man in his second year to continue in literature, take up French, instead of following the indeterminate course of study that had herded him directly into law school, a voice that could stifle the urge to propose to the former Ellen Pritchard (his now ex-wife) after a fling with one of Ellen's friends? He couldn't remember her last name, Lisa something-or-other, this woman he had taken to bed six days before his first marriage, who in the false comfort of afterglow belittled his nervousness, telling him not to worry about his impending vows, since getting divorced was easier than buying a house, and he, Richard MacMurray, had already bought a house.

Now that house was four years sold, and his ex-wife, Ellen, lived in central Virginia with a gentleman farmer who planted a half acre of herbs every spring. He spent his spare time holed up in his workshop, building ever more elaborate cabinets and dining room tables and refinishing antique furniture while Ellen tended to rosebushes and grew peppers and tomatoes and three kinds of squash, putting them up in mason jars each summer. Once every six months or so, Richard and Ellen spoke, whenever a stray piece of mail floated to the wrong ex-spouse, or on the rare occasion when Richard's work merited a mention in a wire-service story that had been copied and pasted into the morning's *Richmond Times-Dispatch*. The truth was, they had hated each other for a while and choked it down, and now they didn't hate each other anymore, if only because keeping up the hate had proven more tiresome. Still, the taste lingered, and required Richard to literally shake his head to push away the onslaught of memories.

An unfamiliar voice emerged from Richard's molded-plastic earpiece, saying, "You're up. We're live in twenty seconds," and in the background, he thought he heard Toni saying, "We've got one, and a mobile unit," and he knew the background chatter was about something else. A different control-room voice said, "Standby camera. Intro package one." On the monitor at his feet, Richard saw the pretaped image of himself paired in split screen alongside Congressman Bickley. Then the graphics flew in, and the music began.

28

JENNY DROVE, and Jeris sat in the passenger seat, fiddling with the camera, playing the tape over and over, watching the playback in the two-inch viewfinder. Jenny's sister Tara leaned into the front seat and tried to see what she could over his shoulder. It did not occur to her that she had left her maid's cart sitting outside room 118, or that she'd left the rest of the rooms along the west side of the first floor untended. Tara would receive a phone call the next day asking her not to come to work.

She had no idea where they were going. Movement was simply required. The reflexology of disaster made it impossible to stand still.

Jeris hugged the camera nearly to his chest, bringing the viewfinder to eye level and then holding it at arm's length, as if he were a middle-aged man trying to deal with the unexplained disappearance of his reading glasses. To Tara, the scene on the video looked like a model rocket, sputtering in near circles, leaving a trail of black smoke. Then the camera went back close to his face, and the radio, which Tara had not noticed, announced itself with a quick theme, four attention-getting tones and a pre-recorded announcement—*From FBN News in New York, this is a special report*—and Tara ordered her sister, "Turn that up."

"Chaos." That is how the fire chief at the Dallas–Fort Worth International Airport describes the scene this hour following the crash of Panorama Airlines Flight 503, which fell to the earth some twenty-seven minutes ago. Initial reports say the plane had not signaled an emergency, and that all aboard—that's some seventy-seven passengers and six crew—are dead.

And Jeris tapped at the viewfinder and said, "Do you know what I have here? Do you know what this is?"

Only Tara answered. "Gold."

29

CHADLEY WAS watching a twenty-four-hour news channel, the volume muted but the closed captioning on. "They're talking about my company," Chadley said, pointing at a roundtable discussion that the graphics on the screen titled *Corporate Fraud: The Worst Offenders*.

It took a moment for the room's temperature to register on the skin of Cadence's bare legs, and for the noise of the city, even through the insulated windows, to whisper to her, *Chicago. The Magnificent Mile.* Her headache announced itself once Chadley turned on the bedside lamp, and her mildly sour stomach turned a bit when he poured a glass of orange juice. "I'd offer you some breakfast, but they brought the food about an hour ago. You slept."

On the other side of the bed was a room-service cart holding a carafe of juice, a pot of coffee, and a pair of plates smeary with grease and ketchup. Once she had been able to eat like that, omnivorous. The best cure for her hangover had always been a bagel piled high with an egg, cheddar cheese, four slices of bacon. Now whatever she ate got weighed, portioned, cataloged, written into a food diary. Never more than 30 percent of calories from fat. Nothing after eight o'clock p.m. She avoided processed foods, nitrates, milk with hormones, and yogurts with too much sugar, and all she wanted now was a cup of coffee, a liter of water, to work up enough of a sweat on the treadmill so that the hint of her hangover would break like a fever.

Chadley poured her some coffee and handed it over. He turned the sound on as the anchor asked the panel, "The more pressing question is this: just how likely are more indictments?"

"Very likely," answered Chadley. "Bordering on inevitable."

The screen cut to file footage of executives being led into the United States courthouse on Pennsylvania Avenue, the sandy-colored stone edifice that Cadence remembered from every other Washington scandal. Chadley tapped her on the arm with the remote control. "That's my boss. My boss's boss, anyway." United States marshals escorted a man in his late fifties—black suit, no tie or belt, hands cuffed in front of him but the cuffs hidden beneath a raincoat—through the courthouse doors.

Cadence wasn't surprised. Her bosses had long considered dumping Chadley's company as their auditors, a decision that would be made above her pay grade, something she did not worry about. She did manage, however, to keep up with the narrative in the papers, Chadley's firm under constant heat, growing questions regarding the practices of offshore sub-sidiaries, the tax treatment of preferred stock, an excess of deferred executive compensation.

Chadley had stylish three-button suits and dress shirts with their elongated, European collars. But he was what, twenty-six? and she knew it to be a costume. It was hard for Cadence to believe that at the heart of Chadley's career was anything re-sembling conviction. In her quieter moments, Cadence often wished that she was married to some absolute beliefs that re-quired her full attention; she wanted a vocation, not a career.

She did not want to be one of the zombified salarymen she saw emerging, hobbitlike, out of the subway tunnels each morning. She did not want to be an interchangeable part. Her career was what it was, a job, one that provided for her, gave her an ample safety net, allowed her to send money home to her father, fulfill this sense of duty that grew in her as she got older. But she could turn the job off at night. All she required then was peace.

With Chadley, she could see the end game. Her view of his future felt clairvoyant, his path the inevitable one that meant he'd bail out of consulting, take the LSAT, attend law school, followed by a few years of backbreaking associate's work in a white-glove law firm, billing his two-thousand-plus hours, then a hasty stab at marriage and a move to Bethesda or North Arlington, a pair of children in quick succession. Nearly everyone who had disappeared from her social life went down the same path. But Chadley didn't have the ability to view himself with brutal objectivity, and Cadence could not provide it for him. Sooner or later, something might jar him enough to provide a massive dose of self-awareness, but that would be a problem for the next girl, or the one after the next.

Or maybe that jolt was already on its way. His Chicago project was going poorly. Chadley's company was supposed to be auditing the books of the Department of Aviation, the massive bureaucracy that ran O'Hare Airport, trying to find a few hundred million dollars that had slipped between the sofa cushions. No one could pin down an exact number. But the newspapers had dredged up evidence of people skipping off to St. Barts for executive retreats; machines the airport bought from Cadence's company either didn't work or sat uninstalled, unpacked from their shipping crates, in a distant hangar. The news this New Year's Day reported indictments and a congressional investigation, pressure on the airport authority to save money across the board. Everyone knew the firings were coming. Chadley might survive the turmoil of the Chicago project with his job intact, but she doubted it.

Chadley was an auditor, and at work, his only responsibility was deciding between competing realities—spreadsheets versus corporate reports. He spent his days poring over boxes of financial documents; finding the bad seed of exaggeration meant days of entertainment. How little he understood the real world of middle management, memoranda, and mortgages he was assigned to disturb and uproot. Chadley often called Cadence to talk about the mild malfeasance he had uncovered, business lunches at strip clubs, gambling markers covered with a corporate MasterCard, executives with expense-account girlfriends tucked into suites at the InterContinental, the Four Seasons, or the Drake. He'd clearly been left out of the larger machinations of the firm. Now the audit of Chadley's Chicago project had already claimed careers—two transfers and four retirements—before anyone opened a box of paperwork.

Chadley spoke over the report, which showed B-roll of office buildings and cartons of documents in a federal courthouse. "We're disappearing a division at a time. Every time I'm back in DC, more cubicles get dismantled. The receptionist left on maternity leave, and they replaced her with one of those automated systems: *If you'd like a company directory, press two now.*"

Cadence thought of the carnage as a disaster movie, red circles on a map, spreading and overlapping, tracking the growing reach of the epidemic. The broadcast report moved on to an unfortunate videotape of one of the firm's senior partners telling a room full of stockholders in some client company how his stock options were *more profitable than cocaine, for chrissakes.* The news networks loved to show the tape over and over, an emblem of runaway corporate greed, a visual that translated to television better than a five-thousand-dollar shower curtain or a wine cellar paid for by stockholders. The conversation that morning was punctuated by a repeat of the video Cadence had already seen, the same partner doing the perp walk into a federal courthouse.

Cadence kept expecting Chadley to change the channel, but he didn't. Finally, he said, "I'm in trouble at work."

"The firm's going under. No one will blame you if you're one of the rats that jump ship. Maybe you should get your résumé together, talk to a headhunter."

"Not that kind of trouble."

"What, then?"

"Someone," he announced gravely, "has been auditing the auditors. Which means I'm fucked."

She knew that if she waited him out, she would get the rest of the story.

"When I started, right out of school, everyone was on the same gravy train, you know? We got performance bonuses, holiday bonuses. On one project, the lead auditors got to take their whole team to the Cayman Islands for a month to finish up a one-week job. Last year, people on the Chicago project got a Christmas bonus in an envelope, cash. No one said where it came from. Just an envelope, understand?"

Cadence thought of her long-dead grandmother in northeastern Pennsylvania, her uncertain English, the immigrant way she punctuated every sentence by asking, *Do you understand?*

Chadley reached under the bed for his briefcase, extracted an expandable folder, pulled out a spreadsheet. "By my own calculations, I'm into the firm for something like eleven thousand dollars. The attorneys told us on Friday that the key to avoiding prosecution is restitution."

"That's quite a chunk of change. What for?"

Chadley ruffled some receipts, looked at the list. "All things that used to be copacetic. Steakhouses. Bar tabs. Upgrades to business class. Tickets to this and that. Laundry. You know how we used to choose the wine for dinner? We'd order the third-most expensive bottle on the list. Room service, and"—he averted his eyes—"in-room movies."

Cadence gave him a wide smile. "Don't you know? *Movie titles do not appear on your room bill,*" she said, in the kind of voice announcers save for the fine print of car advertisements.

"I just don't have it," he said, and it took Cadence a minute to realize he was talking about the money.

Chadley exhaled, somewhere between a sigh and a deflation, and Cadence interpreted his silence as an admission: He was going to be fired. Everyone on the Chicago project was going to be fired. The guys at the top were likely headed to a country-club prison; the guys just beneath them were plotting their bloodless coups, and the guys beneath them were the scape-goats, the endpoint of the avalanche that was going to smother Chadley and his burgeoning career.

Cadence could see Chadley struggling with whether or not he could ask her for help. And she debated whether the easiest path out, out of this Chicago hotel room and out of this relationship with this boy, was simply to write him a check. Would he even have the balls to ask?

Chadley said, "I can't watch," and ran through the channels, past college football, country-music videos, and a pair of cooking shows, before settling on a different news talk show.

The anchorman said, "This afternoon, we'll tackle the issue of free speech in America's public schools. Does the right to speak your mind end at the schoolhouse door? Our guests, Congressman Sammy Bickley, Republican of California, and Richard

MacMurray, attorney for the Students' Committee Against Censorship."

After the theme music faded out, the anchorman described the kids as eighteen-year-olds James Terrance Scott and Riley Wayne Kiddings, using the three-name construction news writers reserved for serial killers and presidential assassins.

Cadence immediately grabbed for the remote, but Chadley played keep-away.

Whenever she saw Richard on television, she expected him to rise to his usual theatrics. But today he seemed calm, measured. She watched him say, "Parody, satire, sarcasm, and biting humor might be unpleasant. But they enjoy total constitutional protection. The real issue here is political, that a superintendent with thin skin doesn't like either the manner or the substance of what these young men have to say."

The anchorman recited the teenagers' names off the prompter again before holding up a copy of the offending student publication and pretending to read from it, asking, "Isn't it counterproductive for these young men to compare that same superintendent to Joseph Goebbels?"

"I don't think that was their message at all. We have very few absolute freedoms in this country, but one of those is an absolute freedom of the press. These young men used their own time, their own initiative, to put out a newspaper that was parody, a bit caustic, perhaps, but entirely factually correct. And that meets, to the letter of the law, our definition of protected speech."

Cadence held her hand out for the remote. "Why are we listening to this guy? He sounds a little off."

Chadley held it away, and Cadence receded to her side of the bed. "It smells like sex in here," Chadley said through a smile. "Sex, cigarettes, and cheesecake."

He pulled a cigarette from a crumpled soft pack on the bedside table. "That guy doesn't sound off." He pointed at the TV with a twitch of his head. "It's those kids he's talking about. Probably walking around the halls showing off their new piercings."

"It's the inalienable right of every teenager to feel alienated." Cadence pinched the cigarette from Chadley's hand, took a drag, handed it back. "Trouble in the land of Presbyterians. Shocking. But can we change the channel now, please?"

"Nothing much else to watch. Unless you've developed a sudden passion for college football."

"Let's watch the Weather Channel. The hotel information. Pull up your bill on the TV and see how much damage we've done. Anything but Richard."

"Richard? You know this guy?"

Cadence moved to the chair in the room's corner, cleared off her clothes. She grabbed a dirty T-shirt to cover herself. Every difference between them suggested fundamental ways they were incompatible, even the clothes they'd worn yesterday working out together in the hotel fitness center. Her T-shirts advertised charity events, race walks to cure breast cancer, or 5K runs to fight AIDS. Chadley's were freebies promoting light beer, bar crawls, and a brown liqueur that tasted like cough syrup, which Chadley referred to as a "gateway drug."

Cadence felt she was sitting in a hotel room with the very definition of extended adolescence. She used to think that she was envious that Richard came to her with a past that she would never be able to truly inhabit. He had a certain worldly authority. But there, looking across the bed at Chadley, with his hairless back and the upper arms that he shaved, she knew she'd been wrong. She'd run her hands over the stubble on his triceps and think, *What a fool*—not just Richard, but herself too. Chadley was a boy who had made only a boy's mistakes.

The Richard she was watching on television came across as unflappable. He wasn't just comfortable in his skin, he inhabited it with an undeniable confidence. It wouldn't bother him to see one of Cadence's ex-boyfriends on television. She'd never known him to lose his composure, not on television and not on the phone with attorneys and producers and editorial boards and the other random public people that populated his contacts, and certainly not with her. He could change the oil in his own car, break apart a fifty-year-old faucet to replace its cartridge and washer, and pair a bottle of wine both reasonable and right for the occasion with almost any of the whimsical foods that she'd chosen to order.

She sat fidgeting with her hair and decided to come clean. "He's the lawyer I told you about. The guy I was seeing." She wondered if seeing Richard on television had changed the preconceptions Chadley must have had. Lawyers by definition existed as older, well groomed, wealthy. Richard looked that way on television.

Chadley said, "'Seeing.' As in 'dated.' As in the past tense?" A disembodied voice coming from the bathroom, his tone flat and matter-of-fact, until it cracked and the end of his sentence rose like a question.

"We're not going to have this conversation now," Cadence said.

"Just when are we going to have it? One of those nights when I call at two in the morning and you don't answer? Or when I get off a plane to find a message that says you can't see me Saturday night, but maybe we can squeeze in brunch Sunday morning?"

"I'm not sure we're ever going to have that conversation. What's the point? We've had a good thing here, but that's just what it is. A thing." Cadence gathered clothes from the floor, more from the foot of the bed. She was proud of herself for resisting the urge to use the word *temporary*.

"And what do you have with him? Is that a thing?"

"A complicated thing. I don't have to explain it."

"It *is* complicated, or it *was* complicated?"

Chadley moved back to the bed and attempted to rub Cadence's shoulders. Cadence shook off his touch and went to the closet and began depositing her clothes in an overnight bag. "He's been in the past tense for about two months. That's how long it's been since I've seen him. I called him one night at two in the morning and hung up. I'm just not sure that he isn't in the present tense, or the future tense too. It's complicated."

Chadley lowered his head, sulking. "I guess that means *it is,* as opposed to *it was.*"

"I'm heading to the airport. We can share a cab if you want," she said as she zippered her bag shut. "You sound more like a fucking lawyer than he does."

30

THE NETWORK cut to a tease for the next game, a sportscaster inviting viewers to the *granddaddy of them all*. When they came back from commercial, the anchor read a one-minute summary of the underground newspaper and its aftermath. "Richard MacMurray, I'm asking: what's a fair punishment for these problem students?"

Richard's media training had taught him to reject the premise of the question. Somehow, when politicians did it, people got irritated, but anyone who hadn't stood for election could get away with it routinely. He stuck to his talking points. "The word *punishment* suggests that these boys did something wrong when they didn't. They're exactly the kind of students you want in honors journalism. Their heroes are Murrow and Cronkite, Woodward and Bernstein. But it doesn't help anyone when the principal, who is white, goes on the local news and calls two African American high school seniors uppity. Any reasonable person knows that at best, that's a poor choice of words, and at worst, it's a code word, a slur."

The congressman sat forward. "This is the same argument he gives anytime he's wrong. Anyone who doesn't want to sanction pornography is suddenly a Nazi. And let's be clear. What these kids put out is pornography. But I should have expected that, since your guest here makes his living defending the indefensible."

And that's when Richard knew he had the congressman; he'd made it personal, and with Richard, the argument was always about a theology of freedom, the right of a true American to be left alone, especially by assholes. "I love the fact that a member of Congress thinks that the First Amendment is indefensible. You took an oath to defend that right, Congressman Bickley. To defend the entire Constitution, not just the parts you like that week. Those Founding Fathers you are so fond of quoting had enough wisdom to know that we didn't need a Ministry of Propaganda. The right to speak freely doesn't end once you pull into the school parking lot," Richard said.

Then the stage manager jumped forward and gave Richard both hands up, a stop sign; he moved so abruptly that Richard and the congressman both reflexively checked the monitor to see if he was in the shot.

The anchor set it up. "We're getting word of a breaking story out of Dallas. For more on that, we'll go to headquarters in New York."

A technician materialized in front of Richard, unclipped his microphone and battery pack.

From FBN News World Headquarters in New York.
   Two words: *Special report.*

The monitors filled with the two-word graphic that even now in Richard MacMurray evoked irrational memories of childhood terror—in his short life, dead popes, dead presidents, celebrities dead in car crashes, millionaire philanthropists missing in their hot air balloons, assassinations and near misses, Three Mile Island, blindfolded hostages being paraded around the embassy compound, the sinking of an overcrowded ferry three-quarters of a world away, volcanoes that awakened after decades of percolating slumber, tornadoes that took aim at Walmarts and trailer parks, the sixty-plus-car pileup on a fog-shrouded interstate, car bombings in Gaza, the springtime Mississippi creeping malevolently past its banks, that one summer when so many young blond girls disappeared into the teeth of evil, and now, according to the chatter in Richard's earpiece, the sudden disappearance from radar of a commercial flight. *Special report*. The two words triggered in Richard an immediate reaction: fear.

Special report. The first time Richard remembered hearing those words, they'd been about his father.

It was the disillusioned autumn of 1978, the president begging us to drive fifty-five and turn the heat down to sixty-eight, the shah of Iran about to wander the globe in search of the Western miracle of chemotherapy. Ron Guidry of the Yankees had just picked up the Cy Young Award for his one miraculous season.

Lew MacMurray was the chief of staff to a member of Congress, and one morning he walked into a Rayburn Building anteroom to find a group of parents from San Mateo waiting patiently, hoping they might convince their congressman to investigate just what had happened to their daughters. Two families telling the same story: she'd once been the shining light of their family, they said, and now was off in the Guyanan jungle in the grip of some Svengali.

They'd seen news footage of the Reverend Jim Jones peering over the dark lenses of his Ray-Ban aviator sunglasses, the kind favored by state troopers. He kept telling the children how the time would soon come for the *dispensation of judgment.* These parents had written letters, epistles of heartbreak, but the congressman could not understand how this was a governmental matter and shuffled the letters off to Lew, told him to make it go away. And Lew picked up the case. The parents told him there had been reports: the minister was having sex with the children; it was more like a *commune;* they were growing weed; they were trying to create a master race; they were holding people against their will. The Reverend claimed they were building a utopia in the jungles of South America, and he'd begun to say some strange things; he was too fond of quoting Revelation, stories of horses carrying plagues, stories about the end of times. But in his correspondence with congressional investigators, the Reverend was surprisingly lucid, inviting them to come on a fact-finding visit to the plantation—a thousand Californians living a simple agrarian life in the Guyanan jungle, raising their own livestock and growing their own vegetables, weaving rope and fabric out of the hemp they grew. They hadn't given up the comforts of home entirely, the Reverend said; a plane came in from the States once a week with mail, toilet paper, magazines, and Hershey bars.

And so Lew advised the congressman to visit.

After a miserable fourteen-hour flight, they landed on an old airstrip built by the British twenty years before. They made a cursory tour of the farm, expecting no problems, expecting to be poolside in Caracas by dinnertime. Then the people, in their twenties and thirties, dislocated from the cocaine-and-gold-chain California of the seventies, started talking. They'd come to Guyana because they'd seen the future visions of the corporate wars, and they were tired of all that, oil prices and odd-even gas rationing and stagflation and land wars in Asia. Tired too of the pressure to discover what was next, so they'd fled to the jungle, and their problems had followed them there. Out of earshot of the leaders of the church, they asked the congressman, *Take us home.* Begged him, really. There had to be seats, certainly, on such a big plane. And then on the tarmac, as the congressman and Lew MacMurray and thirteen members of the cult were preparing to leave, men who worked for Jones, men who feared everything was about to be taken away, rounded into view on a jeep with a .50-caliber machine gun bolted in the back.

When the special report aired, a reporter in his 1970s-issue safari jacket narrated the disaster. Twenty-year-old Richard saw his father's recognizably rumpled khaki suit, the repp-striped tie (Brooks Brothers number one red). His father's hair was mussed, tangled, his body facedown on the tarmac that had been carved out of the Guyanan jungle. The congressman almost made it to the trees.

His father's body, via satellite, the first in a chain of death that would be known by one name, Jonestown. He'd never see his father's dead body except on television; the casket came back from Dover already sealed, draped in the American flag.

Lew MacMurray's death became a recorded case, something indelibly American, the mere presence of a large gun making everyone feel safe for a time. That scene, replayed over and over, slowed down and sped up, diagrammed and telestrated the way Vince Lombardi used to draw up the power sweep on the chalkboard—how the cult members emerged from the jungle at the far end of the longest runway, waving arms, white flags. Flags of surrender. The bait for murder. A few hours later, film of those displaced Californians, those dreamers of a tarnished dream, facedown in the lush subtropical grasses of Guyana, delivered to the Almighty by a glass of a poisoned kiddie drink.

31

PEOPLE COME to Utah, as they always have, to escape. That's the history of the place, God's chosen people chased out of the breadbasket of Missouri and Illinois. They took to the western trails in search of deliverance from the enemies of the Lord. Mike had seen the land with his own eyes, such magnificent desolation that first time; he felt like an astronaut soaring high enough to see the curvature of the earth. Just a few days before, as he had arrived by passenger jet, on the long and slow descent into the airport, the landscape below became obvious in its beauty: if Brigham Young could have taken the same circuitous flight path, a seamless descent over the valley and its perimeter of copper hills and peaks, among the expanse of the immense lake and its surrounding flatlands, with the clearing jolt of the zephyrs filling his lungs, the land teasing him with the promise of shelter on three sides from all enemies foreign and domestic, it would have been even more apparent than it already was to this leader—tired of the backstabbing and the internecine politics and the blood atonement that came with being a visionary—that this great basin, this Kingdom of God on earth, was the place.

What it might take to convince Mary Beth to feel that way, Mike Renfro had no earthly idea. He hoped she'd be drawn to the landscape the way he was, a feeling of homeplace, that whatever was planted here would grow solid and tall. Instead she'd answered his enthusiasms with more questions, rhetorical ones, repeating one word over and over again with a shake of her head and an upward lilt in her voice that made even the simplest declaration sound like a question. *Utah?*

Time would render Mike Renfro's recollection of the afternoon a muddle, clear only in snapshot. His most persistent memory would be standing next to a rented Jeep along the frontage road that dropped gradually into the bathtub-like expanse of Montezuma Canyon. The house he intended to look at that afternoon stood on eighty-two contiguous acres of land dotted with sandstone and red rock, and the agent who was supposed to meet him at the property was late. Mike entertained himself with daydreams of being a gentleman rancher, raising organic chickens, buying himself a thirty-year-old red truck to drive to and from the mailbox in the late afternoon, a large and overly friendly mutt riding shotgun, lolling his head out the passenger window.

Only as Mike saw the approaching truck, with its feathering trail of red-brown dust, did he step back into his own car, intending to turn off the radio. But he heard the familiar four-note overture of the FBN network, heavy on tympani and synthetic brass, and then this: *From FBN Radio News in New York, our top story this hour is the crash of Panorama Airlines Flight 503, on approach to Dallas–Fort Worth International Airport. The flight, which originated in Salt Lake City, carried seventy-seven passengers and six crew. Early indications are no survivors.*

The real-estate agent arrived in an extended-cab pickup truck covered with dust and road salt, and Mike watched him approach, his slow gait meaning he likely hurried for no one. Mike felt this insistent pressure on his ribs, realized he'd collapsed against the top frame of his car door, hung his arms limply over it. Tears fell to the ground, to the tops of his shoes. There was no heightened awareness, none of the clarity that adrenaline provides. His recollections would be unreliable, factually incorrect; he was after all a man of action and had spent his career helping others plan for just such developments in their own lives, and what good was a man if he wasn't good in a crisis?

This crisis demanded action, and as Mike sobbed over the door, he tried to imagine what he could do, what action he might take. Excuses could come later. The real-estate man would be the type to return to his truck to give Mike a chance to gather himself. That would take some time. Instead Mike slid into the driver's seat and wiped his nose, childlike, on his jacket sleeve. His rented Jeep kicked back an impressive spray of gravel and chalky mud as he spun away. Mike turned the radio off, wanting to be submerged in the quiet hum of tires over the highway, but there was the sound of his wailing, and he could not be consoled.

32

IN THE bathroom of Mike Renfro's palatial house, Sarah Hensley and this guy Carter came together naturally, the kind of temporary alliance that happened between single people in their twenties. Sarah untied her bikini top at the neck and it hung down her torso. She eased herself down, working at Carter's button-fly jeans and worrying about the toll of the tile floor on her kneecaps. Carter offered reassurances as to the rightness of this particular sexual transaction, telling her, "You're gorgeous," and tracing her jaw with his right hand. Her posture, his mumblings about God, suggested some crypto-religious overtones. She wondered if maybe Carter was married and having second thoughts, or gay, because when she took him in her mouth, he softly said, "Don't."

He lifted her by placing two fingers under the curve of her jaw and gently suggesting that she stand up. "I ought to buy you a proper dinner first," he said, a thought she could almost accept as sincere before he added, "Besides, there are a lot of people around who could talk, and you never know what one of them might say."

Sarah slipped out of the bathroom first and headed instinctively for the kitchen, away from this Carter guy and away from the hum of the party. She'd never known a man who had refused a blow job. She made herself a stiff margarita, doubling up on the Herradura Silver. She gathered her drink, wrapping the stem of her glass in a paper napkin, and when she returned to the great room, the spectators, her party guests, were all standing around the television. *We're getting reports of the disappearance of a passenger jet, a Boeing 727 bound from Salt Lake City to Dallas, vanishing from the screens of air traffic controllers just moments before its scheduled landing at Dallas–Fort Worth International Airport, apparently crashing into the Texas countryside at approximately 2:05 Central Standard Time.*

She felt the tension in the muscles of her jaw, her teeth tight, one deck against the other; she used two fingers to inspect the racing of her drug-afflicted heart as it announced itself in her carotid pulse.

Sarah managed to think about the child. Who can say what he saw?

She did not think of herself as maternal, but surely Mary Beth would have wanted to shelter the kid from news of the disaster du jour that he couldn't possibly understand. He was a curious one, that Gabriel. Just a few minutes before, passing idly through the den, he looked up at the football game long enough to ask the room the difference between field turf and regular old grass, and no one knew to answer him. That was his M.O. He'd been watching those end-of-year wrap-up shows and pestering her with questions: What is the Palestine Liberation Organization? Who is Al Gore? Where's Yugoslavia, Chechnya, Vanuatu, Kashmir? What's the euro? He'd watched the weather and explained the polar vortex and the jet stream to Sarah, and seemed to have at his disposal a tremendous amount of useless information for a first-grader, the kind of things that couldn't help you at all in the real world but made you a hit at parties and a wizard at Trivial Pursuit.

Gabriel stopped playing with the Lincoln Logs and the Legos and the pack of cards and the Matchbox cars and the blanket, ignored the small plate of nacho-cheese tortilla chips and the plastic cup filled with America's number-four-bestselling soft drink. Instead he stared at the television as the anchor repeated the lede.

A Boeing 727 bound from Salt Lake City to Dallas has crashed on approach to Dallas–Fort Worth International Airport, some thirty-eight minutes ago. You are watching continuous live coverage of the crash of Panorama Airlines Flight 503, lost on approach to Dallas–Fort Worth International Airport. We have crews on the way, and we'll continue to bring you the most news and information on this developing story after a short break.

The news seemed to stop the party. A handful of people moved closer to the television, and a voice, indistinct, demanded that they turn the volume up. The silence stunned the child.

Minutes before, he had himself prescribed the deaths of the entire civilian population of one of Asia's largest cities, but now he stood in front of the screen as it showed an aerial shot, the news helicopter hovering at a discreet distance from the crash site, the only sign of tragedy the presence of fire and rescue vehicles, the men in their turnouts loitering truckside in the midday sun. Gabriel stood there, in front of the television, mouth open with the intent of making noise. The helicopter shot moved higher to show a scar, a burning field. Who can say what the child saw?

33

RICHARD WATCHED.

He hadn't removed his IFB device, so he could hear the New York producer narrating the story into the anchorman's ear. "What we know," the voice said, "Panorama 503. A Boeing 727 en route to DFW from Salt Lake. The rest is going to come at you hot." Richard knew enough to deduce: *crash.*

His interview canceled, he unplugged himself and made his way into the tight quarters of the control room. He mouthed, *We're done?* and Toni nodded, paused her shuffle of phones to point up at the large monitors and turn on their audio feed. A fly-in graphic, then introductory music, ten seconds of backing track, long enough for a voice-over to say, "From FBN World News Headquarters in New York, this is a special report. Reporting from our Washington bureau, here is *FBN News Now* anchor Max Peterson," and on the camera monitor, Richard saw the anchorman fiddling with his lapel microphone. A third hand, some technician, reached in from stage left to make one final adjustment of the mic before a voice in the background, bleeding through on the control room audio, said, "You're in the goddamn frame!"

The anchor said quietly, "Steady, people." The guy was un-flappable. Another newsman of the trench-coat-and-safari-jacket era; he'd covered George Romney's quixotic 1968 run for the White House right up to the moment the governor claimed he'd been brainwashed; he'd found time to smoke hash with the fine gentlemen of Second Battalion, Fifth Marines on a few days of mop-up patrol in one of South Vietnam's hottest sectors. A plane crash wasn't going to make him lose his shit.

On the main monitor, the graphic dissolved, the animation fading as the anchorman lowered his head to begin: "Good afternoon. We're interrupting to bring breaking news out of our Dallas bureau. This afternoon, Panorama Airlines Flight 503, a Boeing 727 passenger jet bound from Salt Lake City to Dallas, vanished from the screens of air traffic controllers just moments before its scheduled landing at Dallas–Fort Worth International Airport. Weather in the area has been reported as clear. And now FBN is confirming"—he pushed his earpiece farther in—"based on police and fire department sources, that Panorama 503 has crashed on approach. A crew is en route to the scene, and we'll take you there for a live report. But first, a short break. Stay with us, this is FBN."

A bumper. *If it's news, FBN is there.*

Television, Richard thought. The perfect messenger of death. Plane crash, but first a word from our sponsors. He'd seen this movie before. His own father, facedown on the tarmac of a military airfield in a third world country he'd never heard of. The tableau he remembered: his father's body in the foreground, surrounded by plain men in sack suits who had conjured up handguns and automatic weapons. One guy barked orders, a Secret Service earpiece dangling against his collar. This was a special report, rendered in the grainy realism of 16-millimeter film. For emphasis, one of the agents waved around a compact submachine gun—a weapon he was not supposed to have, a gift of fealty from a Mossad colonel—and no one, not even the millions who saw the film (it was still on film) a day later on television, noticed the proscribed weapon. His father's body, followed by a commercial. *How'd you like a nice Hawaiian Punch?*

Richard made his way to what he hoped was an unobtrusive spot in the rear of the control room and watched the live feed. The room pulsed with the urgency of disaster, people making and receiving phone calls, doing the leg work of solid reporting, figuring the capacity of the aircraft, its flight schedules and maintenance history, obtaining a copy of the passenger manifest. The familiar faces of on-air personalities scurrying back and forth to the desks in the newsroom.

One of the other monitors showed a young female reporter milling around the crash site, flipping pages in a reporter's notebook, trying to push flying tendrils of her hair behind her ear. At the edge of the two-lane road that led to the airport fire station, a sterile area had been carved out by lines of yellow caution tape running between a perimeter fence and an idling fire truck. A firefighter in full turnout gear was pushing the reporter gently toward the truck.

Richard watched the satellite feed, the pretty young reporter stopping to set up her stand-up, then moving her lips in such an exaggerated fashion that Richard recognized it as a warm-up exercise. Behind her, scattered in the grazing field, purses and wallets, soft-sided duffel bags, magazines. The cameraman had already shot footage of severed limbs and viscera that appeared to have been decoupaged and baked onto what remained of the airframe, a priest's collar and the shoes that dotted the landscape at random intervals and the intact water bottles and the briefcase with its engraved brass nameplate—the initials G. C. W. clearly visible even through a layer of soot. The rear section of the plane shrouded in the foam of white fire suppressant, and a kid, couldn't have been more than seventeen, who was missing his clothing from the waist down but still had on a T-shirt bearing the words CLASS OF 2001 and a list of names silk-screened across its back, and a hand, a well-manicured hand with painted fingernails and a wedding set on the ring finger in platinum and diamonds in the art-deco style; the hand clutched an open cell phone, but the casing and the screen and the numbers had begun to melt, and the hand rested on the blackened ground in a puddle of what appeared to be motor oil next to a woman's facedown body covered in what must have been melted plastic. Richard had seen enough; he knew that the raw feed he was watching would never make broadcast. This was that human compulsion, to see what could not be forgotten, but television news focused on telling us what happened, while we pretended not to want to look.

Cut to the New York–based anchorman giving the briefest possible introduction: "We go now to the crash site, on the outer edges of the Dallas–Fort Worth International airfield, where Graciela Martín is standing by."

In front of the truck, the reporter began her stand-up, with the tail-rudder section of the plane visible over her left shoulder and the bright American sunlight of the plains now fading into a more seasonally appropriate grayness. Her Michelangelo-veneered teeth glowed with such radiance that they looked almost blue under the camera light. "You are looking—" she started a second time and stopped herself; she had the nervous habit of smiling when reading copy over stories about flesh-eating bacteria, colleges struck with outbreaks of viral meningitis, tourists robbed and dismembered in Colombia, explosions in a corn elevator, forty-car pileups on the interstate, four promising teens killed in a crash involving alcohol and excessive speed. She was still smiling broadly, and someone in the control room said into their headset, "You better frame her up. Or give me some field shots. Don't shoot that fucking smile talking about dead people."

She had it cold, first on the scene. The airport police had established their perimeter, which meant FBN would be the only team on site for at least the next hour. Her report went through the basics, Flight 503, departed earlier this afternoon from Salt Lake City. Obligingly, the broadcast monitor filled with reference shots: firemen milling around with no specific duties. This was a recovery operation, not a rescue now, an entirely different protocol. The reporter read what little copy she'd written down, then couldn't figure out any exit line beyond "Back to you."

Max Peterson reset the situation, and the cameraman turned to record the departure of the first-responding engines and the firefighters stacking plastic-bagged bodies in an open field; the largest part of the fuselage had come to rest in the grazing lands of a ranch just off the flight path five miles to the west, and now the aircraft-rescue and firefighting teams stood around their equipment, wiping foreheads and cadging cigarettes, little left to their mission except the recovery of body parts and personal effects. Forty-seven wallets, twelve purses, carry-on bags, four laptop computers, an array of small electronic devices melted from the heat of impact's fireball, one miniature replica license plate from the state of Utah, stamped with the name Gabe.

Richard wasn't really paying attention anymore; he stared at a shot from the still store, a briefcase with a doe-colored stuffed bear beside it. The monitor audio broadcast the anchor saying, "Here is what we know so far," and Richard answered him half-aloud, "Nothing. We know nothing."

And nothing for him to do except head home.

He turned his collar up and ventured to Pennsylvania Avenue. Finding the wide promenade empty save for the odd

Metrobus and the white-and-red cars of the District police, he decided to walk until he reached a Metro station or spotted a roaming taxi.

A plane crash was enough to shake anyone.

Special report. Six blocks up Pennsylvania, Richard found himself ducking into a CVS drugstore for some Camel Lights, hard pack. When he was a kid, CVS had a more honest name, Peoples Drug, which seemed a perfect place—the only place— to buy cigarettes. Back outside, he struggled with the cellophane and foil of the pack, then tried to remember which pocket held his matches; halfway through the survey, he produced a single copy of his own business card from the right-hand pocket of his suit coat. A gift from Cadence. *Richard MacMurray, Defender of the Republic.*

The card, his matches, the muck of subway fare cards and membership IDs that filled his wallet—*his* personal effects— were the sundries that defined who he was. He thought of the crash, how tonight workers would hit the grazing field under the glow of diesel-powered mercury lights to gather the surviving briefcases, shoes, earrings, and cuff links. Some unlucky relative would get them in the mail once the investigation was complete, another unwanted reminder of just how fleeting the optimism of a New Year truly was.

One thought of Cadence and one unsatisfying cigarette, his first in a year and a day, and Richard found he had wandered west maybe a dozen blocks. At the gothic tower of the Old Post Office, he turned north, toward the welcoming cacophony of the subway. The morning's weather had begun to turn. An insulating blanket of clouds rolled in from the west, dense, thick, a light gray that seemed more in tune with January, more in tune with his mood. She wouldn't approve of the midday cigarette any more than she would approve of his morose mood, and he found himself wadding the pack into a ball and tossing it in one of the brown garbage barrels that stood sentry at the exit to the Metro Center station.

As he turned, the eldest from a group of Japanese tourists huddled around a laminated map shyly approached Richard, seeking directions to the Smithsonian in fractured yet competent English.

Richard took the map and turned it over and, through a combination of elementary sentences and Marcel Marceau gestures, showed the man and his group how to take the Blue and Orange Lines the few stops to touristland. As they departed—the men in the group all offering the same slight bow—Richard turned and took his first step smack into the black-suited chest of Don Keene.

"A bravura performance," Don said. "Overcoming the language barrier to communicate in precise and effective terms."

Richard laughed and shook Don's offered hand. "It's not like I'm the great communicator. In this neighborhood, people only want to find two things, Metro or the museums." Richard started to walk, expecting Don Keene to follow him, but Don did not move. He stopped, asked, "Headed back to the hotel?"

"I'm at the Pilgrim. I was thinking about catching a cab," Don said, using his head to point over his shoulder at the street behind him, a gesture that said he was worried about the weather, or maybe just in a hurry.

Richard stepped to the curb, and a purple cab sidled over from the rear of the line at one of the other grand hotels a block away. Once they had settled into the backseat, Don opened his soft leather briefcase and extracted a file folder, placed the case on his lap and rested the folder on top. "You didn't forget, did you? I'm here to hire an anchorman."

34

CHADLEY AND Cadence shared a silent cab ride to O'Hare that lasted thirty-five minutes. All his overtures to conversation had been answered with monosyllabic grunts or dismissive smirks that reminded him how often Cadence made him feel like a child. He'd never thought of their age difference as significant; his own parents had been a dozen years apart yet somehow became old at the same moment. But Cadence seemed serious where he was slight, the kind of shameful, gnawing knowledge that ate away at him like an ulcer. He was not serious and had no idea how to become that way. Even his clothes—a leather motorcycle jacket that looked too new to belong to anyone who actually rode a bike, jeans and a brand-new Ramones T-shirt that had been chemically distressed to resemble a twenty-year-old Ramones T-shirt—made him feel like he was wearing a costume.

At the gate, a harried attendant informed Chadley that the entire ebb and flow of air travel back east was clogged in a mess of occluded fronts, high-altitude thunderheads, defective equipment, and, of course, the temporary closure of the airline's hub in Dallas. The crash was being discussed at length by newscasters whose images flickered on the soundless televisions at gate C73.

Cadence, however, had chosen to pursue détente and delivered a humongous Diet Coke and a lemon poppy-seed muffin. In between glances at the *Chicago Tribune,* she would lean over and avail herself of a long draught on the drink straw. The third time she did so, Chadley simply handed the drink to her, and she busied herself with a copy of *Forbes* and a bag of cherry licorice.

To get on an airplane in the aftermath of a crash, to watch the continuous live news coverage while sitting in the molded plastic chairs surrounding gate C73 at O'Hare International Airport—indeed, even to believe in the principles of thrust and elevation and the microprocessors that control the hundreds of infinitesimal calculations that manipulate the avionics—was the ultimate expression of faith.

The flight to DC was only half-full. Once the drink cart came around, Chadley ordered two screwdrivers and dug in his pocket for a ten-dollar bill, but the flight attendant waved off the money.

She put the drinks on the edge of Chadley's tray, between his elbow and Cadence. "Someone said you two were newlyweds," the flight attendant said.

Cadence looked at Chadley, then answered, "Not us."

"Oh, I'm sorry. But you do have that look. Half-excited, half-scared."

The flight attendant unlocked the cart with her foot and slid past, and Chadley thanked her before saying to Cadence, "She's right about the half-scared part."

Cadence raised the corner of her mouth. "Is that really all you have to say?"

"Before. In the hotel. I was going to ask for money, you know."

She nodded. "I know." And then a pause. "Why didn't you?" She put her finger in the book she was reading to look him in the eye.

"Because I knew you wouldn't help."

"I'm saving my help," Cadence said, "for someone who really needs it."

He said nothing, then lowered the window shade and hoped he could sleep. They would land in late afternoon, and by Wednesday, he'd likely be out of a job, perhaps escorted out of the building by security. A week after that, his personal things would show up in a box at his door. The question was whether he was going to pay for his mistakes all at once, or if he could spread the cost out over time.

His most specific memory of Cadence would always be the touch of her right hand, their last moment of physical contact. Standing in the crush waiting to exit the plane, Cadence reached out to touch his cheek. Chadley thought that she was going to lean in for a kiss, but in the end all she did was some reflexive grooming, wiping away a stray eyelash, before condemning him with one remark: "You have been nothing but a scared child."

And she was exactly right. He would remember her departure as the point when he knew he was going to have to ask for help. He pictured following her off the plane, down an escalator to the baggage carousel. Underneath the terminal they would slide into the line and wait for separate taxis. At some point, with their two cars veering off into opposite directions—Chadley's home to his near-empty condo, on the margins of downtown, Cadence's disappearing into the grids and diagonals of the city—she would begin to recede, back to whatever secret life she craved.

35

THE TAXI Don and Richard hailed outside Metro Center smelled of incense and bitter orange. The driver, white, wore his hair piled high under a tam knitted in the colors of the Jamaican flag.

As Richard entered the cab, he noticed a plastic bottle filled with what was almost certainly urine rolling around on the front seat. Downside of the job, he guessed. The radio coughed out a thirty-second report on the plane crash: *Federal authorities are on the scene in Dallas, where a passenger jet has crashed just minutes before its scheduled arrival,* etc., and a few minutes of local news, *Traffic and weather, together on the eights,* and Don Keene listened to the broadcast intently, eyes closed, a sommelier sampling a wine for the first time. He nodded his agreement, then winced when the announcer stumbled over a live read of a commercial for a local mattress dealer.

"I didn't know anyone still listened to AM," Don said. "Other than me, that is."

The driver headed across town on I Street. Don's immersion in the news made Richard glad they hadn't taken a more southerly route that would have sent them past the Treasury

Department or closer to the White House. The statuary and fountains of the parks often felt oppressive to Richard, ever since the Reagan-era homeless appeared in Lafayette Park with their army surplus blankets and five-pound blocks of cheese and signs proclaiming that we were living in the end times— John on Patmos warning about the coming apocalypse— hand-lettered signs with the simplest of declarations, all in the imperative voice: *Repent! Peace!*

The past year had been the year of taxis. Richard took taxis everywhere. Taxis to and from work, taxis at the lunch hour to meet the four or five other men in the city who performed this same indescribable work. At lunch, they mocked each other for ordering a salad or not ordering a drink. Over steaks and potatoes, the men talked about what they would that night talk about on television, practicing their phraseology, coming up with the rhetoric of the week. They used to joke about it: if you took away the medium-rare fillet and the midday cocktail, the conventional wisdom would disappear like the passenger pigeon. They coughed out these little catchphrases in the bluster of a buzzy lunch, and later that afternoon, production assistants transformed the words into the flyover graphics and chyron'ed letters that appeared during the five o'clock hour superimposed over their chests as the men talked on and the screen reminded everyone that it was *Day Seven of the Budget Impasse,* that they were discussing *Breaking News,* or that Congress was still debating *The Repeal of the Death Tax.* Then a taxi back to the office, later a taxi to the news bureau and an appearance on the five p.m. national broadcasts, followed by a taxi to a fund-raiser for a gentleman who represented the good people of Tennessee's ninth congressional district, a few more drinks. Some insouciant flirting with the endless crop of twenty-two-year-old congressional staff assistants. Then a taxi to a bar where a veteran lobbyist from the cement industry who preferred his gin and tonics in a pint glass could be counted on to provide a decent steak, a bottomless bourbon and ginger ale, a Marlboro 100, a Montecristo No. 2 cigar handed over with a conspiratorial laugh: *Here, this is the kind that Castro smokes.* A taxi home.

Apparently Don felt the same way, that taxis meant business, which meant he shared Richard's reluctance to engage in small talk. He didn't know Don well enough to engage in anything deeper, but had Don asked, he was ready to tell him everything he knew about his city.

Washington wasn't a city that you inhabited so much as one you survived. You told people you lived in the city and people shook their head and you knew they were thinking about the violent streets and the crack-smoking mayor. You endured the traffic as you did in any cosmopolis, and you endured the incompetent government that couldn't remember to pick up the trash, couldn't plow the streets when it snowed, couldn't check to see whether its schoolteachers were criminals or had actually gone to college; the trains never ran on time, hardly ran at all in inclement weather.

Don covered the taxi fare, and together, they walked through the revolving doors at the hotel's Connecticut Avenue entrance and moved silently toward the bar. Its narrow entryway, lined with signed portraits of five decades' worth of members of Congress, Supreme Court justices, and presidential appointees, suggested an exclusivity that had always intimidated Richard, as if the waitstaff might accuse him of being an impostor and ask him to leave.

He'd taken Cadence here on their first date, an occasion that seemed almost as distant in his mind as his marriage or passing the bar exam. It had been a strange place to suggest for a date. He'd been out of the game long enough to know that it was wrong, but Cadence never mentioned it. Richard liked the way she'd handled herself, the banter with the bartender who'd teased her about her fruity drinks and threatened to ID her. He remembered thinking that it wasn't a date until he'd noticed the details, her fresh pedicure, her newish shoes, the way her lips looked with their well-appointed lushness and their gloss. Her mouth reminded him of the women he saw reading the news on television, a wide smile that started in one corner and spread until it lit the entire face.

These hotel bars were where so much of Washington business got done; all the city's nicer hotels made Richard feel the same way he had on that night with Cadence, as if he were a twelve-year-old boy dressed in one of his father's suits, and mostly he wanted someone, another man, to explain to him why that was. Even now, at forty-two, he still felt as if he were playing dress-up, that an unbelievable stroke of good fortune had delivered him into a life of $2,500 bespoke suits and $150 ties of French silk. Sooner or later the grown-ups would come home and relieve him of his duties.

Don Keene hardly looked like the type to sit idly by for these emotional unzippings. Men did not make friends in their forties; they had activity partners and drinking buddies. Richard had professional acquaintances and guys who were not much more than familiar faces at the bar, guys who were good for superficial conversation but did not know his last name or home phone number. The men who had once been the great patriotic confidants of Richard's 2:00 a.m. musings now lived thousands of miles away, alienated from Washington and a decade removed from their few common bonds. A phone call from any of them was as likely as a total eclipse. What Richard got out of those long-term friendships now was an email on his birthday, a Christmas letter filled with pictures, dogs in Santa hats and children he had never met.

Listening to whatever Don had to say would take half an hour, tops, and might give him a story to tell at the bar later that week. Of course, it bothered Richard that he could not think of anyone specific that he might tell the story to.

The bartender moved in front of Don and Richard but never stopped wiping the zinc-topped bar. Richard ordered a Bloody Mary with peppered vodka, and Don said, "God, that sounds good," but when the bartender asked, "One for you, sir?" Don shook his head and ordered club soda, two limes, a dash of bitters.

"Sour stomach?" Richard asked.

"Actually, I was in bed by ten, up at four forty-five, and had to tip a guy at my hotel twenty bucks to let me into the gym. Forty-five minutes of cardio and forty-five minutes of trying to do some decent weight work with twenty-pound dumbbells. All followed by a fruit-and-yogurt parfait and a pot of coffee for the low, low Pilgrim Hotel price of twenty-eight dollars."

"I hope that wasn't a New Year's resolution. You're going to make me feel guilty," Richard said, filling his mouth with a handful of bar peanuts.

Don put a slate-blue folder embossed in silver foil with the logo of his television station on the bar top. "Instead of making you feel guilty, how about I try to make you feel wanted? You should know two things right from the get," Don said, tapping the folder with his index finger. "What's in here is negotiable, within reason. It's a four-year contract, with a station option for two more. A good-faith gesture that we're committed. It contains certain easily attainable benchmarks that would allow you to automatically renew for another two years after that. That is, if you are the successful candidate."

"Candidate for what?"

"I thought you'd be one step ahead of me on this one. You're the number one draft choice. *Eyewitness News at Six and Eleven, with Richard MacMurray and Anna Sogard. Thom Rollins on sports, and Gordon Helmer with your Doppler Eight Thousand forecast.* Your reel tested off the charts. Our focus groups say that middle America would believe just about anything you tell them."

"I didn't even know I'd applied for the job. Until this morning, I didn't even know I had a reel."

"Well, what you need to know now is that, while you're the leading candidate, you're not the *only* candidate."

Richard had used this ploy himself during his years of hiring research assistants and paralegals. The pay wasn't much, he'd say, but the experience was invaluable, the same bullshit salt-of-the-earth rap his father must have given to the decidedly earnest young people who wanted to work in a congressional office. *It's not the dollar, it's the experience,* he could imagine Lew saying, especially since the entry-level jobs on Capitol Hill didn't pay much more than McDonald's. His father had been full of clichés and a fervent belief in a peculiarly American brand of opportunity (or was it opportunism?), often sounding like a cross between Elmer Gantry and Zig Ziglar. Twenty years after Lew died, and Richard could still hear him bungling messages together into malaprops like *You have to leave the door unlocked for opportunity.*

"How do I know I'm not the other guy?" Richard asked.

Don looked pleased. "What other guy?"

"The second choice. The fallback. The one that the other reporters *really* want. Say, a veteran network correspondent who's being phased out of Washington because his Q rating is too low or he tests as too old."

Don motioned for the bartender. "That guy doesn't exist anymore, and even if he did, we couldn't afford him. He's got a second wife and a kid at Williams or Bowdoin that's costing him something like forty grand a year, so he abandons the true calling of journalism for public relations or corporate communications and makes the world safe for special-interest organizations and comes up with slogans like *Beef, it's what's for dinner.*" Don narrated the slogan in the resonant fakeness of a voice-over artist, but when he started talking again, any hint of artifice was gone. "And as for Q ratings, well, your Q rating isn't much greater than zero. They've seen your face before, maybe even know you're on television, but they can't quite place you. The focus group described you as conventionally handsome. That beach bum who lived with O. J. Simpson, he's got a higher recognition factor. You, my man, are the proverbial blank slate. Give me six months, and I'll convince people that you've been doing this for twenty years."

"Kato Kaelin."

"What?"

"The beach bum. The freeloader. Before I even give this serious thought, you need to tell me one thing. Why me? What do I bring to the table?"

Don's answer came quickly enough for Richard to think it had been scripted. "You bring the fresh face, the new perspective. You bring a tiny bit of gravitas, but you do it at a small-market friendly price."

"As in cheap," Richard said.

"I prefer to think of it as value," Don said, smiling.

"I don't know what they say in television, but in politics, you never want to be the guy who succeeds a legend. You want to be the guy who comes after that guy."

"If you start next month, during sweeps, you can be the guy who works alongside the legend. His name is Jack Shea. Been everywhere for every network. Vietnam for CBS, White House correspondent during the illustrious Gerald Ford administration. Anchored the Sunday-evening news, though he didn't get to do the broadcast very often because they'd preempt for tennis and golf and football running long. Shit, you grew up here. You'd know the face. Guy looks like he was born wearing a trenchcoat. When he shows his vacation pictures around the office, you half-expect him to begin narrating in his on-air voice. 'Good evening tonight from Paris, where in just twelve hours, all parties will gather once again around the famous round conference table to begin a final set of peace talks.'" Don's voice came in staccato breaks that sounded more like Johnny Carson imitating Cronkite than anything else, but Richard knew the type. The MacMurray dinner table had always meant Cronkite blaring in from the Magnavox in the living room, *Marvin Kalb in Saigon, Bernard Kalb at the State Department, Bert Quint near Khe Sanh, South Vietnam.*

Richard said, "So he's not getting forced out. He's retiring?"

"Not exactly. He's dying."

"Jesus. What happened?"

"The guy's diet consisted almost entirely of fast food and Marlboros for the better part of three decades. Who knows what happened? Maybe time. Maybe Jack got a flu he couldn't shake. The insurance company sends him for a physical. He gets some blood work. There's an elevated this or that, so they call him back for more tests. And those tests spell out a particularly aggressive form of lung cancer. Five-year survival rate is zero. He's making a series. The unrepentant anchorman faces his mortality, tonight at six. We'll send camera crews with him to chemo, to the lab for blood work, to his support groups. You'll help him edit it for a series of two-minute drop-ins during sweeps."

"What exactly am I getting into here?"

Don took a handful of bar nuts. "Let me tell you a little story. For the first four years Jack Shea was on the air up there, he was in third place. For sixteen consecutive quarterly-ratings books, he wasn't within four points of the lead. Right up until this one afternoon when he's filming a stand-up in front of the oldest furniture store in Wilkes-Barre. He's there to tease the night's feature story, thirty seconds, when a woman across the street gets her purse snatched. She starts screaming, and the camera follows her voice, and the thief runs right toward them. Jack Shea tosses his cigarette aside, very casually jogs across the street and clotheslines the guy, just a little close-combat hand yoke to the fucker's throat. The guy falls backward onto the sidewalk, comic book–style, out cold. And the camera guy is right there, and Jack just picks up the purse, daintily pushes the tissues and lipstick or whatever back into the bag, and walks up to the lady and says, 'Ma'am,' like he's Sergeant Joe Friday or something. Then he looks at the camera and winks. He's been in first place ever since."

"How long?"

"Since 1983," Don said.

"That isn't what I meant. He's got what, six months? I'm not sure I'm ready to help someone put together a grand theorem on mortality."

"Why not?" Don asked, a question for which Richard had no prepared answer.

The only person Richard had ever known who died of cancer was his mother, and she hadn't exactly been the poster patient for a dignified last few months. She had gone to her general practitioner several times with minor complaints, and he'd frowned indecipherably at computer printouts, EKGs, and lab results, and then one afternoon, she went on a referral to a gastroenterologist, who sent her for some sort of scan—Richard couldn't remember what type—and before the afternoon was out, was telling her, "It's time to put your affairs in order." There were options that would shrink, but not eliminate, her tumor. There were synthetic opiates for her pain. Injections to keep up the platelet count so that she could endure more of the treatments that would shrink, but not eliminate, the tumor. After her diagnosis, she'd lasted fourteen months.

Suddenly Richard was aware that if he failed in his new gig, he'd become the answer to a trivia question. Conversations that began, "Whatever happened to...?" were the city of Washington's greatest pastime. One week, you were the young politico of the moment; the Secretary of State was at a party at your rented Georgetown townhouse, drinking white wine from a gallon jug and hitting on the intern from the Style section of the *Post,* and you were being lampooned in *Doonesbury;* the next week, you had fallen so spectacularly that people avoided your phone calls, and a few months after that, the Style section of the *Post* was running a feature on you, five thousand words in a tone best described as postmortem.

"Tell me why I'd even want to do this," Richard said.

"Of all people, I'd think you'd understand what it means to shape the news. To understand the power there."

"Here's what I know about the news. The news suggests death, decay. News is over. It's a thing of the past."

Don smiled. "Just the opposite. News connects us with the parts of our past you think are dead. It's resurrection. If you want to see it as a monster, then it's a perpetual monster. And the thing is, this monster can't be killed. Last year we did a series of two-minute features. Your basic whatever-happened-to stories on all the things of our childhood. Whatever happened to the guy with the ridiculously long fingernails?"

"The Indian guy? From the *Guinness Book*?"

Don poked Richard in the arm, a quick and unobtrusive jab that said, *Yes, you understand.* "Who still hula-hoops? Do children even buy Slinkys anymore? Why is it that nearly every guy around my age knows that the fastest car on the planet was once called the Blue Flame? Or how that kid Mikey from the cereal commercials was supposed to have died from mixing Pop Rocks and Coke?"

"Eddie Haskell got killed in Vietnam."

"That was an urban legend. Hell, for a while, it was rumored that Eddie Haskell was actually the porn guy. Johnny Wadd. But people don't want to hear about that. They don't want to hear about the former child star who robbed the video store to feed her crack habit. They want to remember everything just the way it was. They get nostalgic for the totems of their childhood. The Legos and Lincoln Logs, GAF View-Masters, Gnip Gnop, Tang. They get homesick for places that no longer exist. It forces us to adapt to our environment. Harry Reasoner came to ABC to make five hundred thousand dollars a year, and then he was bitching about Barbara Walters and her million-dollar contract, and then he was back with the geezers of *Sixty Minutes,* and a few years after that he was dead, and you never hear anyone at some journalism school lamenting the grand old legacy of Harry Reasoner. Why? Because he didn't adapt. The future tapped him on the shoulder, and he said, *Not now. I'm busy.* And right now you are being tapped on the shoulder, and I want to know if you're ready to face the future."

"And you expect me to say what, exactly?"

"I expect you to say yes," Don said. "I can't believe that what you are doing in DC is enough. Being a pundit. Smoothing over a message that someone else has already shaped."

"I look at it as trying to correct the record."

Don tapped the folder. "What's in here is an opportunity to *be* the record. The first draft of history and all that. Unless you're going to tell me that you're satisfied being a hired gun."

Richard figured he'd play the scene out, no matter how preposterous it sounded. "I'm a hired gun who gets to speak, for roughly four minutes a week, to about three point four million people per quarter hour. But just for entertainment value, let's say I'm actually interested. I'm interested despite the fact that the job is in the farthest reaches of Transylvania. Despite the fact that, outside of college, I've never lived beyond a radius of about seven miles from this very bar stool. Or despite the fact that I've never done the news. I didn't even work for my high school paper. Other than that, I'm a logical choice."

"I'm not going to shit you. You're a long shot. Most likely you're going to fail, and you're going to do so in spectacular fashion. But if you do fail, you're not going to fail alone. If you fail, it's because I've failed you. You come up to Scranton and spend four weeks shadowing Jack; you'll watch *Action News at Six,* and then you'll do it again, live to tape, at seven o'clock. Just for us to critique. After the four weeks are up, we'll send our co-anchor on a little assignment, and you can anchor side by side with Jack for a week. We'll take some publicity photos, get you fitted for a wardrobe, have you do some local promotion work. We'll get you an official anchorman's haircut," Don said, laughing, showing his brightest smile. "So what say I run this by your agent?"

"I don't have an agent. I get a phone call. I take a cab to a news bureau and unwrap my IFB and appear for union scale, sometimes more, and I rarely if ever negotiate. A few weeks later I get a check in the mail. Once every couple of weeks, I give a speech to the annual meeting of the National Association of this or that. They have a breakfast where I inhale a Danish and nod gravely at the idiotic opinions of Earl from Milwaukee, who owns the largest feed store in all of whatever county. I pick the most obvious thing that he says, and when no one is looking, I jot it down on a napkin, and then, when I get up on the podium, I applaud his political skills and tell him he should be the one on *Crossfire,* and the other guys at the head table slap him on the back. I congratulate them for being dedicated enough to fly down to Washington and for being smart enough to hire me to talk to them. And then, because I'm on television, I stand there and repeat the exact same things that were in that morning's *Washington Post,* and somehow, the mere act of repeating it makes it true, and for those two hours I pocket a check for ten thousand dollars."

"You're what passes for conventional wisdom." Don laughed.

"In other words, I'm already a newsman."

Don slid the folder over to Richard and excused himself. "You can think it over for as long as you want. At least as long as it takes for me to piss."

Richard mulled the offer. *Mulled.* He thought the unfamiliar word. Serious decisions required more than mulling, didn't they? You don't change your life because you've had two Bloody Marys and decided that the best strategy for the New Year is to look opportunity in the eye and say, *What the fuck.* Or do you? This is probably what it felt like to go to the crossroads and be offered a deal with the devil. The devil probably borrowed Don's black suit for these sorts of things. Still, in nearly every facet of conversation, Don Keene had been right. It wasn't enough, being on television for one o'clock here, two-thirty elsewhere. His mind flashed on a memory, the women who'd worked for Lew wandering, stunned, through the MacMurray kitchen after the funeral. Lew's whole office had that feel, of teamwork, of family, and Richard got exactly none of that feeling from what he was doing now. He needed courage, and if he found some after two drinks, *what the fuck?* Some spontaneity could do him good. A tandem jump from eight thousand feet above the Mojave? *Sure, why not, what the fuck.* A long weekend in Tulum filled with margaritas and naked tanning with a woman you'd met the evening before? *What the fuck.* Try that Japanese soup that might kill you? *What the fuck.* Buy a house he'd seen only pictures of? *What the fuck?* That lack of spontaneity had always been an issue in the previous regime, his first wife and her ridiculous calculations and her research at the library—a Saturday afternoon wasted as she pored over magazines, seven months of back issues of *Consumer Reports*—all to buy a $40 blender. He billed his time at $380 an hour, and once he'd had enough, he finally told her that he might have to charge the same rate if she was going to make everything *such a goddamn ordeal,* and it had been *a dick thing to say* (her words), and he knew she was right.

Surely it was ego to think he could slide right into the anchor chair and make jokes about the hapless Phillies and then be serious about two dead, four wounded, in a shoot-out at a Wilkes-Barre branch of some monolithic national bank. Why would he even think he could do this job? The Greeks knew this feeling for what it was. Hubris. Richard supposed it couldn't actually be hubris if he was aware of it, but that didn't mean he was going to turn the job down. He would have to be vigilant for any omen that augured his failure. That's what *hubris* really meant, after all: "failure." Hubris meant flying too close to the sun on his handmade wax wings, hubris meant saying the ship was unsinkable, it meant building a plane the size of an ocean liner only to watch it rise a mere eight feet before falling, as did Icarus, into the sea. The time felt right for that kind of leap. He could picture the handful of reporters and assignment editors he knew shaking their heads at the word *Scranton*. Still, what did Washington have to offer him now? Subpoenas and bureaucrats. There was nothing left to tether him here. Washington was over.

36

FOR TWO years now, Sherri Ashburton had worked at the Canyon Room Tavern and Grill, four nights a week, either as a bartender or as a cocktail waitress. If Ash was around, she played it straight, wore a modestly short skirt and hose with black seams running up the back. When things were tight and her husband wasn't behind the bar, she switched out the hose for thigh-highs and kept some bills for change in the elastic around her right thigh. Her tips went up by twenty or thirty bucks.

Her preshift duties included cutting four dozen limes and four dozen lemons, refilling the maraschino cherries in the service trays, and pestering a busboy to deliver ten five-gallon buckets of ice for the drop-in coolers of bottled beer. Never once had the ice been in the cooler when she punched in, and never once had someone fetched it without complaint. The bar manager stayed focused on the larger things, like the bottom line. He'd bought these syrupy premade mixes for the fancier cocktails and had the soda gun switched from name-brand sodas to generics. The tonic water tasted more like rust than quinine, and that meant Sherri constantly had to buy back drinks, and buying back drinks meant she got the same three-dollar tip for pouring the same drink twice, no matter how weak or strong she poured or how many buttons of her Stay-Prest uniform blouse she left "accidentally" undone.

On this New Year's Day, only a handful of skiers wandered the hotel, these impossibly hardy families who'd braved I-80 or I-15 in their minivans, hoping for a few days of fresh powder and reasonable winds. The sun today turned the busiest runs to gunk, and the arriving winds and falling temperatures tonight would turn them into skating rinks and make even the bunny slopes fast and slick; all that meant people would stay tethered to the hotel, order their food at the bar. Since it was a holiday and her husband was on a plane, she'd picked up an extra shift, and there was no one to help her and the cooler still needed ice and the register drawer needed to be counted, eighty dollars in change to get the night going, though she could count on one hand the number of checks that got settled in cash; everything got charged to the rooms or to a credit card. She wished Ash wasn't on his way to see his mother, that he'd show up at eleven p.m., the hour that passed for last call in these parts, and produce a key to a room that he'd connived from the night manager. He'd be back in a couple of days, she thought, and she counted a roll of quarters, two rolls each of dimes, nickels, and pennies, seventeen dollars in ones. Making note of the shortage in her audit journal, she flipped through the pages and found a business card, the insurance man who'd been working them even on New Year's Eve. She slipped it into her apron pocket and spotted the remote for the overhead television behind the first row of call liquors. Why couldn't people put things away at the end of the shift? Almost as strange as the fact that she could flip channels from 2 through 200 and back again and couldn't find any of the football games.

She knew the late bowl game was on FBN; the omnipresent

promos with incongruous animated robots and cartoon fruit had aired all morning. The network came back from commercial, and Sherri saw the reporter saying, "You are looking live as firefighters tend to the final resting place of Panorama Airlines Flight 503, which crashed just short of runway 13L here at Dallas–Fort Worth International Airport about two and a half hours ago."

Sherri would not remember this, the remote trembling along with her hand, her finger remaining on the volume key, the voice growing louder and louder, distorted. Then the ridiculous notion that it was all a joke, a misunderstanding. Any moment now, Ash would walk into the bar with a room key, flashing that smile that told Sherri he'd saved up forty-five dollars, enough for a couple of drinks and an order of those Tex-Mex spring rolls he liked so much, and a carefree night in the hotel with the password for the in-room movies and a couple of extra pouches of self-serve coffee for the following sluggish morning.

She dropped the remote, flung it away, really; the cover opened, and the AA batteries rolled across the floor. As she scurried, crablike, across the green carpet, gathering up parts, she became aware of how loud the television was as the screen showed the reporter telling the world, "Initial reports, now confirmed, say all seventy-seven passengers and six crew members aboard were killed." Sherri fumbled with the remote, its reassembly. The reporter's face disappeared, but her voice reset the entire story, and the network went to commercial with the correspondent saying, "You are watching continuous live coverage of the crash of Panorama Airlines Flight 503 on FBN."

But Sherri could not find the battery cover, and the bar manager heard the television, wandered in to find his bar empty, the bartender crying on the floor, the cash-register drawer open, the television blaring a commercial for an over-the-counter remedy for upset stomach and diarrhea.

37

DON KEENE loved hotel bars. They reminded him of the era of
oak telephone booths in the lobby and gimlets and Rob Roys
at lunch. The Pilgrim Hotel reminded him of the very first time
he'd been to Washington, as a wire service reporter just out
of college in 1968. He'd gone "Clean for Gene" McCarthy, and
the combination of an old-school haircut and a degree from
Columbia meant he'd never looked the part of a revolutionary.
Universities up and down the eastern seaboard manufactured
boys like Don by the thousands. He just walked into one of
those young establishment jobs, already equipped as he was
with the narrow ties and lapels.

He hoped MacMurray wouldn't ask him for advice, because
when people asked him for advice, Don Keene had a strong but
only year-old tendency to tell the truth. In television, this was
a considerable handicap. Not telling the truth was incompatible with his newfound sobriety, and if that wasn't the way that
Don was interpreting the twelve steps that week, it was almost
certainly the way that his sponsor would. His sponsor was the
kind of hard-ass who made him pick up the phone and apolo-
gize, the kind of guy for whom making amends meant making

immediate amends, none of this taking inventory and ritualistic letter writing. His sponsor was a man of action, and after a few months of working the program this way, Don had decided that, for him, the easiest and softest way to live his life was to just tell the truth, all the time, and damn the consequences. He'd suffered through meetings in which people asked him, "Don, are you bored?" and he'd said yes. After a few sorrowful dates, one woman had looked at him askance and remarked, "It's almost like you aren't attracted to me in the slightest," an accusation that Don answered with body language that said, *Yes, but what's your point?*

So when Richard dared to ask, *Why do you want me?* he'd wavered on telling him. Hiring a rank amateur to anchor northeastern Pennsylvania's lowest-rated evening newscast represented acceptable risk; he could get Richard at a discount price and save the $20,000 it would cost his station to use a headhunter. He'd save the station another $30,000 on what he was going to underpay the new guy, and if it worked, Richard would be a perpetual bargain.

If Richard didn't ask, he'd keep his mouth shut and let the guy figure it out for himself. Don didn't have the stomach for focus groups and test reels and tryout weekends when some stranger flew into town and did the Saturday six p.m. news. And Don didn't feel like taking the three harrowing connecting flights on the kind of turboprop planes better suited to running guns to Salvadoran rebels, flights that would deposit him in Cedar Rapids, Iowa, or Battle Creek, Michigan, where he'd see some consultant who would tell him things that were best described as common sense: anchormen shouldn't wear flashy suits, and anchorwomen should be slightly deferential, wear earrings no larger than a nickel, and be about as sexy as June Cleaver. Don couldn't help but think of those small planes as the ones that featured drunk pilots, failing equipment, ownership that cut corners on keeping the aircraft clean and well maintained. More often, those were the planes, Don thought, that fell burning out of the sky.

Richard could be an experiment. Don saw him as the kind of guy that people wanted to invite home and tell about the kids, and that was the gift that Jack Shea had too. But first Richard had to display an awareness of his limitations, an understanding that he was being set up to fail. At the very least, Don wanted someone reckless enough to say yes without really thinking about it, and smart enough to ask for a little more money. After Don had pissed and washed his hands and left a message for his boss, he walked back to the bar.

"Where were we, exactly?" he asked.

Richard tapped the folder and sipped off the vodka the bartender had floated on top of his Bloody Mary. Don could smell it, medicinal, the hints of pepper and horseradish that bit at the back of his nose. Ever since he'd gone clean, his nose could always be counted on to find these sensory reminders of his past. The vodka. The female bartender who wore the same slight perfume as one of the women at the station. When he'd gotten out of his four weeks of residential treatment, Don had walked barefoot along the facility's cut grass, and the smell had made him feel eight years old. His father had made a ritual out of cutting the lawn: mow and trim, rake up the clippings, wash down the sidewalk, a victory cigar and a beer. And Don's mind felt so sharp, so associative, that he imagined the smell of the gasoline and the oxidized rust burning off the mower's muffler and the hints of wild onion and berry that grew in his parents' lawn and the vodka and horseradish of Sunday dinner.

It was all too tempting. He had to get out of the bar. He never noticed how much business was conducted in bars until he had a reason to avoid them entirely. Don tapped his pencil, then pulled a couple of cocktail napkins from the holder and started doing some figuring on them. Richard watched as he added a trio of six-figure numbers.

"You've got that look," Don said, "the one that says you want to call time-out."

"That's not it," Richard said.

"Well, then I'd say that you aren't as smart as Toni said you were. You should call time-out and take a step back and figure out your next move. Heed the advice of learned counsel. Isn't there someone you'd like to talk with before you sign on the dotted line?"

"There is. Was. I'm not sure," Richard said. He looked pained by the admission. "Tell me why this has to happen today."

Don knew he meant a woman. He debated whether or not he should put the cap on his pen, slide the sheaf of papers back into his file folder, start the pantomime of packing up. "The whole point of this is that we want to put you in the chair next to the guy you are replacing. Make you look like the anointed one. Jack Shea is going to do everything short of kissing you on the cheek and telling Luzerne County that you are the goddamn heir apparent. His tumors are so advanced that the doctors can't believe he can read the news, much less walk. You're going to come in there, and Jack's going to tell everyone that you're the next man up. So no, technically, it doesn't have to happen today. But if it doesn't, and he dies, then it might not happen at all."

Richard said, "I thought this wasn't a high-pressure sell."

Don gathered up his overcoat and briefcase. He put his case on the bar and extracted a pair of discs and handed them to Richard. "This is your predecessor. The living legend. Eight hours of his greatest hits over thirty-two years on the air. The last eighteen as the anchor of *Eyewitness News at Six and Eleven*."

And Don wouldn't realize until a week later that he'd made a mistake in asking Richard, and that he secretly wished Richard would be consumed with a sudden awareness of his limitations and say no. He could just hand the discs back to Don and shake his head and say, *You have the wrong man.*

"Eight hours?" Richard said, putting the discs into his own briefcase.

"Think about that. Ninety minutes of broadcast, five days a week, forty-eight weeks a year. And then, because you're dying, an intern boils it down to eight hours of highlights, and the last two duties we're going to ask you to perform are this: we'd like you to train your replacement, and we'd like you to document your own illness. From the moment the doctor comes in and worries about that spot on the X-ray until the day it takes us thirty-seven takes for him to utter, *Tonight is my final broadcast.*" Don took out forty dollars and half-threw it to the bartender.

Richard said, "What do I do with those discs?"

Don finished his club soda and used the cocktail napkin to wipe his mouth, then left it in a ball on the bar top. "We'd like you to edit those eight hours of tape into a two-minute-and-twenty-second highlight package that you'll write and narrate, and we'll broadcast it the day he dies."

There wasn't much more to explain that wasn't in the folder. The salary was guaranteed and even for this small market bordered on astronomical, and Richard would be just as much of a fool to say yes as he would be to say no. As Don stepped behind him to make his exit, Richard picked up the folder and swiveled around on his bar stool.

"Well, what do you say?" Don asked. Richard opened the folder and shook his head. The salary was there on the first page. He added $25,000 to it, mumbling something about moving expenses.

Don took the pen, initialed the change, and said, "I take it that's a yes?"

Don, or more likely someone who worked for him, had thoughtfully affixed little yellow stickers that said SIGN HERE in each of the places where Richard's signature was legally required. The last time he'd seen little reminders like that, he was signing the sheaf of documents that dissolved his law partnership, transferred the deed to his house, enforced a qualified domestic-relations order dividing his meager retirement savings in half, paying his wife back for suits and ties and prescription medications and every damn thing she could think of, and he'd never had the pleasure of telling her that it was worth every penny to get the fuck out. He smiled and signed. As he was about to hand the folder over, he turned it around so Don could watch him scribble a quick note on its cover, tiny block printing that said WHAT THE FUCK.

38

IN HER most recent personnel evaluation, the receptionist working the front desk of the Dallas bureau of FBN had been praised as an efficient gatekeeper and traffic cop. Important skills, because the news brought out weirdness in flocks of threes and fours: whistleblowers and their more generic tattling counterparts, self-styled vigilantes with fourteen hours of camcorder footage they thought might be the key to solving the lasting riddles of the Kennedy assassination. Sitting at that desk thirty-seven and a half hours a week, you learned to recognize all the great and dangerous things a city assembled, even a city with as benign and polished a facade as Dallas, which at times seemed to Sally Doerfler to be made entirely out of mirrored glass.

Then came the news alert, a red banner across her computer monitor, followed within thirty seconds by a chorus of ringing phones. Sally knew enough to say, "FBN Dallas Operations, please hold," and never wait for a reply. "You've got thirty seconds, go," she said to each caller that filled the eight blinking lines. She took notes, gathered the relevant intelligence—plane down at DFW; the conspiracy theorist on line two said, "Ground-to-air missile, Panorama Airlines Flight 503"—and, because it was a holiday, didn't wait for the assignment editor or the bureau chief, just called it out to the correspondent herself.

Sally didn't have time to mess with frivolous things. She'd worked here seventeen years and knew how to take initiative, knew what the pressures of the business and the twenty-four-hour news cycle meant. Sally sent the crew to the airport, telling them what the bureau chief would have said, because it was a motto around these parts, and she knew it—they all did—without his having to say it: *Get it first and get it right.*

In just ten minutes, the calls accounted for two pages in her handwritten call log, a total of seventy-four tips, neatly categorized into convenient categories: false starts, pranksters, conspiracy theorists, and, on maybe one call, valid information. She had passed along to the reporter two separate reports of a man with a bazooka at the airport (later this man would be identified as a sound technician for a competing network carrying a boom microphone and a tripod) and was now on the phone with someone from one of the hospitals who said they'd activated their trauma response teams at Baylor and Methodist and Texas Children's and Parkland, but someone from the airline or the NTSB (the nurse wasn't sure) had already told them to stand down. That was as good as confirmation: *no survivors.*

She was still on the phone, taking tips and callback numbers, when the monitor cut to the reporter doing a stand-up from the airfield, the stopped airport traffic visible over her shoulder, the screen filling with a column of noirish smoke and the now-useless emergency personnel.

Then this teenager emerged through the front door and walked up to her desk. He looked like a good kid, like he was waiting for permission to speak. He had the long, hungry look Sally had been taught to recognize as ambition. He was followed by a girl, and to Sally, they registered immediately as a couple. He opened up the playback window on his video camera, turned it to face her, and hit Play.

Sally watched a plane spiral clockwise into the ground.

She couldn't remember who she'd been talking to, just hung up. She raised the volume on the monitor to hear the network feed, then flipped to the other news networks. They were all on-set shots of the anchor desks in New York or Atlanta. FBN would be first with actual video of the crash, just as they'd been the first to have someone in the field.

Sally called the bureau chief and said, "Someone needs to come down and take a look at this," and when the chief wanted to know what exactly she was referring to with that indefinite pronoun, she told him, "The gold standard. Flight 503."

The bureau chief sent a production assistant, who didn't bother with introductions, just took the camera from this teenager and asked if it was cued up, hit the Play button and watched the video, grainy, shot handheld and underlit. *Holy shit.*

At that point, the PA hit Stop and just said to the room, "Come with me," and Sally and the kid and the PA went together into the control room. In the crush of the busy afternoon, no one noticed the chime of unanswered calls while Sally narrated for the kid what was going to happen next. "We'll get someone from Legal on the phone, and you'll have to sign a release." Somehow they'd agreed on a price without anyone thinking how strange it was for these de facto negotiations to have been conducted by the receptionist; Sally had shuffled enough paper in the past to anticipate every argument, and she spelled it out for the bureau chief: they could label the kid as an independent contractor to satisfy the standards-and-practices people and the attorneys who kept insisting that this network wasn't in the business of paying for the news.

The accountant on duty would cut the kid a check in the low five figures. All the kid wanted was his name on the screen, *Footage courtesy of Jeris McDougal,* and the bureau chief had to sign off on that.

The production assistant dumped the tape into a deck, and the monitors in the control room split into two distinct categories: those showing the live network feed and those showing the plane in its final moments. The bureau chief was on the phone to New York control, saying, *I know you think I must be some kind of fucking Huckleberry, but the kid has the shit,* and, *He's got it on tape,* and, *We've got it cold,* and, *No, no one else has it,* and finally exasperation took hold and he shouted into the handset, "He has the crash on tape. The plane. Right into the fucking ground!"

The kid kept trying to say *My name is Jeris* as he stood in the control room of the Dallas bureau, watching the tape with a paternal pride, expecting a high five, because to him the tape was the first verifiable evidence of his powers of persuasion, documented and incontrovertible, and he knew the technicians were alternating between watching the monitor and watching him.

At time code 0:00:12, the abrupt presence of horizontal lines fluttered across the tape, as if the control room had tuned in on a vintage, tube-powered television. The interference was caused by a camera powering up at random, and the tape had a bit of vertical roll to it, which made the producer in the room think of his childhood, the old nineteen-inch Philco black-and-white, the first television he had ever known, and his afternoon struggles with a rabbit-ear antenna, all for the pleasure of watching the local UHF channel, its grained and snowy broadcasts of Japanese kids' shows, *Marine Boy* and *Ultraman.*

In the foreground, a girl—freckled and prematurely endowed with the prominent curves and sun-damaged décolletage of a much older woman—sat on the edge of a motel-room bed. The voice of some young man, presumably the same one who was now standing in the reception area, started cajoling her to remove her top. The girl who'd arrived with Jeris couldn't make eye contact with anyone in the room; she could tell by the way they were looking at her that they only wanted to know just how far the girl on the tape was willing to go.

The image of the girl working at the buttons on her blouse, a midriff-baring silver number stretched across her ample chest, and a voice asking, *What you gonna do, are you going to suck my cock? You know how I like to watch you do that*—and *Christ*, the editor thought, *she has to be the same age as my little sister.* The voice told her, *Undo another button; stand up and show me what you got on under that skirt.*

Then the kid went running out the motel-room door and into the parking lot, and the sudden flush of daylight saturated everything into such bright hues that on the control-room monitors, the light of the sky and the color of the cars and the glint of this girl's silver shirt as she appeared in the corner of the frame—standing in front of the cameraman by about a foot, she asked the question everyone asks of a man holding a camera at a moment of crisis, *Are you getting this?*—it all appeared with the shining brilliance of an old Kodachrome snapshot. The camera began to move, and the editor thought, *Yes, yes, kid, follow the action.* The guys who worked in television—the VTR and chyron operators, the video editor—they too felt a certain vicarious pride that the kid had been smart enough to know he *had* something, a passenger jet and its continual spiral of right-hand turns, the inevitability of its uncontrolled descent.

To the film editor, a man in his early sixties, the images looked like the handheld battle footage he'd shot himself in Vietnam, the camera with its distinctly first-person point of view, *These are the men of the air cav, First Division, First Squadron, Ninth Cavalry; this morning they dropped in An Loc, fanning north toward the Cambodian border, and you are there.* (In the sixties, he'd shot tape in Danang, shot the aftermath of Tet, and the proudest moment of his career was when his 16-millimeter Bolex got loaned out to one of Cronkite's guys, who toted it between hot zones.) He marked out the first twenty-five seconds with a digital tag, the part with the girl in the top and the aborted motel-room fucking of two kids. The bureau chief told him to cut in the fluttering of those vertical lines, the camera powering up, so that the tape opened with the plane, visible, already in its final spirals. The time code on the digital display said that the relevant segment—the plane as unidentifiable streak in the sky, gleaming and silver, to the moment that implied impact, the plane disappearing at the bottom of the horizon and the view obstructed by the corrugated-steel warehouses and sprawling three-story office buildings that surrounded DFW Airport—ran thirty-two seconds.

The rewound tape went straight into the broadcast feed. Everyone at the network listening on a headset or an earpiece heard the director saying, "Cue chyron," and "Thirty-two seconds of tape," then the director's quieter, "Roll VTR in three, two, one." Anchorman Max Peterson watched his own image depart from the monitor, and the fly-in of chyron that gave the event FBN's official title: DISASTER: THE CRASH OF PANORAMA 503. He'd covered the elections of three popes and five presidents, and whenever he had to fly by the seat of his pants, he eased forward in his chair, and his voice, always mellifluous, slowed down, and he could hear the sentences forming in his mind before he spoke them, an unattributed gift springing from a source he never understood. "You are watching an FBN exclusive, amateur footage being fed to us now, live and unedited, from our

Dallas bureau. The last moments of Panorama Airlines Flight 503 captured on tape, as it struggled in an apparently futile attempt to make an emergency landing earlier this afternoon at Dallas–Fort Worth International Airport."

Concurrently, a voice on the tape said, *Oh, Jesus, look at that.* The camera moved past the obstruction of an office building covered in mirrored glass panels and reacquired the target, a plane moving through the air; *careening* was a better word. The left wing turned skyward, a movement the engineers would study and alternately decide meant some system had either failed or just started to work again.

The plane continued its trajectory, its route expanding into circles that drew closer and closer to the ground; the sound from the tape became a litany of gasps and exhalations of disbelief from seventeen-year-old Jeris McDougal and his girlfriend, a soundtrack that contained numerous utterances of nearly all the FCC's prohibited words, audible even over the anchorman's narration.

At the Pilgrim Hotel, half a country away, Richard MacMurray watched the coverage on the bar television. The anchorman's words, *This isn't happening*—Richard had said the same thing at seeing his father's body on the tarmac. But at the remove of two decades, he couldn't remember if he'd said it while watching the special report, or if it was the phrase with which he'd begun to narrate the whole week's worth of events: the air force officer who explained about the repatriation of his father's body, the soldiers at attention as the aluminum casket was offloaded at Dover, the stricken look on his mother's face in the American sunlight the afternoon of the funeral, the way he'd had to remind her to extend her hands to accept the offered flag, that symbol of thanks from a grateful nation.

*   *   *

The nation watched.

This isn't happening, repeated by Max Peterson in the most studied and solemn version of his voice, and the thirty-two-second tape—the plane spiraling from the upper right-hand corner of the frame and disappearing behind a landscape of warehouses and two-story office parks and freeway overpasses, the moment of the crash obscured at the horizon, the video offering only the concussive shake of the impact, followed by the thick column of rising black smoke—was over.

The director went back to a one-shot, tight on the anchor, who had nothing to say. In his ear, the producer was telling him, "Twelve seconds to cutaway; we'll take a break and then reset at the top of the next segment," and she was counting, "Nine seconds, eight..." He vamped for time, shuffled the stack of papers in front of him; he was the only one who knew that they were a prop, the script to a newscast that was some twenty-one hours old, a useless artifact. The television critics who saw this continuous coverage would look at the anchor, his pausing and obvious effort to collect himself, and to a person they would comment on how refreshing it was to see this small demonstration of humanity, proof that at FBN, real people still populated the news division.

In the collective memory of everyone who watched this broadcast, the anchor had teared up. Whether it was emotion or the very real consequence of being on the air for thirty-nine consecutive minutes and the rush that came with an unscripted live broadcast, or the fact that there was no water under the desk, when the voice in his IFB told him, "Five seconds and we're out," he put the papers down, then said only, "This is not happening." His voice broke, a slight adolescent waver. The anchor hadn't even noticed the playback monitor showing the tape again: the fuselage beginning to separate, what the engineers writing in the incident report labeled *Catastrophic failure of the airframe*; the tongues of fire; the noise of the impact; and the smoke rising in three distinct columns of dark-blue haze, with the camera zoomed in to its mechanical limits. And then the tape, and the utterances of the two teenagers, went silent.

"This is not happening." The voice recovered its usual stentorian tone and pace. "We'll return after a break."

39

THE EARLY afternoon at Salt Lake City International Airport should have been filled with just a handful of solemn (read: hungover) travelers and the occasional harried businessman. Now, in the immediate aftermath of the crash, the relatives of the dead began to congregate, wandering near the ticket counters, increasing in numbers, all coming to the only place where they could imagine finding an answer, standing together in the stunned silence of their grief.

The survivors moved in the disoriented and staggering steps of the near-dead. They wanted to huddle together for comfort. They'd driven a loved one to the airport, and the last thing they saw, the last image, was a tepid wave or the obligatory blowing of a kiss from the other side of the security checkpoint. They scanned the terminal in search of a sign that what they had been told was a mistake. The hope was that their loved one, just this once, had missed the plane. It must have been a different airline, a different flight, they told themselves. But their hearts were already becoming accustomed to the truth. They practiced the ways and means of saying it aloud. They made phone calls. They shared pictures from their wallets and purses.

They wandered the corridors in the hope of random comfort. Their anxiety was a tangible thing that they carried and passed among themselves.

In the antiseptic hallway of terminal 2, around the displays that showed the arrival and departure times of every flight, a group began to gather, their murmuring conversations attracting the attention of Bob Denovo as he mopped the linoleum floor. Bob, like the rest of us, was a voyeur, inclined to eavesdrop. He often used an old push broom to cursorily sweep under the chairs of the waiting area just to hear one side of a telephone call. He looked around the gate and began making up stories for each distressed face that he saw. Bob craved to be connected, to be returned to the bosom of friendship; he wanted to be a confidant, an ambassador of consolation.

A large man in a navy blazer stared at the monitor, moved close enough to take his finger and run it along the screen at eye level. Bob couldn't say why he felt drawn to this man, but he pushed his custodian's cart toward the screens and began mopping in his general vicinity. Bob wrung out the mop in its metal press and placed down a bilingual caution sign, WET FLOOR/PISO MOJADO, even though most of the people who spoke Spanish at Salt Lake City International Airport were the Salvadorans who arrived each night to buff the floors.

As a few more people arrived, Bob gave up the charade of his headphones and simply joined the crowd, listening to the chatter as it became discernible: Panorama Airlines Flight 503 was no longer listed on the departure board. Not canceled or delayed. Just gone.

Bob thought about returning to his mop, but for some reason the image of his father passed into his head. Saturday afternoons of Bob's childhood, watching NBC's *Game of the Week* with Joe Garagiola and Tony Kubek. His father had been a catcher, and among the few things he'd taught Bob was the nickname for all his gear, the mask, the chest and shin guards, the protective cup; he called them "the tools of ignorance." "The tools of ignorance"—Bob said it out loud as he looked at his mop and bucket; pushing a mop was what he would be doing for the rest of his shift. Twelve hours on and twelve hours off, he thought, the workaday rhythm of a loser. He was a grunt, un-skilled labor, an afterthought. He tried to be a good worker, to distinguish himself by volunteering to work holidays in place of the guys who were married and had families, and absolutely no one had noticed. He could put his mop and bucket back in the custodial closet and drive out into the high desert, and some-one else would take his place by the next day, as if the airport spontaneously regrew the people it needed to serve it.

His thinking was interrupted by the quiet arrival of two men and two women in matching poly-blend blazers, the ubiqui-tous uniform of the airline customer-service rep. The partic-ular shade of blue identified them as employees of Panorama Airlines—Bob could not see the blazers without thinking of the airline's commercials, the flight attendant who stopped to pick up a dropped teddy bear for a five-year-old, the slogan We Fly the World intoned by one of those film noir actors. Bob wandered over to the newsstand in the main concourse, where a second small crowd had formed beneath a television monitor. Bob heard the narration before he saw the screen: "You are watching continuous live coverage of Panorama Air-lines Flight 503, which crashed on approach to Dallas–Fort Worth International Airport just over one hour ago. Initial re-ports say everyone on board the flight, which originated in Salt Lake City—that's seventy-seven passengers and six crew—has perished."

And then the video began.

*　　*　　*

The crowd watched the monitor as it replayed *amateur footage, an FBN News exclusive, you are getting our first look at the final moments of Panorama Airlines Flight 503,* followed by the appearance of the gleaming jet lurching through the sky as it moved right to left across the screen.

The image they all would remember: contrails of black smoke, the fuselage moving at its catastrophic speed. They remembered the image because television took the intangible and gave it authority, eliminated any doubt; the network brought in an aerospace engineer to telestrate the destruction of the airframe, his drawings explaining the pieces missing from the aircraft as it loomed into view. The engineer talked about stresses and shearing forces of the compound elements of the airliner, and already they were trying to answer the peculiarly human question: *Why?* The thirty-two-second clip became the Zapruder film of personal loss. Everyone had seen it. Everyone knew how it ended.

To the question of *why?* there was no answer. It did not depend on an overlooked checklist or a faulty indicator light or a pilot distracted by the holiday or any singular factor. It was a confluence of events, a series of contingencies for which there was no preparation.

The television went to commercial, broadcasting an appeal for one of those emergency-alert services for the elderly, and a voice behind Bob's shoulder said, "I have no snapshots." Bob thought the voice was talking back to the television. Most of the assembled dozen kept watching the monitor, but Bob turned as he heard, "I don't think I have a single picture of her," and whether it was the tenor of the voice or how each word came between the heaving breath of his sobs, Bob made eye contact with this great, bearlike man, saw in the light of the televised glow a highway of tears marking his face. The man rifled through his wallet as if he'd misplaced a driver's license or a credit card. Bob stepped close and took the man into his arms, the benevolent touch of consolation.

Before Bob could respond, a man in a suit stepped in front of the assembled crowd, reached up to turn down the television, and said, "You're about to hear a series of announcements. But if you believe that you knew someone on Flight 503, I'd like you to follow me. We're going to escort you to conference room C upstairs, where you'll be briefed by representatives from the airline and from the National Transportation Safety Board."

Bob expected a barrage of questions to follow, but the group stepped in one direction and began to toddle slowly down the hallway. Only then did the large man step out of Bob's embrace, the entirety of his story on his face, the look that betrayed all the persistent tortures of hindsight, its sadness and regret, a look that Bob knew well. He knew it from his own mirror, a look halfway to the madness of shame and grief.

40

THE AIREDALE'S name was Maestro. When the time came for his afternoon feeding, the kennel handlers found him running up and down the fence at the far end of the property, a few hundred yards to the left, a few hundred to the right, chasing imaginary rodents and romping through the grass in a path that his paws had trampled over the past four days. A guy from the local organic-foods market had delivered some marrow bones, as he did each Monday. Maestro took his out to the far end of the property and alternately chewed on it and used a whip of his neck to toss it as far as he could, another toss to throw it back toward where he started.

When the handler on duty, Tommy Campbell, called his name, Maestro ran back toward the pen and took a seat at his feet. Tommy hand-fed him pieces of lamb kibble and corners of cheddar cheese and tried to explain what he'd heard on the news. Maestro's master had been working that doomed flight. Tommy just said it to the dog, already suspecting that Maestro, and maybe all dogs, knew far more than we give them credit for. Who knows what it was that Maestro responded to, the tenor of Tommy Campbell's voice or even the disappearance of what had moments before promised to be a never-ending supply of cheese. This was a story Tommy would tell his wife; he'd read that wolves use different vocalizations to announce their location to other members of the pack when they are separated, and that must have been what Maestro was doing, sending up an effervescent wail, a howl, rising in timber and volume until most of the dogs at the kennel joined in and filled the yard with their mournful tune.

41

THESE WERE Richard's preoccupations on his way home: his self-congratulations at walking off the two drinks he'd had with Don, adhering to one of his lesser resolutions, to walk more through a city that had been built for the traveler on foot or horseback; his loneliness; and the gathering of clouds that had thickened into the heavy blanket he had come to know as a harbinger of snow. The unpredictability of the weather itched like a bite. He felt a trickle of sweat loosen itself along his spine, pass down through his waistband and into the crack of his ass. He wished that he could turn toward the river and feel the drop of the barometer in his knees or his arthritic pinkies. The ache of a twenty-year-old boxer's fracture in his hand predicted the weather almost as well as the guy on channel 4. Richard wanted muffler-and-topcoat weather, the silence of heavily swaddled commuters padding through the Metro. He longed for a cold snap brutal enough to feel in the framework of his bones. Instead, as he rounded the corner toward home, he saw the blinking bank clock at the circle of Connecticut and Massachusetts Avenues, a block from Cadence's old place. Time and temperature: 5:05 p.m., forty-eight degrees, the wind picking up and the temperature beginning a precipitous drop.

A few years back, Richard would have walked up the avenue to wait at a neighborhood bar for a familiar face, someone interested in watching the tail end of the Rose Bowl while pretending to celebrate his new job. But when you were forty-two and not twenty-two, holiday obligations meant that friends were out of the city, the bars in the afternoon filled only with the odd tourist and bored waitstaff.

He took the steps to the fourth floor two at a time. He thought he'd put his feet up and settle into his couch. The room's only window let in a dim gray light, the few recognizable parts of Washington's skyline occluded by an oncoming bank of clouds. By evening, they'd collapse into a low ceiling, insulating the city, a sure sign of the end of three days of springlike weather. He expected the forecast on the *Eyewitness News at 6* to hedge its bets, use nonspecific language, "a wintry mix." Richard liked the idea of a catastrophic storm, schools and stores closed, the government on liberal leave, the radio broadcasting calls for volunteers with four-wheel-drive vehicles to escort doctors and nurses to and from work.

He turned the television on and lowered the volume until it provided only the slightest of background noise, then picked up the copy of his new contract from his cluttered desktop. It contained all the usual contingencies: a personal-appearance clause in which Richard was asked to guarantee that he'd never gain weight, that he would be obligated to endure both medical and surgical options if necessary to keep his lustrous hair. A further rider prohibited him from profiting from endorsements, while a disturbingly vague "morals clause" suggested that nearly any misbehavior could result in termination.

Underneath the contract were the two discs Don Keene had

given him, the greatest hits of a retiring local icon. Inside the jewel case, Richard found a folded piece of paper in what he assumed to be Don's handwriting: *Good. You've already proven that you're willing to do your homework. Disc one is a career retrospective. Disc two is all local, all recent. Watch them in order, please. Call me when you're done.*

The disc player whirred to life, and a saturated color video appeared, a man standing in front of a building, wearing a gray suit, a beige trench coat belted at the waist. "Jack Shea reporting tonight from Paris." He wore combat fatigues in tiger-stripe camouflage. "From the Mekong Delta with First Marines, this is Jack Shea reporting." From San Clemente, from the Republican National Convention in Miami Beach. A denim jacket and khakis at a free concert in Golden Gate Park. From the Pentagon. From the campus of Kent State University. From the Johnson Space Center in Texas. From Cape Canaveral. Then from the same spot, now called Cape Kennedy. From Plains, Georgia. The picture wobbled a bit. Jack Shea was wading through three feet of muck on a city street somewhere, the familiar floodscape of rescue boats and dogs barking on rooftops and helicopters hovering over the scene. Shea held the microphone cord out of the water as he spoke. *Forecasts said the damage from Hurricane Agnes was expected to be almost insignificant. But the first storm of the Atlantic season stalled last night over the mid-Atlantic region, and residents in this corner of northeastern Pennsylvania awoke this morning to a Susquehanna River eight feet past flood stage, and the city of Wilkes-Barre under two feet of water.* Richard used the remote to speed through the stories at double time, from NATO headquarters in Brussels, from Tel Aviv, from Jerusalem, from Cairo, from the Sinai Peninsula, from Camp David, from the Golan Heights (each time appearing on camera wearing a beige safari jacket and a powder-blue shirt dotted with sweat). Jack Shea watching President Carter walk the route of his inaugural parade. Reporting via satellite from Phnom Penh. Jack Shea, reporting live from Harrisburg, Pennsylvania, in the early hours of Three Mile Island. It was history's cavalcade, Jack Shea reporting.

And there it was. The sudden jolt of memory.

Richard pounded the Play button, let the video resume at normal speed.

Jack Shea standing on the tarmac of a military airstrip in Guyana, in the immediate aftermath of Jonestown, narrating the video as the panel truck pulled up and the elected gunmen of the People's Temple opened fire on the escape plane. Wounded in the firefight: an NBC News cameraman, reporters from the *San Francisco Chronicle,* the *San Francisco Examiner.* Dead: one member of Congress, four departing Temple members, one congressional aide. Even in Jack Shea's reports, they didn't mention Lew by name.

Jack Shea in his safari jacket and, behind him, the gray-and-white United States Air Force jet that would be used to repatriate the bodies. A pair of corpsmen wheeling the aluminum caskets up the cargo ramp of the jet. Jack Shea began, *They came from the tree line*—gesturing toward the edge of the airfield—*shouting for the visitors to stop. Members of the People's Temple, asking to be taken home. Followed by a second jeep, this one filled with gunmen intent on letting no one leave.*

Jack Shea's voice-over narrating filmed helicopter shots, the famous shot of corpses linked arm in arm. A quarter century on, and Richard found he could recite the narration from memory: *They came in search of a new life in a new land, a place they thought might be nirvana. What they found instead can only be described as hell.*

Richard shook his head, tried to force out the memory.

He hit the Forward button. Jack Shea in Geneva, talking about the Iranian revolution. Jack Shea at the Winter Olympics, 1980. And then, the longest cut, Jack Shea calmly walking across the street to stop a robber, as cool as any television detective. He'd even paused to stub out his cigarette first. He watched that scene, thirty-one seconds of it, again and again, Jack Shea handing the purse back to a grateful old woman; Richard imagined her purse filled with coupons and an uncashed Social Security check and lipstick and tissues and wild-cherry Life Savers, his mother's purse. He didn't even realize that he was tearing up until he had to blot at the corner of his eye.

Nor did Richard remember turning off the disc or the television, but he had, falling into the elastic narrative of an unplanned and nightmare-riddled nap.

42

THE EMERGENCY plan for Panorama Airlines involved deploying a series of response teams, each armed with duties and procedures sanctioned by consultants and executives who had extensively gamed every scenario. Each responder had received special training in crisis management, grief counseling, bilateral negotiating tactics, cardiopulmonary resuscitation, first aid, federal privacy laws, and martial arts tactics of leverage and hand-to-hand self-defense. The enemies of orderly airport operation are unanticipated crowds, gossip, and speculation.

It fell to the Angel Team to clear the terminal—locate the stricken and grieving, then discreetly usher them out of the sight line of passengers who were waiting to board a passenger jet of the exact make, model, and vintage as the one that had just fallen from the sky. They herded the family members and friends into the controlled and sterile environment of a conference room; here, sustained by doughnuts and watery coffee, the bereaved could listen to the news or seek comfort in the waiting platitudes of members of the clergy from every imaginable denomination. This part of the plan was executed nearly simultaneously at the departure and arrival airports.

The airline itself required answers, and ideally before anyone else had them. Getting the information first meant staying ahead of the story. This was where the Go Team—mostly mid-level executives from the flight-operations division—came in. They worked with federal investigators to determine exactly who was on board the flight, whether they had checked a bag, and where they had been headed, preparations for the messy business of notifying the family.

The general counsel had produced great sheaves of memoranda outlining the desirable qualities that members of each team should possess; Angel Teams were without exception men because they conveyed a competence and an authority that strangers responded to in predictable ways. Prematurely gray hair was seen as an asset.

The requirements to be part of an Adam and Eve Team were more flexible, written in familiar human resource jargon; members should be self-starters, levelheaded, willing to work unpredictable schedules. The general counsel kept secreted in his safe printouts of correspondence from a consulting psychologist who claimed that the grieving were much more likely to confront people with obvious flaws in their skin, hair, teeth, or nails; inside the company, it was a widely known fact that members of Adam and Eve Teams needed to be attractive, proportionate, with a body mass index within the range defined as generally healthy. Finally, written in pencil at the bottom of a yellow legal pad, a page that would be produced as documentary evidence in at least two lawsuits that sprang from the crash of Flight 503, a final quality added by the general counsel himself: *Needs to be good in a crisis.*

Adam and Eve Teams were dispatched to notify—in person whenever possible and practical—the next of kin. The Adam and Eve Teams also had to learn a new vocabulary—or anti-vocabulary—because they reported to the corporate general counsel, who had written a list of thirty words that any airline representative was prohibited from uttering. The most verboten was, in fact, *next of kin*. They could not say *passenger,* as in *Seventy-seven passengers were killed,* a word prohibited after a specific incident following a minor crash in Denver, when the father of one of the victims beat an airline-reservation clerk senseless, saying, "My son is not a passenger; his name is David," each time his fist struck flesh. Airline employees could not say *crash,* as in *Flight 503 crashed on approach,* if only because in the mind of one astute litigator (a second-year associate who briefly had considered a career in personal injury law), the word *crash* implied a relationship between cause and effect, the ultimate judgment of who exactly was at fault. So it was that a crash became an *incident;* investigations and reconstruction became part of the *incident report.* And a crash like this afternoon's—the disintegration of the airframe, the inability to precisely identify human remains, the concomitant likelihood of ongoing litigation—became not merely an *incident* but an *incident* of *uncontrolled flight into terrain.* The airline was willing to make extraordinary efforts following the death or injury of *a loved one* in an *incident.*

Team members were prohibited from referring to themselves by name. They were prohibited from identifying themselves as anything other than representatives of Panorama Airlines. They spoke in the communal voice, using the plural personal pronoun *we* whenever possible. The singular *I* was prohibited. *We want to know what we can do in this difficult time. We can accommodate any number of special requests. We stand ready to help. How can we serve you?*

They called the next of kin *the contact,* like an operative behind the Iron Curtain in an old spy thriller, someone who could materialize with an envelope and a smuggled weapon without attracting too much notice. Use of the words *widow, widower, orphan,* and especially *victim* was not tolerated, nor was the use of any word that described the relationship of the passenger to the next of kin, which abrogated *husband, wife, child. The contact* was an honorific that did not imply any power relationships, did not evoke a default response of sympathy.

Among the fifty-odd people crowding the conference room of the tower offices of Salt Lake City International Airport, more than half were representatives of Panorama Airlines. The other half sat stunned and motionless. Some were grieving, some thinking of miracles.

A folding table had been converted to a buffet, a mercy meal of hamburgers and barbecue sandwiches and pizza slices and cinnamon rolls and great, steaming urns of coffee that went almost untouched. Still, men in white uniforms came and went every half hour, carrying in a new urn, departing with the old one.

At the front of the room, four Panorama employees outlined the next twenty-four to forty-eight hours on a series of hand-written posters that they taped to the wall and then read aloud.

Investigators from the National Transportation Safety Board, accompanied by the Go Team, were en route to Dallas to take command of the incident scene.

A ticket audit was under way to confirm who was on board the aircraft.

Official notifications would begin within the hour.

The Dallas County coroner had agreed to expedite the issuance of notarized death certificates for those needing documents for banking and insurance purposes.

They did not mention the bodies, and it was Mike Renfro

who raised his hand and asked, "There's no delicate way to say this, so I'm just going to. Have they begun to recover the bodies? Are there even bodies? What exactly are you telling us?"

"We're not prepared to discuss that particular issue," one of the men at the front said, and moved on to the next question. Mike saw the man's suit, his continual habit of referring to his black binder, and guessed *Corporate counsel.*

Mike was surprised at how docile the crowd was. He stood up. "I'm sorry, but I'm going to need more than that. We've been here for forty minutes, and you haven't told us a damn thing. You're behaving like we didn't just see a burned-out jet smash into the ground on network television. Prepared? Prepared? None of us were prepared to discuss this today. It's the holidays, for fuck's sake. Excuse my language, but I need to know. We all do. We've all got questions. What exactly happened? When are we going to be told something that matters? Are there any survivors? We've ruled out bad weather and another plane being involved, but only because we watched it all on television. But are you going to take us to Dallas? Will we be able to see the site? I asked about the bodies. Have the bodies been recovered? Are there even bodies? Can we even tell if the people are who we think they are? I don't have any idea how to get her dental records, but isn't that what people do, they go get dental records? I don't think any of us has any idea what to do, and so far, none of you seem to either. Can you tell us anything at all? Or does that notebook tell you just to come up here and bullshit until the lawyers arrive? You're not telling us anything that I haven't already heard on the news." Mike took a deep breath and sat down. He thought he'd spoken in his usual, mannered tone, but the reactions of the people around him—the open mouths, the way the two women nearest him rocked back in their chairs—suggested that perhaps he hadn't.

One of the men from the front of the room walked to the buffet table, picked up two small plastic bottles of water, and then moved to Mike's seat, took out the chair next to him and turned it around, straddled it. He handed one of the bottles of water to Mike. It was a ten-ounce bottle, narrow and thin, and it disappeared into Mike's meaty hand.

"I'm sorry that we haven't had a chance to speak individually," the man said. In his jacket pocket was the same laminated script that each member of the Angel Team was required to carry, offering an apology on behalf of the *airline's chairman, our shareholders, and, most important, the friends and family we work alongside each day.* "But I'm sure you can understand that things are still very much in flux. There's so much we don't yet know, and it would be irresponsible to speculate. As a matter of fact, I am going to step outside and say exactly the same things I've just told you to the reporters who are waiting in the hallway. But friends and family have to know these things first."

"I understand," Mike lied. He did not understand. This man had one job, and it was to pacify him. This was new territory. Mike coughed out a small laugh: No one in this room had spent more of his life helping to prepare others for the unthinkable than he, Mike Renfro; hell, it was part of his sales spiel. But no one had ever helped him. He did not know how to ask for what he wanted and never had. After Mary Beth kissed him on the forehead, he had not known how to ask her to please not leave him with such a chaste and sisterly kiss. He wanted to have stayed up all night with her, to have had any conversation she wanted. He didn't want to have found her as he had at 4:00 a.m.; he'd gone to take a leak in the middle of the night, and there she was, half-asleep in the bathtub, resistant to his efforts to wake her and relocate her back to the warmth of the bed.

His shoulders were tight with the tension that came from

knowing he wanted the impossible. He wanted kisses of reconciliation and reunion and a hero's welcome at home and a
begrudging hug from her kid. He had this feeling in his throat,
as if he were coming down with something, allergies, maybe.
His eyes felt dull, heavy lidded. Yes, his wants were much sim-
pler now. He wanted a happy ending. The same faces that had
looked on him in disgust at his outburst now looked away from
his tears; there was nothing uglier than seeing a large man cry,
his bulk heaving with sobs, his nose beaded with mucus and
his breath coming in sharp snorts. As he cried, he could feel the
skin of his face flush, the pink of rare meat.

The airline employee gave Mike a stack of paper napkins
from the buffet table, and Mike settled enough to blow his nose,
the sound a resonant, trumpetlike blurt.

"Tell me your name," the man from the airline said.

"Sorry," Mike said, and introduced himself.

"Who did you know onboard Flight 503? Your wife?" The exact question the training materials said never to ask.

"Her name was Mary Beth."

"And she was related to you?" A required question, taken
from the laminated card. Physical clues (no ring) suggested
Mike was not married, and the man from the airline had memorized the draft passenger manifest, and there was no one with
the last name Renfro on board.

"No. We were dating. She was my . . . I don't know what you'd
call it. She worked for me."

"I'm not sure I understand. What was her full name?"

Mike answered, "Mary Beth Blumenthal," a phrase that told
the man from the airline *seat 26C.*

"I would imagine that you are going to find this entire process
very frustrating, Mike. It is all right if I call you Mike?" Clearly
whoever had written the training materials for the airline had

experience in sales, because Mike could anticipate how the man was going to try to solicit him to say the word *yes* as many times as he could in the next few minutes.

"Sure," Mike said. He regretted being so docile.

"We won't get confirmation of anything other than the ticket audit in the next several hours. If you'd like, we can put you up at a hotel here for the next day or so, until...," and then the man from the airline trailed off.

"What is it? What were you going to say?" Mike resettled in his chair, and the pressure against the molded plastic back of his seat made him aware of how soaked his lower back was, how his skin had gone clammy with sweat.

"If you'll excuse me," the airline rep said, "I've got to look into one thing."

Mike knew when to call the question. "Tell me right now. What were you about to say?" Mike stood up and knew that he'd raised his voice. The same people who had turned away at his grief now looked on at the spectacle. Mike was about a foot taller and a full hundred pounds heavier than the man he was speaking to.

"I was going to say," the airline rep stood and almost whispered at Mike, "that the airline could put you up until we can get you on a plane to Dallas."

"Sounds reasonable. Let's make that happen," Mike said.

"That's what I need to check on. I am not certain that we can. But if we can, we will. We've bumped all the passengers from the next two flights in order to accommodate family members. The earliest I can get you on a plane is going to be around this time tomorrow. Maybe. I don't mean to be blunt, but there's going to be a problem here. We're prepared to deal with husbands and wives and parents and children, but you fall into what we might call a gray area."

"A gray area," Mike repeated.

"I'm not sure you have any legal standing here. You're not a designated emergency contact for Ms. Blumenthal, and you aren't a relative. At this point, it's unclear whether I should even be talking to you."

"Just what exactly is your name?" Mike demanded. The sensation he felt was stunning. His anger ran out of him, his shoulders fell. The pressure in his neck suggested that he was nearing the limit of the stresses a man could tolerate. He sat down and almost missed the chair, stumbling into it. His legs thumped against the conference table.

The man from the airline opened the other bottle of water and handed it to Mike. "You need to eat something. And you need to relax, if you can. Do you think you can do that for me, Mike?"

Once Mike nodded, the man from the airline pulled out a small pad and made some notes, then tucked the notepad into his jacket pocket. "There's no polite way to tell you this, Mike, but your situation...," and he trailed off again. Mike knew the pause was deliberate. "My name is Arthur McDevitt. Call me Art." He palmed a business card to Mike. He wanted to say something to Mike that committed him to nothing. "I can't do anything for you that might infringe on the rights of Ms. Blumenthal's family. It's just a strange situation. You're someone we hadn't anticipated. A gray area."

Mike gave a cursory nod that meant *I understand.*

"Do you know who she might want us to contact? A relative? A parent, perhaps?" Art asked.

Mike took another of his business cards, wrote a name and number on the back of it. "Her brother."

The man from the airline stood and went to the front of the room, where he conferred with another man, the two of them glancing at Mike every few sentences. What could he give Mary Beth now? He would forever be in that gray area between boss and husband and boyfriend, and maybe it was odd, but they hadn't said a thing to him about the body or the procedures, and, most of all, they had not once mentioned the boy. The boy. Gabriel had no idea.

How do you tell a child? That would be the thought that consumed Mike the rest of the afternoon. His mission now. To protect the boy. To be the one constant in his life, the one source of comfort.

The man from the airline returned, accompanied by two more identically dressed men. They flanked Mike on either side, as if he'd been a disruption and was being escorted out of the room by security. One of the men was folding a stack of papers, tucking them into his inside coat pocket.

"You didn't tell us that she had a son," one of the new men said. "Where is he now?"

Mike explained the situation. "I want to be the one who tells him."

"When there is a minor involved and there are surviving family members, we leave those decisions to the family."

The three men nodded in agreement, and Mike assumed what he was seeing was relief that they would not be asked to take on this disheartening duty themselves.

They made their way out of the conference room, into a hallway that was nearly empty. It made Mike realize they were afraid of him, of some volcanic eruption. Mike repeated himself, "I need to be the one who explains things to the boy."

Arthur nodded, extended his hand. It was the tone of his voice, the perfunctory "Of course," that told Mike the man was lying.

*   *   *

Before Mike understood what he was doing, he had made his way out of the terminal to the parking garage. He got back behind the wheel of his rented Jeep and started his way east on the interstate. When he saw the mileage sign for Cheyenne, he thought to stop and fill the tank, made the call to arrange to keep the car for a few more days. We perform our duties out of custom or obligation, and this one, this last bit of service to Mary Beth, was somehow both.

At the first exit, he pulled off and bought a portable Rand McNally atlas, a large Diet Coke, and a cheeseburger that had been kept warm under a heat lamp. Back on the highway, he thought about Mary Beth at the office, about the ebb and flow of their Mondays, when she would review his calendar for the week, the every-other-Thursday sessions when he signed payroll checks. She'd come into the office with a stack of checks and a stack of documents affixed with yellow stickers that read ACTION REQUIRED.

Action required. He said the words to himself. He knew exactly what he was supposed to do now. The mileage charts in the atlas told him it was almost 1,300 miles to his house in Dallas. At some point he'd have to stop again and call Sarah Hensley and make arrangements for her to stay another night. He'd be home by lunchtime tomorrow, sooner than he would if he waited for the next available flight, and he could be the one to take Gabriel onto his lap and tell it to him, man to man. He owed Mary Beth that much.

43

IT HAD been fourteen years since Panorama's last crash, when an L1011 had failed to achieve adequate lift on takeoff, slid off the runway at Denver's old Stapleton Airport. Thirty-seven dead and twenty-three injured, ten with life-altering burns. In the language of the reports, *a minor incident, with fatalities.* A contretemps between pilot, copilot, and head flight attendant captured on the cockpit voice recorder led to new rules promulgated in the Code of Federal Regulations requiring a sterile cockpit, that all conversations be directly related to the operation of the aircraft; the pilot's inquiry, "Anybody get laid last night?" would become as famous in the industry as the last words recorded on the flight deck of Panorama 503, First Officer Bill Zimmer's almost involuntary *Oh, shit.*

The decade-plus gap between the two incidents meant that of all the teams assigned to the task of in-person notifications, only the Washington DC–area Adam and Eve Team was staffed with someone who'd done this before. That was Carol Nessen, senior vice president of corporate communications, chosen specifically because the day-to-day rigors of her normal job required a certain discretion. She was also the only one who had volunteered to work this crash; this was the kind of duty that left its mark, and the few people who had been on Adam and Eve Teams after Denver and were still with the airline stayed silent in the manner of combat veterans who no longer wanted to talk about the shit they'd seen.

Nessen drafted an attorney named Brad Lemko as her teammate. He was one of the airline's fourteen associate general counsels. Tall, well built, and tan, he flew Warthogs in the naval reserve and kept himself in flying trim. The last time he'd been in the simulator he'd test-crashed any number of planes, gaming the possible outcomes: a slide off the runway at Logan into the tea-black muck of Boston Harbor, hitting hard and short at Reagan National, getting buffeted by tropical crosswinds approaching no land 30 (a pilot's nickname for runway 30R) at Miami International. Like most pilots, he gave off an aura of competent authority, one that the teams depended on in the event of a particularly difficult notification.

Nessen and Lemko had traveled together often enough on unrelated matters to have a rhythm, as if they were long-partnered cops. But those trips usually involved a lawsuit, human resource issues; they flew in, checked into a hotel, took a deposition in the morning, had lunch, reviewed the preposterous and contradictory facts during their flight back to Dallas headquarters. On their travels, Lemko always picked up the rental car, and he always drove, and at the airport, Nessen always asked, *What kind of car?* Lemko, while kicking the tires and watching the rental attendant note the scratches and dings and cigarette burns, always managed to mumble, *This is not your father's Oldsmobile,* whether it was a Ford Taurus or a Toyota Camry or any of the other indistinguishable sedans they rented.

As they rode from Reagan National, skirting the river and

passing the landscape of monuments, Carol felt they were driving right onto the back of the ten-dollar bill.

The first contact lived in a small saltbox colonial just over the Key Bridge, in one of Northern Virginia's tonier suburbs. The Adam and Eve Team knew her husband had been seated near the back of the plane; he'd be among the most easily identifiable victims. The contact answered the door wearing a bathrobe over a red cashmere sweater, and from the sight of the tissues tucked into her sleeve cuff, Nessen assumed that she already knew.

"This is about Clem, isn't it?"

Nessen nodded, kept the speaking to a minimum, standard procedure. She asked the contact if she was related to a Clement Benjamin, employed by the United States Department of Labor.

The woman answered, "I'm his wife. Diana." She directed them to sit, a conciliatory gesture. Nessen remembered from her training that this was an early sign; there would be no trouble here.

The wife kept repeating, "I'm just not sure what you people are doing here."

The training dictated letting the contact talk. "I was watching the news," she said. She hadn't realized her husband's flight connected through Dallas, she explained, even though every flight seemed to connect through Dallas or Atlanta these days. At least, she hadn't realized it until she saw his sweater, lime green, the color of sherbet and toddler's toys; the sweater had been a gift from their daughter a couple of Christmases back. "I told him that he should never wear it. Not outside the house. That's what a good wife does, right?"

Mrs. Benjamin laughed, a quick snort, then used her palm to wipe the underside of her nose. "He looked like a fucking Popsicle," she said between sniffles. Nessen realized that the daughter she'd been thinking of as an adult was probably something like ten.

Mrs. Benjamin said, "I didn't even know he was on that plane," until she saw the news, the hint of green sleeve awash in a charred field. She'd hoped against hope that her husband would be the exception, the miracle of Flight 503, but she'd already gotten confirmation from an overzealous reporter who had called to confirm details for the obituary. "A wife knows these things in her heart," she said, but only because she'd seen the broadcast footage of her husband's sweater and, within it, his lifeless arm.

She said *wife,* and Nessen thought *contact,* and Lemko thought *widow.*

A widow she was, beautiful and wronged; Lemko secretly hoped she would get angry and stay that way, break things and get violent and pound on his chest with closed fists. Trying to imagine himself in this situation, indeed trying on any cloak of empathy, felt impossible. What did he know about the subworld of death? He was a bachelor; his parents were not only alive but healthy, even in their mideighties. His father played tennis every morning, and his mother swam in the cold chop off Narragansett Beach every afternoon, weather permitting. He'd be the one who died with no one to remember him.

Lemko's briefcase contained a heavily annotated paperback of Kübler-Ross, part of the short course in required reading for each Adam and Eve Team, and here was a woman whose reactions were textbook. Lemko guessed Mrs. Benjamin to be thirty-four, thirty-six tops, and among the contingencies of her new life as a widow would be a settlement check from the airline and a settlement check from a credit card company (the airline's ticket audit noted that the contact's husband had purchased travel insurance, that frivolous lottery ticket). Perhaps the $750,000 of accidental-death-and-dismemberment coverage could push her past stage one of the grief cycle, denial.

She kept repeating "No, no, no," and with each sob her resolve seemed to soften, until each breathy *no* seemed affixed with a question mark at its end, followed by a series of more assertive *no*s, exclamations that Lemko's legal mind appreciated; there was something beautiful about the process, denial followed by its almost imperceptible transmogrification into fury, the anger of conspiracies and incompetencies that almost all litigation, at its heart, was built upon.

Contact number two answered the door while on the telephone with the fraud prevention department of his credit card company. From what Nessen and Lemko overheard, they gathered that the contact had telephoned a mortuary to pay the final $1,000 on one of those prepaid funeral-arrangement plans and had suffered the embarrassment of having not one but two different cards declined.

Nessen thought briefly of burying her own mother, how the funeral director had stepped out of the room and sent in an underling to talk about payment plans and options—*Darla here will talk to you about financing*. Nessen, whose own credit cards never carried a balance, signed a contract without even looking at the amount or asking Darla to explain how much. The casket had cost as much as a good used car. And now this contact was explaining into the telephone how demeaning it was not to be able to pay the final $1,000 for his wife's casket, or for the transport of her body back to the Washington area (she was one of three people on Flight 503 who had been continuing on to the next leg of the flight, from DFW to Reagan National). His wife's cards had been canceled because she was deceased, but his own cards had inadvertently been marked *Deceased* as well, and it would take at least forty-eight hours to correct the error. Nessen wanted to interrupt, to be assertive just for once, to defy her training and rip the cordless phone from his hand and end the call.

She'd explain how Panorama Airlines would make everything okay, bereavement tickets and no charge for the transportation of the caskets and first-class upgrades and limousine service and tarmac permissions to stand at the baggage area and supervise the loading and unloading of the loved one's body (a service that a surprising number of the next of kin accepted). But the very purpose of the visit—the notification of the contact—had already been subverted by the inability of a pair of computer systems to communicate with each other. They had no need to tell him what he'd already learned. Nessen was left to watch as the contact sank into his sofa, hung up the phone without comment.

The drive back into the northwest section of the city took only twenty minutes, thanks to the relative quiet of a late holiday afternoon. Nessen was happy to let Lemko drive; he'd grown up in the Maryland suburbs and knew his way around the Beltway and the parkways and bridges. He piloted while she read and reread the dossier on the next contact. *Only known living relative.*

They double-parked illegally in the middle of California Street, and Lemko stayed with the car while Nessen used the buzzer to try to enter Richard MacMurray's building. She rang his apartment, but the automated entry system was connected to the telephone, and there seemed to be some problem with the phone line. The operator she called for assistance verified the line as in service, suggested that the phone was simply off the hook.

After ten minutes of waiting at the door, she gave up. Lemko drove them to the yellow loading zone directly in front of the Third District police station on V Street Northwest, just three blocks away. They moved with the assurance of people tasked with an important mission, and to everyone in the building—the detectives and patrolmen and even the mechanic who changed the oil in the Crown Vic police sedans—Nessen and Lemko looked and behaved like cops.

They introduced themselves to the desk sergeant, produced laminated identification in the manner of so many films and detective shows, and Nessen explained their purpose. The sergeant escorted the Adam and Eve Team out through the Police Officers Only exit. Nessen started heading back toward the car, but the sergeant restrained her, gently, at the wrist, saying, "No place to park. It's faster on foot. In this neighborhood, everything's faster on foot."

When they again reached Richard's building, at the summit of the small hill on California Street, Lemko had to hunch over, hands on knees, and catch his breath. He checked his pulse against the dial of his diver's watch and thought about upping the intensity of his cardiovascular conditioning. He'd hardly realized their pace.

The sergeant radioed back to the station for someone to try Richard's phone. Through his Motorola handheld unit, he could hear his colleague, a second-year policewoman, mumbling over and over, "Pick up the phone."

Lemko thought to dial another apartment on the entry console, and the person who answered did not say a word, just pressed the entry buzzer. They bounded up the stairs. At the door to apartment 33, the sergeant had the disconcerting sensation of knocking on the door and then hearing the report of his knocks again, with the slight delay of transmission, through his radio. The policewoman's voice told whoever had answered the phone, "You need to go to the door now."

The voice on the walkie-talkie kept saying, "You should be talking to one of my officers," whatever that meant. Lemko worried about not having his briefcase. It was his security blanket. He'd left it in the car. He carried in his briefcase intelligence estimates on the average life span of a plane, its hours of service, its entire history. He knew he could pull out the papers in a practiced bit of theater and use them to calm a particularly agitated family member. He knew from his experience as a litigator that so much of what he did, day to day, was performance; the papers were a prop, but a useful one, and almost always had the desired effect—anything in writing made it true. *I can tell you the last person who put in a roll of toilet paper,* he'd planned to say. *If someone touched that plane with any tool, tightened this or loosened that, or even spat on the windshield and rubbed it off with the sleeve of his coveralls, I can tell you who it was and when, and certify that his saliva was drug- and alcohol-free.*

But encountering vitriol was rare. He tried hard not to be taken as the typical asshole lawyer and served up such serious attitude only to plaintiff's attorneys, the guys who represented the passengers in the lawsuits that Lemko tried to make disappear: the morbidly obese passenger who could not buckle his seatbelt even with the seatbelt extender and sued the airline for causing his acute embarrassment; the child whose peanut allergy meant that his flight to Toronto had ended with an injection of epinephrine in his neck at thirty thousand feet and an emergency landing in Cincinnati; the sales manager who suffered a mild concussion when another passenger's trumpet case sprang from an improperly closed overhead bin.

Lemko's briefcase contained the file folder with the page of information about Richard MacMurray and his relationship to

Mary Beth Blumenthal of Garland, Texas. In the Comment field of the form, someone from the corporate office would have written the reason that Richard MacMurray of California Street Northwest merited in-person notification. After all, the Adam and Eve Teams were performing a service required by exactly *none* of the fifteen thousand pages of federal regulations that outlined what was and was not necessary in the aftermath of an incident. If Lemko had reviewed that form, remembered to bring that form with him, had that form with him now, he would see that Richard MacMurray was not only the next of kin but the only one left. *Only known living relative.* Somewhere in the byzantine world of the main corporate office, it had been decided: Some things could only be said face to face. Sometimes death merited looking a man in the eye.

But inside the airline offices, no one had to be told why they did it; Lemko knew it boiled down to a cost-control measure: put a human face on the corporation, and it became a lot harder for someone to sue.

Then there was the matter of the half-awake man on the other side of the apartment door, this confusion in the hallway and the dull tintinnabulus of bells and alarms in the background. None of it disturbed Richard's continuing dream. During his unintentional nap, Richard's mind had constructed a dreamscape that was an impossibly confused pastiche of his past: a child playing in Richard's childhood bedroom, with its blue walls and the laundry chute that dropped straight to the basement and the closest thing Richard had to a secret lair, a window seat. In both the dream and later in his memory of it, he would assume he had been watching himself.

The bookshelves of that bedroom had been filled with oversize volumes of children's tales, *The Three Little Pigs,* the only one Richard could actually remember, and so in the dream, all the books became *The Three Little Pigs,* in hundreds of different editions, embossed leather covers and glossy consumer paperbacks with cartoonish drawings wherein the Big Bad Wolf wasn't so much a villain as a charming and obsequious neighbor; he'd somehow morphed into a cartoon, more Wile E. Coyote than anything else, a huckster, a con man, a rogue and a rake, a wolf neither big nor bad.

But the house that contained his room was no house Richard had ever seen, a center-hall colonial built on maybe forty acres of land, with a stocked pond and three chocolate lab puppies romping across an expansive, rolling lawn. The child called to the dogs by name—Sonny, Sam, and Frank—and even in his disquiet, Richard recalled that those were the names of the guys who called the Redskins games on the radio. The dream slowed as Richard tried to remember whether Frank was the one who did the play-by-play, the one who for twenty years could be counted on to botch the name of the Redskins' punter.

The backyard was huge, with a deep carpet of bluegrass and natural sideline of pine trees, and a woman was calling him in for dinner. Richard had the awareness that he was watching himself as a child, saying something about his dad, and he thought and maybe said *Lew* as this woman waved to him. In her outstretched hand was a metal spatula, and the dream filled with the smells of charcoal and cinnamon as he waved back. The arm that waved the spatula became the arm that rang a dinner bell, back and forth as the clapper slammed into the brass and the peal became constant, then doubled in intensity, a ringing and a buzzing, and in the distance, he heard the howl of his alarm and maybe even a banging inside his head that he felt obligated to investigate. He opened his eyes to see his navy suit trousers over the desk chair. He was wearing only his white shirt and his boxers and a pair of high-rise wool socks that had dug into his calves and made him itch, and he scratched out of instinct, and the ringing wasn't an alarm clock at all but a phone, the cordless handset that he couldn't locate.

He could not locate the phone because it had been in his right hand the entire time. He pressed the Talk button, and a voice identified itself. "This is the Metropolitan Police. You need to answer the door. You should be talking to one of my officers now."

He harrumphed. He put on pants. The voice on the phone kept speaking. "Sir. Sir? You're going to need to open the door."

Richard uncracked the door slowly. Lemko was surprised there was no security chain, if only because most of the neighborhood looked as if it were still deciding whether or not to reject its recent, sketchy past.

Richard looked rumpled. A bit of white gunk littered the corners of his mouth. "What's all this? What's this about?"

Still on the line, the police sergeant said, "Sir, could you identify yourself for these people?"

"MacMurray. Richard MacMurray. What's wrong? What time is it?" He looked at his wrist but wore no watch.

Nessen thought she had heard the last name somewhere, MacMurray. "It's a little after six. May we come in?" Her training instructed her to inventory the scene when she arrived, and now she was doing just that: couch, desk, armoire containing a large television and various home-entertainment equipment. Speakers hanging from brackets in the high corners, walls of horsehair plaster, not just a prewar building but pre–the war before that. Framed posters from a handful of exhibitions and charity events and political campaigns, and only two pictures— Washington standard-issue grip-and-grin, autographed photos of Richard MacMurray with each of the last two presidents. In the second one, the president had his hand on Richard's shoulder and leaned in close, looked to be talking directly into Richard's ear with the whisper of a conspirator. The contact looked familiar, like someone she'd known in college. No pets. No pictures of family. No potential weapons.

The contact turned and walked deeper inside the apartment and stopped at the point where the wide hallway spilled into a cave-like living room. "I'm not big on the small talk, so why doesn't someone tell me what's going on here?"

Procedure meant Nessen was supposed to offer an explanation, but, saying his name over and over silently, she could think only of *My Three Sons* and Fred MacMurray. Twice already today she had braced herself to be the airline's appointed messenger of death—to show up unannounced on someone's doorstep and present a business card and ask to be let inside— and twice the next of kin had already received the news. This was in the briefing books too. People already knew; they heard radio broadcasts, saw special reports, watched the plume of smoke trailing out the fan exhaust of engine 3, overheard the first responders on police scanners. In their most common iteration, they simply showed up at the airports and wandered without purpose or direction until an airline employee could corral them and get them into a conference room, out of the sight of the general public.

Lemko thought only of their duty; the purpose of an Adam and Eve Team was to round up the stray family member, a next of kin to sign the requisite paperwork for the acceptance of the body, someone of close-enough relations and standing in the family and/or community that their signature was legally enforceable.

Then Richard made an offer of some hospitality. He poured three glasses of orange juice, handed them around, then put a small ramekin of cashews on the corner of his cluttered desk. "I'm sorry, but I don't really have much more," he said.

Nessen murmured a thank-you. She sometimes wondered how she'd even gotten into this career; her degree was a master's of social work, and she had done enough clinical work to identify Richard MacMurray as a man under severe stress, perhaps indeed shock, but it was not likely caused by the plane crash or the afternoon's events. Her mind flashed to a case study she'd read in graduate school, and here she was, perhaps a bit unprofessionally, diagnosing Richard MacMurray, forty-two, as someone who existed in a constant state of trauma. He absently touched his pained forehead and adjusted a nonexistent necktie. He suffered the look of the afflicted.

Before Nessen could say, *Perhaps you'd like to sit down and talk to us for a moment,* Richard moved to the couch and took a seat on top of a week's worth of newspapers and asked, "Now what can I do for you?"

Lemko whispered at her, "Procedure," which Nessen took as a reminder that there should be no shortcuts here, no mistakes.

She started to read from the small laminated card that contained a series of statements that had been prepared by the general counsel and vetted by outside attorneys. The lawyers asked the Adam and Eve Teams to read from the card verbatim, but Nessen preferred to make eye contact; the instructions in the procedures binder specifically warned against this, as did the lessons of her training. The contacts' reactions were wild and varied; no application of science or reason could predict who would cry, who would argue. The card was supposed to suit every contingency. Yet already today she had read it to two contacts who already knew everything she had to say, and here on an enormous couch was a man who clearly didn't know what was about to hit him, and the card couldn't possibly tell him what he needed to know.

We are working in concert with local, state, and federal author-ities. Our primary purpose in these difficult hours is to assist the family members of the passengers and crew of Flight 503 in any rea-sonable way.

She had a script but could not say the words. Lemko whis-pered at her again, "The card." This was how mistakes were made, how cops who'd said the Miranda warnings a few thou-sand times ended up watching a criminal skate because they didn't feel like reading what was on the card. She tried to chase the irrelevant details from her mind but instead kept thinking of a movie in which the cop kept his Miranda card inside his hat.

"On behalf of the chairman of Panorama Airlines, Ellison Gem—" she began, and Lemko showed her a palm.

"You're forgetting the confirmation," he said, pulling a piece of paper from inside his jacket pocket. He still sounded out of breath.

"Right. Forgive me." She took and unfolded the paper and read from it instead. "You are Richard Llewellyn MacMurray, brother of Mary Elizabeth MacMurray Blumenthal, age forty-seven, lately a resident of Garland, Texas?" Nessen was aware that she had just identified the deceased in the exact manner of newspapers and anchormen.

Richard nodded.

"I'm sorry, sir, but our procedure requires that you verbally answer the question. She is your sister?"

Richard said, "Yes. My sister. Where are you going with all this? I'm going to need you to spell it out."

Nessen moved back to the card and read from it. "On behalf of the chairman of Panorama Airlines, Ellison Gem, and our entire family of employees, we wish to offer our sincere condolences. Your sister, Mary Elizabeth, was a passenger on board Flight 503."

Richard stood and smoothed his shirt and looked at Carol Nessen, held her gaze until she broke eye contact and lowered her head. He looked so familiar to her, but she still couldn't place it. He went to step past her, but the police sergeant—who until this moment had busied himself with inspecting the books and magazines around the apartment as if conducting a forensic examination—was in his way, and they both stepped in the same direction, as if dancing.

The sergeant said, "Sorry."

"If you'll excuse me," Richard mumbled, then headed out the door to the balcony.

Nessen began gathering up the juice glasses, ate the last couple of cashews. She fidgeted when she was nervous, Lemko knew that. In a minute, she'd start fluffing pillows and dusting blinds.

"Carol. Stop," he said.

She took the pile of newspapers at the edge of the couch and began ordering them all in the same direction. "I just can't get over the feeling that I know this guy from somewhere."

The sergeant said, "You do. Television."

44

GABRIEL HEARD everything, every mention of the words *weird* and *strange*. They were the words most familiar to him because he heard them at school, the daily mantra of his tormentors. He accepted them as an accurate definition of his personality.

On his fifth birthday, when his mother asked what he thought he might want to be when he grew up, he knew enough to understand that she expected him to say something that would please her, astronaut or doctor or lawyer or even insurance man (those were really the only jobs he'd heard of). But he could not resist the truth, its awkward blurtings, and said, *Lonely.* When she questioned him, he repeated himself—*I will always be lonely*—because even then he equated *lonely* with *strange.* As an adult, he would remember those words not as a self-fulfilling prophecy but as deft insight. He was lonely on his fifth birthday, and so still he was lonely now, playing on the floor in the solitary games of his imagination.

Weird and *strange.* He heard those words being whispered by the partygoers, and it made him want to be strange. He wanted to astound them with his acts of defiance, his weirdness.

When his mother returned, he was going to propose a

remedy, a manner in which he could pretend to be more like the other kids. He needed a sidekick. A dog, maybe, but more likely a brother. He'd have to look into this, see if it was possible somehow to have his mother find him such a protector. For now, what he needed was a friend. But there were some issues that needed to be addressed. First, there was the fact that no kids lived around him. His mother's apartment complex was filled with well-meaning young professionals who liked mixed drinks by the pool and loud music and spent most of the summer outside grilling burgers at one of the four built-in community grills; from them Gabriel had learned another word: *mascot*. He was the office mascot, too.

He was smart enough to know that the women of the Mike Renfro Agency who surrounded him with minor affections did so because they felt sorry for him. He did not know enough yet of the larger world to understand why, but he knew he was treated differently, that his concerns were addressed with the utmost seriousness, that conversations in his presence frequently stopped or devolved into whispers. He suffered the truest indignities of being an only child: School became a safari into the unknown wilds of torment; an amusement park was a place where he was forced to sit next to strangers on rides that shook him until he was terrified. He feared showing his classmates the width and breadth of what he knew, how he could look around the room and see how they were going to end up. It wasn't clairvoyance or any particular gift other than being observant; he spent hours lost in books and in the elaborate fantasias of his mind. His stuffed animals were chattering misfits. He was trailed by a cadre of imaginary friends. Herewith, his own prayers on New Year's Day were not to be left alone, never again to be consigned to the care of the women from Mr. Mike's office, who passed him around that afternoon enough that he embarrassed them all when he asked, "What's a hot potato?"—another phrase he'd learned by observation and repetition. He wanted the camaraderie of team sports, the bonding and instruction that came with it. He prayed again for a sibling, someone with whom he could create the private language of brothers, someone to whom he could teach the intricacies of Legos and video games, someone he could volunteer to play with so that his mother would not have to leave either of them alone with these people. All of these things—he knew from six years' experience watching television—required a father.

45

THIS, THEN, is a portrait of Richard's grief.

Grief is the American flag, folded in tricorner pattern and stowed in a Plexiglas case, an oft-overlooked relic that sat on the corner of a desk cluttered with newspapers, magazine clippings, small electronic devices and their associated chargers. Grief is the oil stains on the heavily ribbed grosgrain of military medals, fingered as talismans by the surviving members of a dead man's family.

You never wanted grief to be like this, dull and ordinary, delivered to your front door like the *Washington Post*.

Grief, too, meant these strangers in his living room.

Grief is the phrase that he'd overheard the woman use to describe him: *only known living relative.*

Richard did not know what to call the people from the airline, the ones who came to tell him that his sister was dead. And what the hell was a cop doing there, standing in the kitchen, drinking his juice and talking on his telephone? He couldn't even remember who poured the juice. Richard walked straight past him and out onto the balcony; he'd seen in that woman the flash of recognition that usually meant the person *knew*, but could not place, his face.

They know me from television. Richard did not know when the habit of narrating his own life had begun; now this omnipresent voice spoke to him like a stage whisper, stating the obvious whenever the obvious thing appeared at the core of his unconscious mind. How did people on television grieve? They didn't. They kept it together until they could retreat. He'd seen the clip of Cronkite telling the world about Jack Kennedy, taking off his glasses: *From Dallas, Texas, the flash, apparently official, President Kennedy died at one o'clock p.m. Central Standard Time, two o'clock Eastern Standard Time, some thirty-eight minutes ago.*

And today that internal voice had been particularly insistent. The walk home from the television studio had been riddled with reminders of his past. The voice had said, *You are now walking on Thirteenth Street Northwest.* The place where Richard first saw a prostitute; he was eleven years old, and the street then was nothing but liquor stores and Doc Johnson novelty shops with their twenty-five-cent peep shows. On this street, an ancient janitor in military greens had offered to give him twenty dollars for his Fruit of the Loom underwear, and Richard asked for twenty-five, because to a kid of that vintage, twenty-five dollars was a nearly incalculable sum, a lottery's worth of mischief and pinball and junk food. He stepped into the restroom of a liquor store that wasn't even there anymore. He remembered the man's callused hand palming him the bills, his breath medicinal and sharp as he said, "You are an excellent businessman. A tough negotiator."

He didn't tell his mother until years later. And even once he'd admitted it, in the manner of her generation, she simply denied it. "I don't remember you saying that at all," she'd say back to Richard as she put together a cheese tray or refilled a wineglass. "I *would* remember that," she insisted, but never once looked him in the face. "If a thing like that had actually happened."

He told his sister that very afternoon. Mary Beth's reaction: she marched him by the wrist to the police station, found the desk sergeant, and told him the whole story, never once letting go of Richard's wrist and making him feel very much the little boy. The sergeant smelled of juniper and sweat and came around from behind his desk to appraise Mary Beth, a predatory look, the look older men give to teenaged girls that says, *My, how you've grown*. Richard slipped from his sister's grasp, bolted out the double doors and into the cleared lot across the street. Mary Beth found him sitting on a short stack of cinder blocks at the edge of the construction zone; he had crossed his arms over his chest and rocked gently back and forth as if he could not be consoled, and now he recognized that as the very moment his internal voice began to speak, the message ex cathedra of Catholic guilt and fear: he'd be punished for losing his underwear, he'd have to give back the money; he worried most that he'd have to tell this story to his father, whose intolerable dinner-table soliloquies were about the decay of modern society and the predators who roamed the modern city.

Now, at a distance of some thirty years, Richard could identify the janitor who asked for his underwear as nothing but an old drunk with an Eastern European accent so thick and comical, Richard had not even understood his request until the visual clue of a twenty-dollar bill was there to help him decode the entire sentence. What the voice said to him as he prayed for consolation on that pile of cinder blocks was the same message he kept hearing now, on his balcony, his hands tight on the steel safety railing as his knuckles whitened with the fierceness of his grip: *You will always remember this*. His face gathered its musculature into a mask that spoke as well, saying, *Here is a stricken man,* his body a conversation unto itself. *This is a moment you will always remember.*

293

And what would happen to his nephew now? Gabriel. Named after the messenger of the Lord, he'd joked after the child had emerged in full-throated howl. That was the message. And this, then, was Richard's vision: Gabriel running in a backyard as wide as a meadow. The afternoon unbearably bright, the sky yellowed like an overexposed snapshot from thirty years past, and the boy wearing a T-shirt in candy-cane awning stripes, utilitarian green shorts, a functional garment whose pockets could be counted on to be filled with penny candies, odd-lot pieces of Legos, chewing gum, even a goldfish in a plastic sandwich bag. Richard imagines the boy running and ticks off the distinguishing characteristics of the landscape: a toolshed, a short course of feed corn growing in five-by-five rows, a barn that he'd once watched burn as a teenager. He knows this is not literal, this is Gabriel running through time, and to Richard, grief is not the dour monochromatics of a winter's day but vivid and bright and rendered in primary colors.

He tried to force his mind to focus on his sister. Yet the city intruded, the street four stories beneath him percolating with the sounds of a holiday evening: shouts and car horns, but also the low and dull moans of idling traffic and the trumpeting of cars and buses accelerating away from a too-long signal light and the conversations of lovers and groups of friends headed to the restaurants that dotted his neighborhood. Everything about the place felt like a diluted imitation of more famous and progressive neighborhoods in larger cities. The weather had turned, and the breeze carried a cutting chill, a reminder that said *January*. At the Hilton Towers, a few hundred feet to his right, the window lights glowed with the dim refraction of televisions, the curtains closed and permitting just the hint of escaping light. Death arrived with duty. He understood this instinctively and could think of only the one duty that would be required of him: the boy.

The first weekend of his life as a divorced man, four and a half years before, he'd stood on this same balcony with Mary Beth; he supposed that had been her last visit to Washington. They'd had a few drinks and pretended as if divorce weren't the end of their known worlds. It was Independence Day, and Richard's place provided a great view of the fireworks, the sky filled with concussive shocks, colored phosphor raining down in patterns that looked like stars.

His father had been a sentimental man and liked to preach a bit on the holiday. He talked about parades and memorial services, about how his own father used to make him cut the grass around the base of the stone monument to the soldiers of his hometown who had died in the First World War. Somewhere in that anecdote, Richard knew, was an explanation of why his father always teared up at the sound of the "Star-Spangled Banner," even when he was watching the Redskins and having a few pops with the boys from the office.

Richard knew he wasn't remembering a specific holiday but an amalgam of many: Lew inviting the neighbors over for hamburgers, homemade with his two secret ingredients of Worcestershire sauce and powdered onion-soup mix; Lew behind the grill, dousing the fatty flare-ups with a stray ounce of beer. On the Fourth, Lew smoked a cigar, a gift from his boss, the congressman, claiming to his son that the cigar smoke chased away the mosquitoes. At dusk, as the fireworks exploded over the National Mall, Lew and Richard and some other kids from the neighborhood wandered out onto D Street, in the shadow of the Capitol, and lit off firecrackers and bottle rockets, Lew igniting the stubborn fuses with the burning cherry of his stogie.

Richard knew that most of what his father had been teaching him was how to be a man, and those were lessons he could pass on, the difference between a Windsor knot and a four-in-hand, shaving first with the grain and then against it, all of Lew's little rituals that to this day Richard unconsciously followed. Lew allowed Richard to hold the cigar and light a bottle rocket, and hold the cigar and pantomime taking a puff, and Richard fetched cans of beer out of the basement refrigerator, the one with the wonky-sounding compressor, and Richard pocketed the pull tabs because his mother had asked him to keep count, a request he hadn't understood until years later.

Lew let Richard sit on the edge of a redwood picnic table on the brick patio that took up most of their postage-stamp-size backyard, and all of Capitol Hill rang with fireworks, and maybe, Richard knew now, gunshots. Lew asked him to hand over the pull tabs, and Richard asked, *How did you know about that?* and Lew laughed and said, *I have been married to your mother for a very long time.* He talked to his only son about the responsibilities of drinking beer and told him it was something he needed to learn, the ability to drink most of the day and not lose his composure, and to the nine-year-old Richard MacMurray, composure meant a clean shirt and a freshly shaven face and his father, almost always immaculate and smelling of beer and Aqua Velva.

Richard could not tell his sister these memories, because she would want to know what her place in them was, and the truth was that she had so little place there; she had been a spectral presence, a dervish that hustled in and out each summer and around the holidays, and before that she'd been the moody girl in the bedroom next door to his who yelled at her parents and ridiculed her little brother's clothes, or hair, or teeth. The truth: the most distinct of Richard's memories of his sister centered around tragedies—packing up Lew's personal effects at his office and arguing over which child was going to get the flag that had been draped over Lew's casket.

It felt like he had lived on this balcony for years. What he remembered most of that last visit of his sister's was the party upstairs, a world he had never been invited into; he'd spent his reckless twenties pretending to be first responsible and later married, and he had abdicated any interest in the more surface recreations of his friends: weekends at the beach and softball and drinking games and charity bar crawls. His neighbors upstairs samba'ed and cha-cha-cha'd and generally had themselves well lubricated by sundown, and the girl who lived in apartment 43 was there too, and she'd leaned out over the fire escape and shouted down, inviting Richard and Mary Beth upstairs, and his sister was halfway up the escape ladder before Richard could tell her that he did not want to go.

He was a stranger at the party and sulked and didn't really talk to anyone. Mary Beth brought women back to the sofa to meet him and kept repeating, "You gotta get back on that horse," as she gave the briefest of introductions: "This is Lori, she works on the Hill." He'd forgotten that his sister was, at her core, as much a Washingtonian as he was, inherited her brusque manner from the same father. He dreaded these kinds of party conversations; he kept up with the Redskins not out of a true love of football but because it felt like the only neutral thing anyone in the city was prepared to discuss. Half the women he met were interested in networking, not dating, and the ones that announced their interest in dating carried their insecurities with them like some sort of ritual scarifications, as if they had realized just that morning how most of their friends were now doting suburban parents. He was in his forties and had never learned how to talk to a woman without introducing that famous Beltway question, "Who do you work for?" as if it were still the era of the Roman Empire and you were defined by who owned the product of your work.

At the end of the party, Richard had nothing but heartburn and a pocket full of business cards of women he never intended to call. His sister was staying at a friend's house in Silver Spring and had to leave in time to catch the last Red Line train. When she left, she embraced him, her head against his chest. He'd been taller than Mary Beth since he was twelve but never realized just how much; as he rested his chin on the top of her head, he could see the emergent gray hairs at the roots of her part. That couldn't have been the last time he'd touched her, but he could conjure no other memory, no other likely time they had hugged or even kissed each other on the cheek.

He conflated memories of his sister too. His sister as a teenager, slathering her arms with suntan lotion, his sister at their childhood home, with her shelf full of facial cleansers and herbal shampoos. He could not remember what she smelled like or if she wore perfume or even what she had been wearing that July. Had that really been the last time they'd seen each other? *You should be talking to one of my officers now.*

He felt the cold, abrupt and shocking; he had been standing on his balcony for who knows how long, and three strangers stood whispering in his living room, the specifics of what they were saying lost in the drone of the television—*Continuous live coverage of the crash of Panorama Airlines Flight 503*—telling him again and again that his sister was dead. His sister.

This city was his childhood, and how much of it he'd spent heeled at her side. She'd taken him to the Smithsonian to see Charles Lindbergh's airplane and John Glenn's space capsule and bought him a bootleg FBI T-shirt from a Korean street vendor whose cart was a cornucopia of pizza by the slice, soft pretzels with huge, glistening crystals of white salt, and ice-cold seven-ounce bottles of Coca-Cola. Together they'd waited in line to see the touring treasures of the Egyptian king and sat in the House gallery on the day that the Judiciary Committee voted to impeach Nixon and then ate lunch in the cafeteria of the Rayburn Building with their father, who took Richard back into the committee room and let him sit in Chairman Rodino's big leather seat and even take a crack or two with the chairman's weighty gavel.

Later that same afternoon, his sister took him to the top of the Washington Monument, and Richard asked her if the first president was buried on the grounds; Mary Beth laughed and asked why, in the patient manner of a mother, and Richard said, "Because it looks like a tombstone." And the view from the monument's small windows was not much different than the one from his balcony.

His building was situated at the crest of two intersecting hills. To his right stood the hotel where President Reagan waved to the lone gunman. Though the clouds had thickened into what forecasters called a low ceiling, visibility was still good enough that Richard could see all the way south to the new tower at National Airport, which rose like a parapet. His eyes roamed across the cityscape, all its polished granite and etched concrete, the monument built of marble blocks carried on the backs of Union Army carts, and that was when it struck him: there were monuments to dead cops, and a black granite tombstone hundreds of yards long inscribed with the names of the dead from America's most foolish war; there were plaques to honor the dead army nurses from the two world wars, and in the suburbs there were eighty-three stars blasted with a pneumatic hammer into a marble wall at Langley, two and a quarter inches tall to represent the life of an intelligence operative lost in the line of duty, a cenotaph so inconsequential that the sculptor who chiseled the recesses into stone never even knew the names of the dead.

There was life, a future, but not here. His nephew was the only necessity now. Dallas, that modern cartoon; how could a boy live there? Gabriel needed space and sunlight and the soft undulations of a half-acre lawn. He needed a dog. A room with a desk for his homework, and a captain's bed with secret compartments and comic books. None of that was here, not in this dour apartment and not in this disappointing city. There were cities of angels and cities of light, windy cities, and cities of night, cities that never slept, cities of magnificent intentions, cities of big shoulders and kisses and promises, cities of balconies, and brotherly love, but it was this city that had been poisoned for him; what the young Richard MacMurray had once seen among the marble and granite landmarks of his hometown was a living history, where now every notable building of this city he had once loved with all his heart was nothing but a monument to the fallen dead.

46

LEMKO NEEDED to develop his own theory about grief, about how and why people reacted the way that they did. He had been well trained in the aphorisms of the legal profession. You never asked a question unless you were absolutely sure of the answer, and he was sure that guilt and anger and self-recriminations came quickly. He wanted the contact—say, the husband, contact number two—to offer him coffee, tell him stories of how he had met his dead wife, and flip through the photos from last summer's trip to the Greek Isles. Death, however, was proving to have a variable effect.

The contingency plan limited the visit of an Adam and Eve Team to thirty minutes per stop, but he secretly wished he could stay longer, until the contact disassembled himself into a hysteric, convulsive mass. Just once he wanted to see flagellations and mortifications of the flesh, to see the tangible presence of grief right there in the room.

Contact number three, *MacMurray, Richard L.*, had offered him orange juice and cashews, and Lemko at the very least could understand why. Probably raised Catholic, wakes of Irish whiskey, brisket sandwiches, and pitchers of beer at some dingy bar where the bartender wore black slacks and a white shirt and kept a shotgun or a Louisville Slugger or both in the beer cooler. If Nessen hadn't been there, MacMurray probably would have offered him a shot and a beer; he looked like the shot-and-a-beer type, Lemko thought, because Lemko himself looked like the shot-and-a-beer type. Shot-and-a-beer guys wanted action. They didn't want paperwork and explanations and promises.

This thought coincided almost immediately with the slam of the balcony door. Lemko found Richard MacMurray digging through the bottom of his closet and emerging with a small suitcase, the kind just big enough to fit in the overhead bin. Richard pointed at a leather dopp kit on the dresser, and Lemko simply zipped it and tossed it to him. He nestled it in among two T-shirts and two folded blue shirts and sets of underwear and socks for a couple of days. Lemko thought about his own bag, how being part of an Adam and Eve Team meant keeping a go bag packed in your office or the closet at home. He kept two, winter and summer, and was always raiding it for a spare shirt or a pair of socks, and now he'd be spending the night in DC with not much more than a toothbrush and a disposable razor, rethumbing his heavily annotated copy of *On Death and Dying*.

Richard zipped up his bag and yanked out the retractable handle and said only, "I'm going to need a ride to the airport."

Lemko said, "Why?"

"My nephew. What will they do with him until I get there?"

Nessen had apparently dismissed the cop and had busied herself rinsing out the empty glasses of orange juice and putting the cashews away. She stepped out of the kitchen, drying a glass with a bright-yellow hand towel. "There's a nephew? What nephew?"

"Christ. I thought you people were supposed to know these

things. My sister has a son. Gabriel. He's five—no, six. He's six, I think. Your file doesn't say anything about him?"

He took the yellow hand towel from her, refolded it, and hung it on the handle of the oven door, then pushed past her, preparing to leave.

"Unbelievable. Somebody better take some initiative and find out about the kid." Richard pointed, making clear that Carol Nessen was the somebody he had in mind. Turning to Lemko, he said, "If you want to do something for me, you can get me to the airport and get me on a plane to Dallas, and if you can't do that, then you can lock up because I'm going downstairs to catch a cab."

Lemko would have to write this up in his incident report to the general counsel, the justification for expensing the ride to the airport, the comped ticket to Dallas. Mostly, he'd have to explain why they hadn't known about the boy. Richard and Lemko sat in the back of the cab and did not speak. They rode in silence until Richard noticed the coat sitting across Lemko's lap, and took it from him, started playing with the black velvet collar. The coat fell open, and Lemko saw the tag: *This coat tailored especially for Lew MacMurray.* They did not talk, not even when they crossed the river and the ominous clouds began to unleash a heavy blanket of snow.

47

IT TOOK Nessen over ninety minutes of working the phones from Richard MacMurray's apartment desk to confirm that there indeed was a child, Gabriel Llewellyn Blumenthal, age six. The Dallas County Office of Family Protective Services was closed for the holiday, so phone calls went to the airline first, where a recheck of the ticket audit and a call to the airport Angel Team confirmed that the child had not been a passenger on Flight 503. The Angel Team at Salt Lake airport had called it in; the kid was in the care of a coworker of the deceased. Nessen scribbled notes, made more phone calls.

She managed to reach an FPS caseworker, who promised to locate a qualified court-appointed special advocate to retrieve the child and watch over him until the uncle arrived. Again Nessen referred to Richard by the phrase *only known living relative,* and the caseworker was relieved because, in the entire spectrum of emergency-custody cases, a sole surviving relative was perhaps the easiest to deal with. They understood what duties were now required of them.

The child wasn't in the system: no notices of neglect, no complaints to FPS. He presented no special needs, no history. The mother, at least the parts of her narrative that could be discerned from her presence in various databases (Division of Motor Vehicles, Harris County Traffic Court, even Internal Revenue—a call that was technically illegal but that the case-worker made anyway), was squeaky clean: no delinquencies, no outstanding traffic tickets or library fines, a solid credit score of 754, registered to vote at her current address, which was a garden apartment in a reasonably safe neighborhood.

Nessen kept having to thank people for getting involved on New Year's Day, for interrupting their afternoons of football, and each person she spoke with breathed the heavy sighs of the put-upon bureaucrat; each thought that the pay of a municipal employee was not nearly enough to justify holiday work, that they would never get those hours back. They moved into action only because they were parents themselves and a six-year-old was involved.

As Nessen told the caseworker, "We're putting the uncle on a plane now," she felt as though this was the most important duty of an Adam and Eve Team, to shepherd the relatives through their final obligations to the deceased.

The caseworker wanted to know, "What's the uncle like? Are there going to be any problems there?"

Nessen took the cordless phone with her into the kitchen, tore the doodles she had made while on hold into a series of long strips, and tossed them into Richard's garbage can. "I don't think so. He's a pretty solid guy."

"Solid? In what way?" the caseworker asked between smacks of her gum.

Nessen coughed. "As in 'employed.' 'Familiar.' His name is Richard MacMurray. You'll recognize him the minute you see him." She heard the caseworker's computer keyboard clicking in the background.

The caseworker laughed. "Oh, *that* guy. From television."

48

AMONG THE tariffs and wages in the latest collective-bargaining agreement, the customer-service personnel of Panorama Airlines had negotiated a clause, little noticed by management, that expanded the definition of holiday and double time, all while reducing the number of customer-service advocates (the term used in the contract to describe the polyester-blazered attendants who printed boarding passes and threw luggage onto the conveyor) on duty on a holiday evening. Just one red-jacketed employee stood at the gate, and when Lemko and Richard MacMurray approached, Lemko discreetly moved to the head of the line, told Richard to take a seat, that he'd handle everything.

Richard hadn't gotten two feet toward the chairs when a loitering passenger voiced his objection. "I guess waiting your turn doesn't apply to guys in suits."

Richard knew how Lemko would defuse the situation: by telling the saddest possible version of the truth, that the man over his shoulder (Richard saw Lemko indicate him with a slight jut of his chin) had just lost his sister, and that if no one else in line objected, Lemko was going to borrow this gate agent for five minutes to get Richard a boarding pass and to make sure someone was on the other end of the flight to greet him in Dallas and take him to the hotel reserved for victims' families.

Lemko spent five minutes explaining before stepping around behind the desk himself to type at the second terminal. The gate agent went back to waiting on the people in line, and as each subsequent passenger came to the counter, they pretended not to look at Richard. He was not just a familiar face from television; now he was the literal face of a plane crash. A survivor.

The man who had complained about being asked to wait took his itinerary and boarding pass, went back to the newsstand to make a few purchases, then came to Richard and extended his hand. And there was something about his demeanor, his approach, that suggested sincerity. He was a supplicant. Richard wanted to end the encounter and thought the quickest way was to stand up; his father's teaching again, reminding Richard in the voice of decades past how rude it was to shake hands sitting down, how rude it was to shake hands with gloves on. Richard realized that he'd never put on his coat, but also hadn't removed his gloves.

Among the many moments of this New Year's Day, here was one that neither Richard nor this passenger Samaritan would ever forget.

The man said, "I'm sorry for your loss."

Lemko walked over from the ticket desk, waving a handful of papers at Richard to get his attention, and Richard stepped away with a mumbled apology.

"We're not putting you on this flight," Lemko said. "Actually, there isn't going to be a flight."

"Mechanical problems?"

"We don't have a pilot. The aircraft arrived from Cincinnati, but the crew aboard is already too far into overtime to make the flight to Dallas."

As they walked toward the security entrance, Richard's face betrayed his anger. Lemko had expected this too. Emotions come to the surface faster, and with more violence, in the presence of stress. He was quoting that from somewhere in his training but could not cite the source.

In the terminal hallway, workers were removing silver garlands and snowflakes, those secular holiday symbols that public spaces depend on. In the newsstand, a turbaned woman was using a razor to scrape off the painted-on material that made the windows look like they were frosted over by snow and ice.

Without warning, Richard veered off into the men's room. Just inside the bathroom door was a two-chair shoeshine stand, the attendant nowhere in sight. His supplies and rags were still there. Bending down, Richard linked him to the brilliantly polished and thick-soled black work shoes visible in the first stall. The bathroom smelled well worn and close, the air heavily ammoniated. Burnt urine, Richard thought. All the sad intransigence of bus stations and train stations and seaside amusement parks with their broken attractions, the tea-cup ride at the Delaware shore where he'd vomited all over his sister's shoes, the stadiums he'd visited as a teenager that had long ago been torn down, his mother's soiled hospital linens and medicated lotions and alcohol wipes, all of his past was present in that smell. Richard couldn't think of anything else but bathrooms.

He needed to think, and in order to think, he needed quiet. He slipped into one of the shoeshine stand's polished chairs, and from the stall, the man said, "No more shines today." Richard was unable to answer, and the voice repeated itself, adding, "I'm done for the day. Going to go home and see my family for dinner." The man exited the stall and kept talking to Richard as he washed his hands. "Watch some football and, I'll be honest, drink a beer or three."

"Sounds nice," Richard said. "I could use an evening like that."

The shoeshine man stepped back to the stand, entered his catcher's crouch, and began packing up his polishes, sponges, brushes, and cloths. "You going to watch?"

"My sister was on that plane. The one that went down this afternoon."

There was a long silence. Then the man snapped a towel open and said, "Stay right there." He reached into his case and extracted a tin of black Kiwi polish, spat on the corner of a brush, and started working on Richard's shoes. "This one is on me. Can't have you showing up to home with shoes looking like that."

Richard managed, "Thank you." He shut his eyes for a moment, and when he opened them again, Lemko had entered the men's room and was tipping the shoeshine guy what looked like a ten-dollar bill.

Lemko said, "We've got you on the 9:40 a.m. flight, first class direct to Dallas." When Richard raised an eyebrow, he sputtered out a detailed but nervous explanation. "No pilot now means no flight at seven o'clock tonight. No flight at seven means the nine o'clock is overbooked by twenty percent, and even if I asked for volunteers, we wouldn't get any. I tried every other airline. We checked Dulles and Baltimore and even Richmond, but with the snow and the backup in traffic"—Lemko stopped and looked at his watch—"and the logistics problems caused by the incident, well, it just isn't going to happen tonight."

The shoeshine guy went back to packing up his kit. He unlocked the small locker next to his stand and started putting away his brushes and rags. "What the man here needs is someone to talk to. Times like these, you need to be with your family."

"Once we were four," Richard said.

The shoeshine man shook his head.

Lemko held out his cell phone. "Is there someone you'd like to call?"

There was no obvious call to make, no one left to be informed. *Only known living relative.* He knew then what he had always known, that the history of the telephone itself is a history of heartbreak.

Heartbreak from its very beginnings, as in the story of Elisha Gray, inventor, in his race with Alexander Graham Bell to perfect the "speaking telegraph." History paints a kind picture of Gray's archrival, ascribes to him noble motives; his wife having lost her hearing to scarlet fever at the age of five, Bell did what so many of us do in our daily lives: he dedicated himself to undoing the damage of the past.

The truth, as always, is more nuanced and complex. Bell was a curmudgeon, a notorious grouch. As a child, his experiments included provoking the family terrier into a constant growling state in an early attempt to induce speech. As an adult, he berated his celebrated assistant, the poor Watson, for his inability to carry a tune. It was the harmonics of singing that Bell thought could be most easily reproduced. Watson sang into Bell's conical microphones; he sang drinking songs and college anthems and ditties about wayward women and Civil War marching songs until his throat went raw from the effort.

Meanwhile, in Illinois, the person passed over by history toiled on his own inventions. Elisha Gray filed a notice of intent to patent his version of the telephone on February 14, 1876, saying in part: *Be it known that I, Elisha Gray, of Chicago, in the County of Cook, and State of Illinois, have invented a new art of transmitting vocal sounds telegraphically, of which the following is a specification: It is the object of my invention to transmit the tones of the human voice through a telegraphic circuit, and reproduce them at the receiving end of the line, so that actual conversations can be carried on by persons at long distances apart.*

Elisha Gray's notice was the thirty-ninth official document filed that day at the United States Patent and Trademark Office; Alexander Graham Bell's application for a full patent was fifth. History tells us about some apparent skullduggery—Bell's attorneys bribed or threatened the patent examiner, a vulnerable rake of an old man to whom $100 meant the eradication of his debts, and whiskey in endless rivers. Bell's patent contained explanations and diagrams that did not, and could not, work. His later filings featured drawings of an apparatus nearly identical to the one that appeared on Gray's application. Nonetheless, the details of these stories are lost to the erroneous wash of conflicting memories. It would be years before Watson would invent that convoluted story about Bell's clumsiness in the lab, the spilled bottle of acid that led to his pleading, *Watson, come quickly, I need you,* but the anecdote would provide exactly the type of humanizing narrative the telephone needed to succeed; the Bell Telephone Company and Gray's Western Union Telegraph Company sparred for years, with suits and countersuits, until Gray's name fell away from history, consigned to the scrap heap of crackpot claims and marginal contributions.

This lesson of heartbreak Richard MacMurray had already committed to memory.

There had been a phone call about his father.

There had been a phone call about his mother.

Richard rarely thought of the particulars of her death; she had lived out her days in Florida on Social Security, a lump-sum settlement from the federal government, and Lew MacMurray's congressional pension. She'd been fine one day, maybe it was a Monday, and by Thursday, her physician had found some polyps and wanted to schedule more invasive diagnostic procedures, and she was just too embarrassed to talk about it with her son or her daughter. A week later she'd been admitted to the emergency room in Pensacola with nonspecific bleeding, and he knew the end was rapidly approaching. Mary Beth couldn't decide whether or not to bring her husband, or even if she could take time off work, and, besides, it was a nearly ten-hour drive, and Richard was already at the hospital. He'd spent most of his mother's final hours talking on the phone to his sister, who kept promising to come when things stabilized a bit, assuming there would always be more time. But there wasn't more time, things never did stabilize, and Mary Beth arrived about twenty minutes after Richard had finally given up and allowed his mother's body to be taken from the room.

He had made all the final decisions, and his sister's only comment at the funeral had been, "Mom would be appalled to know that you put her in that dress." Richard had looked at his sister and hissed under his breath, "Well, she'll never fucking know, will she?" and then hadn't talked to Mary Beth again until the day she had called to tell him that she was pregnant.

He remembered the exact time of each of those phone calls (4:48 a.m. for his father, 5:30 a.m. for his mother), and, however coincidental it was, it seemed he could not look at a clock in the predawn hours without the time displaying one of those two moments exactly, as if the minutes between did not exist.

Lemko said again, "Surely there's someone you'd like to call."

49

CADENCE WOULD remember the phone call as the call that changed everything. She'd just walked in the door, where she was confronted with both the message light on her answering machine flashing its metronomic blink and the phone ringing its insistent digital chirp. She fought the temptation to let the call go to voicemail. The caller ID screen read LEMKO, BRADFORD R., a name she did not know, accompanied by a phone number and area code she did not recognize. The call couldn't be more uncomfortable than any other thing that she had done that day—like sit for almost three hours on an airplane next to a man she would almost certainly never see again—so she picked up the phone.

"I need to see you," Richard announced.

"Richard. I wasn't expecting you," Cadence said.

"I don't know anyone else I can talk to about this." His voice wavered, enough that he heard it himself, wondered if it made him sound weak.

And it was from his voice, the shake in it, its fluttering pitch, that Cadence took her cue. She felt obligated, at least somewhat. "Talk about what, Richard? What's happened?"

He recognized the repeated use of his first name as a device;

in our most intimate relationships, we use any excuse not to call someone by name. He'd called Cadence all sorts of things— Cate and Catey-Cat and Cat and just C.—when he wrote her notes, and he didn't much like Cadence using his first name; it sounded like he was being scolded.

"I need to tell you in person. You're going to have to have faith," he said, resisting the urge to use her name. "Can you come see me?" he asked, and knew immediately from her sharp intake of breath that she would refuse to come to his apartment precisely because it was his. "That isn't what I meant," he said, trying to preempt the argument that rested just under the surface of their conversation. She'd say something about how she wasn't going to go home with him, not under any circumstances, and he'd say whatever he could to avoid that part of the discussion. He worried that Cadence might hear the irritation in his voice. "I just need…" He stretched it out; how strong the urge was to blurt out what had happened, to just admit how strange everything had been in the past seven weeks, in the last several hours, but to admit it required more strength than he could muster. If there was one thing that could make this evening better, it would be the solace of Cadence, his familiar. The story of his life was getting bad news on the telephone, and he wasn't about to contribute to it now. "I need to see you."

Lemko and the shoeshine guy tried their level best to maintain a discreet distance, but the three of them were standing in a cramped men's room, so Richard just walked past them out into the terminal corridor and headed to the exit. Lemko fell in behind him, a good three steps back.

"I need you," Richard said. "I need help."

That, for Cadence, was enough.

She wouldn't meet him at his apartment, she said, and she did not have to explain to Richard the reasons why. "My place is a mess," she parried, as if anticipating his suggestion. "I'm repainting my end tables, and there are brushes and newspapers everywhere."

"I guess that leaves the Cleveland," he said. A favorite bar. A demilitarized zone almost exactly halfway between her apartment and his. It occurred to Richard that they'd spent the entirety of their time together floating around the city, going from event to event, happy hour to fund-raiser to concert to the Kennedy Center to cultural evenings at the Smithsonian. He wondered how many times they'd simply spent the evening inside, cooking dinner together, afterward lounging on the sofa while he absentmindedly rubbed her feet. Not often enough. He wanted nothing more than that kind of quiet now, a woman nestled against him, a dog at his feet. Gabriel.

"One hour," Cadence said, and hung up.

Lemko took his phone back from Richard, and they stopped in front of the next airport newsstand. "I've never understood why they sell luggage at airports," Lemko said, pointing at one of the open stores. He was desperate to lighten the mood. A combination of bureaucracy and a confluence of unimaginable events—a dead pilot, snow, another overworked crew, unusually heavy traffic to Dallas—had defeated him in his only task for the afternoon, which had been to see to Richard MacMurray's safe delivery to Texas.

Richard let him off the hook with an easy laugh. "For people who plan to do a lot of shopping."

"Maybe." Lemko handed Richard the papers he'd been toting around. "This is a boarding pass for tomorrow morning—9:40 departure, gate B25. There's a voucher in here for airport parking if you need it, and instructions on how to keep track of your expenses. And I want you to know that if you need anything, you can call me direct at these numbers." He produced a business card.

Richard started to leave, and Lemko grabbed him by the shoulder, turned him back around.

"Is there anything else I can do? Something I've overlooked? We can put you up at a hotel closer to the airport. I can send someone back to your apartment to pick up some things. Hell, we can sit down at the bar over there and have a drink."

Richard took the business card and tucked it into the inside pocket of his overcoat. He extended a hand, for what reason he was unsure, and Lemko took it as his absolution, shook it vigorously. Richard could see in the lawyer's face that he was deciding whether or not to pull him into a hug (despite the express prohibition of such personal interaction with a contact). He took his second hand and put it on top of their grip, keeping Lemko at a distance. "If I think of something, I'll let you know."

Lemko headed back toward security, and while Richard wanted very much to be out of his visual range, he instead found himself wandering into the newsstand. Meeting Cadence required at least some semblance of preparation. He grabbed a toothbrush and a travel-size tube of paste, some cinnamon-flavored gum. How much time had he spent at airports in the past four years? Were they all like this, incongruent? He'd landed in Florida somewhere at eight p.m. one night, and the only thing open had been the bars in the international terminal. Kansas City looked like Milwaukee, which looked like Memphis or maybe Nashville. The terminal in Bismarck, North Dakota, was built according to the same blueprints as the original terminal in Prague. Richard didn't know if he could face another airport. He was supposed to get on a 9:40 a.m. flight to Dallas, pick up a six-year-old boy who was essentially a stranger, and explain to him that his mother was dead and that he would be coming to live with Uncle Richie.

The woman at the register repeated herself—"Will there be anything else?"—and Richard walked over to the shelves displaying all the junky Washington DC memorabilia—Redskins T-shirts and miniature monuments and paperweights in a heavy plastic that were supposed to resemble the lead-crystal paperweights of the Capitol dome that congressmen sometimes gave as Christmas presents in the days before ABSCAM and the Congressional Post Office scandal and the check-kiting scandal and the scandal with the boy interns and the one with the girl interns. He saw the perfect gift. A miniature license plate. He'd given his nephew seventeen of them, one from each state he'd traveled to in the past few years, but somehow never a Washington DC plate, and there was one at the bottom of the first row that spelled out GABE—not GABRIEL, but it would have to do—and Richard added it to his purchases. He would not arrive in Dallas empty-handed.

50

POLICIES AND procedures meant that Carol Nessen and Brad Lemko were expected to produce a written narrative accounting for their whereabouts in fifteen-minute blocks; their report would identify shortcomings in the notification process and point to potential improvements. The general counsel, an obsequious little bastard named Gullett, had already warned Nessen to make her recommendations detailed and specific. His management style mimicked whatever business book was in vogue at the moment. She could imagine hearing him even as she made notes for her report: *Don't identify a problem unless you can identify its solution.* Nessen knew also that Gullett hated her because she was taller by a good six inches and had never worked airside, whereas Gullett took every opportunity to mention how he'd loaded baggage carts every summer of college.

Nessen hated Gullett because he covered her desk with inconsequential memos on policy and procedure, and because he wore his hair plastered to his head with Vitalis or VO5, some old-fashioned goop that smelled like the feet of senior citizens tarted up with lilac. And since the reports went to Gullett, it made sense to find Lemko, compare notes, agree on a strategy.

Lemko was Gullett's anointed successor, and if Nessen could get him to sign off on her ideas, she was golden too, if only by association.

With no standby pilot, a piece of defective equipment taken out of service in Cincinnati, and the East Coast bogged down under a winter storm stranding some 940 Panorama passengers in the Washington metropolitan area's three airports, a morning flight back to Dallas was a long shot. Seating preference would be given to passengers paying full fare, so Nessen made arrangements for them at a decently luxe hotel in Pentagon City, just a five-minute taxi ride to the airport.

By 9:00 p.m. Nessen had retrieved the rental car, left it with the hotel valet. Lemko had seen Richard MacMurray off in a taxi and taken the Metro to the hotel, where he waited in the lobby for his partner. He stood to greet her, and the bellman who wheeled in their two bags stopped a few feet away.

"Don't you even have a topcoat?" Nessen asked.

"In the bag there," Lemko said, pointing to his suitcase. "Going to join the fire department?" he asked, giving her yellow rubber footwear an obvious once-over.

"They're loaners from our friend the sergeant. Can't do the job without the proper equipment, he says. Besides"—Nessen held up a small plastic grocery bag—"my shoes are ruined. It's snowing. Note to self: more than one pair of shoes is required on each trip."

They handled the business of check-in and reconvened in the hotel's top-floor lounge. Nessen came loaded down with the policies-and-procedures binder and a laptop, looking entirely like a woman expecting to work.

"Wouldn't you rather deal with all that"—Lemko used a tilt of his head to indicate the notebook, the laptop, the report—"in the morning?"

"I want to hit it while it's fresh in my mind."

Lemko sighed. "I don't know that it will be any different. I keep thinking about how I'd explain what I did today to anyone who didn't work for us. 'What did you do at the office today, honey?'" he said in a pitch-perfect falsetto. "'I knocked on doors and told people that a person they loved was dead.'"

"How else should it work? You want to call them on the phone? Send a telegram? A priest and a pilot, like in those old war movies?"

"It's a horrible duty. You're brushing your teeth in the morning and thinking that you've got this two-day swing to Buffalo but you'll be back in time to drive little Benjy to soccer practice, and *wham!*" he said, his flat palm making a solid *thwack*ing sound in a tiny bit of condensation on the bar top.

Nessen was older and, as such, felt entitled to play the role of a grizzled veteran. "You did good work today. It won't feel like it, not for a while. But you have to trust that how *we* tell them is better than hearing it from the neighbor or watching it on television. If you can't do that, then at least you can sleep knowing you put a human face on the faceless corporation."

Lemko shrugged and gestured with his drink to the corner of the bar, where a duo—jazz guitar and stand-up bass—picked up their instruments. Nessen turned to watch them begin, hoping the music might offer some distraction. She was expecting a Christmas song for some reason, but they launched into something syrupy, a pop melody she couldn't place. She felt pressed up against the very limits of language itself; what more could she possibly tell Lemko to make him—to make herself—feel good about the job they had done? She wanted to forget about the contacts and her plans and get drunk and half-lost in her favorite songs. Instead the guitar player vamped between two chords, and she realized she was waiting for the vocals to begin but hadn't seen a microphone. The words were what had always been most important to her. The songs that transported her were always about the narrative. Now music that she had once loved, college-radio bands from Athens, Georgia, or the UK, floated in the background as she picked over organic produce at an upscale grocer's on her way home from work. The hope of the future, *four lads who shook the world,* reduced to Muzak.

Outside, the wind picked up, and she imagined the building moving with the slightest perceptible sway, the way certain skyscrapers did, the Sears Tower, World Trade. Snow clotted on the windowsills and blew past the picture windows, almost whiteout conditions, the storm and the lights of the city together casting the room in a soothing gray-blue glow.

She stood and leaned into Lemko a bit, took his hand and sandwiched it between hers. It did not mean anything other than a moment of connection. Later, alone in her room, she would think of how good it felt to touch someone—to touch a man—at the end of the day; she wanted to be lost in the sensation of strong fingers on her shoulders, her wrists, warm breath at the base of her neck.

"It's just too cold for me," Lemko said.

"What? My hands? The weather?" Nessen swallowed the last of her drink. She was leaving and didn't want to give the impression that her impulsive grab had been an invitation, tried to deliver the brightest, warmest smile she could muster.

"All of it. The city, the weather. Every damn thing."

51

DESPITE THE snow, the Metro was still running at a regular clip. Richard took the train from the airport, transferred once, and was at a table in the back room of the Full Cleveland within twenty minutes. The bar stood at the top of the service road that led local traffic into the Dantean confusion of Dupont Circle, and its clientele were almost completely removed from the world of politics that was Richard's orbit. It was a dive, and its patrons were failed musicians, chain-smoking graduate students, and young professionals just out of college who'd spent the fall learning how quickly the city consumed the paycheck of someone who worked in a nonprofit cubicle farm.

The taps at the Full Cleveland were filled with beers that had once belonged to the blue-collar man—Pabst and Ballantine—and the coolers were packed with tall-boy cans of Black Label and Schaefer, which Richard couldn't see without singing the jingle from the commercials of his childhood: *Schaefer is the one beer to have when you're having more than one.* His father had often come home from a Redskins game at RFK stinking of beer and singing that song, talking about how he and his boss, the congressman, had gone out for a few pops with the announcers from that game, Lindsay Nelson and Paul Hornung, Lombardi's own golden boy.

One fall afternoon, after a Redskins–Packers tilt, old Lindsay Nelson had taken a shine to Lew MacMurray, so much so that they had actually traded sport coats, Lew's Brooks Brothers navy hopsack for Lindsay Nelson's Hart Schaffner Marx Gold Trumpeter label in a cacophonous houndstooth of red, white, and black that would have been more appropriate as one of Bear Bryant's hats. Lew had worn that jacket with a white turtleneck and gray slacks to the stadium nearly every Sunday for the rest of his life. "This jacket was given to me by the voice of Notre Dame football himself," he liked to say, and from a good Irish Catholic, there could be no prouder statement.

It had been almost six hours since he'd eaten anything, and that was just a handful of peanuts at the Pilgrim Hotel bar. The smells from the Italian restaurant next door wafted in, reminding him of his hunger. Richard and Cadence had eaten maybe two dozen meals at that Italian place, evenings when inertia had dragged them into the welcoming comfort of the familiar. The restaurant was part of the city's legacy and made only two kinds of pizza, sausage and four cheese, and the red sauce, heavy with garlic and basil, was something Richard once thought he could eat every day of his life, but he'd never eaten there without Cadence. On one of their first dates, he'd stolen an ashtray—*Mamma Agnelli's Ristorante Italiano,* pink lettering on black ceramic; it now sat in the corner of his desk, a souvenir he could see traveling with him for a lifetime. Only now Cadence wasn't part of his day-to-day life, and he hadn't eaten at that restaurant in more than two months; a FOR LEASE sign had appeared in the building's front window.

With no conversation to distract him, Richard for the first

time noticed how much of a true drinkers' bar the Full Cleveland really was. Over the table was a chandelier on a dimmer switch, the arms of the fixture covered with a dark-gray fake fur that looked like the balls of dust and lint that collected under his bed. At the end of each of the eight arms, a bulb glowed a quiet pink-yellow that reminded Richard of the tubes of the old Magnavox console television from his parents' basement. He was lost in thought enough not to notice Cadence's approach to his tableside.

"That's where the polar bear head used to be," she said, pointing to an old wool pennant for the Toledo Mud Hens hanging diagonally above them.

Richard stood, and they gave each other a timid hug. He thought about kissing her on the cheek, a noncommittal move, but he hesitated, and Cadence used the moment to slide into the booth.

There was a twinge of weird there, a moment he was certain she felt too. In the early days of their dating, Richard used to insist on sitting on the same side of the booth with Cadence, something he never saw any other couple do. He wanted the same vantage point, the same frame of reference.

Cadence reached across the table and pulled a hair, one of hers, from Richard's white shirt. It was long and straight, the dark brown-black wire of the kind he used to find in his bathtub or on the floor of his bathroom. He wondered if it was vanity that she always wanted him to look perfect and presentable, or if it was a little reminder that she once possessed him, a way of asserting that she knew she could again. Maybe it was one of those Discovery Channel mating instincts, like rhesus monkeys grooming each other to remove lice and nits, or simply the last reflexology of a dying love.

"There," she said, sliding back in her seat. Richard noticed the definition of her lipstick, the same color as the burgundy-black vinyl that covered the seat of the booth, and took it to be a good sign.

"I'm perfect now. All fixed." He decided to play along. The conversation was going to be hard enough. Maybe after a drink, he'd relax.

"It's a start," she said.

Richard watched her hands fidget in her lap. Soon they would search out some other imperfection; perhaps she'd touch up her lipstick at the table or take a napkin and begin wiping the surface of the tabletop.

It was difficult for Richard not to blurt out all the news he had in a series of impulsive comments. *My sister is dead. I'm expected to fetch my nephew and bring him to live with me. Oh, and I have a new job, two hundred miles away.* Instead he indulged in the self-flagellation of nostalgia. He wanted to revisit all the high points of his relationship with Cadence, if only to reassert for himself that those lovely things had actually happened. Like the fixing. That impulse had been there in her from the very first. After crashing her shopping cart into the door of Richard's car, she had taken out a tissue and tried to wipe away the scratches. Ten days later, between their second and third dates, he had found Cadence on her knees in his parking garage with a can of rubbing compound and a tube of no. 70 Metallic Candy-Apple Red touch-up paint. He liked that she was willing to get her hands dirty.

It occurred to Richard that maybe he had been a reclamation project the whole time. There were new shirts, shoes, CDs, and thrift-shop knickknacks, like a Fiestaware vase for his apartment that Cadence kept filled with cut flowers. She fed him salad, even on the nights when he wanted nothing more than to restore himself with pepperoni pizza and a six-pack from the weird Greek-Italian-Mexican deli on the corner. They would go to a restaurant, and she'd talk gently about the many different varieties of fish, the benefits of omega-3 fatty acids.

Richard was nervous, but he stopped trying to censor himself and just started talking. "We came here on our second date."

"You tried to get me drunk."

The waitress came, and Richard ordered two beers. "How did I do? Was I successful?"

After a long gulp and a swallow of her water, Cadence said, "You twisted my arm." A satisfied smile expanded from the corners of her mouth.

Richard took her arm at the wrist and turned it a quarter clockwise, pantomiming that he might twist it further.

"That's exactly what you did," she said. "You twisted my arm. I was just happy you were touching me." She pushed some hair behind her left ear and raised her eyes to meet his.

"I missed that." Richard was still holding her, his fingers encircling her remarkably thin wrist, an autonomic response. When she looked down at his hand, he shyly released his grip.

"You missed a lot."

"I meant I wasn't sure you'd want me to touch you. I wasn't even sure it was a date," he said.

"What convinced you?"

The beers arrived, in frosted glasses, already dripping rings onto the tabletop. "When you straddled me on my couch, I was pretty sure," Richard said, and the departing waitress rolled her eyes toward her overdyed Bettie Page bangs. "I think that's how I finally figured it out."

He slid his fingers back into Cadence's, interlocking them like a child's mismatched plastic building blocks; they fit together, but something wasn't right, either the tension or the alignment, so he withdrew and used the same hand to pick up a napkin and move it around the tabletop. It left a wet sheen across the brown Formica like a Zamboni resurfacing a hockey rink. "It's really something," he started again. "You never expect to get to someplace like this. What are we even doing here?"

Cadence picked up the napkin Richard had wadded up, put it in the ashtray, and moved the ashtray to the edge of the table near the aisle. "We're having a beer. We're being friendly."

"How friendly are we going to be?"

Cadence smiled because this sounded like the usual innu-endo that passed between the two of them until seven weeks ago. "I'm not sure. Friendly, but perhaps not as friendly as we used to be, for example." She laughed.

The humor felt one-sided to Richard, like joking with the clerk at the DMV. There was no easy way to say what he needed to say about Mary Beth, about the ways in which his life had ir-retrievably changed in the past few hours. It seemed ridiculous to blurt it out and equally artificial to wait. For now, he chose silence.

"We are going to be friendly, right?" Cadence had her hands on her knees, as if she was ready to spring backward, up, out of the booth.

"And civilized."

She took a decent slug of beer and shook her head as she swallowed. "So what couldn't wait until tomorrow?"

He finished the last ounce of his first beer and thought about fleeing to the men's room. How he hated the telephone, but now he would have given anything to have blurted out the truth the hour before and avoided this moment. His stomach tight-ened, and he felt a sudden pressure in his temples as if he'd been squinting at a document riddled with fine print. All he could manage was, "It's my sister."

52

IN THE four days that she had been Gabriel's temporary care-
taker, Sarah Hensley had gotten used to summarizing his activities for his mother, shaping the routine events of the day
into a narrative that sounded as if his solitary efforts at play
had been great teachable moments. She had no reason to think
that this was anything other than an ordinary holiday. She was
watching the news, almost inadvertently, as a live shot of the
rescue equipment and floodlights that brightened the edge of
the airfield filled her screen. She'd been flipping channels, looking for something to pacify the kid, and now that she was
paying attention, she saw the chyron along the bottom of the
screen: 77 PASSENGERS AND 6 CREW. FLIGHT 503 WAS HEADING TO
DALLAS–FORT WORTH INTERNATIONAL AIRPORT FROM SALT LAKE
CITY. She checked her watch. How random. Mary Beth's flight
wouldn't be in for another two hours. She'd need to start the
daunting task of cleaning up the house but was having a hard
time getting motivated. She flipped past to another football
game. Gabriel played along, unimpressed.

Sarah sank into the couch to watch as Gabriel played with
Lincoln Logs and Legos, designed the imaginary skyline that

made up the cityscape of his mind; she watched as he built houses and office buildings and the secret lairs of millionaire superheroes, populated the mise-en-scène with the appropriate set of vehicles, and then swept it all to untimely destruction. Monsters from Tokyo Bay, tornadoes, and hurricanes.

Gabriel took a break to eat a repast richly loaded with trans fats and American processed-cheese food product, washed down by a fruit punch that contained no actual fruit juice. An inadvertent nap followed, wherein he slept for about ninety minutes while the party went on around him; Gabriel nodded off, leaning against the couch in the den, and Sarah carried him to the quiet retreat of his room, then eased into the bed next to him. Contorting herself around his body was a challenge, given the twin mattress. Gabriel pushed closer to the wall. Sarah spooned in, and when he awoke, they watched football. During the halftime report, Sarah switched the channel from an update about the crash of Panorama 503 to a channel in the middle of a *Looney Tunes* marathon. Gabriel sat transfixed by a cartoon in which the child was not a child at all but a Martian superbaby, misdelivered by the stork into the comforting custody of a suburban family; the cartoon boy built himself a flying saucer for his escape from earthly bonds, the return trip to Mars. "All he wants to do," Gabriel said, "is see his dad," clearly admiring the Martian boy (his name was Yob) and his single-minded purpose. Mary Beth had never spoken to Sarah about Gabriel's father, and neither had Gabriel, as if the word were absent from his vocabulary.

Soon after, the party dissolved in the usual way, one person leaving and many following. Sarah had not even noticed as the bulk of the crowd began to leave; a few girls she didn't really know had bagged up the plastic cups and paper plates, taken out bags of garbage. One of the other women from Mike's office still sat on the leather couch in the den, talking on the telephone with her legs folded beneath her, giving every appearance that she was moving in. Sarah went to clean the kitchen, where she found the counter still strewn with dishes of half-eaten snacks, congealed melted cheese, smears of ketchup and salsa and guacamole; a hubcap (she had no idea where it had come from) had been inverted and used as an ashtray, and she guessed there were more than a hundred cigarettes crushed out in it. The disposal's maw was stuffed with the snapped spines of limes. Pizza boxes covered the round table.

She put Gabriel to work finding bottles all over the house, promised him a nickel for each one, a trick she'd learned from her grandfather when she was about Gabriel's age. Sarah opened the garage door and carried out more garbage. Gabriel emerged from the den with his arms loaded down with brown bottles. A woman in a pantsuit that Sarah did not know stood behind him, and she bent to Gabriel's level and took the bottles from him one by one, placing them on the counter.

Sarah jutted out a hip, asked, "Can I help you?" A challenge. This wasn't a random partygoer.

The woman in the suit ignored Sarah and talked to Gabriel. "We're going to need to get your things together. Do you think you could help me do that?"

"I'm not supposed to go with strangers," Gabriel answered. He was well trained in this area. All men and women Gabriel did not know, anyone he had never seen in his house, they were all strangers.

Sarah stepped forward. "Do I need to call somebody? In other words, what are you doing in my kitchen?"

The woman in the suit picked up her briefcase, cleared off a small space on the kitchen counter, and opened it, produced a stack of documents. The answer was there in the papers, but the woman spoke anyway. "There's no need to call anyone. In fact, I have sheriff's deputies sitting in a squad car in the driveway. I'm hoping that it won't be necessary to involve them, that we can manage everything that we need to do here and keep our focus on the larger issues."

Sarah peered out the kitchen window to confirm that there was in fact a police interceptor sitting in the driveway, engine and signal lights running. Perhaps a neighbor had called the cops. Who knew? She told Gabriel to play in the den.

"You can put the TV back on. There are more cartoons," she said. He turned to leave, and Sarah noticed that he was still carrying two mostly empty bottles. She pointed, and the woman in the suit stopped Gabriel, took the bottles from him.

Sarah turned back. "And just what are the larger issues?"

"The best interests of the child, of course."

The perspective of the woman in the suit: the best interests of the child were easily determined by observation; the first step in protecting him would be to get him out of this house. That's what the deputies were for, in the event that any of the persons on the premises decided to interfere. The paperwork in her hand and a laminated identification card and badge gave her name as Maura Valle, court-appointed special advocate, and she was there to take temporary custody of Gabriel, oversee his transfer into foster care for the evening and ensure his appearance the following morning in family court, where presumably a surviving family member would appear before the judge. The name of the family member was there somewhere in the paperwork, but the crash had called her away from her own dinner table, and she hadn't really even had time to look over the temporary custody order for any other detail beyond the child's name.

Now, looking around the kitchen, Maura hoped that this

woman in front of her wasn't a blood relative, would have no claim to the child. The kitchen looked as if a party had been going on for the better part of a few days (true), and the young woman—wearing jeans unsnapped at the waist and a man's white T-shirt on top of a navy-blue bikini top—had all the appearances of being under the influence of alcohol and perhaps narcotics. Identifying the telltales of substance abuse was part of Maura's training too, but she did not need any expert help to know a sad scene when she wandered into one. Food moldered in open containers, the house smelled as if something had recently burned, and beneath the cluster of nauseating odors in the kitchen was something rank enough to make Maura keep looking around for a forgotten pet.

"The best interests of the child?" the young woman said. "I would think the best interests of the child will be covered once he goes back to his mother. She should be here"—she checked her watch—"before too much longer. Ninety minutes tops."

This was the worst part of the job, in Maura's experience, having to tell people things they didn't know. She often had to tell people their neighbors had reported them as potential abusers, that their stepdaughter had accused them of molestation. She knew it to be an exaggeration, but at that moment, she felt as if never once in six years of being a child advocate had she given someone good news, and now this woman clearly did not know. Maura was going to have to be the one to tell her.

"Could you tell me, please, how it is that you are acquainted with Mary Beth Blumenthal?" Maura asked.

"After you tell me how it's any of your business." Sarah returned to the busy work of cleaning the kitchen. She used the spray nozzle and began rinsing the sludge out of the sink.

"That is a card you don't want to play. Trust me. I've got a reason to ask. I'm going to need to see some identification."

Sarah found her purse among the countertop clutter and meekly handed over her driver's license. "I work with her. We work at the Mike Renfro Agency. This is Mike's house. Mike and MB are away for the holiday, and I'm watching her kid, but, like I said, I'm expecting her at any moment."

Maura looked at the floor. No one had told this woman, at least no one from the airline. The answer popped into her head. They would have no reason to tell Sarah. They would be looking for a spouse, a blood relative.

When Sarah said it, *I'm expecting her at any moment,* this bureaucrat in the kitchen refused to meet her eyes, and the lack of eye contact told her the enormity of it. Maura could see the series of deductions as they registered on Sarah's face, as her expression sagged with the demonstrable recognition that Mary Beth would not, in fact, walk through that door.

Gabriel returned to the kitchen carrying a stack of small plates, a handful of crumpled napkins. The two women went to him, and they both crouched in front of him, to his eye level. Maura knew that whatever words she could find to begin to explain the mysteries of death to a six-year-old boy would take away the unbridled brightness of childhood from his eyes, most likely forever.

Sarah thought, for her part, this was not her duty. Not what she signed up for. She let her legs go slack, sank to the floor. Jesus.

53

RICHARD HAD learned precious little from his past except that bad news needed to be delivered quickly, with a minimum of equivocation. Certainly she'd seen the news about the plane, Salt Lake City to Dallas. Just the facts. There had been a crash. His sister had been on the plane, but not his nephew. Cadence did not make Richard spell out the details. What more did she need to know, anyway? He'd given her the outline, thin on the specifics because he simply did not have any. Seventy-seven passengers and six crew. Tomorrow morning, Richard would get on a plane and fly to Dallas, and when he arrived, he would walk into his uncertain future.

Once she had said everything that a person was expected to say in these types of conversations, she found herself at a loss.

She felt encumbered by her body. It was something she didn't want at the moment. It interfered with her thinking. The comfort she felt in Richard's presence was a distraction. She loved the solid manliness that he presented—another thing she'd missed for the past seven weeks. He wasn't the kind of guy to pose, and he certainly wasn't going to shave his arms so he looked better at the gym. Still, she did not want to be thinking of his body, the comfort she took from being across from him. She hoped her being here would give him some peace. She wanted the crystallized thinking that came from adrenaline and movement and cold air in her lungs. She wanted to put her hands on Richard's face and see if she could intuit his thoughts, like a Vulcan mind meld.

Cadence felt his pain would be impossible to measure. He rarely talked about his sister except to identify her as the only other living member of his family, as if he often forgot entirely about his nephew. She was used to looking at Richard, and just from his face she could tell how serious the wound was, how invasive a treatment would be required. Now she had nothing for him, nothing except this body, and so she slipped out of her side of the booth and onto the seat beside Richard, and once she was there, he began to speak.

Her first thought was of the boy, and she did not even have to ask the question, because now, for the first time since she'd known him, his concern for the boy was primary and all-consuming, and she could see it.

"I'm going to Dallas tomorrow to get him. We'll have to do some things with lawyers, I guess; I don't know how these things work in Texas. I don't know how any of this will work. We'll get someone to pack up his things, and then I'm coming back. *We're* coming back. Jesus." She imagined that he was only now beginning to understand the duties that fell to him, not just the boy, but dealing with practical things, his sister's apartment, her clothes, her bills. Jesus.

She held his hand, ran her fingers over it. He kept on.

"Before Gabriel was born, I read those baby books, and I stayed with Mary Beth for two weeks. This one pamphlet they had at the hospital talked about all the things that needed to be secured, removed from your home, in preparation for the birth of a child. I just can't remember what things. I keep thinking that if I'd read each of those pamphlets, actually studied them, I'd be better prepared. My dad always said that you need to be prepared for every eventuality. But really, how can you be prepared for something like this? Something random. Who is his pediatrician? What does he like to eat? What is he afraid of? And then I look at my apartment and I wonder where he's even going to sleep. Shit, I don't even know what school district I live in. And suddenly that seems like something I need to know."

It was a daunting prospect, enough to merit a long silence punctuated by swigs of beer and one or both of them again mumbling *Jesus*.

Richard talked for nearly twenty minutes without interruption, a few highlights about his sister, the occasional story of a particular visit. "Sometimes it feels like all we ever did was go to restaurants and fight. There ought to be more to tell," Richard said.

He wasn't thinking about anything other than how he could muster the strength to say what he needed to say to Cadence; when her hands found his under the table, he realized she was content to wait until he discovered some way to say it, and she wouldn't permit an interruption. She dismissed the waitress by showing the palm of her hand.

"When my mother died," Cadence said, "I was in the middle of moving here. I'd just bought my first place, and it was supposed to be a celebration. I had friends waiting with champagne and pizza, and I was at my old apartment, on the phone with my father. He's telling me how I have to come home to Pennsylvania, and there are three men in my apartment tapping their feet and waiting for me to hang up so they can take the chair I was sitting in." Eons ago.

The waitress brought the check, and Cadence paid cash. "Do

you want to get something to eat?" she asked Richard. "At the very least get out of here? Have you eaten? It's always good to eat something." He answered each thing she said with an affirmative nod, and she pulled him toward the door.

Out on the avenue, traffic was stopped by a minor accident, a bus having broadsided a taxicab, apparently after sliding through the traffic light at very low speed. There did not seem to be much damage to the cab, and nothing was visibly wrong with the bus. The passengers milled around the sidewalk like they were in a church social hall on Sunday morning, pre-formed groups of two or three closing ranks to keep out strangers. But they seemed in good spirits, as if dancing in the falling snow.

Cadence and Richard stopped in front of a diner where they had eaten together often, ordinary dinners, late-night cravings for milk shakes, and morning-after breakfasts. At their first breakfast together, Cadence had slid the remainder of her hash browns onto Richard's plate without asking, and he was thinking of that moment, how effortlessly beautiful she looked with her hair balled up under a baseball hat, wearing his white T-shirt, everything about her perfect, down to the playful way she licked ketchup off the blade of her knife, and he knew at that moment he would keep that memory forever. Maybe that was his first inkling of falling for her, of falling in love, wanting the night to hurry up and be over so that he could watch her again, even just her usual, yogurt and fruit and one cup of coffee, black. That morning had smelled of spring, the fragrant blush of fruit blossoms that somehow settled on the city on a Saturday morning in late March.

"Here?" Richard asked, and moved to the door.

Cadence reached across her body to take him by the arm and pull him back into the flow of pedestrian traffic. "No, not here."

The crowd on the sidewalk forced them to walk single file, and before Richard realized where they were going, they were standing in the circular driveway of Cadence's building. She took out her keys, handed them to Richard, and fumbled in her purse for something else, saying, "Let's order in. We can talk upstairs. Spring rolls and chicken with lemongrass, maybe?"

"Garden rolls," Richard said.

"I never remember the difference."

The first time Richard set foot in Cadence's apartment was the day she moved in, when the weather had not yet fully committed to summer and a surprising thunderstorm brought bone-cold rains, as if it were still March. The night before the move, they had fought over something inconsequential, and Cadence had released Richard from his role in the day, told him not to bother, then enlisted an army of her friends to help with the rental van, the carrying of furniture. Richard decided to help anyway, but the heavy lifting was finished by the time he arrived. The shower in her bathroom was broken, the water pressure just a trickle; he bought a new diverter valve and whittled the afternoon away installing that and a new showerhead. After he finished, Cadence slipped into the shower and then leaned out of the bathroom, carefully hiding herself behind the door, to wave an invitation. Richard joined her, washed her hair, inscribing circles on her back with one of those nylon puffs that came with the body scrub she liked to use. They ordered pizza, watched a rerun of *Saturday Night Live*, and slept. The second time was seven months later, the night after Cadence had explained how things were not working out. She'd left Richard a telephone message, a short list of all the items she could remember leaving at his apartment (a pair of gloves, a hairbrush, and a blow-dryer, no mention of the Polaroids) that she wished returned. He'd shown up at her door with a small paper bag filled with her sundries and had been allowed inside long enough to accept the return of a handful of CDs, two books, and a neon-green fleece scarf; she handed the items over without even a perfunctory comment, as if they were artifacts from an era of agony.

This was the third time.

It occurred to him how strange it was that they'd spent most of their relationship at his apartment or in bars and restaurants.

Inside her apartment, Cadence turned on the hall light and excused herself to the bathroom. When she returned, she undid her ponytail, using her fingers to rake through her hair. She lit a pair of stocky candles on her glass-top coffee table and turned on the stereo, a classical piece Richard didn't recognize. She patted the couch, and Richard dutifully sat next to her.

"Can I get you anything?" she asked.

Richard said, "Maybe later. Nothing right now." He picked up a disposable lighter from the coffee table and flicked it maybe a dozen times before she took it out of his hand and put it on the corner table farthest from his reach.

She turned so that they were facing each other. Her legs were folded beneath her, and their knees grazed each other. "It's okay, it's just me," she said. "When are you leaving?"

"I've got a ticket for the morning. 9:40 a.m."

She searched for something consoling to say. "I'm just sorry you have to go through this by yourself."

"I've done a lot by myself in the last few weeks." She grimaced a bit, and Richard added, "I'm sorry."

"No. That's fair."

"I probably could find a nicer way to admit that I've missed you. But I have. I do."

"Of course. Me too." Their hands were touching.

Richard said, "I'm not quite ready to leave."

"I'm not kicking you out," she answered.

Richard reclined against the back of the couch, and Cadence came over to him, sat in his lap facing him, half on top of his body. He pushed some of her straying hairs behind her ear.

"I didn't think you were. But I don't want to leave, period. I was hoping I could stay." Cadence was quiet, and Richard started to say something more, whatever his anxious mind could come up with, but instead Cadence smiled and pressed her finger to his lips for a moment. Their faces were nearly together.

They kissed a few more times before Cadence stood and slipped her shirt over her head, then led Richard by the hand to her bedroom, where they fell together out of what Richard hoped wasn't habit, convenience, or, most of all, pity.

Cadence let herself collapse facedown onto the mattress; Richard straddled her, reached for her arm, gave it a gentle twist. But the angle was awkward and she yelped a little, so Richard eased up on the tension. She rolled over underneath him, laughing, and said, "If you're going to go for the pain, we might as well get out the handcuffs," and Richard smiled because this was a woman with whom he had shared just about every kind of bedroom adventure; he took her wrists together and raised her arms up over her head, moved in on her unprotected mouth and neck. He let go of her arms, and she eased out of her bra, pulled his shirt over his head without undoing the buttons.

Richard knew what was going to happen.

He knew what was going to happen because he was returning to familiar territory. There was no need for any posturing or ritual storytelling and especially not the negotiations that had reduced most of the sexual contact he'd had in the era between his divorce and Cadence to sad transactions. He liked that when he had told Cadence about his slight dominant streak, she'd only laughed and said, "Maybe because you are a man," and when he asked what she meant, she added, "It means that you like fucking."

Through her actions over time, Richard had learned to translate that discussion. It meant that Cadence enjoyed ceding control occasionally, which, given the mildness of his own proclivities, was enough. He'd suffered enough awkward and mechanical lovemaking for a lifetime. He always dreamed of being a libertine, but what he realized with Cadence was that he did not dream of opportunities missed or strange and exotic behaviors or newer and less inhibited partners. He dreamed of intimacy, of not just *doing* everything with Cadence, but of *telling* her everything as well.

Her mouth tasted of beer and bar nuts, and he swore he could discern the thin and inoffensive film of xylitol, the sweetener in her omnipresent sugarless gum. He was thinking of the past too, how in the first days of their relationship, lunch had meant sneaking home to frantically immerse himself in her, the kind of fucking performed by a man grateful for the opportunity, who still sees all things female as somewhat exotic and on the verge of extinction.

On a good day, they had ninety minutes. In that block they would manage to fuck, inhale some insubstantial snacks (he particularly enjoyed when Cadence's mouth tasted of a sliver of a Granny Smith apple smeared with peanut butter), and fuck again—the second time always more like a thrill ride, if only because Cadence could let go. Any of the residual shame that either of them felt, those mutual fears at letting out whatever secret things either desired, those passive and desultory ways in which lovers endure the uncomfortable, all of that was gone. Fucking her meant adrenaline, and there wasn't a bar across his lap to keep him from being ejected from the ride.

During intermission, he knew that Cadence would slide into the nook made by his shoulder and upper arm and, contented by the sound of his breathing, allow her hands free purchase across the expanse of his chest. He thought of it as a miracle—not that humans did these remarkable things to each other in the privacy of the dark, but that he in particular had been invited to participate in love's wild gift. He knew too the difference between men and boys and that to boys (or even to the childish version of himself that persisted well into his twenties), the eye always searched out any imperfection, sought to enumerate it, to add it to the list of potentially disqualifying attributes. Now that he was a man, he could say honestly that he relished imperfections; equally he knew that Cadence would never believe him if he attempted to articulate his appreciation. Richard chose to love the small scars on Cadence's breasts from a late-childhood battle with the chicken pox; he chose to love the tiniest archipelago of moles that arose in the center of her back, each no bigger than the stray dot made by a pen. He chose to love the irregular bumps around her areolas, and the hairs that found their way into his mouth, and the rough edges of her fingernails as they dug into his shoulders, and the way her left breast was maybe 5 percent bigger than the right; he loved every part and needed no further evidence of her body's exquisite and purposeful design than the way it felt in relation to his. He had learned these thrills early, in the era of concealed secrets of lingerie and the decadence of mussed hair and smeary mouths and the satisfaction of watching her return to her office wearing different underwear than she had worn that morning.

She had been an ambassador sent from a faraway land to

teach him how to be human again, and his greatest pleasure had not been skin on skin or even watching her ecstasies but the fabric of the intimacy they built; he loved how she could laugh and make love concurrently, and the way in which she used his boxer shorts to clean both of them after the act. He loved the long stray hairs that took purchase in every crevice of his body and that he found hours or sometimes days afterward, or even the way in which he made himself late for whatever appointments he had in the afternoon by the simple act of lacing his fingers behind his head and watching Cadence move around his apartment. What else was love if not the recognition that we were all deformed, scarred by our pasts, and chose to love each other anyway?

There was passion fueled by the added gas of grief.

He knows what is going to happen. He knows the way in which this woman's finger fits to his lips, telling him not to speak, because she has asked this of him before. He knows too the way her lips fit his, an embouchure with the gentlest suction and glide, and how preferable this particular sensation is to the sensation generated by the other women who have kissed him, or who have allowed themselves to be kissed. He knows this kiss because it has been repeated without number, because the uncountable repetitions coincide with the placement of her hand on his cheek.

Being present requires that Richard no longer think of himself and Cadence in the past tense, because he looks now at the immediate future, and the immediate future is the merging of their breath, the galvanic rhythm of the two of them together, his hands on her hips and the litheness with which she steps out of the remainder of her clothes, the shy fumblings and the more aggressive ones, the thrust and parry of fingers and, yes, the darting of tongues and the chime made by his brass belt buckle as it falls to the hardwood floor and the pleasing sound of his hands as they smooth across the shoulders of a woman who is incontrovertibly beautiful. Richard is grateful again, because he has arrived at the moment wherein the two of them cleave to each other in the darkness, steady hands and the ship no longer rudderless, this is safe harbor, and the voice in his head relents for once and does not need to speak, does not need to predict what will happen next, and when it is over, only Cadence will sleep, his Cadence, and the light is out.

54

SHE KNEW he would need reassurance. He was a lovely man and the best fuck she had ever known, and over a glass of wine she once told her closest girlfriend that what made Richard a great lover was that he knew the exact moments to make things all about himself. She used the word *lover,* and it felt pretentious coming out of her mouth; in so many ways she still felt like an awkward fifteen-year-old girl mustering the courage to reach for her boyfriend's fly. Richard knew when and how to take command of the moment, and that Cadence was aroused by that assertiveness even though it went against everything she had been taught; it wasn't the self-actualized message for which she, as a post-feminist career woman, was supposed to be a standard-bearer. Sometimes she liked to be *fucked,* and sometimes, she liked for the guy who had just fucked her to get up and leave.

Richard wasn't going to leave. He'd taken a beachhead here among the extra pillows, and God only knew where his other shoe had ended up, and now he wanted to talk about his sister, and Cadence felt she owed him an effort at conversation.

"It was nice, wasn't it?" Richard asked.

Cadence propped herself up on the pillows and pulled the sheet to her chin. Somehow she hadn't noticed his turning the light back on, but turning it off now meant getting out of bed and making the walk diagonally across her enormous bedroom, and she didn't want to face the cold, so she stayed put. "The whole thing? Very nice. Best in a long time," she said, and then winced at her own words.

Richard sped past the reference to other lovers. "Best in class. Best in show. It's good to know the talent is still able."

The talent. As in, *The talent is waiting in the green room.* The very language of the contract he'd signed for Don Keene earlier that afternoon. *Talent agrees to maintain a visible presence in the community. Talent agrees to maintain his weight in the prescribed range. Talent agrees that any material change to his physical appearance without the express written consent of station management shall constitute a breach of this agreement.* He still hadn't told her.

"The talent has always been blessed with certain abilities," Cadence said, and then decided to brave the cold and turn out the light. There were no coded messages in showing Richard her naked ass. She was still as embarrassed as a teenager at the way she inflamed men, Richard especially. On occasion, he liked to confess little things both vulgar and sexy; depending on her mood, they either gave her a racy and Taser-like charge that kicked her body into another level of arousal, or, more often, annoyed her into changing the subject. If nothing else, Richard had learned how to read her well enough to know when not to make the jokes.

As she walked to turn off the overhead light, she liked knowing that he was looking, that his eyes went to her legs. She stifled the urge to turn around or bend over or make little teasing and lascivious gestures with her tongue because the air of

Richard's grief had returned, expertly defusing the sexual charge she had been feeling.

The light was out.

"You're waiting for me to say something," she said.

Hearing her say it was like diving off a dock and into a frigid lake. Her voice had taken over his. How to explain such a frightening prospect? She nestled against his shoulder and wrapped one leg over his for warmth. Richard wanted the room to fill with sound, any sound but that of their voices. He rummaged in the sheets for the TV remote, and the set snapped on to images of the crash, *amateur footage from earlier today of Panorama Airlines Flight 503, which crashed on approach…*, and Cadence reached over to take the remote from him and turn off the set.

"I swear, if you tell me that everything is going to be fine, I'll be sick."

"It's a ridiculous thing to say," Cadence admitted, "but I'm obligated to, contractually."

"I hope all this"—Richard patted the bed—"wasn't out of some sense of duty."

Cadence took her leg off his and rolled onto her back with a loud exhalation that Richard translated as *Jesus Christ*.

"Sorry," he said. "It's been a hard day. Hard to even remember what's normal. I don't know what's expected of me except that in the morning, I'm expected to fly to Dallas and pick up a six-year-old kid who by some accident of birth is my nephew but is in reality nothing more than a short stranger, and by the time the return flight touches down, we're supposed to have bonded. Instant father."

Cadence raised herself up on two pillows, and Richard slid closer to her, wrapped his leg on top of hers, and held on. She said, "You're going to be just fine, and when you aren't, you're going to learn that it's okay to ask for help. Plenty of people will help if you just ask."

"I need help," Richard said. He liked the sound of it in his mouth, so he said it again.

"You can teach Gabriel all sorts of things. Man things. The difference between thirty-weight and forty-weight motor oil. Never to order a steak well done. How to shave around the cleft of his chin. When a team should hit and run. How to slide into second base. When to use a fairway wood. How to check the air pressure in the tires of his first car. How to place a bet. When to double down at blackjack. How to put that little dimple in his tie. He can be a mini-you. In summer, you can take him camping and teach him how to tell the difference between a harmless snake and a poisonous one."

"Who's going to teach me that shit? What is the difference?"

"It has something to do with where the eyes are on the head. I've never really understood."

Richard physically felt the challenge of the next few years. It emerged as a tightness in his musculature, and he absentmindedly grabbed at his neck while he talked. "I'd just like to know how everything is going to turn out in the end."

"Sit up," Cadence said, and she took over rubbing Richard's shoulders. "It doesn't work that way."

"Children might as well be invaders from another planet."

"You and Ellen never wanted children?"

He could tell she expected him to say yes based on the proportionate increase in the pressure she was applying to his knotted trapezius. How he hated to talk about his ex-wife in front of Cadence, if only because Cadence had always been greedy for details. She wanted to know what they'd fought about, how they'd made up, where they used to live, whether or not Richard considered himself a good husband or had managed to stay faithful, even whether or not Ellen had been a good fuck and a good wife and if she'd liked to suck his cock on long drives or show up at his office with no panties on beneath her summer dress. Cadence could retell every detail of every relationship she'd ever been in with cold precision. To Richard, telling Cadence about the life that he and Ellen had lived had seemed like one last betrayal of his ex.

"We'd go for a walk around the neighborhood, maybe to Dupont Circle, and stop for coffee. We'd sit at the corner tables at this café over by the Scientology building and watch the young families go by. I'd look and think I was seeing my future. But then some couple would roll up with their new baby, the kid in a stroller that cost more than my rent. Ellen always looked at those kids and sneered and said, 'I'd never want that. It's like having a parasite take purchase in your body,' and she'd end it with this little theatrical shiver. It was hard to even suggest sex after that."

"But you wanted a kid, yes? You saw the allure."

"I'd see a father lift a kid high over his head, and I'd think only about that kid's face, half laughter and half terror. And I'd think about how I had no memories of anything like that from my own childhood. None. I can't recall anything I did with my father."

"Never tossed a baseball? No family vacations?"

"Do you know what my family did for vacation? We'd rent a house at Rehoboth Beach, and he'd pack the backseat of the car with exciting reading material like the conference report on the Consolidated Omnibus Budget Act of ninenteen-seventy-whatever. While I swam by myself, my mother slept off the drinks from the night before and my father waded out into the ocean up to his knees and read stuff for work. Some kids could tell you who played right field for the Orioles. I could tell you the names of all the minority counsels for the House Judiciary Committee."

"That's not really a marketable job skill for a ten-year-old," Cadence said.

"I was never ten. Anything normal kids did, I missed. I grew up in the city, and all my friends and their parents disappeared to the suburbs, poster children for white flight. I missed out on all of it, lightning bugs in a jar and setting ants on fire with a magnifying glass, soft-serve ice cream, dogs named Clyde, candy cigarettes, going to the beach on the spur of a moment with a $1.49 Styrofoam cooler. I missed it all."

Cadence's face brightened with a wide smile, the kind that came with a specific memory. "We did that. Before my mom died. Styrofoam cooler and two bags of ice and about twenty different sandwiches, potato chips. We'd go to Wildwood for the day, and at sunset, we'd all ride the roller coaster. One of those old rickety wooden ones that tilted side to side in the wind." Somewhere during her story, she stopped rubbing his shoulders. Richard fell back into the bed, and she snuggled up beside him.

He said, "If we went to an amusement park, it would just be me and my dad, and he'd find a pay phone somewhere and an excuse to call the office about something, and I'd end up riding the roller coaster next to a stranger."

"You got to go, at least. That has to be worth something," Cadence said. "There has to be one pleasant memory in there."

"Oh, sure. Skee-Ball. Afternoons at the beach when it rained. Lew would hand over a roll of dimes. That's how long ago this was—each game cost a dime. I'd play hours of Skee-Ball, and Dad would sit under the awning on the boardwalk and smoke a Hav-a-Tampa. At the end of the week, I'd have a million tickets, and Dad would find some downtrodden-looking kid at the arcade and make me give them to him." Richard was aware that he sounded greedy, petulant, so he smiled his way through the last half of it.

"It doesn't exactly sound traumatic. How good were the prizes, anyway?"

"Like a pot of gold. Squirt guns. Itching powder. Baseball cards. Invisible-ink pens. Those snap-pop things that blew up when you threw them on the ground. Toy handcuffs. The Chinese finger torture. Plastic sharks and plastic army men. A yardstick made entirely out of bubble gum."

The only light in the room, the pale blue wash of the television, flickered to black at the end of a commercial. When the news resumed, Richard looked up long enough to recognize the footage of the crash, its broadcast loop starting again. He shook his head, turned away from the TV. "I don't even know what kids do these days."

"They do what kids have always done. Tell me, counselor. What kind of father will you be?" she asked.

Richard was proud for having anticipated the question, the way a good lawyer should. What Cadence really wanted to know was, Can you be reliable? Can you get out of bed at four in the morning to fetch Gabriel a glass of water in a spill-proof plastic cup imprinted with scenes of superheroes and cartoonish reptiles? Can you take his temperature? Can you provide three meals a day, complete with fresh fruit and vegetables? Can you make time for father-son picnics, after-school conferences, emergency room visits, movies on Saturday afternoon, carpools to and from everything? Can you remember the orange slices for soccer practice and the cookies for the Christmas party and the dozen miniature cards and tiny candy hearts for the girls in his class on Valentine's Day?

Richard wanted to give the kid a normal childhood, and he wanted Gabriel to know he would always stick up for him in a spat with his fifth-grade teacher. He wanted Gabriel to have what he hadn't, tennis lessons and sleepaway camp and lake swimming. He could coach Gabriel's Little League team. That all sounded normal. Normal meant skinned knees and minor accidents that resulted in stitches, bee stings and chigger bites, seventh-grade make-out parties and car dates and getting so drunk you get sick the first weekend away at college. That was what Cadence had done, only she often claimed not to remember it. Her childhood was a secret buried out in the backyard, and she hated to dig it up, portioned it out in rations. He knew she was making an effort here for his sake.

Richard wanted to tell her that he loved her, past and present tense, that she belonged where she was. Her left hand fell in the center of his chest and absently played with his chest hair, and though he had always been vaguely ashamed at the amount of fur there, she pulled it through her fingers and stroked it against the grain and smoothed it back down enough for him to know that it was not a nervous tic but a gesture of affection. What more could he ask than that, he thought, the eye or the hand that saw his imperfections and decided for whatever reasons—expediency or closeness, passion or the simple fear of being alone—to love him anyway.

She tapped him twice on the chest, a sign that she actually expected an answer to her question.

"What kind of father do I want to be? One that tries. Hard."

Cadence lingered in the bathroom, dawdling in front of the mirror. She wanted to tend to her upkeep, to floss her teeth and use the makeup mirror to direct a surgical strike on blackheads, her eyebrows. She wondered how long she could stay in the bathroom, how long she could avoid opening the door to Richard's sadness. Too much of her adult life had taught her what sadness looked like: it looked like her father's prescription bottles filling the top shelf of a medicine cabinet, his weekly pill trays whose plastic compartments overflowed with a cornucopia of meds—drugs for hypertension and high cholesterol, diuretics, blood thinners, Proscar, B-complex pills, and vitamin-E capsules, gelatinous and golden—that smelled to Cadence of hospital beds and urine.

She'd been waiting for the thunderclap, some grand announcement that she was on the right path instead of just committing herself to one option or another. Work meant a hotel and a minibar and a series of allegedly guiltless assignations with someone whose loneliness was as tangible as hers. Her judgment, which she had once thought unassailable, had led her in what she saw now as a big fucking circle, and now she stood in her own bathroom washing off the semen of a man she'd never thought she'd sleep with again.

He was a fixture, as prominent as a piece of furniture. He belonged.

And it was time to say something, time to admit it. She returned to the bedroom, and there he was, riveted to the screen again, because he wanted answers too. He had a natural inclination. He looked at the television and then at her and then back at the television, and if for no other reason than that she was afraid she might be in love, Cadence said, "I need you to do something for me." He raised an eyebrow in response, and she snapped the overhead light on. "We are not watching that again. Absolutely not," she said, and Richard knew her well enough to wait for the alternative she undoubtedly was about to propose.

She started rummaging in her bedroom closet; when she moved in, she had removed the closet door and replaced it with a beaded curtain, which at the time had seemed charming, a little personal stamp on an otherwise generic condo. Now, in the late night, it looked childish, and the clacking plastic beads were nothing but an irritant. She turned the closet light out and told Richard, "Turn around."

"I'm in bed. Where am I turning around to?"

She laughed. "Cover your eyes, then. Okay, now you can look."

She knew him well enough to realize that he half-expected lingerie, some erotic costume, but instead Cadence emerged clad in black ski pants, a down parka in a brilliant silver nylon, her head topped with a knit hat that peaked in a giant felt pom-pom of a bright tomato red.

"Very nice," Richard said. "I had a hat like that as a kid. Mine had a Washington Redskins patch on the forehead. What exactly are we doing?"

"Get your coat," Cadence said. "We're going to remind you how to be a kid."

55

IN A hotel located between terminals at the DFW airport, six-year-old Gabriel and his temporary guardian, Maura Valle, tried to make the best of it. She'd lied to the boy at least three times; they were going to meet his mother's plane, she would be late, she would be home tomorrow. She couldn't imagine lifting the psychic weight that it would take to tell him the truth. The evening felt driven entirely by her guilt. She let him order dinner from room service; she'd worry about who was paying tomorrow, and if it came out of her pocket, it would be the price she had to pay for her lack of courage and her well-intentioned lies.

While Maura made phone calls to various executives at Panorama Airlines, establishing that there was indeed a responsible party (the boy's uncle) and that he would be arriving in the morning, Gabriel flipped through the channels, at least twice skipping beyond footage of his mother's crash. Maura took the remote, brought up some animated film from the pay-per-view movies; Gabriel collapsed into one of the two queen-size beds and pronounced his judgment: "That's kid stuff."

She picked up the phone and dialed the number that had been forwarded to her by one of the angel teams, the home number for the boy's uncle. Three hours' worth of phone calls in fifteen-minute intervals, and she'd gotten the same recording each time: "You have reached the voice mailbox for Richard MacMurray. If you are calling about an on-camera appearance, please leave a number that is available after hours, and I will return the call as soon as possible."

She hadn't left a message. She would call, and keep calling, until he answered. Some things should be said only from one human being to another.

She knew too that feeling was hypocritical. She couldn't find a way to say it to the boy. Maybe it would be easier to explain in the morning, the both of them well rested. Easier still would be to wait until the boy's uncle arrived, but that seemed callous. She knew she'd already made mistakes here, enough that she felt frozen, unable to act.

Maura managed to suggest that he brush his teeth, then put on the pajamas that she'd salvaged from the mess in Mike's guest room.

"It's time to get ready for bed," she gently reminded him. Gabriel had a certain deferential quality, hadn't once questioned her authority or why someone who was effectively a stranger had shuffled him off to a nice hotel. She'd blown off his questions at Mike's house, and he'd been mostly silent during the forty-minute drive to the airport. After she'd decided to stop lying to the boy, all she'd volunteered was that his uncle was coming to visit. She was still working out how to broach the subject. She'd read reams of stuff, the best practical advice on grief, on talking about death with children, and now the entirety of it ran together in her head, a well-meaning muddle. She'd seen other court-appointed guardians struggle with this stuff in the past; that was to be expected. The heartbreaking part usually came later, some remark that showed how the child did not understand the permanence of what had happened. An orphan girl she'd chaperoned for a week kept repeating that her father had gone to sleep and would be up soon; Maura kept thinking how so many of us approached any conversation about death solely with euphemisms, trying to sneak up on the subject. The doctors were the worst. Ever since she'd worked in child protective services, she'd never known a doctor to use the words *dead, death, dying.* They would walk out of the operating theater still draped in their sterile smock, saying, "We tried heroic measures." But to have a hero, you had to have a victory.

She did not know for certain how long she'd been in that reverie, only that Gabriel had returned from the bathroom and was standing in front of the television, his toothbrush in his hand, and had changed the channel to FBN and its continuous live coverage. *A plane en route to Dallas from Salt Lake City, which earlier this afternoon crashed on approach.* There were only so many ways you could say the basic facts. It looked to Maura as if each of the repeated details drew the child a step closer to the screen. The part that Maura would always remember, even more than the sight of the boy running across the terminal to his uncle the following morning, was his hand, in this moment; it dropped from his mouth to his waist, then slowly to its full extension, down, and the toothbrush tumbled out of his grip onto the hotel room's carpeted floor.

56

It is a kind of delicious cheating to flip ahead, to know how everything turns out; to read the last page is to learn exactly how inevitable the events are in a particular story. But the *idea* of an ending as inevitable is less than modern. It is quaint and disquieting in all the most pejorative ways. Said another way, the neat ending is directly contrary to the massive disorder of life.

Bob Denovo, Heavy Metal Bob, walked out of the Salt Lake City airport on New Year's Day and never returned, not even for his final paycheck. Without bothering to gather the few items in his almost-barren apartment, he withdrew what little he had from the bank and drove through the high desert into Wyoming and kept heading north. He entered Manitoba on the afternoon of January 3. Today he works illegally as a short-order cook at a Greek diner in Winnipeg, where the owners pay him in cash under the table.

Funeral services for Captain Grady Williston, fifty-five, of Westlake, Texas, were held on January 7; federal investigators would keep his remains embargoed for forensic investigation for several months' time, which meant that the centerpiece of his viewing was an empty casket. At the Elder Brothers Mortuary—whose promotional materials include a quarter-page Yellow Pages advertisement with the disclaimer *not to be confused with the original Elder Brothers Mortuary*—the funeral director provided the casket as a prop for the material benefit of the widow and the dead pilot's friends and colleagues. Two other captains made repeated trips out of the viewing, to the lobby, to discreetly take telephone calls placing them in charge of the flights scheduled for Captain Williston for the next fourteen days.

Mike Renfro ordered his office closed for the foreseeable future, and then, because he was first and foremost an insurance man, realized that the progression of loss that created the need for insurance would not stop just to make accommodations for his grief, so he rescinded the order. Closing the office was like trying to fight the very notion of what it meant to be human.

He arrived home after his overnight drive to Dallas, expecting to find Gabriel and Sarah; instead, a cleaning lady he did not know was on her hands and knees in the kitchen, and Gabriel was on his way to the airport to be reunited with his uncle. He woke Sarah with an early-morning call, wherein she provided the name of a child advocate and a number for someone at the family court. Mike thought of getting back into the car and driving to the airport, but what would he do once he got there? His duty was to Mary Beth, and by extension that meant some obligations to her son. But Gabriel wasn't *his* son, a point that even a six-year-old could make with a surgeon's precision. Mike could see no way to impose himself into Gabriel's life that didn't require lawyers and hearings and social workers, hours of paperwork, sworn depositions. Perhaps his duties had ended with the crash; he had spent his adult life selling people the idea of security, and that was the word that came to mind when he understood what it was that he could do for the boy. He could provide security. Instead of a harried trip to the airport, he decided he could take action. He busied himself with the details of creating a tuition fund for Gabriel, filling out the paperwork, making sure he had the liquidity to start it with a large cash contribution.

After a week in Dallas, he did, however, return to Utah to view a few possible homesteads. He checked back into the same hotel in Salt Lake and took his dinners at the Canyon Room Tavern and Grill, where he kept looking for Ash the bartender and Sherri the waitress, his well-qualified leads. The new girl behind the bar did not know either of them by name. But on the third night, as Mike tried to muster some newfound enthusiasm for his overdressed salad, he asked a manager what happened to Ash the bartender, and the manager simply said, "503," the state-sponsored shorthand for the crash.

Each evening, he would check in with the office via telephone, and each evening, Sarah Hensley would ask him when he was coming back; signatures were requested and required. But Mary Beth had years ago thought to have a stamp made with a facsimile of Michael David Renfro's signature, and as long as there were Speedy Ink rollers and pads, his signature could pay the bills and endorse checks and write payroll. Once he'd heard of Ash's death, Mike avoided the grill and took to his bed, ordering three or even four meals a day from room service, watching reruns of television series that were two decades old.

In one serial drama about a law firm, the name partner had died, and the junior partners staked their claim to the corner office even before passing the hat for a nice display of carnations whose ribbon spelled out *Beloved leader, mentor, and friend.* He realized there would be no wreath for Mary Beth, no ribbon; Mike would ask one of the girls to clean out the personal items from Mary Beth's desk, and the girl (it would be Sarah Hensley) would find in the rear corner of the top drawer two pieces of saltwater taffy, desiccated and fossilized, their wax wrapping paper knotted together at the ends. Sarah was enough of a romantic to recognize a souvenir when she saw one; she slipped the taffy into her pocket, and later, it took up residence in her desk. In a little more than five months, after a discreet period of mourning, Sarah Hensley was promoted to office manager of the Renfro Agency and moved into Mary Beth's old office.

Howdy Ard got a literary agent and with her help wrote a book proposal, which turned into a book called *The Chief: Leadership for Tomorrow's Crisis*. It saw mediocre sales and spawned another book with even fewer readers.

After a brief hearing that occurred in her absence, Sherri Ashburton was named the sole beneficiary of her mother-in-law Geneva's estate. Geneva died of complications from the pneumonia that set in just a week after her hip surgery. She was buried next to her husband in the family plot, and a headstone was added to represent the body of her deceased son Warren. His seat had been in the part of the plane that had been engulfed in the fireball, and Sherri chose not to go through the charade or the expense of burying an empty casket some fourteen hundred miles from where she lived. One afternoon she took a pair of her husband's jeans and doused them in lighter fluid and burned them in the chamber of an old Weber grill that Ash had purchased at a yard sale the summer before; she scraped the ashes into a small metal can that had once held some English toffee and kept the can in her closet.

Eighteen months after the crash of Panorama 503, the National Transportation Safety Board's forensic reconstruction of the incident would appear in executive summary, omitting the unnecessary statistics such as airspeed and pitch angle, and providing the story of the death of seventy-seven passengers and six crew, as follows:

The aircraft leveled off at 11,000 feet and rolled out of a fifteen-degree left turn, gear still retracted, autopilot and auto-throttle systems engaged. The aircraft entered the wake vortex of a Delta Airlines MD-80 that preceded it by approximately forty seconds. Over the next three seconds, the aircraft rolled left to approximately eighteen degrees of bank. The autopilot attempted to initiate a roll back to the right as the aircraft entered a wake vortex core, resulting in two loud "thumps." The first officer then manually overrode the autopilot by putting in a large right-wheel command, yet the airplane never reached a wings-level altitude. At 14:03:01, the aircraft's heading slewed suddenly and dramatically to the left (full left-rudder deflection). The aircraft began to oscillate in pitch. The aircraft pitched down, continuing to roll. Gaps in instrument data were inconsequential, likely caused by onboard power fluctuations. Performance of the craft during the incident was verified by amateur videotape of the crash. At 14:03:07, the descent rate reached 3,600 feet per minute. At this point, the aircraft stalled. Left roll and yaw continued, and the aircraft rolled through inverted flight. A compressor disk likely disintegrated, rupturing fuel, oil, and hydraulic lines. The nose reached ninety degrees down, less than a half mile above the ground. The plane descended fast and impacted the ground nose first.

Likely cause: A manufacturing defect, complicated by failure to perform both routine and emergency maintenance.

57

FOR YEARS, the boy will dream of his mother.

In those dreams, she is young, filled with an illusory beauty. She is part of landscapes that Gabriel Blumenthal finds no way to describe in his waking life. He has few true memories of her. Instead he has the tangential planes where memory intersects with subconscious hope; his own desire for a well-ordered ending suggests that being orphaned is a burden, which of course it is, but the largest part of Gabriel's burden will be these dreams.

In each, his mother is vibrant and very much alive. He has grafted images of her from photographs into surrealist tableaus. On the few occasions when he encounters adults who knew his mother, he will ask them to share their memories of her, a ritual that he eventually stops in his teens, saddened by the inconsequential nature of what these strangers recall: *She was nice, She had very straight teeth, She didn't like white bread, She hated the Doobie Brothers, She kept the office humming right along.*

The functional details of his life: As an older preteen, he will play a competent small forward in rec-league basketball. He will hit the floor with abandon in pursuit of loose balls, work tirelessly on the off-hand dribble and on maintaining good defensive position, spend hours shooting the same shot over and over, in the quest to develop a decent touch on his jumper from the left-hand corner. He'll box out for rebounds and deftly follow his shot to the offensive glass. He'll shoot free throws at a near 90 percent clip. He'll play a steady if unspectacular second base from T-ball through Little League and on to Babe Ruth; he'll learn the art of the drag bunt and hit for high average, but in high school, he'll ride the bench for only a year. He will begin to seek his escape in comics and graphic novels in which the world of morality, though still murky and situational, is far more clearly defined than the confusing world in which he lives.

Gabriel suffers the serial angst of adolescence and the embarrassments of eighth-grade gym; the pleasures of furtive kissing in a basement closet will elude him, but instead he will find happiness in the discovery of music, namely the recordings of bands that speak to his sense of alienation and displacement. Secure in his place, the older Gabriel will favor solitary pursuits.

His uncle will teach him the strategies and offenses of competitive chess and the joy found in a library of hundreds of books. Richard will convert the basement of his home into a makeshift gymnasium with free weights and exercise mats and a stationary bicycle as part of his own last-ditch effort at self-improvement, but it will become more Gabriel's equipment than anyone else's. Gabriel will get the rest of his exercise as a long-distance runner. By seventeen, he will be a letterman on his high school track team, a threat at the five-thousand- and ten-thousand-meter distances. Running will be the only place where he finds comfort in his surroundings, the place where his breathing, his own rhythm and function, become part of the natural order of things. The teenaged Gabriel will spend his quiet hours alternately doing his road work or hiding behind the closed doors of his bedroom, practicing diligently on the electric bass guitar, becoming competent enough to mimic the wandering bass lines of Jack Bruce, the pentatonic rumblings of Paul McCartney. He'll take hours to do this, playing the complications of "Crossroads" until his fingers can keep up with the Clapton-is-God-era picking. Gabriel will not join in bands or casual basement jam sessions; he will not ever perform in public. In other words, if you need a clinical assessment: he is going to grow up; he'll become a teenager; he is going to be fine.

58

THE WINTER prayers of schoolchildren are limited in their ambitions, invested only in the idea of school closings, unconcerned with the consequences of squalls that lock in traffic for days, the historic conflation of a pair of Atlantic low-pressure systems stalling over the eastern seaboard, the kind that bring blizzard conditions and a record three inches of snow per hour. The local eleven o'clock news reported tomorrow's cancellations—banks, libraries, recreation centers, shopping malls, all closed—as the lead stories. The city obligingly ground to a halt.

The solitary light from a news camera illuminated the intersection where Richard and Cadence walked. The cameraman was a freelancer who sometimes worked for FBN, and he knew Richard by sight, waved and shouted his last name. He turned the attached external light on Richard and shot a few seconds of footage, Richard taking a quartet of short and choppy steps before sliding across the packed snow in the middle of the street. He kept the camera on as Richard and Cadence tossed small, puffy snowballs at each other, Cadence's first throw striking Richard in the upper chest, the cameraman catching the powdery explosion on tape, lit by the battery-fueled spotlight and by the yellowish sulfur of a decades-old streetlamp, the two competing lights giving the evening an almost buttery glow—followed by Richard's sudden lurch sideways to avoid Cadence's second missile, then his laugh, the openmouthed and uninhibited roar of it.

Nearly midnight now, a Metrobus eased down the hill, riding its brakes and knifing gently sideways, barely in control. At the bottom of the hill, it slid in front of Richard, blocking the cameraman's view. The bus was trailed south by a cabal of young Salvadoran kids on foot, some of whom were seeing snow for the first time. A handful of unsupervised rogues strolled up and down the nightclub-and-restaurant district of Eighteenth Street, testing the packing abilities of the newfound blanket of snow, compressing projectiles from the moister slush at curbside, scraping grapefruit-size balls off the trunk lids of parked cars, test-firing them against No Parking signs. The kids took the opportunity to belt the bus with a fusillade of iceball artillery, the impacts sounding out like snare drums across the quiet nightscape. The bus, displaying its Out of Service sign, slowed to a halt, and its driver stepped out to gather up snowballs for a retaliatory strike. He was outnumbered six to one, and Cadence and Richard quickly came to his aid, Richard fanning out to the left and lobbing snowballs up in the air as far as he could, baiting the kids to watch, and, each time they looked up, firing a fastball on a straight line right at the ringleader, who retreated after being struck twice in the chest, once in the leg (the driver). As the kid withdrew, he got truly smoked by a snowball thrown on a perfect straight line by Cadence, a hollow-sounding *thump* hitting against his wool hat. The teenagers threw back a few more half-hearted volleys and began a full-fledged retreat.

A four-lane midcity street, the bus driver laughing and brushing himself off before tipping his imaginary hat at Cadence, reboarding the bus, the light of the camera going dark. The safety gates of every storefront had been pulled down hours ago, all except a small French bistro where the waiters and kitchen staff appeared to be singing a karaoke version of "La Marseillaise," the familiar overture audible due to the entirely absent traffic. Enough snow in four hours to close the bars, empty the buses and the parking lots. As Richard and Cadence walked through the intersection, the lights blinked red in all four directions. In the middle of the street, Richard pulled Cadence to him.

What is every kiss but a prelude, an invitation? The composer Schumann, himself no stranger to the disorders of the mind, described Chopin's preludes as "ruins, individual eagle pinions, all disorder and wild confusions." The Chopin analogy here was a direct parallel, the preludes twenty-four individual pieces, intended to be at once separate and unified. What better description for these kisses, those short pressures that added up to a constant state? Richard kissed Cadence, and Cadence returned the kisses, her hands in the pockets of his overcoat, his scarf flying backward over his left shoulder; the cameraman, had he been more of a voyeur, could not have resisted circling the two lovers, but instead he recognized the moment as both beautiful and private, and set about packing up his gear. In the snow-packed middle of a quiet Eighteenth Street, the moon occluded by a low blanket of clouds and the scene scrimmed by a curtain of snow falling to the ground in large, featherweight clumps, Richard and Cadence kissed, and then kissed again.

It was impossible for him to shake his desire to speed up the events of the next few days, to see how everything would turn out. He wanted some confidence that he could take care of the boy. He wanted to know he could do this ridiculous new job he'd accepted on a whim. He wanted to know if the faith and confidence that Cadence claimed to see in him were real qualities, the kind that made him appear a trustworthy presence on the news at 5:00, 6:00, and 11:00. He wanted to know whether the things he viewed as the possibilities of a better life actually were. He wanted to know if he should buy or rent. Could he afford a house with a few dozen acres, the kind of large and inviting kitchen that he could fill with new friends and their children? He wanted to know what Gabriel liked to eat, what color he'd want his new bedroom to be, whether or not he'd ever dreamed of having a dog. But mostly he wanted Cadence; definitions could come later. She always resisted him when he tried to put labels on things, and in between pressing his lips to hers, he told himself he did not need a name for it; he just desired her presence, its calming influence, the possibility that when they did define it, it could be something permanent.

Cadence took a second armload of snow and shoveled it at Richard. He stepped toward her, halving the distance between their bodies, and as the powdery snow fluttered down, it left its momentary traces on his overcoat. He lifted one foot in the air, pointed to his wingtips, standard-issue Washington wear, and said, "I don't exactly have foul-weather gear on." The cuffs of his pants were starched with ice. The wet pom-pom on the top of Cadence's hat fell limply to one side, and Richard stepped in, brushed the snow off her shoulders while she did the same for him, then used her scarf as leverage to pull her in for another kiss before they headed back to her building.

59

INSOMNIA. The middle-of-the-night city noise conspicuously absent. No deliveries, no garbage trucks in the alley, the only sound the mechanical grind of the snowplows as they cleared the streets, burying the cars parked streetside under decaying mountains of gray-brown slush. When Richard looked at the clock again, it was nearly four o'clock, though he did not remember slipping into the maw of sleep. His view out the window was of a city covered in the cold, dull film of rain.

Beside him, Cadence breathed at a steady pace, one Richard assumed to mean she was deeply asleep. That sonorous breathing he associated with the sound of his own childhood, summer nights when his father broke out the transistor radio and together they listened to Chuck Thompson broadcast the Orioles games on WBAL. Richard had grown up in the no-baseball-in-DC era, between the city's second and third major-league teams, and hadn't even seen a game in person until he was twenty. He made the drive up to Baltimore on a Sunday afternoon to sit in the upper bowl of the old Memorial Stadium, section 9, eat three hot dogs and drink four National Bohemian beers. A foul ball from light-hitting shortstop Mark Belanger sailed over his head, into the lap of a kid who looked like nothing so much as the five-year-old version of himself. He'd not thought of that afternoon in years, but he knew he was really thinking about Gabriel, how to teach a boy the unspoken things—about baseball, about . . . He tended to forget how he'd learned these things himself, listening to the Motorola transistor from Lew's workbench, his father arranging two nylon-webbed folding chairs in the backyard.

On those nights, Lew taught Richard the proper way to light a cigar, how to tamp its fat end and how much of the tip to cut. In that great haze of smoke, his father promised that next summer they'd make the drive up to Baltimore together and see the O's and their crazy manager, who was so fond of the three-run home run. The next summer, Richard's mother sat at the dining room table studying for her real-estate licensure exam, right up until the day that a man from the General Services Administration showed up with a settlement offer from the government, and Lew was dead.

When the alarm sounded, Richard experienced a momentary dislocation, not knowing much of the situation beyond the time, 5:27 a.m., displayed in the bright-green digits of the clock. In the early days of his career, and again in the first furious months after his divorce, there were weeks of eighty-plus hours and bar nights that went on until three in the morning, and going back to work meant a quick shower, a change of underwear, a new shirt and tie. The era of guest beds, foldout couches, strange apartments, temporary women. He knew this clock. Cadence.

She stirred, rolled to one side, and he clicked on the television, which faded in during the local forecast; the confluence of low-pressure systems was moving out into the Atlantic. Rising temperatures overnight had changed the precipitation to a steady rain. But on the heels of this system came another, pushing cold air down from the north. Temperatures were expected to dive later in the morning, leaving the city encased in a thick shell of blue-black ice. He had to get out now. This morning.

The weatherman began to narrate some footage of last night's snow, and Richard recognized the intersection as the same one where he and Cadence had come to the rescue of the Metrobus driver, fended off the snowballing marauders. He tapped Cadence on the shoulder, and she rolled to see the television, pulled her down comforter up and tucked it beneath her chin.

"If I'm going to drive you to the airport—" she began, then stopped to point at the screen. "Hey. Hey! That's us," she said, hitting Richard on the shoulder for emphasis.

The camera zoomed in and followed Cadence as she packed a snowball, then unleashed it in the direction of the teenagers. "We look like we're having fun," Richard said. "Excellent form you've got there."

Cadence shimmied out from under the covers and headed to the bathroom, then glanced back over her shoulder. "Turns out you knew how to have fun the whole time."

Just a few hours ago, Richard had told someone he was a firm believer in happy endings, and now he couldn't see any reason for that to change. If that was naive, so be it, but he'd seen the possibilities of his happiness in that televised clip, the two of them frolicking in the snow. He'd stop thinking about whether or not he was going to be okay and start working toward a specific goal. Happiness. This was revolutionary thinking. Happiness meant a family and a home, and it was hard not to notice how those feelings had returned after only a few hours back in Cadence's company. Even her apartment felt like a home, he thought, with all its telltales: a welcome mat in the hall, a place by the door to leave the keys, actual curtains on every window.

The pleasing chime of her shower rang out, the water echoing off the porcelain tile, the ancient tub. Richard heard the sound of the curtain being pulled back, the barely discernible change in pitch as Cadence moved her body under the water.

The sound of the running water jogged his memory. He hadn't thought all that specifically about his sister in the intervening few hours. *The* intervening few *years,* he corrected himself. She'd made it clear that she wanted to handle the challenge of raising Gabriel as her own cross to bear, didn't want Richard's money or counsel, hadn't brought the boy back east to visit what little family he had left. That meant that Richard had adopted a kind of defense mechanism; he waited for his sister to call, or to write, and often she did neither. It wasn't unusual to hear from her only at the holidays, for the conversation even then to be all about how she wouldn't see Richard at Christmas, the functional greetings of the emotionally distant.

Richard's new life was going to require honesty, most of all honesty with himself. Still, he found it difficult at times to trust his memory. His memories usually behaved like a blue-and-white afterimage, as if someone had taken his picture with a flash too close to the eyes. But on this he was clear: he had helped his sister into a shower in the delivery room of the hospital where Gabriel was born. They wanted her to relax, stretch; she wasn't dilating fast enough, and it had been eleven hours since her water had broken. Though Richard suspected the shower had little medical value, he was grateful for the memory. Mary Beth used his arm and shoulder for support as she slipped off her dressing gown and eased under the stream of water. She took his hand and put it on her belly near a spidery distension of red marks, and he felt an insistent and rhythmic tapping coming back at him. He was the second person to hold Gabriel; he had cut the cord.

The news was in that last dead thirty seconds before a station break, and the weatherman was riffing on about January blizzards when the anchorman stopped him midsentence. The anchor pressed his right hand to his earpiece, and Richard expected an update on the aftermath of the crash, maybe the discovery of the black boxes.

The anchor said, "We are getting word out of Chicago this morning of a train accident, on the city's famous El, the Orange Line. Early indications are there are injuries, some serious, and for more details, we're going to listen in to our local affiliate for live coverage on this breaking story."

He turned the television off, moved to the kitchen, and took out a carton of orange juice and a honey-wheat English muffin from the refrigerator. On the top shelf of the fridge, there was a glass dish containing what he could identify only as a salad, with unrecognizable greens, cherry tomatoes, chunks of cucumber, crumbles of a moldy and odiferous cheese. Next to that, two Cornish hens, identical, golden-skinned. The door shelves held exotic mustards, prepared horseradish. Ketchup with no sugar added. A dozen brown eggs. Sweet creamery butter made on a mom-and-pop organic farm. Organic skim milk in a wide-mouthed glass bottle. A pitcher of filtered water. The shelves were filled too, a bowl with apples, lemons and limes, grapefruits. A jar of egg whites. Peach-mango salsa. The produce drawer held unlabeled plastic containers of four different kinds of herbs, and Richard opened one, six-inch stalks of green-black, and breathed deeply and thought, *Tarragon*. He hadn't bought fresh herbs in years, could not remember when cooking had not meant something as mundane as heating spaghetti from a can. A bulb of fennel. Green beans. Almond butter. There was nothing in his refrigerator and everything in hers. It was the refrigerator of a mother, he thought hopefully.

He didn't realize Cadence had come into the kitchen until she announced herself. "Why don't you put on some coffee?" She wore a lush terry-cloth robe that looked as if it had been stolen from a resort, and her hair was turbaned in a towel.

Richard took out the coffee, the filters. "When are they expecting you back in the office?" He knew Cadence essentially made her own schedule; in a typical week, Tuesday through Thursday was reserved for client visits, checking on the machines she'd sold last year. When they were dating, they'd had standing dates for Thursday through Sunday nights.

"Not until next Friday. I'm headed to Houston on Tuesday to oversee the install of a new machine," she said.

Richard found two navel oranges in the fruit bowl, began peeling them and breaking them into sections. It occurred to him that he could not remember the last time he'd eaten a piece of fresh fruit. "Tell me you aren't tired of that life. Airplane, hotel, conference room, restaurant, airplane, repeat."

Cadence puttered over to the cabinet and extracted a pair of coffee mugs. "Of course I'm tired of it. I've got platinum status on three airlines, and about the only thing it gets me is free drinks and upgrades to business class." She threw some bread in the toaster, and Richard glanced at the bag, a ten-grain loaf, honey sweetened, unbleached and unbromated flour. He made a mental note to look up what *unbromated* meant.

Cadence took a seat at the kitchen table and blew across a too-hot mug of fresh coffee.

"I want you to come with me," Richard said. "Come to Dallas, and then head back here for a few days to close up some loose ends, and then, eventually, Pennsylvania. I need to look for a house."

"Pennsylvania?"

They both knew why he wanted her to come. She could call it whatever she liked, desperation, or even love, and she would be right.

The summary of what he was prepared to say: He could not inflict this city on a child. Not without giving Gabriel the extensive armature of a better neighborhood and $35,000-a-year private schools he could not afford. There was a certain intransigence to Richard that didn't fit in the city. Unlike Lew, he'd never been comfortable in a culture that said things like *You can wear any tie you want, as long as it's red.* In Pennsylvania, he could have acreage and dogs and, most of all, a homestead. If the kid voiced a desire for a horse, a horse could be provided. Moving meant no more apartments, no more fumbling for quarters just to have a clean T-shirt. No more hollering drunks in the alley, no curbside fistfights over a parking space. No flyers for *2-for-1 draft beers, no cover* left on his windshield, and no bicycle messengers sliding Chinese menus underneath his apartment door at 4:00 a.m. The dreams that were available to him in Pennsylvania weren't just speculative, they were achievable.

Richard hadn't yet told Cadence about the job that was waiting for him. That was a conversation that could wait until the airplane, for whenever it was that the two of them would sit down and see if they could imagine themselves a future. Tomorrow. He checked his watch. It already was tomorrow.

"We never ate," Richard said.

"Like the old days," she answered, and he knew that she meant the first few evenings of their relationship, back when they had every intention of going out to dinner but never left

Richard's apartment. "Are you hungry?" she asked. "I could make something. Pancakes?"

"I could eat a double stack," he said. "Like at Waffle House."

Richard wanted to leave now, drive to Dallas with Cadence in the passenger seat, pretend there wasn't any urgency in the situation. Pretend. There was no reason this had to be decided today. The road would give them cover, time to talk. They could take turns behind the wheel, four-hour shifts fueled by diet sodas, eat their meals at any place along the side of the road that served twenty-four-hour breakfast and good, strong coffee. It sounded equal parts pleasant and implausible. How much of his grown-up life had been like this, imagining what he wanted to do versus doing what he knew he must? He had to get to Gabriel; his only thought now was about the boy. The fact that he'd had to wait through the night ate at him. Already he was talking himself out of his fantasy drive with Cadence. He needed to be on a plane, and quickly. He was leaving in an hour. She could come with him or not.

Cadence pulled down a box from the cabinet, retrieved a mixing bowl. He was thinking about the restorative properties of a solid breakfast. His new house would need to have a spectacular kitchen, spacious, where each day would begin with a family breakfast. These meals would be the relaxed ceremonies that kicked off an era of good feeling. They could, Richard thought, lapse into a routine. When he heard Cadence's blow-dryer click off, he'd pour the coffee, then the milk on Gabriel's cereal right after that. For his new kitchen, he could buy an unobtrusive thirteen-inch television, and in the mornings they'd tune in to *The Today Show* for the weather. The forecast would always be for American sunlight, nostalgic and kind, the kind that dominated his memories. Cadence would come to the table and read the front-page headlines over Richard's shoulder.

When everything was normal in the world, the three of them would begin to eat.

Cadence ladled the batter into a frying pan and said, "I didn't know what you were going to tell me last night. When you wanted to see me, I was expecting some sort of grand announcement. I thought maybe you were seeing someone."

Richard laughed. "Who?"

"No one I know. Some woman who pushed her shopping cart into your car. Somebody like that."

"There hasn't been...," Richard started to say. She brought him a plate with three pancakes, a side of fruit drizzled with vanilla yogurt and a touch of honey, then sat down across from him. The steam rose from his coffee cup in visible streaks. She watched as he doctored the food on his plate with thin-cut pats of butter, a generous dollop of real maple syrup. The pancakes tasted heavy in the way that a good rib-sticking breakfast should, dissolving into a sweetness he could taste on his lips after each bite.

"There's no other girl. There is, however, plenty to talk about. We can figure all this out on the plane," Richard started. "There's never been any real reason for you to stay in DC. Your job is where the machines are." Richard could see her figuring out the logistics, what the trip would entail in time and travel.

"What are you saying?" She took her mug in both hands, warming herself.

"I'm saying I need help. The guy from the airline"—he pulled Lemko's card from his wrinkled shirt pocket—"he can put you on the 9:40 flight with me. I'm asking you to come to Texas."

Cadence picked up her nearly untouched plate, scraped it into the sink, then ran the tap. "What makes you think I know anything that can help? I'll be here for the phone calls and for advice. I can drive you to the airport. I can take care of stopping your mail and locking up your apartment, and I can pick you up when you get back. Beyond that, I can't make any promises."

Richard pushed his plate sideways across the table. "You can't." He regretted how much his inflection made it sound like a question.

She shook her head.

It was decided. Cadence would drive him to the airport, and he'd ride in the passenger seat with his father's overcoat draped across his lap, and for the second time in twelve hours, he would sit by himself by an airport gate and wonder how on earth one talks to a child. At least in his dream, the child had been happy. The boy had Richard's lanky frame and ran with a high leg kick, his heels nearly hitting his butt with each stride. Someone would bring him to the Dallas airport, and as Richard exited security, the boy would shake loose of his handler, run to be reunited with the uncle he did not really know. Or maybe the boy would be running toward the house, and Richard could recognize the house and remember the three dogs and the boy romping across the yard from his dream; only now did he re-alize that he'd never seen the face of the woman there. His vision had been faulty. The house and the dogs and the boy, those things were in his future. The woman, only that part, was fiction.

Downstairs, some of Cadence's neighbors began to dig them-selves out. The sound of snow shovels scraping against the asphalt echoed through the alley. He watched as she walked past him to the closet, extracted her small gym bag. For a mo-ment, he thought she was packing to come to Dallas, but then he watched her fill the bag with cosmetics, a pair of close-fitting black pants, a blouse. Work wear. She stripped off her robe and began the process of sliding herself into the running tights that she wore to the gym, and he knew for certain she would not be coming. For her, today was just another day in a series of days, relatively indistinct. He would be the only variable in her routine.

Richard walked over to her.

Cadence looked up at him with one last question. "Why are you smiling like that?"

Now was the time to tell her. "Because I've figured out how it's all supposed to end."

The drive to the airport was slowed by road conditions; on the radio, the forecast warned again of falling temperatures, the prospects for ice, and, later in the day, the significant accumulation of more snow.

They did not speak. He consoled himself by fiddling with the car's heater and by thinking about the coming hours. Cadence had complained about his inertia, and now here he was, springing into action. Except it wasn't action, just momentum. He'd been asleep in his apartment, and this rogue wave had capsized everything, pushing him forward. Where he would stop was the only part of these events that he could control. Things at rest tended to stay at rest, things in motion stayed in motion. The plan for the days ahead meant DCA to Dallas, and then on to a Dallas County courthouse; he'd brought his passport, for some reason, and he tapped it lightly where it rested in the pocket of his oxford shirt; Dallas back to Washington and the prospects of packing up his apartment. A drive to Pennsylvania. He wasn't going to be taking Gabriel north in a vintage Oldsmobile. Maybe he'd buy a new car, something sensible. Jesus, this was exactly how you became a guy who drove a Camry or an Accord. His mind flashed to his father in the distant past, sitting across a metal desk from some car salesman, the salesman writing numbers upside down on pieces of scrap paper, his father pushing them back across the desk uninterestedly, refusing to buy snow tires, floor mats, undercoating. *Someone in this family had better be good in a crisis.* Richard hoped to God that it was him.

Cadence had asked Richard what kind of father he might be, and now, like any good Washington lawyer, he wanted to revise and extend his remarks. He would *try.* He would try to be the kind of father that Lew had always promised to be but never actually was. He was going to be *present.* What else could he give this child? Safe harbor. A bed. Three meals a day. That sounded more like prison. What could he manage beyond that? Everything he possessed seemed incomplete, not enough. No wife. No house with a room that could be reinvented as a space for a six-year-old boy. No quarter acre of grass to walk across with a push mower, no bright golden dog to greet him and the boy enthusiastically whenever the door pulled open, no spontaneous joy whenever the boy heard the recorded music from the ice cream truck that circled the neighborhood at twilight. Could he teach what needed to be taught, how to lose oneself in books and how to dream, how to throw a tight spiral or a curveball, how to know when a girl wanted to be kissed (he coughed out a brief laugh, thinking how often he'd been wrong in that area), how to learn the joys of discovering what you did not know, and the pleasure when you learned something you'd once thought impossible?

Then there was the practical stuff, how to take care of your body and your mind and even your teeth in the right way, how to keep your nails clean, how to sew a button on your white dress shirt, and how to give your shoes a shine until they glowed with a high parade gloss, how to make your bed, the sheets drawn so tightly as to pass military inspection. He wanted to give Gabriel all those things that came with a family, even the crazy parts, the morbidly obese aunt with her never-ending advice on diet and exercise, the distant cousins who'd squandered their inheritance on women and poker, the self-exiled brothers whose only appearances were at family funerals, the deceased relatives with their alluringly preposterous first names, Marmaduke and Cleveland. Somehow, Richard wanted to give Gabriel that which did not exist, the happy family he himself had never known in the real world but had always seen on television, the Bradys, the Van Pattens, the Waltons. He could teach Gabriel the right way to tie a tie, how to pull the skin taut around the angles of his chin when shaving. He could teach him how to know a burger on the grill was properly cooked and never to press out its fat into the fire.

He shook his head. How many of these were his wishes, and how many Mary Beth's? Here he was awash in an ocean of best guesses and deductive reasoning. How would she feel about Gabriel being a Boy Scout or an altar boy? Playing the violin? Quitting youth-league sports? Would it be better for Gabriel to be a benchwarmer on the football team or a leader in the marching band? Richard wasn't sure how he felt about these things, if his gut reactions were nothing more than long-ingrained prejudices. Grief had been out there, circling, and he did not know which would be more painful, the sadness at knowing what he had missed, or the lasting grief that, like a remora, attached itself to the long, dark underside of his sadness.

He silently noted the landmarks as they passed, the cavalry officer on the horse at Thomas Circle, and even though he'd lived in the city most of his adult life, he drew a blank on who exactly this Thomas was, probably the guy on the horse, and why he was important enough to earn a bronze statue. The radio cycled back to news at the top of the hour—*We are following two major breaking stories this morning*—and he knew in his heart that breaking news was a metaphor for broken lives. It struck him as soundly as an open-hand slap: he had not yet cried. It seemed shameful, even more so if he told Cadence about it, so he remained quiet. He did not need to seek absolution from her, but his face wore the look of it. And of tears he could not gather. He had no idea when he would.

The car meandered out of the city and along the river. Behind and overhead, planes filled with business commuters followed their customary banks and turns, slaloming along the Potomac on their way to National Airport, one arrival every 120 seconds. He checked his watch. He'd have plenty of time to walk to the gate, read the paper, get a coffee, pretend he was one of the airport's usual population of executive travelers. Someone with child protective services would likely be there on the receiving end at the Dallas airport, maybe even with the boy in tow, and that person would be the one who would actually introduce them both to their new life together. The boarding pass that Lemko had handed over last night gave his seat assignment as 2B, first class, on the aisle.

The grayness of the day felt perfect for being lost in thought. He'd been entertaining the idea that the three of them, Richard and Cadence and Gabriel, would manage to be an instant family; now he could see what Cadence had said, that she could not provide much beyond temporary comfort. He wanted to work up some sort of righteous anger, that she'd been so adept at her playacting that he hadn't even noticed; she'd treated him with the benign care that you might give to someone who was dying; she'd done everything short of show up at his bedside with candy and flowers. He was charity.

And then, as he watched her slow the car in the midst of the morning traffic, he knew he was being too harsh. He'd loved her, and she him, and for eight months that had been enough. In the midst of his divorce, he and Ellen had on a few occasions taken comfort in each other, and what a mistake that had been; even as a child, Richard had never been one to simply rip off a Band-Aid with one pull, preferring to pull it off slowly and luxuriate in its pain. Why shouldn't everything be that way, a slow dissolving? He had not been alone in the few hours when he needed to not be alone, and for now, he could convince himself that was enough.

Not until he was on the plane did he realize how thoroughly Cadence had planned her quick getaway. She had not parked the car and walked him to the terminal, choosing instead to pull up curbside. She pressed the emergency flashers and stepped out, came around to the passenger side. She was wearing her gym clothes and a fleece jogging top and a little headband that covered her ears. Her long hair waved in the wind like a pennant, drifting behind her, then back again across her face and into her mouth. She popped the trunk and pulled out Richard's bag.

A skycap came whistling over and offered to take it. "And just where is the gentleman headed this morning?" His hearty and effervescent greeting struck Richard as mercenary, artificial, but before he could answer, the skycap took the bag in his left hand and pointed at him with his right. "You're that guy I saw on TV. Yesterday. Yessir, an honest-to-God expert celebrity. Where you flying off to with this beautiful lady? Let me guess. Antigua. Saint Martin. Puerto Vallarta?" The Vallarta came out strangled and weird, *Vay-ar-tay*.

"Dallas."

"All the glamour spots. Am I right? Turtle Creek." He stood

waiting for instruction, and Richard handed him ten dollars, then showed his palm in dismissal. "Thank you, sir. I'll be right over at the counter, sir."

"You're famous," Cadence said.

"I'm not. I'm just familiar. I look like someone who everyone went to high school with."

She smiled. She looked back into the car and noticed that Richard had left his scarf on the seat. She reached in and grabbed it, then put it over his shoulders, and Richard knew that she intended to say good-bye. She would put the scarf around his neck and pull him in for a kiss, and then she would be gone before he'd even made it to the automatic terminal doors. He could see it in her face.

"It's not too late. You could come with me. We pick up the kid and make a road trip out of it. Try every chicken-fried steak between Dallas and DC," Richard said.

She looked at her feet. He knew not to press her on the issue, that the answer was, and always would be, no. "That's the trouble with us Americans. We want everything wrapped up in nice, neat packages."

Richard was ready to argue with her. He didn't expect all the answers now, but he at least wanted the chance to make his case. He imagined that she knew how disappointing this all was for him, but he'd given her nothing to convince herself; he had no speeches or compelling arguments, and he hadn't even told her what was next, a new job and a new career, Pennsylvania. She'd spent her life trying to smooth the rough edges of coal country out of her voice, her mannerisms, and her thinking, and he could not imagine any developments in their romance that would make her suddenly crave to return to a place she had so strongly denied. She wasn't the kind of person who capitulated. And so they stood there in silence, the cold rain having tapered off, until an airport policeman shuffled over and reminded Cadence that she would have to move the car. The cop swung out his metal baton and used it to tap on the sign: Immediate Loading and Unloading. *Move it along.*

Richard knew if he waited, she would say something. But he expected more than the two words she gave him, "I can't."

This departure would not be as pretty as the one he'd imagined, and in that way, it would be like so many other times when a man left a woman standing in the passenger drop-off line, a series of stifled expectations and disappointments. His new life would begin the moment he went through those terminal doors.

That she was leaving was a fact, and he felt it settle firmly between the two of them. The cop circled back and without stopping said, "Give her a kiss before I have to call a tow truck." And the four of them, Richard and Cadence and the interloping policeman and the waiting skycap, all laughed. He could see that she knew what was expected of her—probably it was the only time all morning she'd given any consideration to the customs of departure and separation. The grayness of the sky and the sting of the rising winds and the bone-chilling wet of the cold foretold a deep and lasting winter. She gave Richard this kiss, a kiss of solemn grace, a kiss because it was the right thing to do, a kiss that would be the only part of her that could remain, a good-bye kiss.

ACKNOWLEDGMENTS

I am grateful for the support of many people during the writing of this book. My wife, Tracy Kendrick, comes first here; she's always been my first reader, my in-house copy editor and proofreader, and sounding board, and she's a diplomat, too. Thank you. Thanks, too, for my agent Wendy Sherman and all her staff. She believed in this book from the beginning. To Ben George, Amanda Brower, and everyone at Little, Brown and Company, thank you for being the true professionals that you are and making this book so much better.

I was lucky to be taught by amazing people who inspired by the sheer eloquence of their example. That list starts with my AP English teacher, Jewell Alexander, who managed to show the ways in which all art was a conversation; I wish she were here to see this day. From the College of William and Mary, Peter Wiggins, Walt Wenska, and Scott Donaldson. At the University of Iowa, Ethan Canin, Edward Carey, Jim Hynes, Elizabeth McCracken, Thisbe Nissen, and Chris Offutt. Connie Brothers, Deb West, and Jan Zenisek made my life in Iowa City so much easier. I was in the last class taught by Frank Conroy; so much of what I say as a teacher and mentor seems to have sprung from Frank's thinking and writing. At Florida State, Julianna Baggott, Robert Olen Butler, and David Kirby shepherded me through. Mark Winegardner shared career advice, fantasy baseball, and rock-and-roll trivia (the Paul Carrack question was mine!). Kurt Gutjahr, Tom McAllister, and Jennifer Vanderbes provided great feedback on earlier versions of the book. President Bill Lennox, Dean Mary Spoto, and my colleagues at Saint Leo University provide daily inspiration, especially Gianna, Pat, Lis, and Brooke.

A good portion of this book was written at the Hermitage artist retreat; I'm grateful to Bruce Rodgers, Patricia Caswell, and the entire staff there for their support of my work and that of so many others. Thanks due also to Josip Novakovich.

A handful of writers offered the necessary encouragements. Thank you, Rick Moody. George Garrett managed the difficult trick of always being a good teacher and a good friend. I never told the poets, George. Cheers to you.

Finally, my family. Thank you, Mom, for everything. Thanks to my mother-in-law, Valen Brown. Patrice and Dave. My cousin Andy showed me how to love books and changed my life. I'm glad you get to see the family name on this book. And, finally, to my daughter Colette; there are no talking parrots, pandas, or polar bears in this one, but I hope you love it anyway.

ABOUT THE AUTHOR

Steve Kistulentz is a graduate of the College of William and Mary and he holds an M.F.A. from the Iowa Writers' Workshop and a doctorate from Florida State University. His fiction has appeared, among other places, in *Narrative* and *Mississippi Review*. He is also the author of two books of poetry: *The Luckless Age* and *Little Black Daydream*. He directs the graduate creative writing program at Saint Leo University in Florida and is currently working on a second novel. He lives in the Tampa area.